THE STORY OF CANADA

THE BESTSELLING GENERATIONAL
SAGA OF AN UNFORGETTABLE FAMILY
WHOSE LOVES, ADVENTURES AND STRUGGLES
WERE THE STORY OF A NEW WORLD

"EPIC . . . ENTERTAINING . . .
The action is compressed and carefully plotted."
Calgary Herald

"A BLOCKBUSTER SERIES . . .
Its considerable strengths are its meticulous historical fidelity and its interesting, lively characters."
West Coast Review of Books

"A CRACKLING GOOD ROMANCE"
Ottawa Citizen

"FANS SEEKING HISTORICAL FICTION AND ROMANCE WILL FIND PLENTY TO KEEP THEM TURNING THE PAGES . . .
Adair and Rosenstock know how to tell a story . . . with physical violence and personal turmoil . . . action fast and furious . . . battles, sex, and narrow escapes . . . keeping the story moving quickly."
Toronto Quill and Quire

"EXCITING NARRATIVE"
Books in Canada

Other Avon Books by
Dennis Adair and Janet Rosenstock

KANATA: BOOK I: THE STORY OF CANADA
BITTER SHIELD: BOOK II: THE STORY OF CANADA
THUNDERGATE: BOOK III: THE STORY OF CANADA

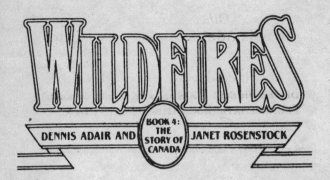

WILDFIRES

BOOK 4:
THE
STORY OF
CANADA

DENNIS ADAIR AND JANET ROSENSTOCK

AVON
PUBLISHERS OF BARD, CAMELOT, DISCUS AND FLARE BOOKS

WILDFIRES Book IV: The Story of Canada is an original
publication of Avon Books. This work has never before appeared in book form.

Produced by Larry and Helene Hoffman, Authors' Market-
ing Services

AVON BOOKS
A division of
The Hearst Corporation
959 Eighth Avenue
New York, New York 10019

First Avon Printing, April, 1983

AVON TRADEMARK REG. U. S. PAT. OFF. AND IN OTHER
COUNTRIES, MARCA REGISTRADA, HECHO EN U. S. A.

Printed in the U. S. A.

WFH 10 9 8 7 6 5 4 3 2 1

ACKNOWLEDGMENTS

The authors would gratefully like to acknowledge the continued excellent work of Jay Myers, the historian and researcher who worked with us on *Wildfires*. Among the reference books used in the preparation of this novel were the following: John Prebble's *The Highland Clearances*; Dr. George Bryce's *The Romantic Settlement of Lord Selkirk's Colonists*; J. Mackay Hitman's *The Incredible War of 1812: A Military History*; Gilbert Auchinleck's *A History of the War Between Great Britain and the United States During the Years 1812, 1813 and 1814*; Pierre Burton's *The Invasion of Canada 1812–1813*; Douglas Arthur Hill's *The Opening of the Canadian West*; Virginia Spencer Cowles' *The Astors: The Story of a Transatlantic Family*; William J. Healy's *Women of Red River*; Harry L. Coles' *The War of 1812*; Glyndur Williams' *Highlights of the First 200 Years of Hudson's Bay Company*; Marjorie Wilkins Campbell's *The North West Company* and her *Northwest to the Sea: A Biography of William McGillivray*.

FOREWORD

In the year of 1812, the United States declared war on Great Britain and attacked British North America, which consisted of Upper Canada (today the Province of Ontario), Lower Canada (now a portion of the Province of Quebec, additional land having been added to the Province of Quebec at the time of the Confederation), and the Maritime Provinces.

In the same year, Lord Selkirk's first settlers reached the Red River in what is today southern Manitoba. They spent their first winter in Pembina, which is currently part of North Dakota. In 1812, the area was called Rupert's Land.

Rupert's Land was a vast land mass owned and governed by the Hudson's Bay Company. It extended from the Arctic Circle down into what is today the Dakotas, Montana, Idaho, and Washington State. East to west, it included what is now northern Ontario, Manitoba, Saskatchewan, Alberta, British Columbia, the Yukon, and the Northwest Territories.

CHAPTER I

September 1, 1811

The village of Queenston was located on the western shore of the Niagara River. Behind the picturesque little village, a deep wood covered the bluffs which rose three hundred forty feet above the river to the flat, rich farmland that curved around the eastern end of Lake Ontario.

Will MacLean, following his father Robert MacLean's profession, owned and operated a trading post in Queenston. He and his wife of thirty years, Jenna Macleod MacLean, lived in the village. The Macleod family homestead of Lochiel was located a few miles away on the flatland above the bluffs, enabling Will and Jenna to visit often.

"I'll go to Lochiel tomorrow," Jenna said as she surveyed the table. She had set out the butter, the brown bread, a large bowl of fish stew, and a plate of greens for the noon meal. "There's too much food," she complained, shaking her head.

Will watched as she finished putting food on the table, knowing she would make the comment because it was a comment she made often. "We'll eat it all eventually," he promised.

"I just can't get used to cooking for two. When the girls got married it didn't make that much difference because my men all had such big appetites, but now

1

that Josh and Ian are gone so much, I always cook too much."

"It's not the first time they've been gone," Will observed.

"I know," Jenna said with a deep sigh. "But before, they usually were gone one at a time. Now they're gone together."

"Don't fuss," Will said with good humor. "But you had better get used to cooking for just us. Either Josh or Ian will be getting married soon and I suspect the other will be off to the fur-trapping country."

Jenna looked mildly disturbed. "Colleen's a wonderful girl," she said carefully. "But it troubles me to have two sons courting the same girl."

"They aren't officially courting her," Will corrected.

"Well, the three of them are always together. If they're not courting, they're certainly doing a fine imitation."

Will smiled. "What can you expect when men outnumber women twelve to one? The girls get married young, the men either remain single or they marry Indian women. Colleen's a real find. Of course they're both interested in her."

"I suppose it is only natural," Jenna allowed. "But I wish something would happen. I wish just one of them would court her."

"When one of them finally asks permission to court, you'll know which one is getting married," Will told her. "Josh and Ian will work things out between them, Jenna. You don't have to worry."

"And what happens if they don't work it out? What happens if she has to decide? What happens to the one who's rejected? Oh, Will, it's just that I don't want either of them to be hurt."

Will reached across the table and patted her hand.

2

"I'm sure it will be all right," he assured her. "Now might I have some food?"

Jenna nodded and passed the bowl of fish stew. "I only worry because of you and James," Jenna admitted. She referred to Will's twin brother, James MacLean—the brother she almost married, the brother who had stolen Will's inheritance. She and Will had never tried to contact James in thirty-one years.

Will put down his spoon, which had been poised halfway between his plate and his mouth. "Ian and Josh are not the same as James and me. Those boys were reared together. They learned their wilderness skills together; they've been in situations—dangerous situations—where they had to depend on each other. They traveled into the western fur country together and they've been East together, too. Jenna, Ian and Josh have the same taste, the same likes and dislikes, the same morality and values. They aren't like James and me—there always was a distance between us; we never had anything in common. Josh and Ian care about each other. They're brothers separated by four years, but they're close, as close as if they were twins."

Jenna did not reply. Left unspoken was the fact that Josh was, in reality, James' son and not Will's. Left unmentioned was Will's inability even to speak of Josh's real parentage. But, Jenna told herself, Will probably was right. The only thing Will and James ever had shared was their desire for her; apart from that, they were totally different. But Josh once had saved Ian's life by pulling him from the frigid water of the Niagara River when the ice had unexpectedly caved in. And Ian—Ian had given Josh his most prized Indian knife as a birthday present when Josh turned twenty-one. Still, Jenna was worried, and her heart went out to Ian. His eyes virtually caressed the lovely Colleen Adams, while hers seemed to rest on Josh. But I would feel just the reverse, she admitted to herself, if I thought it was Ian Colleen really cared for.

Will ate hungrily, wiping up the milky gravy with bread.

"There's plenty more," Jenna said, passing the bowl.

"Good. I worked up an appetite this morning unloading that shipment of dry goods from Montreal."

"I guess that means I'll be in the store next week," Jenna surmised. Actually, nothing could have made her happier. She liked working in the store, especially if Josh and Ian were away. There simply wasn't enough to keep her occupied around the house.

"With the new goods in, we'll have customers from miles around. And winter's coming, time to stock up. Mind you, if you haven't time, I could take on some extra help."

Jenna shook her head vigorously in the negative. "I want to work in the store! I love doing it!"

"I wouldn't deprive you," Will replied playfully. "But it'll mean some long days. The boys probably will be up at Lochiel helping with the harvest. There's plenty of salting to do, and a lot of preserving."

"I don't care. I want to work in the store with you. I like to see what people buy." Jenna chuckled. "You know, a month ago Mrs. Pringle bought a length of cloth for a dress. Oh, Will, you should have seen it! Made up into a dress, it will make her look as broad as the side of a barn! It had printed flowers that big!" Jenna made a sweeping gesture with her hands.

"You can afford to make fun of Hester Pringle. You still look thirty and your figure after four children is as good as it was when you were seventeen."

Jenna blushed. "Do you think so?"

4

Will stood up and stretched. "You're fishing for compliments, my dear." He winked. Then he walked around the table to where his wife sat and bent over. Lifting her long hair, which was pulled back and tied with a ribbon, he kissed her neck and then bit it gently, teasingly.

Jenna jumped. "Oh, Will!"

He kissed her again, then pressing her shoulders affectionately, he stood up straight. "Don't 'Oh, Will!' tease me.

"You're just a sassy tart. Unfortunately, I have to go back out to the dock. Otherwise, I'd stay here and make love to you."

Jenna stood up and turned to face him. She was aware her face was flushed, and it never ceased to amaze her that Will's good-humored flirtations and seductive suggestions still excited her after thirty years of marriage.

"Sometimes I wonder how you are with other women," Jenna commented impishly.

"Not the same as I am with you," Will answered honestly. "Now, if you had a twin, I could make love to both of—" Will interrupted himself abruptly.

He was only making a silly joke, Jenna thought. But James was Will's twin and she had made love with both of them. Will had stopped speaking because the sense of what he was saying suddenly had occurred to him and Jenna knew full well that whenever Will accidentally referred to his brother, he came to a sudden halt while he searched for a way to change the subject. Where James was concerned, Will had a kind of wishful amnesia.

Jenna looked down at the floor and then back up into his eyes. "You're sure that Ian and Josh will be all right?" she asked, allowing Will an escape from his sudden rush of unpleasant memories.

"I'm sure," Will replied.

* * *

5

"Oh, it's a spectacular sight!" Colleen stood on the expanse of grass and stared across at the falls. It was an unusually clear, warm day. But across from where they stood, in the deep, jagged gorge of the Niagara River, a heavy mist rose as a result of the immense power of the water tumbling over the steep cliff.

"No matter how often you see them," Ian observed, "they always seem to look different."

"Have you ever seen them in winter?" Josh was standing close to Colleen and she felt his hand close gently on her arm. "They're wonderful in winter, they turn into an icy fairyland. The water sprays the trees and then freezes on their branches so everything around the falls looks as if it is made of crystal. And the falls themselves look as if they are frozen solid and suspended in midair."

"I haven't seen them in winter," Colleen replied. "I've seen them only once before, when we were on our way to Lewiston." Josh's fingers moved lightly on her arm, and Colleen felt a chill pass through her, a desire to turn and throw herself right into his arms.

"I shall have to bring you here in the winter," Josh suggested. Colleen let out her breath slowly. He had said "I" and not "we," as was usually the case. Colleen thought that it was only last summer that her life had changed so completely. She had met Josh and Ian when she and her father, Richard Adams, had journeyed across the river to the trading post in Queenston to buy some needed items that were not available locally.

Everything had been different almost from the moment she had met Ian and Josh MacLean. Colleen Adams began to know the life she had missed. Ian and Josh belonged to the Macleod–MacLean clan and their family owned the largest farm in the area.

6

Lochiel, it was called, and for Colleen it was almost a magical place.

Josh and Ian went to Lochiel often to visit their grandmother, Janet Cameron Macleod. Colleen, much to her delight, often joined them. She also visited Josh and Ian's home in Queenston, a few miles from Lochiel, down on the shore of the river. There were dances, festivals, and games to participate in, and gradually, though always chaperoned by one of Josh and Ian's cousins, Colleen began to spend nearly as much time with Josh and Ian as she spent with her father.

"You've found a family," Richard Adams told her. "One of those young men will marry you. He'll take you across the river to live."

"Marry me?" Colleen had said, blushing. "They haven't even asked permission to court! We're all just good friends." But Colleen knew her father was right. She, Josh, and Ian rode together, canoed together, and danced together. Ian looked at her as longingly as Josh did.

"And even if they wanted to court me," Colleen had asked her father, "how could I choose?" Ian was twenty-seven with dark hair and deep green eyes. He had a ready smile and a good sense of humor. Josh was thirty-one with sandy hair and laughing brown eyes. Both of them were tall and strong, both were frontiersmen, both were traders, and both were fine marksmen. But unlike most of the men on the frontier, Josh and Ian MacLean both had been schooled in Montreal and both had traveled not only West, but East as well. They gave the impression they'd be as at home in an Indian village as in a palace. They both were rare men filled with fun-loving good humor.

"You will choose," Colleen's father had told her, "if, in fact, you have not done so already."

That conversation had taken place some months earlier and it came back to Colleen now as she stood next to Ian and Josh, looking across at the falls. In her heart, she sensed that the carefree days of the threesome were coming to an end, to be replaced by a more mature relationship involving only two of them.

"The whole family used to come here in the spring," Ian told her. "When Grandmother was younger. Now only some of us come, but it's a special place."

Colleen sighed. "I wonder what it was like before the settlers came."

"They say the Indians used to throw a virgin over the falls every year to appease the thundering waters." Ian laughed and shook his head.

"A virgin—what a waste!" Josh laughed and Colleen felt herself blush, but inside she laughed also. Sometimes their humor was ribald and Colleen knew that their father, Will MacLean, always was making teasing suggestions too, though they always were directed at his wife.

"We should eat soon," Colleen suggested as she turned around and faced the wagon. Little Ronald Macleod, chaperon of the day, was lifting a large picnic basket down from the back of the wagon.

"She's avoiding us," Ian said, smiling. "We hardly ever get serious and now she's avoiding us."

"Serious?" Colleen turned back to them. They looked anything but serious.

"We were about to get serious," Josh corrected as if he sensed her thoughts. "Colleen, the time has come for the three of us to have a talk."

Colleen looked from one to the other. The moment she had both looked forward to and dreaded was at hand.

"We've been seeing you for a long time," Ian was saying. "And it's obvious we both admire you." His voice seemed to be coming from across the river. Colleen moved her eyes, first looking at Josh, then back at Ian.

"One of us wants to court you properly," Josh announced, taking up where Ian had left off.

"But we both want to marry you," Ian put in.

"We want you to decide which one of us will court you, which one of us should speak to your father."

Colleen abstractedly lifted her hand and wiped a strand of long, dark hair out of her eyes. The wind was blowing and in the background she could hear the thundering water as it hit the gorge. Somehow it seemed to match her heartbeat.

She wanted to run into Josh's arms, but found she could not move because Ian's green eyes seemed to hold her in place. They were pleading eyes and they made Colleen reflective and acutely aware of the fact that her decision was going to hurt him. "I—I can't," Colleen said, stumbling. "I have to think about it. . . ." And at that moment she believed herself. I really can't, she thought, I must think about it before I hurt Ian.

"Of course," Ian said as he took her arm. "It's not going to be easy to choose between us. Now, I do feel I should tell you that I'm a very quiet sleeper. You'll never have to worry about waking up and finding me with all the blankets. Josh, on the other hand, is a tosser. Believe me, he won't allow you a single good night's sleep."

"He sleeps so well, you'll have trouble waking him if you want to make love," Josh retorted. "But I will say one thing for him: He makes fine furniture, and the chances are you'll have a better bed if you marry my baby brother."

"That's true," Ian said and laughed. "But Josh builds better houses." He smiled warmly at his brother. "If I were you, I'd choose him. He's more even-tempered."

9

Josh put his arm around Ian's shoulder. "Don't listen to him. Frankly, he's a better catch, younger and more flexible."

"Enough!" Colleen said. She tried to smile, but couldn't quite.

"You know, Ian, there could be a hundred other men who might want to court her," Josh observed. "It's very civilized of us to let her choose between just us two."

"There isn't anyone else," Colleen blurted out. How could they joke about this so? They had put her in the position of hurting one of them.

"Then at least all the competition is in the family," Josh joked.

"I thought we were going to eat." Ian took Colleen's hand and began walking toward little Ronald Macleod, who was sitting under a large maple tree.

Josh reached over and took Colleen's other hand. "We brought a real feast," he told her.

Colleen smiled weakly. Her appetite had fled in the face of having to commit herself. She sat down and folded her long skirts about her.

"We both own a quarter interest in the trading post," Ian said. "And we both have money saved from our fur-trapping expeditions out West—of course, Josh has more than I do because he's older."

"Not much more," Josh jested. "Ian saves all his money. I'm a bit of a spendthrift."

"And we have land near Lochiel," Ian added. "And both of us have worked seasonally for the Hudson's Bay and could go back full time if we wanted."

"In short, our prospects are good and we can take care of a wife, giving her a house, furniture, land, and a future." Josh sounded a bit mocking, as if he were imitating a proper young man pleading his case before his girl's father.

"I'm hungry!" five-year-old Ronald Macleod announced. He began to fish in the picnic basket.

10

Colleen looked at both Ian and Josh. "After a year, I'm aware of your prospects and your experiences. Please, let me think."

"You do have something to think about," Ian said, squeezing her hand.

"Something indeed," Josh added, touching the fingertips of her other hand.

It was Josh's touch that sent the wave of desire through Colleen. "Yes," she said, agreeing with both of them.

Mason James MacLean was twenty-seven years old. He was tall like his father, James MacLean, and he had thick hair, almost black in color. But his eyes were his unique feature: They were brown, until one looked closely. Then one could discern a hint of green, as if Mason James had been born with green eyes that someone had painted over with brown. The result was a deep olive shade that gave Mason James a totally individual kind of good looks.

Mason James MacLean was, by his own definition, a chameleon. Some of his acquaintances thought of him as arrogant, others called him egotistical, and still others complained that he was spoiled. On a more positive note, many people enjoyed his caustic wit, and he did have a peculiar charm. In addition, Mason James was extraordinarily well educated and considerably more erudite than most of his southern colleagues. He was a man of rare taste in what he himself considered a boorish world.

He was tall and strong-looking, with broad shoulders and slim hips. He appeared on first meeting to be a proper young frontiersman. But Mason James' hands betrayed him. His hands were white and unmarked by the calluses that would have denoted a life of labor.

Mason James had surveyed the capital city of Washington and proclaimed it to be "a dismal collec-

11

tion of huts." His was not the most antagonistic of comments. One of his fellow Southerners had called it "a mud hole equal only to the Great Serbonian Bog."

Mason James contemplated a rumor that persistently circulated. It stated, categorically, that the family from which George Washington had sprung once had been called Heartburn and that they had changed the name a generation prior to their settlement in North America. Pity, Mason James thought. Heartburn would have been a much more appropriate name for the capital.

The original intention had been grand enough. General Washington, by then President Washington, had engaged a young French military engineer, Pierre-Charles L'Enfant, to lay out the plans for the new city. L'Enfant's was a grandiose notion, largely because he was given to gazing into the future rather than adhering to the budget restrictions of the Continental Congress.

He did not plan a capital that would be the center of thirteen states and three million inhabitants. "This country will change!" he had proclaimed. "One day it will have fifty states and five hundred million inhabitants. One must not build for today, but for tomorrow." L'Enfant's vision was perfectly sensible, but the Continental Congress was myopic at the best of times. Thus L'Enfant's detractors—and there were many—mumbled that he came by his extravagant ideas in Paris and wanted only to outdo Versailles. His complex was to revolve around the Capitol building, the Grand Mall, and the Executive Mansion. These buildings were to be placed at the end of long vistas, or wide pathways; large, wide avenues were to converge on them, eventually making circular intersections. This, L'Enfant proclaimed, would offer a "reciprocity of view." Beyond the circular drives, he called for centers and subcenters, parks and squares and the like. Washington, L'Enfant had declared, "should be a garden of free minds, a center of the human imagination."

A nice thought, Mason James reflected. A trifle too egalitarian, but not without merit. But, of course, L'Enfant had been dismissed by the money-grubbing Puritan minds that then dominated the Congress—those men from the northeastern states.

To Mason James' eyes, the garden of free minds envisaged by L'Enfant had turned into a patch of grasping weeds. The center of the human imagination had become a mud hole populated by fewer than five hundred persons, most of them self-congratulatory types from the frontier who proudly proclaimed their own ability to survive months at a time without bathing, and who wallowed in the pride of doing their own work. They were quite enough to make Mason James MacLean physically ill.

Fortunately, he did not have to live in Washington proper. He thanked God for Georgetown: for its neat rows of semiluxurious homes, for its taverns that kept out riffraff, for the social graces of its wealthy inhabitants, and, yes, for its slaves.

"A small oasis of elegance in an inelegant world," Mason James proclaimed as he looked on his own well-appointed three-story home. And he was so fortunate to have it! Its original owner had been a Mrs. Susanna Sharp, a strange woman who seemed to dry up and actually shrivel away at the age of eighty-six. Mason James had arrived practically on the day of her death, just in time to buy the house from her footloose grandson before he headed West. It was not as grand as his house in Vidalia, of course, but it would suffice for a time. And who could predict the future? Once Louisiana had been admitted as a state, he might even become a congressman. Mason

13

James MacLean already understood the power of money, and he was just beginning to understand the power of politics.

Then too, in spite of the dreariness of Washington and its limited social life, which constantly exposed him to absurd Southerners like Mr. Clay, who did not believe in slavery, the town did have a few advantages.

The major advantage accrued from the fact that Mason James MacLean actually did not know many people, or to be more precise, not many people knew him.

In Vidalia, in Natchez, and even in New Orleans, Mason James MacLean easily caught the looks people gave him. He heard the whispers behind his back, he felt the sting of a certain restrained acceptance. Money overcame most of the rejection that might have been heaped upon him. People were outwardly nice to him because they feared his father's financial power. Money bought subservience, it bought favor, it bought invitations and polite conversations. It did not buy warmth. And nestled in the back of Mason James' mind, burning in his soul, the whispers lingered. "He's illegitimate," they all said. "He's the product of sin; the issue of incest." But the whisper that troubled him the most was the fact that they called his mother "Mad Maria" and said she was possessed of the devil.

But Mason James did not remember his mother. She had died four days after his birth, and all he knew of her were the whispers. His father denied all the rumors save one: "Yes, you are illegitimate. So are half the children in the South." Then his father would narrow his dark eyes: "I'll make you legitimate, the most legitimate man on the river! Money, power, they buy legitimacy!" But James MacLean never talked of Maria, never admitted that Maria was Mason's mother. And no one could prove the

story because James MacLean had many lovers, and
Maria never had left the plantation house nor seen
anyone for the last five years of her life. "The whispers all come from malevolent slaves," his father
would hiss. "Stop listening to such utter garbage."
In spite of his father's protestations to the contrary,
Mason James more than half believed the stories.
And he now admitted to himself that it was good to
be away from them, good to be where he did not have
to confront a past he did not feel responsible for.
Here, in Washington, he was accepted without question. He had, after all, gone to the finest schools, he
had money, he went to the best parties. He had
money to purchase the Georgetown house, he had his
slaves to attend him, he was able to entertain lav-
ishly, and he felt he had an almost sacred mandate.
He was one of the representatives of the territory
sent to present Louisiana's arguments and petitions
for statehood. It seemed to Mason James MacLean
that all this occurred at the most propitious moment
in the history of the new nation. The population appeared to have shifted somewhat and the southern
states were coming into their own; they would surely
have power in the new Congress.

"Tomorrow I shall be introduced to Mrs. Madison," Mason James said aloud to no one. He was sitting now in the drawing room of his Georgetown
house, a glass of Bourbon and branch water in one
hand. His long legs extended out in front of him and
his feet rested on a pretty blue footstool. "And she
will help me because she is a lady of great influ-
ence." He toasted the air in front of himself.

"Did you want something, sir?" Mason James
looked up. It was only Righteous, his personal slave.

"No, no, just thinking aloud," he said, waving the
old man off. And Mason James resolved, this time silently, to go to the Library of Congress and read
some of the previous arguments given by other

15

states when they were petitioning for statehood. "It's just a grand world," he said. "A grand, grand world."

The old Crippen farm was of medium size and it had two sturdy buildings: a white clapboard farmhouse and a large barn built of fieldstone and wood. Richard Adams had bought the farm some two years ago when, at long last, he had saved sufficient money to settle down.

Having lived a life filled with disappointment, Richard Adams was a moody, discontented man who had searched endlessly for his lost parents. He reckoned himself to be fifty or thereabouts. He had been reared in a foundling home in Boston and when he was near twelve, he had been apprenticed out as a farm hand to a childless couple in Framingham, a small community just outside of Boston.

There, Richard Adams worked till he was in his midtwenties. Restless, he then left to seek work in Boston. After holding down a variety of jobs, he married one Mattie Morrison. Mattie became pregnant almost immediately, but she died in childbirth when little Colleen was born.

Determined not to have his daughter reared in a foundling home as he had been, Richard Adams struck out westward with the infant in tow. He worked whenever he could, saving as much as possible. Wherever he went, women took pity on the motherless child who accompanied him, and thus little Colleen Adams came to know many temporary mothers.

Colleen had been twenty when he bought the Crippen farm. "It's the first real home I've ever had," he had confided. Then almost sheepishly, he corrected himself: "*We've* ever had."

Colleen had smiled with understanding and given her father a hug. He was a brooding man, a man so

16

much alone that he didn't even seem to miss her when she was gone. "You'll be marrying one day soon," he kept telling her.

It was as if he didn't want to get too close to Colleen, fearing that he would lose her completely. Or that, like his parents, she would disappear from the face of the earth.

"When I marry, I'll bring you your grandchildren, we'll be together. We'll be a family!" Colleen always promised her father, but he would only shrug and turn away. "You'll go away," he would mumble.

Colleen knew her father suffered over his origins. He must have had some veiled memory of his mother, for he yearned to know her name.

"Adams isn't even our real name," Richard Adams would lament. "It's only the name they gave me in the foundling home." He made a funny noise when he talked about his name, a sort of a snort. "They said I ought to be happy to have the name of one of New England's first families."

Colleen was not like her father. She had learned to make do, and in her head she carried her own imaginary family. The child who had known a hundred mothers would say, "Wherever I go, the people look different, but the mix is the same." And so it seemed to be. Colleen's substitute mothers were bustling women; farm women who worked hard and always had large families. Colleen always had a couple of substitute sisters and it always seemed as if one loved her and the other did not. She had substitute brothers too—little boys who pulled her braids and chased her around the barn. The faces were all different, but somehow the personalities always were the same.

When Colleen and Richard Adams first came to the farm outside Lewiston, it seemed an isolated place to Colleen. There was no other family living in the farmhouse, there were no substitute mothers,

17

sisters, or brothers. But as time passed, Colleen grew used to it and used to being alone with her father. Richard Adams enjoyed this life and constantly praised the quiet of his own parlor.

In the evenings, Richard Adams wrote letters. The letters seldom were answered, and if they were, it never was with the words Richard Adams wanted to read. He wrote to this person and that, always trying to find clues to his parentage. He kept in constant touch with the foundling home lest anyone, even after all these years, make inquiries about him.

Colleen had no letters to write, and her leisure time was spent sewing and preserving. That was until she had met Josh and Ian. Then, just as her father predicted, her life became quite different.

When Colleen returned from her picnic, she told her father what had happened.

"And on which young man have you decided?"

Colleen had bitten her lip and shrugged. "I have to think," she murmured.

Several days passed and her father finally confronted her. "You know which one you will choose," he told her. "You are only worrying about the one you reject."

"Yes," Colleen agreed. "You're right."

"Time will make it harder for him. Sit down, write your letter, and speak your mind. The longer you wait, the more anxiety you are causing."

Colleen hung her head. "You are right," she agreed. Then, seeking out his eyes, "How do you feel, Papa?"

"It has to be," he replied. "You're a woman. Women get married."

"We won't be apart," Colleen reiterated.

But as usual, Richard Adams only mumbled.

Jenna eyed the letter pouch on the table. A messenger had brought it over an hour earlier and now it

18

sat there, staring up at Jenna ominously. It was a small brown leather pouch sealed with red sealing wax. "Drat!" Jenna said. It was for both Josh and Ian, and clearly it was from Colleen. If it had been addressed to either one of them, it might have offered her a clue. But it was addressed to both. Inside, there was a letter, a letter that undoubtedly rejected one of her sons. Jenna's curiosity was piqued, but it was tempered with apprehension. "Drat!" she repeated. Josh and Ian wouldn't be back for at least an hour. "Now what will I do?" Jenna questioned herself. Since the arrival of the letter she had cleaned the parlor, constantly circling the missive, looking at it now and again and dusting past it. For a time she had sat down and looked at it as if staring at it would make the message inside visible to her.

Finally, Jenna put her cleaning rags away and got out her sewing. She sat down in front of her frame and continued the embroidery she had begun so many weeks ago, glancing every now and again at the letter pouch.

"Aren't we busy?" Will burst into the room and broke Jenna's concentration.

"Oh, you startled me."

"I made plenty of noise; you're either going deaf or you're lost in thought."

Jenna didn't answer, but instead motioned toward the letter pouch. "It came an hour ago," she commented.

"And you can't wait to know what's in it."

"I'm worried," Jenna countered.

"You're curious. And you want to know who we'll celebrate for and who we'll mourn for."

"I wish you wouldn't make a joke of it. It's quite bad enough to have Josh and Ian so . . . so damn offhanded. I'm not sure either of them ought to get married if they care so little."

"They care a lot," Will said in a serious voice.

19

"Colleen may not be the only white woman they've known—certainly there must have been some in Montreal when they were being schooled—but she's the only one around here. They've sown their wild oats with Indian women for the most part, so Colleen is something quite different. There's certainly no use spending time in competition for a woman who doesn't love you. I think they're being really sensible. It's Colleen's decision whom she loves and I'm damn certain that while she likes both of them, she only loves one of them."

"Do you suppose the one who is rejected will marry an Indian woman?"

"Do you object to that?"

Jenna shook her head. "No, not really. I guess I think it might be difficult for their children, and I'd hate to see that; there's a lot of prejudice against half-breeds, you know."

"I know," Will conceded. His eyes returned to the letter pouch. "A considerate woman—at least she didn't keep them waiting too long."

"What do you think?" Jenna queried.

"I daresay they both have their merits," Will said with a smirk on his face. "Good Lord, don't ask me to choose between my sons. I'm not the one who has to, thank heaven."

"I'm sorry," Jenna apologized. "I couldn't choose either."

"At least you won't have to wait much longer to have your curiosity put to rest." Will had moved to the window and looked out. "I thought I heard their horses."

"They've been up at Lochiel helping with the harvest," Jenna told him. It was a large harvest and all the members of the family who were not otherwise occupied had been called upon to help.

Josh and Ian entered the house laughing. "I dug

20

up a turnip today that will last all winter!" Ian announced.

"You have a letter. It's here."

Both men stood in the doorway of the parlor. Jenna looked at both of them intently. "Do you want us to leave?" Jenna turned and glanced at Will uneasily. He had put his feet up on the footstool and was making himself comfortable.

Josh took the pouch from his mother's hand. "It's from Colleen." He turned it over slowly, then handed it to Ian. "You open it," he suggested.

Ian took the letter pouch and carefully broke the lump of red sealing wax. He unfolded two parchments. "One for each of us," he smiled, handing Josh a letter with his name on the outside.

Jenna studied their faces as they read in silence. "Oh, Ian," she said after a moment. His face clearly revealed his rejection, his eyes misted slightly. But there was no hesitation. He turned to his brother instantly and grasped his arm.

"You'll be a happy man!" he said enthusiastically. "She's a beautiful, kind, and loving woman."

Josh's face was flushed. He grasped his brother in a bear hug. "You're a good man, Ian. No man deserves a brother like you!"

Jenna let out her breath and was certain everyone heard her. "I've been so worried," she said in a small voice. "Oh, Ian, I'm so sorry—and Josh, I'm so happy! And I don't know what to say."

"Now, now, I'm not married yet," Josh said, putting his arm around his mother.

"Nor am I dead and buried," Ian put in.

"There was more to our pact than allowing Colleen to decide," Josh offered. "But that's your story now, Ian."

"More?" Jenna looked at her two sons and then at her husband. "I don't understand."

21

"When we decided to end our friendly competition over Colleen and ask her to decide between us, we agreed that whoever of us lost would take the position the Hudson's Bay Company offered."

"What position?" Jenna asked. "What are you talking about?"

"Lord Selkirk is planning to recruit Highlanders—refugees from the clearances—and bring them to North America. He plans to settle them on the Red River, in Rupert's Land near the border of the Dakota territory."

"Miles MacDonell already is in Scotland recruiting settlers," Ian put in. "Now I guess I'll be joining him."

"In Scotland!" Jenna's voice sounded the amazement she felt. "You're going to Scotland? It's so far!"

"Bet your mother said that to you when you went to New Orleans," Will said.

Jenna blushed and thought it was true, she sounded just like her mother. "And then what?" she asked.

"Then the settlers will be taken by ship to York Factory and from there down the river system to Pembina."

"My Lord," Jenna gasped. "That's a long journey!"

"I've been West," Ian said.

"Yes, but not with settlers. And you haven't been to Scotland. That's across the sea!"

Ian laughed. "Grandmother survived the trip in 1746! I suspect I'll survive in this more enlightened year of 1811. It hardly takes a month now!"

"Enough!" Will interrupted. "Josh, you ought to be on your way to see Colleen's father. And Ian, I don't suppose you are leaving tomorrow?"

"Not quite," Ian said, smiling.

Will walked to the cupboard and withdrew a container of brandy. "I think a double toast is in order."

"I guess it is," Jenna allowed, suppressing her surprise at the full extent of Ian and Josh's bargain. "I guess I'll have to get used to losing all my men at once."

"Hardly all of them!" Will laughed, slapping her playfully on the bottom. "Besides, it will give you more time to work in the store. Let's drink to Josh's coming engagement and to Ian's adventure!" Will handed them each a glass.

"And to the harvest," Josh added. "Even though it's not all in yet."

The next day, Josh crossed the river, leaving from the dock at Queenston. The Niagara River was at its narrowest here, a mere two hundred fifty yards across, but they were rough, turbulent yards and one normally reached the far shore somewhat downstream.

Once on the other side, Josh rented a horse and continued on to Colleen's, which was outside Lewiston. There, he formally asked Colleen's father for her hand in marriage and permission to court her.

"It's what my daughter wants," Adams admitted. "I told her she would be able to marry for love, though I understand you're not poor."

Josh smiled and extended his hand to Adams. "I think I can offer her a good life. I have property, I own part of my father's trading post, and I have money from my fur-gathering expeditions out West."

"And once you're married?" Adams asked. "Are you going to wrap up my daughter in a Hudson's Bay Company blanket and take her West like an Indian squaw?"

"No, sir. I have land near Lochiel, but I also invested in land around Fort York. We might go up there and build. The land is right on Lake Ontario.

23

We could open a trading post there. I've thought about it quite a lot, and I do have the money to get started."

"Inherited?" Adams asked, raising one eyebrow.

"No, sir. I made it on two successive fur trips West."

Adams grunted and then silently poured some whiskey and drank a toast with Josh. "To a good marriage," he toasted.

Later, Josh and Colleen walked in the woods. "The leaves are going to turn soon," she said and smiled. They followed a narrow, rutted path that led to a small brook that intersected the farm. "Papa says he'll clear this land next year, add to what's already under cultivation."

Josh stopped short. "This is the first time we've ever been alone."

Colleen looked into his eyes. "I know," she replied, her huge blue eyes searching his. "It's strange, I feel I know you so well. I feel I always was alone with you."

Josh reached out and took her hands in his, pulling her toward him. "I love you, Colleen Adams." He looked down into her face. "I love everything about you."

Colleen bit her lip. "Did Ian take it too badly?"

"No, I suspect he'll recover. Though he was as smitten with you as I am."

"And would you have recovered had I chosen Ian?"

"After a few hundred years." Josh smiled.

"And Ian?"

"Ian needs a feeling of conquest," Josh told her. "If he doesn't conquer a woman, his ardor soon fades."

"Oh, and will your ardor fade because you didn't have to conquer me, because you knew I loved you from the start?"

"Not if you give me simple lifelong adoration,"

24

Josh said good-naturedly. With that, he pulled her into his arms and kissed her full on the lips, moving his mouth on hers and pressing her against him sensuously.

His large hands moved across Colleen's back and she could almost imagine she was naked in his arms. Every inch of him was pressed against her tightly, and the outline of him seemed to press through her. She felt light, dizzy, and helpless in his arms. Her skin seemed to glow warm, she felt small, and all her senses seemed to vanish in her rising desire for the man who kissed her so passionately.

Colleen felt his hands moving across her back, over her full hips, even to her firm breasts. But they did not linger, they moved urgently even as his lips sought hers again and again.

After a few moments, Colleen nearly fell against him, burying her face in his broad chest. "Oh," she moaned in a low voice. Suddenly there were sensations she never had experienced. A dampness between her legs, a feeling of total physical and mental euphoria. "Oh, dear," she finally said and sighed.

And Josh laughed. " 'Oh dear' is right." He let her go and looked at her. "If we kiss like that anymore, you'll be with child on the day we get married."

Colleen's face went pink. "I trust you," she whispered. "I trust you with my life."

"I don't trust myself," Josh told her as he looked into her face. "I want you too much."

Colleen nodded. "And I you."

"On our wedding night," Josh told her. "I love you too much to want you the talk of idle gossips."

He took her hand and they walked hand in hand down the path back toward the farmhouse. "I'll come and see you as often as I can," Josh promised. "And you'll come to Lochiel too." Josh paused and scratched his chin. "Does your father mind being alone?"

25

"No, it's the way he is, alone. Maybe grandchildren will change him, but I don't know. He likes being alone."

"There'll be lots of grandchildren," Josh said, smiling as he gave her a hug. Colleen, Josh decided, was as passionate as she was beautiful, and he counted himself a lucky man.

CHAPTER II

November 1, 1811

All of October had been sunny and crisp. The sky never had seemed more blue and the leaves of autumn never had appeared in more brilliant hues of red, gold, and orange. But now it was the first of November, and the low, sweeping winds and the frosty nights combined to rob the maples, birch, oak, and sumac of their leaves. Fall chased the Indian summer away even as the last birds flew South, leaving their northern climate to heartier creatures.

Still it was a pleasant time. The smell of burning leaves filled the nostrils, the aroma of cooked apples made mouths water, and men talked of the harvest, grateful that it had been so bountiful. Nonetheless, the sky no longer was cloudless. A dark storm gathered around the Niagara, and the heavy gray cloud banks to the north boded a long winter, while those that gathered to the south foretold the end of a tenuous peace.

In the warm kitchen of the white frame house in Queenston, Jenna MacLean paused momentarily to wipe her brow. The paddle of the butter churn had grown difficult to manipulate, indicating that the butter was nearly ready and that the residue of buttermilk could be removed and set aside. The butter, as usual, would be divided in squares and stored in the cold house behind the main house. In the winter, great chunks of ice were brought from the river to the cold house, lasting nearly all summer and providing a cool place to store meat and produce.

Jenna's mind was not on the butter, it was on her husband, Will MacLean, and on her eldest son, Josh. Josh was the child of Jenna's youth; she had been only seventeen when he was born. Josh also was the subject of a family secret, the only secret Jenna MacLean had ever kept from her mother.

Josh was not Will's son, but the son of James MacLean. When Will and Jenna had married, they made a vow to keep Josh's true parentage a secret and to raise the infant as if he were Will's own son.

On three occasions Jenna had regretted their decision to keep the truth from Josh and the rest of the family. The first was Josh's baptism, when Jenna had longed to confide in her own mother. The second occasion was when Josh turned eighteen and Jenna felt he ought to know the truth. The third was now, and her feelings were stronger than they had been before. Josh was engaged and Jenna felt he ought to know. But Will was dead set against it and as stubborn as could be. "He's my son," Will would argue. "Mine as surely as if I had sired him! Telling him now, after all these years, could only cause grief."

It's because he loves Josh so fiercely, Jenna told herself. Will can't face Josh knowing that he's not his natural son. Of course, Will was right on one score. Telling Josh about James MacLean could only raise questions about James and the rest of the family. If part of the tale were told, all of it would have to be told. Josh would want to know all about James MacLean, about his aunt, Mad Maria, and his grandmother, Angelique, and how she died. Jenna shuddered. James MacLean was a mean and selfish creature, and his sister had been pure evil. Some years back, Will had met a trader from Natchez and heard for the first time in over twenty years about

28

his sister Maria and his brother James. "Strange folks," the trader had called them. "Strange, but powerful!"

It seemed James MacLean had amassed a huge tract of land, had built a mansion house to shame the houses of New Orleans, and had made a fortune with cotton. Slaves? Yes, it was said that James MacLean had over a hundred slaves. But those facts were not the crux of the trader's tale. It seemed that in the year after Jenna and Will had run away, James and Maria had lived together and, it was whispered, they lived as man and wife. "The darkest sin of all!" the trader confided. "And it gave issue, there is a child . . . ." And Maria? Will had asked, "Dead," the trader confirmed. "Died when the child was born."

So Josh had a half brother as well as a father of whom he knew nothing. But what bothered Jenna—and made her want to tell Josh—was her fear that somehow he would find out the truth. "He will hate us for lying!" Jenna had told Will. "He might never forgive us. We ought to tell him, epecially now that he's to be married."

"No," Will had replied firmly. "I don't ever want him to know about James and Maria."

That was last night's argument and Jenna felt that all the ends still were dangling. She had not said it all, she had not expressed her greatest fear.

Jenna let go of the butter paddle and flexed her fingers. She had been gripping it tightly in her anxiety. "Oh!" Jenna cried out as she whirled about. "You scared me half to death!"

Will had crept up behind her and wrapped his arms around her waist, squeezing it tightly. "You look quite alive to me," he whispered in her ear.

Jenna looked up into her husband's face. Forty-seven or not, his smile still was boyish and his manner still playful. Too playful sometimes, she thought. But Will's smile was infectious, it mellowed her angry moods. He lowered his head and kissed her on the back of the neck, just below the ear. "I thought you were at Lochiel making preparations for this afternoon. You shouldn't do that to me. You shouldn't sneak up on me."

Will spun her around and kissed her lips, moving his hands along her back and finally punctuating his kiss with a loving, playful slap on the backside.

"You're terrible," Jenna chided. She could not conceal her smile.

"You're afraid I'll melt the butter with my ardent passion," Will answered dramatically. This was Will's way, Jenna knew. Whenever they argued, whenever something came between them, Will came to her playfully, teasing and coaxing her from her worries with idle lovemaking. At such times they both were young again. At such times all was both forgiven and forgotten.

"It's not even ten A.M. and I'm a respectable matron," Jenna reminded him. "We're not courting now."

Will only laughed at her, then swept her into his arms, lifting her feet right off the floor. "I'm quite a young man, thank you. You're a young and, I must say, very desirable woman. I don't feel like being dead and buried. Unless I'm to be buried under a great down quilt with you! Let's go to bed!"

"Put me down, Will MacLean! You're being foolish!"

Will backed away and gave forth with a mock yawn. "I'm so old I can't possibly stay awake to make love to you at night. I like making love in the daytime."

"I have to drain off the buttermilk and wrap up the butter and peel the potatoes and make the pies. . . . Will, I have a thousand things to do before four o'clock, when we leave for Lochiel!"

"A likely excuse!" Will lunged toward her and,

seizing her small waist, hoisted her up and over his left shoulder, carrying her from the kitchen into the foyer and then up the narrow staircase leading to the second floor.

"You're impossible, Will MacLean! Impossible!" Jenna protested and hit his back playfully, though in truth she felt quite excited by his ardor.

"You love it!" Will proclaimed knowingly, and he dumped her on the feather mattress and fell on top of her, nuzzling her long white neck with kisses. Will then lifted his head and, with his chin cupped in his hand and propping himself up on one elbow, he looked down into her face.

Jenna stared back into her husband's impish brown eyes. As always, the argument they'd had the night before was forgotten. Will wouldn't mention it; Jenna didn't want to.

Will leaned over again and this time his kiss was long and slow as his hand traveled beneath her skirts, stroking her thigh, then exploring her more intimately till she ceased all make-believe resistance and pressed herself to him. When he released her lips, her eyes were closed and the look of rapturous enjoyment on her face excited Will further. He loosened her dress and moved his hands over her mature breasts. "Magnificent lady," he whispered in her ear. Will moved his hand away for a moment as he undid his own clothing and removed the rest of hers. She moaned slightly, as if in a trance state.

"You'd think I'd tire of you, after so long," Will teased. Then, burying his face in her deep cleavage, he murmured, "But I don't." Will touched her, moving his hand across her cool white skin lightly. He knew the slow process of arousal was not altogether necessary because Jenna always responded instantly to him.

"Oh, you tease me too much," Jenna said, pressing against him.

"I like to tease you," Will answered. "Tease you and tease you. I like to watch you, the way you breathe, the way your cheeks get hot and rosy."

Jenna groaned in response and Will moved his hand artfully. He felt her tense beneath him and her skin grew warm as her lovely face flushed with excitement and her breath came in short gasps. He waited till she moved upward toward him and embraced him, digging her fingers into his bare back. Then he entered her and they moved together with ease, each reaching satisfaction at the same instant while enfolded in the other's arms. When they calmed, they held each other for a long while, content and warm beneath the huge quilt.

After a time, Jenna sat up and ran her hand through her now tangled hair. "Oh, I must get up." Jenna stretched and Will watched her with warm, loving eyes. Jenna could feel his admiring eyes on her buttocks as she stood. Her skin was white, her breasts full and mature, yet still wonderful to the touch.

Will reflected that beauty came from within as well as from the fortunes of nature. She glowed with contentment and, like her mother, she was intelligent and brave. However silly she had been as a young girl, whatever mistakes she had made, they were past. Today Jenna's judgment was cool, she was secure in her ability to cope with difficult situations, she was loved, and she knew how to love.

Will sat up and began to put his own clothes back on. Jenna dressed quickly. "You know Josh will be home soon. Honestly, how would it be for a grown man to come home and find his parents in bed making love, before lunch!"

Will laughed. "I trust he would have the good manners to say, 'Excuse me.' "

"He'd be shocked!"

"I hope I reared my son better than that!"

Jenna turned to Will with a more serious expression on her face. Will had emphasized the words "my son." It brought back the memory of their recent argument and again apprehension clouded her mind. It was something she just could not shake. She looked at Will pleadingly now, her green eyes wide, unblinking, and filled with concern and love.

"I have to say one more thing," Jenna murmured. "It's the last thing I'll say on the subject: Will, it would be terrible if—if something happened and Josh found out from someone else." Jenna could hardly finish the sentence. It expressed the fear that lurked in the back of her mind, the fear that after all these years something would happen to rip her happiness from her. She feared James MacLean still, the specter of him loomed large.

Will shook his head. "No," he answered simply. "There's only James, and even James could only guess. There's no one to tell Josh, there's no way he could find out."

Jenna nodded. She had no desire to begin the argument again, and Will never would give in. She had expressed her fear and though she felt better for having spoken it, she was not entirely content.

"There's the front door," Will said.

Jenna flushed. "Oh, it must be Josh. He's home. I'll go downstairs and you stay up here. It'll be less obvious that way."

"Less obvious?" The mischievous look was back in Will's eyes. "Come, come now. He must think we make love sometime. How else would he have gotten here?"

Jenna turned quickly away; again Will had said something in jest that stabbed like a pain through her. "Children do not think of their parents that way," she stumbled.

Will was silent for a moment. "All right, I'll play the game. You go downstairs first."

Jenna whirled about, her mind troubled with Will's last comment: "He must think we make love sometime. How else would he have gotten here?" He has come to believe he did sire Josh, Jenna thought. He's chosen to forget the truth himself, to bury it, as if he didn't remember the months of her pregnancy before they were married, before they made love.

John Fraser Murray was a gangling youth of eleven; his eyes were blue like his father's and his unruly hair was golden red like everybody's on his mother's side of the family.

For as long as he could remember, November had been his favorite month. First off, his birthday came at the end of the month and always meant a special celebration. Second, there was the harvest celebration. It was a gathering of the clan from far and wide, a day when the Macleod and MacLean clans joined with their neighbors in a giant bonfire and sumptuous corn roast.

There would be fiddlers and step dancing; more pie than any boy could eat; singing and storytelling; and, of course, a gigantic iron pot filled with ears of corn that could be served up with fresh churned butter; wild partridge skewered over an open fire; rich, dark bread; and a thick, tarty sauce boiled up from wild cranberries sweetened with maple sugar. John Fraser Murray's mouth watered at the thought. He could hardly wait for the afternoon sun to set and for the visitors to begin arriving. In the distance, the men already were making preparations for the huge fire; in the kitchen, the women were cooking.

He glanced at the sun. It couldn't be later than 10:30 A.M. Four o'clock seemed an eternity away.

"And your chore," his mother had told him earlier that morning, "is to repair the rock wall around the house. See that it's done good and proper. No daydreaming, you hear?"

It was not a difficult task, especially since the weather was cool. Still, John Fraser Murray took his time, pausing after he put a big rock in place near the side of the pathway that led from the main road to the long veranda in front of the old stone house. He wiped his brow on his shirt sleeve and looked at his five-year-old cousin, Ronald Macleod, who held a medium-size stone in his small arms. "Where do you want this one?" Ronald asked, displaying a large gap where his front teeth had recently fallen out.

John scratched his head. "Over there," he pointed to a small gap in the wall some four feet from where the two boys stood. Ronald placed the stone carefully, aware that he was only an apprentice to his older cousin. He straightened up and looked off toward the house in the distance. "How old is she?" Ronald asked, indicating his great-grandmother, who sat in the old rocker on the front veranda. From a distance, Janet Cameron Macleod seemed engrossed in her knitting. She sat wrapped in a Hudson's Bay Company blanket and rocked slowly as she worked. By Christmas, as all her grandchildren and great-grandchildren knew, her knitting miraculously turned into mufflers, mittens, scarves, and socks. There always was a special gift for everyone from Grandmother Macleod.

John's face displayed a slight frown as he considered Ronald's question. Pride wouldn't allow him to count on his fingers in front of his younger cousin, so he had to work it out in his head. "Eighty-two," he finally answered. "She's eighty-two."

Ronald's eyes lit up with awe. "That's old! That's older than the house! Older than that old maple, older maybe even than the falls!"

"It's not as old as the falls," John corrected. "The falls are thousands of years old. Great-granny's not even a hundred . . . yet."

Ronald sank onto the leaf-strewn ground, folding

up his legs Indian-style. "Let's rest awhile," he suggested.

John Fraser Murray shot a look toward the veranda. Great-granny was absorbed in her knitting, the men were all out behind the barn, and the women were in the kitchen. "I guess it will be all right," he allowed, judging their task to be near completion in any case.

"Nothing is thousands of years old," Ronald persisted as he abstractedly played with the leaves.

"You only think that because you're five. You just can't imagine anything or anyone being old because you haven't lived long enough yourself. When you're eleven—almost twelve, like I am—you'll understand age a whole lot better."

"Well, I'm going to live a long, long time," Ronald bragged. "Maybe I'll live to be a hundred, or a hundred and six."

"Hardly anyone lives that long," John answered. "The only people who lived that long are in the Bible. They had to live a long time, cause it's such a long book. You know, like Methuselah, whose years numbered nine hundred and sixty-nine."

Ronald looked up from the design he was making with the leaves. They read the Bible every single night, it was the book used to teach the children how to read, and it was memorized. But there were too many big words and so many long names and so much that was confusing. Ronald couldn't keep it all straight. "What's a begat?" he suddenly asked.

John grabbed a handful of tall grass and began braiding three strands together. "A begat?" He repeated the word thoughtfully. "What makes you ask a question like that?"

Ronald shrugged. " 'Cause everyone in the Bible is always begating. You know, Adam and Eve begat Seth, who begat Enos, who begat Cainan and Cainan begat Mahalalel . . . and that's as far as I remember 'cept there's a lot of begatting after that too."

John Fraser Murray looked around uneasily, but no one had noticed the boys had ceased working. The only person around was Great-granny, and she was well out of earshot. "Begatting means having babies," John whispered conspiratorially, hoping that little Ronald would not ask for details on how, exactly, begatting was accomplished.

"Did Mama and Papa begat me?" Ronald asked, a bewildered look on his face.

John shook his head in the affirmative. Ronald was a five-year-old question box. Why do horses have four legs? Why do the falls fall? Why this, why that. But, John conceded, begatting was important. It certainly was more important than the pointless questions Ronald usually asked.

"Your great-grandmother," John motioned off toward Janet, "married Mathew Macleod. Janet and Mathew begat Andrew, Mat, Helena, and Jenna. And they adopted three other children: Madelaine, René, and Pierre Deschamps. Adopting is different from begatting, so let's forget that for now."

"Only Great-auntie Madelaine lives here anyway," Ronald interrupted. "The others all live far away."

John nodded, not wanting his explanation to get more complicated. "Anyway," he continued, "Andrew Macleod married Laurie MacPherson and they begat your Aunt Catherine and your father, John Macleod. And your father married Tara O'Brien and they begat your sister Peggy, your brother Lawrence, and you. Understand?"

Ronald's brow furrowed. "And all Janet and Mathew's children begat too? Is that why we have so many cousins?"

37

John shook his head again, proud of his explanation.

Ronald sighed. "Well, I don't quite understand, but I will when I'm a hundred and six!"

"It'll take at least that long," John mumbled under his breath. John recalled that he had overheard his great-grandmother talking to his Grandmother Helena Fraser at breakfast.

"Why are you still sending presents to René's family in Rupert's Land?" Helena had asked.

"Because they're family," Janet insisted. Janet Macleod's voice was deep and husky; she still rolled her r's in a Scots accent.

"You'd think René could at least write," Helena said.

"He does write, but not very often," Janet replied. Grandmother Helena had turned her face away. No one argued with Great-grandmother Janet. "When René chooses to write, he writes," Janet said with determination. "Miles do not separate a family, nor do years change love."

"Are you children working or playing?" The shout from the veranda jolted John Fraser Murray from his memory of breakfast. His grandmother had joined his great-grandmother, and her attention was directed toward him and Ronald.

John Fraser Murray jumped to his feet, and little Ronald jolted upright. Grandmother Helena was not to be ignored. All the children called her "grandmother," whether they were her grandchildren or not, and jumped when she told them to. On the veranda, in the distance, John could see Helena standing with a broom in one hand. "Winter's coming and I want all those loose rocks piled up where they belong, you hear! You finish your chores like everyone else, or there'll be no celebration for you! And you'll feel this broom across your backsides too!"

John immediately resumed work on the rock wall. "Hurry!" he motioned to Ronald. "She means it. You can fool Mama sometimes, but not Granny Helena."

On the veranda, Janet squinted off into the distance and dropped her knitting into her lap. "They have been working," she told her daughter. "You're too hard on them. They're just children."

"Just children! Just children can get into plenty of trouble. And children have mouths to feed like everybody else. They have to do their share, they have to learn the joy of hard work, or they won't grow up decent. Idle hands are the devil's playthings. You taught me that, I taught that to Abigail, John, and William. And it's what I intend to teach my grandchildren."

Janet smiled, her green eyes flickering with amusement. "Just don't be too hard. Let them have time to play, to explore. For heaven's sake, Helena, let them be children!"

"Mama, I'm fifty-seven, I'm not your baby anymore." Helena set her broom against the wall. "I only sound hard," she confessed. "It's a carefully developed tone of voice that puts the fear of God into them. I'll not have my grandchildren grow up like the blacksmith's children. Lazy and spoiled! I'll not have them think they can spend their lives living off the wealth accumulated by their parents and grandparents. They have to learn to do for themselves."

Janet smiled again, trying to hide her amusement. Helena sounded a trifle annoyed. "You'll always be my baby," Janet answered, "no matter how old you are." Then Janet cleared her throat. "I'm proud of my children, grandchildren, and great-grandchildren." There was a faraway look in her eyes and a few strands of silver-gray hair moved gently across her brow.

Janet's son Andrew Macleod was an engineer with

his own firm. His son worked with him and they were known as Macleod & Son. Mathew would have liked that.

Tom and Madelaine Macleod owned the most profitable mill in the area, and Donald, their son, was with the Hudson's Bay Company, as were Albert Murray, Helena's son-in-law, and Helena's son, William Fraser.

And Janet's other daughter, the youngest of her brood, was married to Will MacLean. Josh, the eldest, was a trader, Lannie had married Tad Miller and moved up to Kingston, while young Ian was on his way to Scotland. Susanna MacLean had married the preacher's son, Steven MacAndrew.

They were a large, powerful family with four farms, a mill, an inn, and engineering firm, and interests in two trading firms. And back in Trois-Rivières, Pierre Deschamps had left a huge estate to his children and grandchildren, and somewhere out in the vast northwestern territory known as Rupert's Land, René, who was a widower, had married an Indian woman and now had grown children by his first wife. René was with the old North West Company.

"I wish your father could have lived to see all this," Janet said pensively as she returned to her knitting. "He'd have been proud, so very proud."

"He lived to see Lochiel restored," Helena put in.

"But not to see Macleod & Son," Janet answered. "He always wanted that most, he wanted to do it himself."

Helena reached over and automatically patted her mother on the shoulder. Without looking, she knew her mother's eyes were misty with memories. Somehow, Mathew Macleod never was far from Janet's thoughts. Although he had died in the fall of 1790, a full twenty-one years ago, it was almost as if he still were there. And often, more often than Helena could remember, she had seen her mother standing by the huge Celtic cross that marked Mathew Macleod's grave. He was gone, but somehow he and Janet seemed in communion. Helena knew her parents had a powerful love, a love that now seemed to cross the boundary that separated life and death.

Helena emerged from her reverie at the sound of the approaching carriage. Janet again dropped her knitting, peering out toward the dirt road that led to the farmhouse.

"It's Donald and Agnes," Helena announced. Donald Macleod was Tom's eldest son, and his wife, Agnes Mackenzie Macleod, was a cousin to Alexander Mackenzie, who, having moved back to Scotland, looked after the business of the North West Company in the United Kingdom. Alexander was best known for his exploration of the North American continent. Some joked that he had walked from Montreal to the Pacific Ocean only because he was too cheap to buy a horse. And that Alexander Mackenzie was a shrewd man was not to be denied.

The carriage came to a rattling halt down by the stone wall and Donald climbed down, lifting Agnes to the ground. Donald was straight and tall; Agnes was hardly five feet and very frail, more like a girl of eighteen than the matron of twenty-seven that she was. It was well that she and Donald were childless, Helena thought, because she might not survive the stress of childbirth.

The couple waved as they walked up the path toward the house. Under his arm, Donald carried an awkward package. "Auntie Helena," he said, beaming. He bent and kissed her on the cheek. "Grandmother," he kissed Janet too, handing her the large package. "A gift," he announced. "Just arrived from Montreal, courtesy of the North West Company."

It was true that the North West Company and the Hudson's Bay Company were in direct competition with one another, and certainly Alexander Mackenzie knew that Janet Cameron Macleod owned shares of the Hudson's Bay Company and that her grandsons worked for it. To another stockholder of the Hudson's Bay Company old Mackenzie gladly would have sent poison, and of course he was not a man renowned for his generosity. But where Janet Cameron Macleod was concerned, business interests were laid aside and Alexander's generosity knew no bounds. The matriarch of Clan Macleod received every consideration from the wily old Scots trader. "In Montreal, when I was but a lad," he would tell his friends, "Janet Macleod was like a mother to me!"

Helena drew her shawl around her shoulders. "The wind's coming up. I think we should have some tea."

Donald extended his hand to Janet and helped her up. Helena took the Hudson's Bay Company blanket and folded it, carrying it into the house.

Helena bustled off to the kitchen to fix tea, calling out "Donald's here!" to Madelaine, who was supervising the preparation of the evening feast.

Agnes arranged herself on the settee, primly folding her long woolen skirt around her and leaning back cautiously as if she thought the back might fall off the venerable piece of furniture. Donald helped Janet to the rocker, then sat down on the low mantel by the hearth.

"Should I open it now?" Janet asked, referring to the package.

"Of course," Agnes answered.

Janet fumbled with the string and pulled away the wrapping. A bolt of heavy wool tartan was revealed. "Oh, that's much too grand for an old lady!" Janet exclaimed. "It's beautiful!"

"And all the way from Paisley," Agnes confirmed. "Cousin Alexander sent three."

"And news too, I trust." Helena came back into the center room and set the tea tray down.

"News as well," Agnes confirmed. "But not very good news." Agnes ran her hands over her skirt and looked down. "There's going to be more trouble between the North West Company and the Hudson's Bay Company."

"There's always competition," Helena observed, "keen competition. Good heavens, what else could you have when both companies are run by crusty old Scots? Do I remember the arguments in this family when we bought those stocks in the Hudson's Bay!"

Donald was leaning back against the stone fireplace. "Legally, Hudson's Bay has a monopoly in all of Rupert's Land; legally, the North West Company has no right to be working the territory."

Helena laughed. "Possession is nine tenths of the law. And the North West Company is there with the métis and they're very successful!"

Donald shook his head. "Didn't matter up till now because the two companies have stayed out of each other's way. But now it's going to be Scots against Scots."

Janet leaned forward in her chair. "Because of the settlers?" she asked.

"Alexander is hopping mad at the idea. He says they'll farm and run off the wild animals. It will be the end of the fur trade."

Janet scowled. "Lord Selkirk's a good man. I approve of what he's trying to do. I gave him my support." Some time ago, Janet had received a series of long letters from Lord Selkirk. He was, she had concluded, a most unusual man. Though he himself was a Lowlander, he had traveled through the Highlands in his youth and fallen in love with the land and its people, even mastering the Gaelic tongue.

"I had memories from those travels," Lord Selkirk had written her. "Now that I can, I want to help the

43

Scots. I want to use my title and my wealth to help the Highlanders in the hour of their need."

And a more needy hour one could not imagine. For years the Highland chieftains in Scotland had rented the land to their relatives. The tenant farms had been divided and redivided as the population grew. In the 1790s the Highland chieftains had decided that sheep were more profitable than the inefficient agricultural economy of the small crofts of land. Sheep produced wool and mutton, and the mills of Scotland cried out for more and more wool, just as the population cried out for more and more mutton. So the Highland chieftains had begun to clear their land; land that could not support both crofters and sheep. Daily, more land was seized; daily, more crofters poured into the Lowland cities to seek work. And daily, partly because the economy was depressed by the ongoing war between the British and the army of Napoleon, the plight of the landless peasants became more serious.

Lord Selkirk took pity on the poverty-stricken Highlanders living in the Lowland cities. He purchased over 40 percent of the Hudson's Bay Company and obtained from them a large land grant in Rupert's Land, on the Red River just north of the Dakotas, where he intended to settle as many Highland refugees as possible. Ian was on his way to Scotland to interview and recruit colonists.

"Cousin Alexander says that when the colonists come, the fur will disappear. Cousin Alexander says it will mean trouble. Cousin Alexander says he doesn't care how many crofters good Lord Selkirk wants to send to Upper Canada or the Maritimes, he doesn't want them in Rupert's Land. Cousin Alexander says—" Agnes was leaning forward and was in midsentence when Janet interrupted her.

"Cousin Alexander is a young pup with a bit of a swelled head!"

44

Her comment caused Agnes to move back, halfway behind Donald. "He's nearly fifty," she whimpered.

"A young pup," Janet reiterated. "But of course, I shall thank him for his gift."

There were suppressed smiles all around, save from Agnes. "I was only repeating what he said," she stammered. "I didn't mean I agreed with him."

Helena wiped her hands on her apron. Agnes was so defensive about her connections. "Alexander Mackenzie is a fine man," Helena said diplomatically, looking at Agnes. "But Lord Selkirk is doing something truly humane. His is a noble act. At least the man is trying to relieve the hunger and the miseries of the crofters. Alexander should know that if every person in Scotland settled in Rupert's Land, there still would be room for him to make money."

Agnes nodded somewhat dumbly. If the truth be known, she could not even imagine Rupert's Land. It extended from the eastward border of Upper Canada to the Pacific Ocean and from the North Pole south into the Dakotas. She had heard it included mountains so tall that their tips were above the clouds, a prairie so flat a man could see for nearly a hundred miles, and great wide rushing rivers. No one could even imagine how many hundreds of square miles there were in Rupert's Land. But Agnes did not express her thoughts or her questions. She always felt intimidated by the Macleod women. Agnes simply wasn't used to women with strong political views. She came from a family where women were not included in political conversations, and even when Alexander Mackenzie wrote to her, the paragraphs dealing with politics and economics were clearly intended for Donald's eyes. Therefore Agnes was the instrument of communication rather than the one actually being communicated with. Alexander would not write directly to Donald or to his old friend Tom Macleod. But Alexander knew that if he expressed himself to Agnes, his views would be passed on to the men as well as to Janet. Everyone makes an exception for her, Agnes thought. She even called the shares in the Hudson's Bay hers, though women could not inherit money or own anything. Actually, the shares were in Tom's name. But Janet made the decisions about what to invest in, and Janet called them "my" shares. And truly, Agnes thought, if anyone went against Janet's wishes, she would probably spank them.

"Rupert's Land is better," Janet said. "I told Lord Selkirk that myself. He tried the settlements in the Maritimes, but there's just not enough room there. And the land is not fertile enough!"

Donald smiled. His grandmother was an amazing woman. Her mind was sharp and alert, her eyes were clear, and her enthusiasm still was evident. She was a young spirit trapped in a body that no longer was functioning properly.

Janet shook her head. "I hate to see the trouble starting again. Scot against Scot." She paused. "Alexander had better behave himself," she muttered. "If he starts causing trouble between the North West Company and the Hudson's Bay, I personally will lift his kilt and take a switch to his bottom!"

There was laughter and Donald shook his head. "It's not bad enough to have the American yahoos warmongering day and night!"

Helena scowled. "I really don't know what that doddering old fool Madison is up to, anyway."

"President Madison," Agnes whispered.

"He's not my President!" Helena snapped. "To me he's just plain 'Mister.' I am quite tired of the assumption that we Upper Canadians share the views of every American. I was over in Lewiston last month and I heard some damn fool saying, 'If the

46

Americans marched right into Upper Canada, the Canadians wouldn't lift a finger! They'd be glad to be a part of the United States and if they're lucky, they will be!' And I said, 'Go to hell!' "

Agnes' mouth opened and closed again without a word being uttered. Grandmother Helena swore in public!

And Helena, sensing Agnes' shock, turned to her. "Don't look so shocked!" she almost growled. "Being able to use plain language is one of the privileges of old age!"

"It's the South," Donald interrupted, ignoring both his wife and his aunt. "They're expansionist bastards! They'll cause a war for certain."

Janet looked down in her lap. She folded her hands. "I hope I don't live to see it," she said quietly. "I've grown used to peace, I like it."

"You don't have to worry," Donald quickly reassured her. "If there's a war we'll win it! There won't be any Americans here! We've got men training, the British regulars are fine fighters! No, Grandmother, you have nothing to worry about—nothing!"

Janet looked up into Donald's eyes. Her hands still were folded and her fingers seemed to tense. "I'm not worried about myself. My time is coming."

"Oh, Mother, don't start talking that way." Helena was frowning, but Janet's eyes still were on Donald.

"If anything should happen to Lochiel, promise me you would rebuild . . . promise. I want it kept and cherished, I want it to be in our family always, a place to come back to. . . ."

"Of course we would!" Donald said.

"I don't want to die without knowing that Lochiel always will stand," Janet emphasized.

"I don't know why you're talking like this," Helena said.

47

Janet looked her daughter in the eye. "We're all going to die," she reminded her. "I may have lived longer than most, but I'm not immortal."

"The bonfire looks like it might reach right up to the sky!" Ronald Macleod exclaimed. In the dusk, the fire roared, giving off warmth. A whole deer was being prepared and the corn bubbled in a huge cauldron, their aromas mixing with those of the boiling cranberries and baking squash.

"I'll bet there's near a hundred people here," John Murray observed. He had tried to count them, but they kept coming and moving about, making his task impossible. Some ringed the great bonfire and others danced in the clearing to the music of the local fiddlers. Tom Macleod, wearing his kilt, danced with his little granddaughter, Jessie Knight, who was nine years old and hardly came up to his waist. They moved more slowly than the other dancers because Tom was sixty-four and the pace of the Highland fling was a bit too much. "I've flung my fling," he kept repeating cheerfully.

Will MacLean was supervising the children in games and races on one side of the far field where, earlier, before the sun had set, the older men had competed in some Highland games. Josh MacLean had won at tossing the caber. In that event, a great tapered fir log some seventeen feet long and weighing ninety to a hundred pounds was thrown outward so it traveled end over end and came to rest, according to the rules, with its smallest end pointing away from the thrower. Of all the Highland games, tossing the caber required the most strength and skill.

"One day I'll win that one!" John Fraser Murray proclaimed. As it was, he had to be content with coming in second in the hurdles races. There were five events in all, less than in the Highland games they might have held in Scotland. But they were enough to wear out the participants. There was the pole vault and a hammer throw, a long-distance race and a sprint race. And while the games were being played, so were the bagpipes. Even now, the melodies filled the open field and competed with the fiddlers' tunes.

"Aunt Helena says we might build a golf course on this field one day," John said. "It's a Highland game, played by old King James himself!"

"Is it as much fun as curling?" Ronald asked.

"Golf is a summer game. You can curl only in the winter."

"Mama's made a new broom for me to curl with. She's giving it to me for Christmas."

"You're not supposed to know that," John chided.

"But I do," the youngster bragged.

Over by the fire, Helena, Donald, and Jenna Mac-Lean stood near Janet Macleod, whose special rocking chair had been carried outside to the ring around the bonfire, where she could talk to all her family and neighbors and where she would be warm in spite of the chilly night air.

"Oh, how I love the bagpipes singing," Janet said. "I wish I could hear them every day."

"They're special because we don't hear them every day," Helena added.

"It's as if they're calling me," Janet said and sighed. Helena smiled silently, aware that her mother's brogue seemed to grow more pronounced during Scottish celebrations.

"Are you warm enough?" Helena asked.

"You're fussing over me," Janet said, shaking her head. Her voice seemed somehow far away, smaller and weaker than usual. But Helena didn't say anything. She suspected her mother was overcome by the celebration and with the homage her grandchil-

49

dren and great-grandchildren paid her. Even John, Helena's grandson, had come to Janet's side and offered her the candy he'd won for finishing second in the hurdles race.

"Would you like something?" Donald asked. "Some brandy?"

Janet nodded in the affirmative and Donald went off toward the table laden with food and drink.

"It's been a good harvest," Jenna said.

"Go dance," Janet urged, touching Jenna's skirt. "I like to see you dance. Seeing you dance is the next best thing to dancing myself."

Jenna smiled. "I remember you dancing. I don't dance as well."

"Yes, you do. Now, off with you. You too, Helena. Off with you. I'm not a relic to be worshiped. Let me sit here alone for a bit and just watch."

"Your brandy." Donald handed his grandmother the brandy snifter and bowed to her, smiling broadly. "It'll warm your insides."

"I'm already glowing," Janet replied. "It's the pipes, the night, and my family." She took a sip. "Go dance with Jenna. Will is still with the children."

"I'll stay here with you," Donald offered.

"No, I want to be alone. I just like to sit and watch. Now go, go on."

Reluctantly, Donald and Jenna went off to join the dancers. Now and again, amid the whirls, shouts, and stamping feet, or during the changing of partners, Donald looked over at his grandmother as she sat stiffly in her chair, alone and apart. One hand was in her lap, the other held her brandy snifter. But soon Donald was lost in the dance. He was part of a great circle within a circle now and the music became faster and faster. Janet had asked to be alone, and they all respected her wishes.

"Papa! Papa!" The piercing scream of young Janet

MacKay, Andrew Macleod's granddaughter, startled everyone. The fiddlers dropped their bows, the pipes wailed themselves into silence. Like dancers suddenly frozen by an icy wind, the celebrants came to an immediate silence and all turned toward the the crying seven-year-old, who stood bewildered by her great-grandmother's side.

Donald reached the rocker first. Janet's eyes were peacefully closed, the brandy snifter lay on the grass, having slipped from her fingers. There was no motion, no sound. Donald could hear the others breathing.

"Great-granny dropped her glass," Janet MacKay said, "and she won't wake up. Great-granny won't wake up. . . ." The child's distressed little voice didn't seem to stop, it merely faded away, getting smaller and smaller.

Donald could feel the tears forming in his eyes; he touched Janet's cheek and it was cold.

"Mama!" Helena was there too, her hand extended. "Oh, Mama . . ."

Jenna dropped to her knees in front of her mother and put her head in the old woman's lap. She had begun to sob lightly and her ears were deaf to the whispers that circulated through the family and assembled guests.

They seemed to come from all over the clearing. Even the fire seemed to have stopped crackling and there was an eerie silence among them. They didn't crowd around the rocker, but stood back in a circle, coming up one at a time, the children first, then the grandchildren, then the great-grandchildren. They came to say good-bye. Some touched her withered cheek, others her shoulder or hands.

Janet MacKay huddled next to Donald. "Granny won't wake up," she repeated. "Is Great-granny dead?"

51

Donald nodded. Then, wiping a tear from his own cheek, he looked down at the stricken little girl and lifted her into his arms. "She died the way she wanted to," he told Janet MacKay. "She died watching over her family."

CHAPTER III

November 15, 1811

Miles Macdonell thanked God for good weather. Though the colonists still had to survive the long winter, at least the cabins now were all nearly finished.

The first batch of settlers had sailed on the *Edward and Anne*, leaving Stornoway, Scotland, on July 26, 1811, and arriving at the port of York Factory on Hudson Bay on September 24, having been sixty-one days at sea.

Miles surveyed the faces of the colonists assembled before him. They were a naïve lot. When they had arrived they had all been impressed because the coast line of Hudson Bay, with its craggy cliffs and low-lying mists, had looked like Scotland. "Where's the factory?" one had asked when told that they had reached their destination of York Factory.

"They were sent to try my patience," Miles had mumbled under his breath. "No, no. Not a factory, my good man," he had answered patiently. "It means a trading post, usually one of the larger ones where the furs are transshipped. And the man in charge of every Hudson's Bay Company post is called a *factor*."

"Oh," the newcomer had replied, a look of disappointment on his face. He had hoped for a manufacturing concern and a good-sized city.

But all that had happened over two months ago, and in those two months the settlers had worked at building their cabins. They were the first of several groups of settlers and numbered one hundred five men, women, and children. They were Scots and Irish together, including Catholics like himself and highly conservative Protestants.

Located on the Nelson River, and a port of entry to the river system that would take the colonists south to the prairie and the Red River, York Factory also was important as a transshipment center for furs.

But it was a dreary place, consisting of a collection of huts for workmen, a few ramshackle dwellings that housed Indian families, the fort, and the Hudson's Bay Company post. The fort and the post lay between two rivers: the Nelson and the Hayes. Miles Macdonell decided the land was unhealthy because it was somewhat marshy, so he moved his settlers to higher ground north of the Nelson, several miles from York Factory itself. The place now was known as the Nelson Encampment.

"You've done a fine job!" Miles announced to the assembled colonists. He thought some praise was in order, even if he himself was not altogether satisfied with the progress they were making. Still, he had to keep reminding himself, one could not expect too much. He, after all, had spent his life on the frontier; he was accustomed to the winters, he knew what to expect. These people were unused to the work demanded of them and they could not even conceive of winter on Hudson Bay, no matter how much he lectured on the subject.

Miles looked out on the sea of expectant faces and unfolded his parchment. "Colin Campbell, John McKay, John McLennan, William Wallace, John Cooper, Martin Jordon, John O'Rourke, and James Toomey. Today I want you to join the tree-cutting brigade." A mild groan of protest went up, but the men turned to join the others who already were in the woods. It would be another day of aching backs and swollen hands.

"I ain't never wielded an ax, Governor," John O'Rourke mumbled. Miles looked heavenward and inwardly counted to ten. At times he wondered what most of them had done, or could in fact do. Miles scowled at O'Rourke.

"You may find your lack of experience a slight handicap, but I'm certain you'll learn, Mr. O'Rourke."

Miles turned his head away from the complainers and looked at George Gibbon, the eldest of the settlers, a man of fifty. "You join the hunting party," he instructed, feeling the man could not take another day cutting trees.

"And I suppose it's back to the mud fill for us?" Betty Campbell asked, rubbing her hands on grubby skirts. "C'mon, ladies, we don't have to wait for orders from the general here."

Miles lifted his hand and more or less waved at her. She was a Campbell and he didn't like Campbells, but at least she and the other women were good workers. Day in and day out, the women had worked filling the cracks in the log cabins with the cold, thick mud mixture he had taught them to make. It was not a difficult job, but it was messy, boring, and chilly.

Miles' eyes followed as Mrs. Campbell led the women off and his gaze fell again on Bonnie Campbell, a lass of nineteen with long chestnut hair and blue eyes the color of cornflowers. Bonnie Campbell was shy and withdrawn, intimidated by her Presbyterian father and his strict rules of conduct. Bonnie was an asset to the colony, but she was a worry too with so many ruffians in the group.

"At least the women go about their work without much complaint," Miles said, turning to Mr. Hillier, the Hudson's Bay Company officer.

"A natural nesting instinct," Hillier responded.

Miles shook his head. "I had hoped these colonists would prove more adaptable than they seem, and God, more ambitious."

"You're tired of hearing their grumbles," Hillier said, shrugging. "Some of them certainly are good, hardworking Scots stock, some are lazy troublemakers. What can you expect from such a grab bag?"

"I could use more experienced woodsmen, men who know their way around, men who are capable of offering some inspiration to others who are willing to work without complaint and have hope of making something of themselves."

"Men like Will MacLean and his sons?" Hillier asked, winking. Miles nodded his head, remembering the last time he had taken supper with the MacLeans in Queenston. He and Will were old friends, they had the same heritage, their fathers had known one another. Both families had settled in what now was Upper Canada, both had traveled the waterways.

"Yes," Miles said pensively. Men like Will and his sons. The comparison was nearly absurd. "They don't make Highlanders the way they used to," he commented.

Hillier laughed out loud. "Every generation says that! By God, man, the wealthy can endure a shortage of tea, but in Scotland the people can't get bread. These people have been dispossessed, beaten into the ground."

"Oh, some of them are more than all right," Miles conceded. "I tend to think only of the bad apples. I forget how many good ones there are. Teaching a hundred fifty people to survive on the frontier is not a holiday! By God, some of them still can't tell one

56

end of a canoe from the other, and when I tell them it's a fifteen-hundred-mile trek up the river system to the Red River they wail, they actually wail!" Miles paused and drew up his scarf tighter around his neck. "Hell, do you know that Will's father, Robert MacLean, traveled out of the Niagara in 1762 and ended up in New Orleans? And Will and his wife, Jenna, came back alone in 1781. By Jesus, I could use some of that experience now."

"You're going to get it," Hillier said, smiling. "Both Josh and Ian MacLean are with the company. Ian's headed for Scotland, I hear. News came with the last ship. He'll be coming back with Archibald McDonald."

Miles scratched his head and grinned. "So Ian will be following us up the river system. . . ."

Hillier motioned Miles off toward William Finlay. "That one's going to give you some trouble," he warned. "I've had my eye on him. He wants extra shares of grog, and I've reason to believe he steals."

"He and several others," Miles acknowledged. "Bad apples in my little barrel." He cleared his throat. "Hey! Finlay! Get out there with the tree crew, get a move on! There's plenty of work to do!"

Finlay grimaced back, then turned toward the deep woods to join the other men. Miles Macdonell, head of Lord Selkirk's first expedition of colonists in Rupert's Land, watched as Finlay ambled grudgingly off. Macdonell was struck by a strong sense of foreboding. "It's not bad enough to have the Nor'Westers at our backs complaining about settlers, we've got settlers who can't defend themselves, or even find their way out of the woods." Miles scowled off into the woods; Hillier made no comment. They both knew that the North West Company might try to cause trouble for the settlers once they actually were confronted with them on the Red River. And Miles Macdonell, soon to be named

Governor Miles Macdonell by the Hudson's Bay Company, was beginning to feel the weight of his responsibilities.

Ominous dark clouds gathered overhead, apparently waiting to open up and deposit a cold autumn rain on the brown grass. The deep oblong pit was as yet empty; the fine hand-carved coffin sat waiting to be lowered into it. There were over three hundred mourners gathered around the gaping grave, their heads lowered.

Andrew Macleod and his widowed daughter Catherine and Catherine's three children stood next to John Macleod and his wife, Tara, and their three children. Tom Macleod and his wife, Madelaine, stood with their son Donald and his wife, Agnes. To one side was Jeanne, Tom's daughter, and her husband, William Knight, and their two children. Helena, now the matriarch of the clan, stood at one end of the grave; near her were Will and Jenna MacLean and their son Josh and his fiancée, Colleen Adams.

Family members who had traveled from other parts of the country for the harvest festival remained for the funeral. They included Lannie, Jenna's eldest daughter from Kingston and her husband, as well as Anne Gagnon and Claude Deschamps and his wife, Giselle Gaboury Deschamps. Anne and Claude were the children of Pierre Deschamps, the eldest of the three Deschamps adopted by Mathew and Janet. Claude also had brought two of his children: Martina, who was a nun, and Francis, who was a priest. The Deschamps had made it a habit to travel from Trois-Rivières for an annual reunion with the Macleods and the MacLeans. This year, because of the funeral, they stayed on longer than usual.

Behind the immediate family, spread out across the wide field, were neighbors who had come from miles away. Interspersed among them were Indians in full tribal dress, men and women who had traveled from as far as Brantford, some seventy miles away. They came bearing gifts and to pay their respects to "the Great White Mother of the Macleod tribe."

As the pipes wailed their final farewell to Janet Cameron Macleod, daughter of the Scottish Highlands, Andrew Macleod, Will MacLean, Tom Macleod, and Donald Macleod hoisted the coffin and lowered it into the grave beneath the seven-foot Celtic cross that stood halfway between the grave of Mathew Macleod and the fresh grave of his beloved wife, Janet.

Father Francis Deschamps stepped forward and crossed himself. The circle of mourners moved closer, and each one in turn lifted a handful of loose earth and tossed it into the grave.

"Dust thou art, man, to dust thou will returnist," Francis intoned in Latin. More prayers were said, and then for the memory of the Jacobites, the entire group recited the Twentieth Psalm: "Let the Lord hear thee in the day of trouble. . . . The name of the God of Jacob defend thee. . . ."

"Why are we reciting the Twentieth Psalm?" young Ronald Macleod asked his mentor, John Fraser Murray.

"Because it was sung by the Highlanders before the Battle of Culloden Moor, back in 1746. Janet and Mathew were forty-sixers, they were Jacobites, supporters of the Stuart Kings and of Bonnie Prince Charlie." Ronald shook his head with understanding and resumed mumbling the words of the psalm, for once not asking another question, John Fraser Murray noted gratefully.

Tears flowed down Helena's face. She was in her late fifties, but at this moment she was a child again—a child running to meet her mother when Robert MacLean and Janet Macleod returned to Fort

Niagara after the Battle of the Plains of Abraham. The memory faded and Helena glanced at her sister, Jenna MacLean. Helena remembered the year Jenna ran away. Abigail had been a baby then; now Abigail was grown and married with a son, eighteen, and a daughter, fourteen. It is not the individual who matters, Helena thought; it's the continuity of our family that's important. We survive; by heaven, we have survived! "Go to Mathew," Helena whispered and tossed her bit of earth on the coffin. "And to Mat who died in battle, the son you mourned so much. Go home, Mother. Go to a place where there is no war, where you can look down on the Niagara and on the green, rolling moors of Scotland. You are one with Father again. It is almost as if you willed it."

Tom Macleod stood straight and tense. He grasped Madelaine's hand in his. Neither of them were blood relations to Janet Macleod, but both loved her dearly. Tom was Mathew's son by his first wife, Ann Macdonald; Madelaine was a Deschamps, one of Janet and Mathew's three adopted children. I loved you as if you were my mother, Tom thought as he looked steadily at the coffin. The memory of his first meeting with Janet Macleod rushed into his mind. It had been an emotion-filled moment when he discovered he was Mathew's lost son. Tom touched his kilt with his free hand, running his fingers over the material and remembering when Mathew had given him his first kilt.

"You treated me as your son," Tom said aloud. "Your memory will always live."

Madelaine leaned against her husband's arm. Sorrow filled her, and the tears ran freely from her large dark eyes. I was protected from my father by you, Madelaine thought, and you loved me as your own, holding me close through tragedy and through joy. I could not have survived without you. She glanced at her own children and grandchildren.

60

Andrew Macleod, the eldest son of Janet and Mathew, remembered huddling in a dark, damp tunnel beneath the burning Deschamps house in Trois-Rivières; he remembered his gentle mother, pistol in hand, protecting him from the wild Indian attacks. We survived, he thought, we survived because you, Mother, were so brave.

And as much as you love this Lochiel, Andrew thought, now you and Mathew and Mat, and even Robert MacLean, can visit in spirit the original Lochiel. Yes, you are free spirits now and you are together again. Maybe you can even feel the heather beneath your feet. He recalled the words of the poet:

My heart's in the Highlands, my heart's not here,
My heart's in the Highlands, a chasing the deer.
A chasing the deer, a following the roe,
My heart's in the Highlands, wherever I go.

Mist filled his eyes and Andrew openly cried with the others. Inwardly, he thanked his mother for teaching him that it was all right for men to cry.

The group finished the Twentieth Psalm written to commemorate some forgotten victory. There was no victory on Culloden Moor, Andrew thought, looking at the graves of his mother and father. But you had your victory; you had it here in Upper Canada, you have it now. He looked around at the children and grandchildren. Your clan rises again, he thought. And stronger than it was before.

As the priest finished the last of the prayers the men lifted the shovels and filled the grave, covering the coffin with cold earth. Each, Helena thought, must be remembering as I am. She lifted her hand and wiped her cheek. Then, turning to John Fraser Murray, she smiled and whispered, "You did a fine job on the rock wall. Great-granny would have been proud."

"Do you think so?" John beamed.

"I know so," Helena answered, just as the first drops of cold rain began to fall.

Jenna let out a long sigh as she pulled on the bow that held her bonnet in place. Carefully, she lifted the bonnet off her head and set it down on the corner of the kitchen table. "I feel old," she said, watching as Will pulled off his boots.

Will nodded, lost in his own thoughts, thoughts of his father's untimely death, memories of the past brought back by the funeral. "It's a time for thinking," he finally responded.

"We'll have to go back to Lochiel this evening," Jenna reminded him. "But I am tired. I need to rest for a while. There are so many people there, I suppose some of them ought to be staying here."

"I hardly think this house is large enough." Will walked to the sideboard. "Some brandy?" he asked.

Jenna nodded abstractedly as she studied the wood grain in the table. "I can't believe she's gone," Jenna observed after a time.

Will sat down and extended a mug to Jenna. His usually merry eyes were somber and sad. "She died peacefully and she was surrounded by those who love her. . . ." Will's voice broke and he thought, Unlike my mother, your mother died peacefully.

"Are you in the kitchen?" Josh's voice called out.

"We are!" Jenna answered.

Josh bent as he entered the kitchen in order to avoid the low doorway. As tall as all the Macleod and MacLean men were, their houses still had the low ceilings and low doorways demanded by the climate. The lower the ceilings and doorways, the less heat it took to keep the house warm during the bitter winters. Jenna looked up and smiled. She was always struck by the irony that Josh, who was not Will's natural son, looked more like Will than did

62

Ian, who was Will's biological son. But then, Ian was a true hybrid. He had his Uncle James MacLean's dark hair but his mother's green eyes.

"It's getting mighty cold!" Josh commented. "The rain has turned to snow and everything is icing up. Ah, brandy. May I have some?"

"Help yourself," Will answered.

Jenna watched as Josh moved to the cupboard. "Where's Colleen?"

"Helping Auntie Madelaine and the other women. Everyone has brought something. I don't think there's a square inch in the kitchen."

"Your grandmother was an important person," Will commented.

"And well loved," Josh added. "Do you know who's come?"

Jenna shook her head.

"Molly Brant's children," Josh answered. "A delegation in full regalia. They've brought a whole deer and a bag of wild rice that must weigh a ton."

"Mama helped Molly when she first came up to Canada during the American rebellion. She helped even though the Mohawk used to be the enemies of the French. Mama always said the Indians were used by both sides, she said that there was no more Christian woman in all Upper Canada than Molly Brant. All her children were baptized and she was wed in the Church. She read the Bible every single day and taught the Christian religion to all her people. She taught that it was wrong to conceive children out of wedlock."

"Didn't a Mohawk bring Grandfather from Boston to Canada?" Josh asked.

Jenna shook her head in the affirmative. "That Mohawk was Molly's cousin. The Scots pay their debts . . . even if it takes years."

Josh smiled and lifted the mug to his lips. "Colleen says she's never seen so many people. It's the first time she's ever seen the whole family together. She can't conceive of it. She says she still hasn't met them all yet and she can't keep the names straight."

Jenna laughed. "Sometimes I have that trouble myself and they're my family." Then Jenna's face took on a more serious expression. "I'm sorry Mother didn't live to see you and Colleen married."

Josh tapped his fingers on the table. "We'll be getting married soon," he said, trying to smile. "I want to have her safely here in Upper Canada. The possibility of war is growing by the day."

"It certainly is," Will agreed. "It's a good idea to cut short your engagement. You'll be asked to serve longer hours in the militia. We're all being asked to put in extra time."

"I want to buy a commission," Josh said abruptly. "In the army."

"Oh, Josh!" Jenna covered her mouth with her hand.

Josh reached out to her, his eyes searching out hers. "It won't matter that much," he said quietly. "If war comes the army won't be in any greater danger than the militia."

"I agree," Will put in.

Jenna looked off into the distance. She knew it was true, but still she didn't like it.

Mason James MacLean sat back in his black carriage and listened as the horses' hooves beat along the cobblestones. In a few minutes he would be home and in a few minutes more, he could lean back in his large chair while Righteous brought him a tall, cool drink. President Madison had recalled Congress on November 4, and the younger Republican element had immediately gained control of the House of Representatives. They were men who would fight for the strong agrarian interests of the South and the West; they were called War Hawks and they clamored for war just as they supported statehood for Louisiana. Indeed, if America were to move against the British—and it seemed she would—statehood for Louisiana was vital.

Mason James MacLean did not consider the possible outcome of war with Britain. He was much too furious. Trade was at a virtual standstill because of the British blockade of the French ports. Moreover, in the course of implementing the blockade, American ships had been seized and searched. America seamen had been impressed into the British Navy, but worse yet, from Mason's point of view, valuable cargo had been confiscated. At the opening of Congress, James Madison had given a speech that still rang in Mason's ears: "With this evidence of hostile inflexibility, in trampling on rights which no independent nation can relinquish . . . Congress will feel the duty of putting the United States into an armor, an attitude demanded by the crisis, and corresponding with the national spirit and expectations."

National spirit and expectations . . . yes, Mason James liked that. He liked the fact that President Madison asked for increases in the regular army, the acceptance of volunteer corps, a larger and better-equipped navy, and more cannon, muskets, and ammunition. New Orleans must be protected, Mason thought. My position, my products, my ability to trade with whom I wish must all be protected. And Mason James liked the growing dominance of the South and southern ideas in Congress. He felt at one with his nation. "The British say America is illegitimate," he repeated. "Just as I am. But we shall both buy our legitimacy, we shall both close the mouths of our detractors."

It had been an exhilarating day. Mason James'

carriage approached the quiet tree-lined street where his house was located. Although he had begun the day in a crisp white ruffled shirt, morning coat, and stylish trousers, he now felt grubby and in need of a bath and relaxation.

He had spent a tiring morning in Congress lobbying for his two favorite causes: statehood for Louisiana and war with the British. He had more than three hours before he was due at the reception being hosted by one of the two senators from South Carolina. I shall take a long, warm bath, he decided, but I shall have a few drinks first. Mason James felt overstimulated, as often he did. However much he hated Washington proper, called Foggy Bottom because it was located in a veritable swamp, he did enjoy politics.

His carriage came to a halt. The black man who drove it climbed down from his perch and opened the door for Mason James. He smiled, bowed, and tipped his high top hat, then extended his crinkled old hand to Mason, who alighted from the carriage, inhaled dramatically, and luxuriated in Georgetown's cleaner and somewhat cooler air. He walked a few steps and the front door was opened to him. Righteous took his cloak.

"A surprise visitor, sir," Righteous told him, rolling his eyes toward the parlor. Mason James frowned and felt annoyed. He was on the verge of mumbling, "Who the hell . . ." when his father, James MacLean, stepped into the doorway of the parlor and, holding his whiskey in one hand, proclaimed a greeting to his startled son. "I suppose you're surprised?"

Mason James blinked. His father stood before him, but he was not dressed in his usual attire of crisp, clean white suit. Rather he wore the dress uniform of the U.S. Army. "You've purchased a commission?"

His voice sounded incredulous and certainly his mind raced with questions.

"I'm going to serve with Winfield Scott," James MacLean replied. "There is going to be a war."

James MacLean led his son into the parlor. "I know we don't always share the same interests," James MacLean said. It was something of an understatement, he thought. Mason James was a strange young man. He was not exactly effeminate, but he seemed more interested in the company of men than that of women, and James MacLean suspected the worst. Still, he wasn't entirely sure of his son's tastes. There had been women, but nothing lasting; Mason James seemed disinterested unless some personal gain was involved. Yet Mason James was not as shrewd and cruel as his father. Mason James was self-centered and inordinately selfish, but he was not wantonly cruel. Then too, he had a sense of humor, which his father lacked completely. "Always laughing at something," James MacLean had said more than once. "No, not like me at all."

Still, between father and son there was affection. And even James MacLean would have admitted that his son worked hard to further the family interests and make yet more money.

"Serving in the army will bring our family a certain prestige," James MacLean announced, "prestige that will be important in the coming years, in politics."

"I couldn't bring myself to do anything so dreary," Mason James confessed to his father.

"Precisely why I'm doing it," his father muttered. "Have you met Mrs. Madison?"

"Oh, yes. A charming lady. I think she really likes me."

James MacLean grunted. "I suggest you pursue that."

67

Mason James tossed his shoulders back. "I surely intend to."

"Have you met any other women?" James MacLean pressed.

But Mason James only shook his head. "None of interest," he replied honestly.

Again James MacLean grunted. He loved his son, but it was worrying. With no grandchildren, who would inherit his plantation? There was no answer to his oft-asked question save one. I simply shall have to sire a child myself, James decided. I shall have to give Mason James a half brother.

Josh guided his horse along the wooded pathway and out into the clearing. He followed the main road now, toward the farm of Richard Adams. He had passed through the village of Lewiston and while there was reminded once again of the absurdity of the warmongering in Washington. Here on the border, it could not have been more peaceful. The people were friendly; indeed, they sprang from similar stock and many families were divided between both sides of the Niagara River, which served as the boundary between Upper Canada, one of the provinces of British North America, and New York State. It seemed unlikely that these peaceful farmers whose grandchildren, cousins, aunts, and uncles lived across the river soon would find themselves at war with their kin. It all was based on a misconception in Washington. Somehow the Southerners seemed to believe that those who lived in Upper Canada were dissatisfied with British rule, but of course they were not. Indeed, the vast majority of Upper Canadians would fight to remain part of British North America. At the same time, New York threatened to leave the new nation if war was declared. For the most part, the New Yorkers and the New Englanders didn't want war. Even if a war succeeded in restoring free trade on the high seas, which seemed unlikely, it would destroy the thriving trade between the New England states and the Canadas—Upper and Lower.

Some Southerners and Westerners in the United States seemed to believe that Americans were a chosen people, chosen to unite the continent and rule it absolutely.

Josh smiled to himself as he approached the farm of Richard Adams. Soon he would marry Colleen and create the same kind of family he had just been thinking about. A family that would not want to be separated by war.

It had been over a week and a half since his grandmother's burial and Colleen had returned to her father's house. Josh had hoped to come sooner to visit her, but there were things to do after the funeral as well as the final preparations for winter. As yet he had not told her that he intended to join the army. There was no need, he thought. It would take some time before his request reached Montreal.

Josh dismounted and tied his horse to the hitching post by the water trough. He bent down, stretching his long legs, then he extended his arms upward, as if he were reaching for the sky. It had been a long ride.

Josh climbed the steps and knocked on the door. "Colleen! It's Josh!"

In a moment, the door was flung open and Josh stood face to face with Colleen Adams, his dark-haired, blue-eyed beauty.

"You've forgotten me," he jested.

"Perhaps," Colleen retorted, a mischievous look in her eyes. "Are you selling wares? Bibles, or maybe bolts of cloth?"

Josh laughed and, circling her waist with his large hands, pulled her forward and kissed her on the nose. "I'm selling kisses," he answered.

Colleen put her arms around him and, standing on tiptoe, kissed his lips tenderly. It was a kiss that grew in passion as Josh wrapped his arms around her and felt the warmth of her slim body pressing to him. "I love you," he said softly in her ear.

Blushing, Colleen pulled away a little. "Come in," she urged. "Papa will be back in an hour or so." Josh smiled knowingly. Colleen was subtly telling him he could kiss her as well in the warmth of the house as on the doorstep because she was alone. He followed her into the house and closed the door. "I'll make you some tea," Colleen said, her blue eyes sparkling. Josh followed her into the kitchen. Her long hair was hanging loose, she moved her hips with a tempting swing, and Josh could all but feel his hands on her.

Colleen filled the kettle and put it on the fire. She turned and came back to where Josh was standing. "Kiss me again," she asked in a low voice.

Josh needed no urging. He kissed her and he felt her move against him. His own passion increased, like a kind of hunger. "I'm afraid hot blood runs in our family," he said, breathing into her ear. His hand moved across her back, around her waist, and upward till he grasped her small, firm breast through the material of her dress.

"I love you," Colleen whispered. "Oh, Josh, make love to me. I want you to hold me, I want you to . . ." She moved about, rubbing herself against him. Josh felt all resolve melt against his own desire to possess her. He lifted her easily and carried her into the bedroom, setting her down on the edge of the bed.

"Your father won't be back?" he questioned.

Colleen shook her head. "Not for a long while." Her blue eyes looked almost moist as Josh lay down next to her.

"Are you certain you want this?" he asked earnestly.

"Will you still want to marry me?" Colleen asked.

70

Josh shook his head. "More than ever, I suspect." He pulled her into his arms and kissed her neck, her ears, her eyelids. She groaned a little as he explored beneath her long skirts and ran his hand along her cool thigh. Josh fumbled with the top of her dress and finally pulled it down, revealing her white skin and small but perfect breasts. He kissed her tenderly till she moaned beneath his hands, then he lifted her skirts and again kissed her, but this time more intimately.

She moaned again and when she did, Josh entered her as gently as he could. She shuddered beneath him, pressing upward. "I do love you," Josh repeated. But there was no holding back for him. He wanted her too much, their encounter had been too erotic.

He vibrated against her and she shuddered again. "No," he whispered in her ear. "I didn't mean to, I . . . tried to wait for you." But Colleen's clear blue eyes were large and questioning. Josh loomed over her. "Close your eyes," he said. "Let me show you." She leaned back and did as she was told. Josh kissed her breasts again and played with them till her nipples grew hard and pink with excitement. Then he moved his hand to the magic center of her pleasure, massaging her gently till he felt her body grow warm and flushed and until she moved her hips two and fro, groaning with desire. Then Colleen gasped and Josh watched as she reached her fulfillment. When she had stopped shaking against him, he kissed her neck and whispered in her ear. "That is how it should be when we do it together."

Colleen smiled. "It takes practice," she said. "But we'll have lots."

Josh sat up at the sound of hissing. "You forgot the tea water!" he said, almost laughing.

Colleen fairly jumped from the bed, replacing her clothes as she did. "Oh, goodness!" Josh followed her

71

as she ran toward the kitchen to rescue the kettle that had overboiled.

"It's just as well," Josh said and laughed. "Your father will be home soon." Colleen nodded. She finished fastening her garments and arranged her mussed hair. "Josh, can we be married sooner?"

"The sooner the better," Josh answered. "How about Christmas?"

Colleen bit her lip and then all but flew into his arms. "Yes, Christmas," she said anxiously. "We'll be married at Christmas."

Richard Adams stood on the dock at Lewiston and stared alternately at the trunk that sat before him and at the letter that accompanied it. He was as excited as he had ever been in his life.

As the letter explained it, a woman had come to the foundling home where he had been reared and inquired after him. Owing to his many letters to the home, they were able to identify him immediately and assure the woman that he was the person she sought. The woman then had left the trunk at the foundling home with the instruction that it was to be forwarded, unopened, to Richard Adams. The woman who had sent the trunk also sent a letter explaining she was a friend of his mother and that by passing on the trunk, she was following the last wishes of his mother's will.

"It is my understanding," the woman wrote, "that in the trunk you will find a series of journals that will tell you everything you might want to know about your family."

Richard Adams refolded the letter and replaced it in the letter pouch. He reached out almost reverently and patted the trunk. "I've waited all these years," he said aloud. "I guess I shall be able to wait till I get home."

* * *

Sir George Prevost was not a man without humor. "My instructions should be as long as my title," he commented wryly. Having arrived on September 11, 1811, his title reflected his position: *Captain-General and Governor and Chief in and over the Provinces of Upper and Lower Canada, New Brunswick, Nova Scotia, and the Islands of Prince Edward, Cape Breton, Newfoundland, and the Bermudas and their several Dependencies, Vice Admiral of the same, Lieutentant-General and Commander of all His Majesty's Forces in the Provinces of Upper and Lower Canada . . . etc., etc., etc.*

Prevost was the eldest son of French-speaking Swiss Protestant parents. His father had also served in the British Army and had been wounded during the siege of Quebec back in 1759. Prevost himself had been born in New Jersey and been educated on the Continent and in England. He had held other posts of distinction since the war with Napoleon began, but he had a sense of destiny about his present position—in spite of the length of his title.

Moreover, Sir George Prevost was yet another example of British concern for the French-speaking inhabitants of Quebec, which now was called Lower Canada. He was Swiss, not English. He was dedicated to freedom of religion, he spoke French fluently, and he had what many regarded as political savvy.

Since his arrival Sir George had appointed some French-speaking Canadians to the legislature of Lower Canada and would have appointed more, had they been willing to serve. Nonetheless, this act had alienated many wealthy English-speaking Montreal merchants, leaving Sir George Prevost in the same position as those who had preceded him. His gestures designed to bring the French-speaking population into the mainstream of life, economic and otherwise, were shunned by nearly all French Canadians save the elite, and disliked by all English Canadians except for rare unprejudiced, bilingual individuals.

But in spite of being ignored by the population, Sir George Prevost believed that if there were a war with the United States, the French-speaking inhabitants would remain neutral. This he believed as a result of his own observations and in spite of the constant nervous predictions of the English-speaking population. Sir George Prevost could see quite clearly that the Catholic Church of Quebec supported such neutrality. The Quebec clergy did not like what was happening to the Church in France under Napoleon, and so the priests urged the French-speaking inhabitants to remain loyal to the British.

But more than neutrality on the part of French-speaking Canadians was needed. Men were needed. There were hardly enough British regulars to spread out along such a long border, and the local militia was not large enough to make up the difference. Montreal might well be the first focus of attack by the bellicose Americans, but the Niagara, Kingston, and Upper Canada generally—that veritable wilderness so necessary to the fur trade—also would have to be held.

At this moment, Prevost sat in his office in Quebec City and thought about Upper Canada. Before him was his trusted aide, Red George Macdonell of the King's 8th Regiment.

"We need a lot more of those," Prevost uttered, an ironic smile on his lips. He pointed off to the gun rack that held the Brown Bess. It was a musket of superior quality, not a muzzle-loader like the muskets used by other armies. It was instead a smoothbore weapon with a maximum effective range of only a hundred yards. It had no sights and was designed for use by well-trained men standing shoulder to shoulder. When the lines were tight, three volleys a minute could be fired. The gun and the drill formation was such an improvement in firepower that it replaced the hand grenade, which had been the infantryman's main weapon. But of course, the army continued to use the term grenadier, though now it referred to the tallest and best-trained soldiers.

"More Brown Besses, indeed," Red George Macdonell agreed. "You're quite right, that's what we need." He rubbed his chin thoughtfully. "Mind you, in Upper Canada you'll have to be careful about just who they are given to. A local militia's fine, but not if they turn on you."

Prevost nodded. He fingered a sheaf of papers in his hand. The story was all there, and it was not the most comforting tale to read on what might be the eve of war.

The militia of Upper Canada numbered nearly eleven thousand men—on paper. But the note on the bottom of the page read, "Of which only four thousand can be prudently armed." The remainder, it seemed, were recent emigrants from the United States, men who would fight for their land, men who did not care what flag flew overhead. They had come because the land was free and because as far as free land was concerned, Upper Canada offered an opportunity the United States did not. But to a family they all had relatives in the United States and their loyalties might be divided, to say the very least.

The four thousand who could be trusted were largely Scots, particularly older Scots families in the Niagara and around Kingston, families like the Macleods and the MacLeans. The remainder were more recent Scots immigrants in Glengarry County, the county that bordered Lower Canada. It was entirely settled by Highlanders, nearly all Macdonells who had served in the Glengarry Regiment of the British Army.

"I should like to revive the proposal to raise a defense corps from Glengarry County," Prevost confided. "What do you think?"

Red George nodded. "My kinsman, Alexander Macdonell, certainly can assist." Father Macdonell had been the original chaplain for the Scottish Glengarry Light Infantry in England and he was the man responsible for their immigration to Canada and their ultimate settlement in Upper Canada.

"They can train at Trois-Rivières," Prevost suggested. "I want you to take charge."

"Talk to Brock about other Scots, about recruits from the Niagara," Red George advised. "I think we can put together quite a decent force."

"We'll need one," Prevost replied. "The Americans are scrapping for a fight. They mean to have another war."

Red George stood up. He was a massive man: Six feet tall, he weighed nearly three hundred pounds. "Have you ever watched a caber toss?" he asked, winking.

Prevost shook his head. "Can't say that I have."

"A caber is a seventeen-foot, hundred-pound log. Now, if a Scot can toss a caber, how far can he toss an American?"

Prevost laughed his restrained Swiss laugh. "Back to Washington, I hope."

CHAPTER IV

December 1811

Mason James MacLean had bid his father farewell and promised to remain in Washington. "Work on building yourself a career in politics," his father had instructed him. "I'll eventually want to see you in the Senate."

Mason James sighed deeply as the servant took his cloak. His father's instructions in the first instance were easy enough; it was his last suggestion that left Mason James apprehensive and confused. "And of course you will have to marry soon," his father had told him. "Because if you don't sire an heir soon, I shall have to take a mistress and have another child myself!"

"I'm seeking out young ladies, but as yet I haven't found one suitable," Mason James told his father. It wasn't true, but he felt pressed to make some excuse.

"Just find someone who is good breeding stock," his father had grumbled.

"Mr. MacLean, dear. I'm so pleased you could come!"

Mason James' thoughts were interrupted by the First Lady of the land, Mrs. Dolley Madison. She smiled a dazzling smile and, taking his arm, guided him into the reception area, which already was crowded with members of the House of Representatives and the Senate.

Mason James was outfitted in his most elegant finery. The shirt he wore was pure silk, imported from Paris, in spite of the British blockade. And that, Mason James thought, makes it all the more distinctive. His waistcoat was muted green with gold trim and gold buttons and had a jaunty cut. His trousers were gray and his boots were shiny and black. His cuff links were a pair of matched blue-white diamonds, and his stickpin was solid gold with a diamond in one end. The cane he carried, not that he actually needed a cane, was made of black ebony tipped with gold. When Mason James MacLean desired attention, he tapped the cane's gold tip on the floor, or on the side of a piece of furniture. Indeed, his cane was his favorite affectation.

There is no one in this room dressed as elegantly as I am, Mason James thought as he quickly surveyed the other guests.

Henry Clay, Speaker of the House of Representatives, was dressed entirely in black. He was trying to look older than his thirty-four years and to impress people with his newfound wealth and position. But never having had enough money to live elegantly before, he simply didn't know how to dress and looked dowdy. Of course, Clay's wife, Lucretia, was not the best-dressed woman in the room either. Mason James had to wonder about Lucretia Clay; she had, after all, been wealthy all her life. She was the source of Henry's wealth and that, Mason James concluded, was the only reason why Clay had married her. She was severe-looking in the extreme, with a nose that could be used for a crochet needle, Mason thought unkindly. Her violet gown was expensive but tasteless, yet another proof that Americans believed expense and taste had something to do with one another.

Mason James considered himself to be a cut above other Americans because of his French background.

Mason watched Lucretia for another moment, noting that her gown accentuated her thick waist and certainly was not the best color for her sallow skin. As he stared at her bosom, he decided that she had stuffed her dress with silk in order to make herself appear more buxom. She was, he noticed, a trifle lopsided.

John Caldwell Calhoun was dressed to the nines. He was adorned in bright red with gold trim, knee-high boots, and an ornate gold-colored ruffled shirt. But his costume, hardly one he would have worn among his earthy constituents, contrasted with his face, which was hardly as cheery as his manner of dress. He had an absolutely square face, a face endowed with a permanent scowl. His wife, Floride Bonneau Calhoun, was round and short with brown hair which was curled tightly in tiny ringlets that somehow appeared pasted to her head. She was well proportioned for one so rotund; indeed, had there been ten inches less of her in the bust, in the waist, and in the hips, she might have had a fine figure. Floride Calhoun, like Lucretia Clay, was rich. In fact, she was an heiress. When he married Floride, John Calhoun had propelled himself into South Carolina society and now, at twenty-nine, was already retired into politics, his sole business being that of a planter-statesman. Just an old boll weevil nestled into the soft cotton ball of South Carolina politics.

"I wonder how history will write about us?" Dolley Madison said. "I've been watching your eyes, Mr. MacLean, dear. You take in everything. You really ought to take up social commentary in the press. Would you be kind to us? I don't like the present press commentary."

"I would be most kind," Mason James lied. Although, he thought, he *would* be kind to Mrs. Madison because she was influential. And small wonder she hated the press. The Federalist newspapers attacked her with an unrelenting venom. First they called her frivolous in the extreme, next they alluded to her having an affair with a former President, Mr. Thomas Jefferson, and of lobbying for her husband in quite unique ways—on a tabletop in the Executive kitchen was the example that stuck in Mason James' mind.

Thoughts of Mr. Jefferson tumbling Dolley Madison amused Mason James. He found himself momentarily hoping that there might be some truth in the accusations made by the papers. He decided that he might be able to stand her company himself; it would certainly make his father happy if he had an affair with the President's wife. She was, of course, older than he. Dolley Madison was forty-three and looked thirty-five, while her husband was sixty and looked seventy. Mason James MacLean contemplated Washington's most famous lady in bed and decided that a woman of forty-two would at least be grateful.

Mason James stole another look at Mr. Clay, who had reached for a drink of Kentucky rye whiskey from a passing tray. The man was positively addicted to drinking, gambling, and womanizing. Quite admirable, Mason James thought.

Another servant passed with yet another tray. It held dainty dishes of ice cream. Mason James took one, happily plunging his spoon into the fresh peach ice cream. "It's delicious," he praised Mrs. Madison, giving her his most seductive smile.

Dolley Madison was a buxom woman with absolutely no need to stuff her dress with silk. She was, in fact, quite spectacularly endowed. She also was vivacious and loved parties. Her Wednesday night ice cream socials at the Executive Mansion were one of Washington's saving graces.

Dolley Madison glided away from Mason James to greet some new arrival at the ice-cream social. Dolley was wearing a rich blue gown trimmed in ivory lace. Her hair was wrapped in a magnificent turban, a style she had only recently introduced to Washington society. Her long, dark lashes fluttered and Mason allowed his eyes to rest on her magnificent cleavage. Lord, he thought, the woman could nurture a nation!

Dolley moved back to his side, and Mason James continued to stare at her cleavage. Her breasts seemed even larger that night than when he had first seen her. Her gown was daringly low-cut. If she bends over, he thought, I shall be able to see her shoes.

But Mrs. Madison did not bend over, she merely leaned toward him, smiling. She carried with her the aroma of magnolia blossoms, and her hand pressed on his arm with what Mason James concluded was meaning.

"My dear Mrs. Madison," he purred, still examining her heaving breasts, "you look stunning and are, without a doubt, the most bountiful—I mean, beautiful woman in all Washington."

Dolley moved still closer, her breasts seeming to thrust forward, touching his ruffled shirt. He lifted his spoon and took a mouthful of peach ice cream.

"You're just a young flatterer, you are." Dolley smiled a devastating smile and drawled her words the way all southern ladies do.

"Madame," Mason James returned in a low, deep voice, "I lack the words to do you justice."

"That I doubt," she cooed.

"Madame, you are a temptress, a virtual Helen of Troy."

"And I would launch a thousand American ships against the British. Imagine the outrage of kidnaping our young men! You do support the war, don't you?"

Mason smiled enigmatically. Mrs. Madison knew full well he might soon become a representative from Louisiana. She was lobbying already.

"I certainly do," Mason replied. "We plantation owners know free trade is a necessity. When we join the Union we certainly intend to stand by Virginia and the Carolinas. We certainly would not support the northern bumpkins. Another southern state, madame, will offer your husband exactly the support needed. Remember New Orleans, madame, it's a major center of trade."

"New Orleans." Dolley repeated the name. "I've always wanted to go there."

"It's a city like no other," Mason James bragged. "The French gave it a certain flavor."

Dolley was pressing ever closer. Her hand idly caressed his sleeve. "I hear it's far from Puritan Boston."

"As far as you can get," Mason James confirmed. As he spoke, he dared to touch her fingertips.

"Are you of French stock, Mr. MacLean? I've been told you come from a family of first settlers out on the Natchez Trace."

"My grandmother was Acadian, from Canada; my father, Scots."

"My, what an exciting combination. Mr. Calhoun is Scots," Dolley lowered her voice and whispered, "but I do believe he could have benefited from some French blood." She paused. "I hear the French are the best lovers." Her long lashes fluttered.

"And New Orleans reflects that talent," Mason answered without blushing or missing a beat.

"I should like to be taken there."

"I shall be *delighted* to tell you *all* about it," Mason offered, careful to put emphasis on certain words. "I should like to paint you a picture with poetry."

She made a cooing sound Mason thought sounded

like a chicken laying an egg, but he did not smile. Her hand pressed his arm quite hard. "Not here, you dear eager young man," she whispered. "But soon."

"Your Wednesday evening ice-cream socials are simply wonderful," Mason praised. Since she wanted to change the subject, he obliged.

"Do you like my ice cream?" Dolley Madison asked, wide-eyed. "It's made from fresh Georgia peaches."

"Southern fruit is succulent," Mason replied, allowing his blatant gaze to return once again to her cleavage. "I just love it in ice cream."

"A good hostess tries her best," Dolley smiled and turned toward Lucretia, who had moved to her side. "My dear, how simply divine you look in that gown. It makes your bosom look so full!"

Lucretia stood stiffly. "I see you've found a new young man."

"Oh, no, my dear. He's found me. But then, who else is there in Washington?"

Miraculously, the snow had stopped falling and the sky was a cloudless, sunny blue. It was still too, as if the wind had deserted the land. The Nelson Encampment was an isolated bundle of huts and one-room cabins. But the sky and the sun were deceptive; it was cold enough to make leather crack, and when a man breathed, his breath steamed in front of him and hung in midair.

The men of the Nelson Encampment were down on the shores of the Hayes River, building the large York boats that would take them all South in the spring. The women were inside their cabins making bread, sewing, and tending the children.

The one exception was the Campbells. Miles Macdonell had sent the Campbells to York Factory on the sled to fetch some supplies. Bonnie Campbell, their daughter, had remained behind. Bonnie had ventured out once to bring more wood from the cabin, but she had quickly returned, realizing how deceptively cold it was. In truth, Bonnie had urged her parents to go to the Hudson's Bay post without her. She enjoyed the solitude because solitude was hard to come by in the Nelson Encampment and even harder when three people shared a single room day in and day out for months on end.

The knock on the cabin door startled Bonnie. "Let me in! For God's sake, a man could freeze out here!"

Bonnie went to the door and opened it a crack. "Mr. Finlay?" She looked into his unshaven face, bright red from the cold.

"Will you open the door wider? I told you, I'm freezing!"

"It's not proper," Bonnie protested, but William Finlay was a strong man and he pushed open the door and strode into the cabin.

"Don't you know you're supposed to share a fire, girl? It's cold enough out there to freeze piss in mid-air! And you in here with your fire and your propriety!"

Bonnie Campbell blinked at William Finlay. He was cruder than the other men, and meaner too. "My father's not home," she told him crisply. "I'm afraid you'll have to find another fire to sit by. And pray, what are you doing here anyway? You're supposed to be on the construction crew."

Finlay grunted and pulled off his gloves. "I've cut myself," he announced, revealing his bloodied hand. "Have you no mercy, now? Are you to be turning out an injured man into the freezing cold? Be a good lass and fetch some hot water."

Bonnie backed off toward the fire. "I'll bandage your hand, then you'll have to leave," she said firmly. The image of her father crossed her mind. "A lady does not allow herself to be alone with a man." Her father had told her that often enough.

She turned from Finlay and went to the fireplace where the kettle bubbled and boiled. She had intended fixing tea from the needles of the white spruce. It was a horrid concoction, but Miles Macdonell had instructed everyone to drink it in order to prevent scurvy breaking out. Bonnie dished out a bowl of hot water and returned to William Finlay, who had made himself at home by sitting down on a large round tree stump that served as one of three chairs placed around the roughly hewn table.

"Well, give me your hand," she said impatiently, anxious to be rid of her most unwelcome guest. Finlay grinned, exposing a space from which his left eyetooth was missing. He extended his hand. Bonnie dabbed at the blood and wiped it away. "It's not much of a cut," she commented, "but I'll bandage it anyway." With that, she left the table. She went to a nearby satchel and withdrew some white cloth, then returned and deftly bound his hand. "There," she announced. "Now off with you."

But Finlay didn't move. "About to have a spot of tea?" he questioned.

"No, just the spruce medication."

Finlay made a face. "Ugh!" he pronounced. "I wouldn't drink that swill for all the whiskey in Ireland."

Bonnie drew herself up. She had a well-shaped but angular face and her hair was a warm chestnut brown. Her blue eyes were framed by well-shaped eyebrows and long dark lashes. "You'll get the scurvy if you don't drink it," she said with an air of superiority. "Miles Macdonell has ordered us to drink it."

"Miles Macdonell is a piss fire. Who cares about the bastard's orders? I'm not a slave! Not even a bonded servant!"

"Can't you mind your tongue?" Bonnie snapped. "You're nothing but a foulmouthed Irishman!"

85

Finlay reached across the table and seized Bonnie's wrist harshly, pulling her forward toward him. "Ain't we pretty when we're so full of it! And ain't you high and mighty for a Scots crofter's daughter, and a Campbell at that! The Campbells are spitting posts for any decent Highlander! And for the Irish too, my girl!"

Bonnie strained against his grasp. "Let me go! My father will be home any time now!" She was bluffing, but Finlay couldn't know when they left, she reasoned.

Finlay leered at her and spit on the floor. He didn't let go of her wrist at all. Instead he tightened his grip and, still holding her, moved around the small table, jerking her to her feet. He loomed over her, expelling his foul breath into her face. "You're a ripe one," he said appraisingly, his eyes moving down her body. With his free hand, the one Bonnie had just bandaged, he reached for her breast and squeezed it through the material of her dress. Bonnie's face flushed and she opened her mouth to scream, but Finlay didn't allow her to shriek. He pulled her to him and kissed her, rubbing his stubbly face across her tender skin. "Hold still, you little bitch!" he whispered in her ear when he was done with the kiss.

Anger and fear filled Bonnie and tears flooded her blue eyes. In spite of her fright, she thrust her lower lip forward and tried to look defiant. "Let me alone! My father will kill you!"

Finlay stared into her eyes and, exerting all his strength on her shoulders, forced her to the floor roughly even as she struggled. But Finlay was too strong for her. He held her flat down with the weight of his body and lifted her long, modest woolen skirt. She shivered as she felt his hands on her upper thigh, and though she wanted to scream, her throat was dead dry.

"Leave me alone!" she repeated. Bonnie struggled and fought her attacker by kicking. His hand muffled her mouth, and he ceased his indecent explorations under her dress momentarily.

"You don't know your Scots Presbyterian father as I do. You'll be disgraced and disowned. He'll say you encouraged me. You'll be the one who gets the blame, missy. You let me in. You broke your father's rule about entertaining men alone."

His words sent a violent shiver through Bonnie. Her voice was gone, and she was shaking with fear as he tugged at her undergarments, pulling them away. There was a respite while he fiddled with the ties of his own breeches. Then he was back again.

"How nice," Finlay slurred as he pulled at her curly brown hair. "And remember, lass, your father will ask how I got in the house. He won't believe you. They believe their women are wanton, sex-crazed bitches. It's you who will get the blame. C'mon. You are wanton, aren't you?"

Bonnie began to cry and shake. Her father's constant words of warning rang in her ears. "Don't talk to these men! Don't ever let them in the cabin! You're not to fraternize, it's not proper! If I ever catch you . . ." Bonnie could see her father's dark brooding eyes, his firm jaw, his mouth moving as he asked for the forgiveness of the Lord. Finlay is right, Bonnie thought in confusion and fear. God help me, he's right!

Bonnie cried out softly as William Finlay prodded at her and finally succeeded in prying open her legs. She muffled a horror-filled scream as he plunged into her and then repeated the assault again and again. Bonnie Campbell was numb beneath William Finlay, numb and terrified. He shook above her and gasped. Then, apparently finished with his act, he rolled off her and stood up, hastily redoing his breeches.

"Get up, you stupid little Highland piece!" He pulled her roughly to her feet and smoothed her skirt down. She was pale and shaking, tears still streaming down her face. "Now you've been mowed good and proper," he bragged. He reached out and caressed her breasts, which were still covered by her clothing. "Next time I'll have ye nude, but no need for nonessentials when a man's in a hurry."

Bonnie stood like a statue, hearing his words and watching him with glazed eyes. She couldn't believe what had happened, it was almost as if it had happened to someone else. She was vaguely aware of the pain between her legs and she knew he terrified her. But he was right about her father, and that was the most terrifying thought of all. She couldn't tell . . . she had been raped and she couldn't tell a soul!

William Finlay was putting on his coat. He turned and brazenly smiled at her. "Nice," he mumbled. "First-class goods. Now be a nice little girl and clean this place up and be a smart little lass and keep your lovely mouth shut." He winked. "I'll be back again," he threatened.

Bonnie Campbell steadied herself against the table as Finlay walked through the doorway and shut the door behind him. A blast of cold air hit her in the face and she wrapped her arms around herself. She moved hesitatingly forward and then, reaching the door, flung it open, breathing deeply till the pain of the cold obliterated all other sensations.

Slowly, Bonnie Campbell closed the door. She picked up her undergarments and put them back on, she straightened up the room. Then she sat down and smoothed out her skirts. Guilt flowed through her as if she were a whore who had slept with every man in the Nelson Encampment.

"Don't swing your hips when you walk!" her father once had commanded her. Then under his breath he had muttered, "You're making yourself a temptation! It'll be no one's fault but your own if some man wants you too much!"

And I didn't scream, Bonnie chastised herself. I can't tell! I can never tell!

Gradually, Bonnie forced herself to be calm. She cleaned the cabin again, double-checking for traces of Finlay. She combed her long hair and, looking in the tin that served as a mirror, arranged it properly, brushing it back. My face looks the same, she observed. Can that be? she asked herself. But in her heart, her fear remained. Her father would be home soon and one day William Finlay would come back too. Bonnie Campbell didn't know which she feared more: the filthy body of William Finlay or her father's wrath.

When Bonnie finally heard the squeaking of the sled on the hardened white snow, her whole body tensed. In moments her father entered the one-room cabin, followed by her mother.

"Whose bootprints are those in front of the door?" her father demanded crossly.

"A man's," Bonnie answered, trembling as she looked off toward the fire. She could not meet her father's gaze. "He came here for hot water."

"Did you let him in?" her father questioned.

Bonnie could hear the accusation in her father's tone. He was ready to condemn her, maybe even disown her. She wanted to throw herself in his arms and seek his protection. She wanted to cry out, "I was raped! He hurt me! And he'll come back!" But Bonnie could not move, just as she had been unable to move when Finlay attacked her. She wanted her father to protect her, but in her father's voice there was no protection, only punishment.

"I sent him away," Bonnie replied. "I didn't let him in. He must have gone elsewhere."

Her father grunted and set the pile of supplies

down on the center table. "You can't trust any man," he warned her. "Besides," he spat, "you have to be watched. You are at the age when you're wanton."

Bonnie turned her face away and back toward the fire. I'm wanton, she thought bitterly. No, I could never desire that! But her father's attitude proved William Finlay right, Bonnie Campbell admitted to herself. I hate men, she thought. All of them!

Josh MacLean studied the leather pouch for a moment, then broke the sealing wax and removed several pieces of paper. He read the letter through quickly, then his fingertips gripped the paper and he reread it slowly, disbelieving the words Colleen Adams had set to paper.

December 2, 1811

My darling Josh,

I'm crying even as I write this letter and I cannot even think of the hurt you will feel when you read it.

I will not be journeying to Lochiel on the twentieth or ever. I have left on a long journey to Boston and I think I will not be returning. It is enough to say that though I love you deeply, there are reasons why our love cannot be. You must trust that those reasons are serious and very real.

Josh, I beg you to forgive me and forget me as I will have to try to forget you. Find another love, Josh. Be happy.

My love,
Colleen Adams

Josh put down the letter and stared at it. What did it mean? It was dated only days after they had made love so passionately. Now it was December 15. That meant that Colleen already was gone!

Josh covered his eyes with his hand and leaned against the table. He had come home early to work on some furniture he was making for the home he and Colleen would share. He had encountered the rider with the pouch en route, taking the message and bringing it into the house to read it. Now, over an hour later, he continued to sit at the table, numb, confused, staring into space.

"My heavens! What are you doing sitting here in the dark? Aren't you freezing? You haven't even started a fire." Jenna had flown into the kitchen, carrying a basket of eggs and unbuttoning her long cloak with one hand. "Josh? Josh, are you all right?"

She leaned over and looked into his face. Even in the fading light, Jenna could read the pain in his expression. "What is it?" she persisted. Then, sitting down, she covered his hand with hers. "Josh, for heaven's sake, you're frightening me. What is the matter?"

"I'm sorry," Josh stumbled. "I can't talk just now, I can't—" He choked on his words and, instead of a verbal explanation, shoved the letter toward his mother. "Read it yourself," he invited.

Josh stood up awkwardly and pushed his hands into his pockets. He strode out the back door toward the woodpile and picked up a hatchet. Jenna soon heard the steady sound of wood being chopped. She didn't call out to him, as she once might have. There already was quite enough chopped wood, but ever since he was a small boy, Josh always had gone to the woodpile when he was upset. He chopped to work off anger, to think things over, to find comfort in hard work.

Jenna picked up the letter and read it, then she set it down and mumbled, "Oh, my heavens."

91

When Josh came back into the house, Jenna had lit the lanterns, started the fire, and begun to cook supper on the potbellied stove. It was the lightest of their three daily meals, since the main meal was always served at noon. Will was still at the trading post and Jenna could only assume that there had been a barge come downriver late in the afternoon. Will would stay to unload it, and the chances were he would be home quite late.

"I expect your father will be late," Jenna announced. "Why don't you wash for supper?"

"I'm not hungry," Josh replied.

Jenna didn't turn to face him, but continued to stir the soup. "I put the letter in your room. Hungry or not, wash up. Come back and we'll have something to drink."

Josh didn't answer but left the room. It's been a long while since I spoke to him with that tone, Jenna thought. I sound like a mother. Jenna searched her mind for some reason for Colleen's actions but could think of none. In truth, Jenna was as mystified as Josh.

"I've come back for my drink," Josh said as he entered the kitchen.

"You know where it is," Jenna said and smiled. She watched as Josh went to the cupboard and got the brandy. He filled two glasses and handed his mother one.

"Do you want to talk now?" Jenna asked.

"I don't know what to say; it's so sudden and I don't understand."

Jenna bit her lip. "Josh, did anything happen the last time you were there?"

Josh shook his head. He could hardly tell his mother he and Colleen had made love. He shook his head and sipped the brandy, trying to remember everything.

"Colleen's father wasn't home when I arrived. I

had to leave before he returned. He went to pick up something. That's all."

"Why don't you go to see her father?" Jenna suggested. "I know he's not a talkative man, but perhaps he can help you."

"I intend to do that," Josh said with determination. "But if he doesn't, or can't, I intend to follow Colleen all the way to Boston!"

Jenna looked into her son's eyes. "Boston?" she repeated. "Oh, Josh. We're on the brink of war!"

Colleen sat primly in the coach as it bumped along the road. On her lap was her satchel and in it were two diaries, one written by her grandmother, Megan Marta O'Flynn, and the other by her great-grandfather, Richard O'Flynn.

Her father had read the diaries, as had Colleen. Unexpectedly, their contents had a greater emotional impact on her than on her father. "Now I know my name," was all he could say. "That's all I care about!" But for Colleen it was different. Her grandmother's diary recounted Megan's love for Mathew Macleod and hinted that he was the father of her child, Richard, who was, of course, Colleen's father.

Josh and I are cousins, we share the same grandfather, Colleen thought once again. It haunted her and pained her. Our love would be—is—incestuous! She closed her eyes and clasped her hands even more tightly. But the diary was not specific, it only hinted. There was a slim chance that it might not be true.

Megan had been a spy for the British. She had come to Fort Niagara and actually cared for the Macleod children. She wrote about loving Mathew, about making love to him one night . . . then there were pages missing until she took up her diary again in Boston. "I cannot keep the child with me," she had written. "It is impossible."

93

Later entries made reference to an acting career and to moving in with a female acquaintance in Boston. She spoke in the diary of how close they were. Colleen stared down at her satchel almost as if she could see through it and read the pages of the books it contained. Megan was dead now and surely her friend, only a few years younger, was dead as well.

Megan's friend, Susanna Sharp, would be in her seventies if she were alive, Colleen concluded. Perhaps her children would remember something. It was a slim hope, but part of the reason why she decided to journey to Boston.

Colleen leaned back and tried to rest her head against the back of the cushioned seat. At least she could be happy for her father, she thought. There was nothing he did not now know about his mother and his presumed father. He knew his mother came from a family of adventurers, a family of spies who knew wealth and poverty. And there was a small legacy as well. Megan had left funds, enough to make Richard Adams, whose real name was O'Flynn, comfortable for the rest of his life.

Into the hems of gowns found in the trunk were sewn jewels—diamonds, rubies, and emeralds. There were gold coins too, enough gold coins to make Colleen and her father rich. And taking the method in her grandmother's dairy, Colleen had carefully sewn gold and jewels into the bottom of her skirt. "Take some," her father had urged. "I don't need them all."

"I have to know for certain," Colleen had confessed when she told her father she was leaving. "And if I can't find out, I will not return. I can't be so close to Josh. I couldn't stand it."

Her father had nodded, then asked, "What shall I tell him?"

"Tell him nothing," Colleen pleaded. "He must not know! Papa, Mathew Macleod was so respected, and Janet Macleod has only just died. Josh would be

94

miserable if such a scandal were to become known. Oh, you must not tell him!"

"It's over more than forty-five years!" her father protested. Then he quickly added, "Of course, I want nothing from them."

"Over is over," Colleen reiterated. "Please, knowing is enough, keep the secret." In the end, to her relief, he had agreed.

As was often the case, the ground on the Canadian side of the border remained bare and cold till the day before Christmas and then, almost as if commanded, a soft white snow fell and the Niagara Peninsula turned into a white fluffy wonderland. But by New Year's Eve, the white fluff had turned to a hard frozen crust, heralding the bitter winds of January.

Jenna and Will MacLean went to Lochiel and together with the rest of the Macleod clan feasted on piglet and wild partridge, brown bread and freshly churned butter. There were carrots and potatoes and meat pies as well. A full hour after the evening meal, the clan sat in the center room of Lochiel, warm, glutted, and sleepy. The children had mostly gone to bed after the meal, or gone outside to play in the moonlight till it was time to come in to toast the New Year. New Year's Eve was reserved for those over the age of twelve, and it was the only day of the year when a large, festive meal was eaten in the evening.

"Looks as if we'll be getting plenty of work from the army," John Macleod announced, not expecting much of a response.

His father, old Andrew Macleod, nodded and said, "The Royal Engineers are few and far between." That caused a chuckle. In both Upper and Lower Canada, there were only four members of the Royal Engineers.

"Fort George needs work; the roads and docks need updating."

Andrew grunted at his son's assessment. "Good lucrative contract work in preparation for war. But it doesn't pay to build the roads too well. You wouldn't want the American artillery to have too easy a time of it."

"Never-ending war," Helena said tersely as she put down a tray of drinks.

"All over the Niagara, and all because of the portage trail," Andrew Macleod added. "It's one bone of contention, a big bone." The portage trail had been held by the British since the American rebellion, and the Americans wanted it.

"Hardly the only cause of war," John put in. "Just the cause that will affect us the most."

Jenna sat next to Will. Her brothers, Andrew and Tom, were older than she by twelve and fourteen years, respectively. Andrew's son, John Macleod, was thirty-one. She was the last of Janet and Mathew's children and always felt as if she were caught somewhere between her brothers' generation and that of their children. She had been a girl during the American rebellion and she had missed most of it because she had run away, going South down the Mississippi. Will had done some fighting in the rebellion, but he had fought for the Spanish. The twenty-seven years since the end of the rebellion had been years of peace, albeit a tense peace filled with warnings of a war that never actually materialized. Now it really looked as if there would be a war. Moreover, it looked as if it would happen right in their own backyard.

"There's been war threatened ever since I can remember," Jenna said with a deep sigh. "We all thought for certain there was going to be one in 1808, remember? I can't believe it will happen now. I just can't."

"It's been building since the treaty that ended the American rebellion." Andrew sounded thoughtful.

"But now there's a Congress full of War Hawks, people who seem to think that uniting the continent under the Stars and Stripes is their destiny. Thanks to those damn Southerners, I think it will happen this time!"

Will looked up and thought about Andrew's comment. He wondered if James had children; it was one of the rare times he had thought of his brother. "You're quite right. It's the South that wants war," he said pensively.

"I don't think the New England states will have a bit of it," Tom commented. "The people there have more sense. They're the most sensible people in the United States."

Jenna lifted a glass from the tray Helena put down. "I don't think I want to talk about war tonight," she announced, standing up. "It's almost midnight and I want to think about the New Year positively! We had a good harvest, and the school is almost built: We have a great deal to be grateful for." Jenna's cheeks were flushed from the wine. "Let's drink to the New Year," she suggested. "Let's not waste tonight thinking about a war that might not happen."

Will stood up and put his arm around Jenna's waist. "Let's drink to 1812!" he said. "Let's drink to the New Year!"

CHAPTER V

February 1812

Claude Deschamps sat opposite John Jacob Astor and studied the man, even as Astor mumbled half in English and half in German. Claude Deschamps worked for the North West Company and he had come to New York to see Astor at the request of the North West Company's head, William McGillivray.

Only last year, John Jacob Astor had become a partner in the North West Company. For Astor, who headed the South West Company, the partnership agreement had been hard fought over because William McGillivray was a wily old trader and prepared to give nothing away. But on January 28, 1811, the two men reached a mutually satisfactory agreement. The North West Company agreed to trade in the Southwest only in partnership with the South West Company, which in turn agreed to limit its operations to the territory east of the Rockies. Each partner agreed to provide half the goods to be traded. Astor would provide goods manufactured in the United States, McGillivray goods manufactured in Britain and imported through Montreal. War between the United States and British North America would threaten this lucrative arrangement, and was in fact contrary to the mutual interests and individual interests of both companies.

"Der Mann ist ein Idiot!" John Jacob Astor fumed.

Whenever he became angry or overemotional, he forgot English momentarily and reverted to his mother tongue, German. And John Jacob Astor was sorely angry with President Madison, Speaker Clay, and the young blustering fool Calhoun. Astor's anger focused on them individually and collectively because they were the most vocal War Hawks. In truth, Astor was angry and disgusted with the whole Congress and blistering mad that the northern states seemed so utterly impotent and unable to stop the War Hawks from blindly marching down the road to financial ruin. Above all things, John Jacob Astor did not want war with the British. War disrupted commerce; war was the luxury of morons.

Good God! He had only just gotten things running smoothly. The new fur lands were neatly divided between the powers present. Riches awaited! It was all very well investing his surplus money in plots of land on Manhattan island, but who could tell if such investments ever would be worth anything? Furs were a known quantity, so John Jacob Astor heeded his own dictum: "Take cash whenever possible."

And Rupert's Land, or at least its western part, had so many little furry beasts to offer! His new arrangement with the Canadian North West Company was almost as lucrative as his arrangement with the East India Company. China was his new market, Rupert's Land his new hunting ground.

It was quite true that the Hudson's Bay Company might offer competition at some point, but Astor decided to deal with that when it occurred. But one need not go to war! One could buy out competition. War was destructive, it upset everyone's applecart.

Claude found he rather liked Astor, perhaps because Astor wasn't British, perhaps because Astor had little respect for the Americans. Moreover, Astor was shrewd and Claude Deschamps liked shrewd men.

99

"We've been on the brink of this war for years," Claude Deschamps said dryly. He looked around the drawing room; the predominant decorative color was a watery blue, the color of Astor's eyes. It was also devoid of ornamentation; Astor was a miser of some renown.

"I suppose my heirs will fritter away my money," he often lamented. "Like the others in this country, they'll forget that books are the only things of lasting value." Yes, Claude Deschamps thought, the man sitting across from him was rare indeed. He spoke of leaving his money to found a library, but while he was alive making that money and holding onto every cent of it was an obsession.

"I can tolerate being on the brink of war," Astor responded in his thick accent, "but war is not a moneymaking proposition."

"Being on the brink of war can be quite profitable," Claude corrected.

"Because fearing a shortage, people buy high and stockpile, true enough. Tell me something of yourself, Mr. Deschamps. You strike me as an odd bird, a man whose tastes and interests represent mixed political leanings."

Claude shrugged. It was a typical Gallic shrug. It had been a long time since he was called upon to explain himself, and in truth he didn't find it an easy task.

"I am open, as are all French Canadians," he said, smiling wryly. "And I am secretive, as are all French Canadians."

"In other words, a contradiction," Astor replied, leaning over.

"It is a contradiction to be among those who continue speaking French on this continent. It is a contradiction to realize that the British are our only protectors in terms of retaining our religion, culture, and language. It is a contradiction to have to support those one naturally dislikes because they are the lesser evil. It is a contradiction to be highly educated and rich in a province of need and, yes, sometimes of intellectual darkness. Monsieur Astor, it is a contradiction to be French Canadian."

John Jacob Astor nodded. "I pride myself on understanding such contradictions. Now tell me, Mr. Claude Deschamps, what can I do for you? What can two contradictions do to stop a war?"

"We can't stop it, at least not in the definite sense. What I have in mind is an arrangement to, ah, deal with certain eventualities. For instance, I believe the English to be better prepared for war than the Americans."

Astor grunted. "That wouldn't take much. The army has a reputation for certain inept acts, some say outright bungling. There's no organization. If I ran my business the way Congress runs this country, I'd be broke."

"The country *is* broke," Claude reminded him. "Now, when a country run by Frenchmen goes broke, you can be certain it is because someone has stolen the money and run away to enjoy it. When a country run by *les anglais* goes broke, you can be sure the money was frittered away in such a fashion that no one enjoyed it. How do Germans go broke?"

"They don't," Astor said and smiled. He paused, then turned back to Claude seriously. "We have two problems," Astor explained. "The first is what some Americans see as their destiny. They want to rule, or, more correctly, think they have the right to rule —given by God, no doubt—the entire hemisphere. On the other side of the political spectrum, you have states still unwilling to yield to a federal system. Well, a destiny which is not at hand does not interest me and, as for the other, I say a country needs a head just like a family. Men conduct commerce and they must be allowed to do it. They cannot do it if the

101

rules change every time they cross a state or territorial border. I cannot abide this nonsense! By God, this country has no destiny till it is prepared to stand as a unified whole. I don't care if the Americans wish to challenge the British right to embargo trade! I don't care even if they try to blockade certain ports. But to get at a British embargo by invading Canada and halting the only lucrative trade is—is— what is the expression? Oh, *ja*, cutting off one's nose to spite one's face."

"Our faces," Claude said quietly. "What we need is advance information—we need to know more or less when war will officially be declared. Now, if we knew that, and if the North West Company offered its services to the British, we might well achieve a decisive victory just as the opening salvo is being fired. It would, I believe, dampen enthusiasm for this war and bring it to a quicker halt."

Astor's eyes twinkled slightly. Clearly the idea appealed to him.

"You have men in Washington, we have a network of the fastest and most competent couriers on the continent. The British could be notified of a declaration of war from Washington even before Washington had time to notify its own armies and state militias."

Astor broke out laughing. "*Ist gut! Ist gut!* I like it."

Colleen returned to the house where she had rented a small room. It was a brick house on Brimmer Street, a short walk from the winding Charles River in one direction, a slightly longer walk to the Boston Commons in the other.

She climbed the narrow staircase and opened the door of her room. It was tiny, but at this moment it seemed like a mansion. She closed the door behind her and sagged onto the bed, grateful to be alone, grateful to be back in her refuge.

"This is a day God can take back," Colleen mumbled darkly. She had been in Boston for some time and she finally had located the daughter of Susanna Sharp, her grandmother's friend.

The woman had turned out to be a great disappointment. She was perhaps forty and as brittle as a branch in midwinter.

"My mother?" she had said, raising an eyebrow. "I don't really know—I have an address in Washington, but I don't know if she's still alive. She was alive last year, but then that was last year!"

Colleen had been taken aback by the woman's attitude. She had always wanted a mother and could scarcely imagine a daughter so unloving and uncaring.

"You do not get along with your mother?" Colleen had ventured.

"No," had come the immediate cold response. "But here's the address, for what it's worth—if anything." Then the woman had leaned forward and confided, "My mother disgraced us. She was a slut. We were shunned."

"But she's near seventy now," Colleen had protested.

"It doesn't matter if she's near a hundred!" the woman had answered bitterly. "I still wouldn't care if she were dead or alive. And I wouldn't care where she lived either!"

Amazed at the woman's hardness, Colleen had taken the address and left after expressing her thanks. But the experience left her feeling empty and alone.

Her visit with Susanna Sharp's daughter had taken place at a little past noon. At three she had kept an appointment with a doctor.

"Oh, Mrs. O'Flynn," he had said, beaming. "You are indeed with child! I know you must be terribly happy."

Colleen had smiled though tears had flooded her eyes. "Overcome," she had whispered before fleeing the doctor's clinic. It was a kind of defiance that had caused her to use the name O'Flynn. But why not? she asked herself. I am, after all, carrying on in the family tradition; I'm going to have a baby out of wedlock! She had walked rapidly back toward Brimmer Street, fighting back tears. But still it seemed that everyone was looking at her, everyone! Now, safe from the prying eyes of passersby, she let herself go. She lay face down on the bed, clutching her pillow and wailing into it. "Oh, Josh! It's too late! Oh, God, help me!"

After a time, Colleen stopped crying and wiped her puffy eyes. "I shall go to Washington anyway," she decided aloud. "There's nothing more to lose."

"How many guns are missing?" Miles Macdonell asked. Hillier looked as worried as he was, and certainly Miles could not afford to take such a theft lightly. Some of the would-be colonists were an untrustworthy lot, rebellious in nature and none too bright.

"Five muskets," Hillier reported. "I knew it was a bloody mistake to bring Irish Catholics and Scots Catholics together with Scots Protestants. Now we have a mixture of prejudice and ignorance combined with cabin fever."

They were in Miles' cabin. Miles tapped his fingers on the table and contemplated what Hillier had just said. Aboard ship there had been rumblings between Protestant Orkneymen and Irish Catholics. Miles already had had to separate them on work crews. Now the tempers that had smoldered so many months ago threatened to burst into flame. On New

Year's Eve, the Irish and the Orkneymen had consumed far too much liquor, and verbal insults had flown. On that night a group of the more bellicose Irish Catholics had beaten one of the Protestants senseless. Of course, Miles had rationalized at the time, if the stupid man had exercised any sense at all, he would not have insulted the volatile Irish in the first place.

"Dare I suspect the Orkneymen are planning their revenge?" Miles pondered aloud. "Or is it the Irish who took the guns?"

Hillier shifted uneasily. "I doubt we'll have to wait long."

Hillier was right. The confrontation began the next morning with what Miles considered a matter of individual discipline. Not surprisingly, the person requiring the discipline was William Finlay.

"I have told you once, I have told you twice," Miles Macdonell said, looking at the unkempt Finlay, "we all take the fir-tree concoction in the mornings. I won't have scurvy breaking out in this camp!"

Finlay stared back, his beady eyes cold. "I'll not drink that bilge water! I'd sooner drink a Proddy's urine!"

Miles swore under his breath and held out the tin cup with the steaming hot drink made from spruce needles. He was well aware that its taste left something to be desired, but couldn't he just do as he was told and drink it? It was known to prevent the dread disease and it certainly was the lesser of two evils.

Finlay swung suddenly and the tin cup went flying. Miles stepped back, his fist automatically doubled. Finlay was questioning his authority and the settlers pressed in from all sides, waiting to see what would happen. If Finlay didn't drink the brew, others would stop too, and they would disobey work orders. Miles would lose his authority over the colonists if he backed down.

105

Miles unclenched his fists and looked around. He had ordered a one-room cabin to be built in case something like this happened. He hesitated for only a second and then he drew his gun, vaguely aware that Hillier was behind him. "Lock this man up in there!" Miles pointed to the cabin. "He's to remain in solitary confinement."

Two Orkneymen came forward. They looked at Finlay as if they could kill him, then they dragged him toward the hut, roughly pushing him in. As the door was shut and bolted, Finlay let forth with a string of nasty oaths.

"Filthy Catholics!" Mrs. Campbell muttered as she turned from the scene with disgust, pulling her daughter along.

As the women and children left the scene, Miles ordered the work crews off to their daily assignments and returned to his own cabin with Mr. Hillier.

"You did the right thing," Hillier assured Miles as the door of the cabin was closed behind them. "If you're to get them safely up the Nelson, they have to learn your word is law."

Miles sat down and poured himself some brandy. He found the whole episode distasteful. He had only just lifted the cup to his lips when he heard the cry go up: "Fire! Fire!"

Miles and Hillier bolted for the door, grabbing their heavy furs and closing them up as they ran. They plowed through the deep snow to the clearing and the hut where Finlay had been deposited only a half hour before.

The hut was ablaze, giving off blinding white steam in the cold morning air. Its timbers crackled. "My God!" Miles exclaimed. Around the cabin, a group of the dissident Irish stood, each of them armed with one of the missing muskets. The door of the burning hut had been kicked open and Finlay stood among his fellow rebels, grinning.

"A good morning fire, Governor Macdonell, to warm me hands and me arse!"

Miles stood stock still, trying to assess the situation. The work crews had come running from the forest, and the women had left the cabins and gathered about in a silent circle.

Five muskets, Miles thought. If I try to take control, people will be killed needlessly.

"Surrender your weapons at once!" Miles ordered, even though he knew it was a futile gesture at giving orders.

Hillier stepped up close to Miles and said, "Listen, given enough rope . . . Miles, where are they going to go? What are they going to eat? Don't challenge them now. Wait!"

Finlay had stepped in front of the men carrying the muskets. "There's a cabin down by the river. It's deserted. My men and I are claiming it. Oh, we'll stay away from your precious little encampment. But we'll not work anymore and we'll not take orders from you anymore, Governor. We'll make our own way."

Miles let out his breath. None of them did much work anyway and when the ships came in the spring, he could send them all back. Hillier was quite right. This was no time to challenge them. There were soldiers at the fort, but not enough. These dissidents would do less damage battling winter on their own than fighting soldiers. And if they stayed out of the Nelson Encampment and out of York Factory, they would be away from the others. Allowing them to go off seemed to have advantages.

"All right," Miles answered with all the calm he could muster. "You're on your own. Just stay out of this encampment and away from the people in it! If there's stealing, if there's any kind of trouble, I'll send the soldiers from the fort for you! And I'll tell them to shoot to kill!"

Finlay spit on the snow and took three long strides, reaching a pale-faced Bonnie Campbell, who stood near her parents on the edge of a circle of spectators. He grabbed her arm and jerked her toward him. "I'll be taking this one with me!" Finlay's announcement echoed through a stunned silence, then in an even louder voice he turned and shouted at Bonnie Campbell's parents, "She's already given herself to me, you know. The day you went into York Factory, I had her and she loved it! A nice little bundle, she is!"

Aghast, the Campbells stepped back, shrinking from their own daughter's side as if she had the plague. A whisper of condemnation moved quickly around the circle. "He's lying!" Bonnie Campbell shrieked. "He's lying! He's lying! He made me do it!"

"Slut!" Campbell spit on the ground. "And I tried to raise you decent! You're just a little wanton slut! Don't you ever come near your mother or me again! You're dead as far as I'm concerned—dead!" His face was nearly purple with rage and he drew his arm back, striking his daughter across the face. Bonnie's knees buckled and she fell to the snow, digging her fingers into it, even though Finlay had grabbed her elbow and was pulling her toward him.

But Bonnie was impervious to the snow and the biting wind. "No, no, no!" she wailed. "Papa, don't let him take me!"

Miles shook his head and then took long strides to reach Finlay's side. He delivered a quick, hard blow to Finlay's wrist, causing Finlay to release Bonnie's elbow. Then, with his other hand, he jerked the hapless girl to her feet.

"You'll take her nowhere!" Miles told Finlay.

"C'mon, Finlay, one woman's not enough for all of us, and you ain't going to have your own!" called out one of the dissidents, waving his musket in the air.

Finlay wiped off his mouth with his hand and

108

moved backward toward his men, accepting their decision instantly. Behind him, Miles could hear the dissidents moving off. There was no sound save the crunching of their feet on the snow. Around him, he was only too aware of the good Protestant settlers as they glared at Bonnie Campbell with hatred and contempt. The women's faces bore the look of the self-righteous; some of the men leered.

"I'll not have her!" Bonnie's father announced. He grabbed his wife and pulled her away. "We've been disgraced! She disobeyed me and invited sin! I'll not have her!"

At Miles' side, Bonnie Campbell shivered and whimpered. "Go to my cabin!" Miles ordered. "I'll send you to stay at the post."

Miles turned wearily. Finlay and his men had just reached the edge of the woods. "Good riddance!" Miles shouted. "And you'll leave this girl alone!"

"She was willing enough!" Finlay called back, bragging.

"Well, she's not willing now!" Miles retorted. Finlay didn't answer. He paused only to spit in the snow, then he and his motley crew strode off into the woods.

Shaken, Miles turned and followed Hillier back to his cabin. Ahead of them, the lonely figure of Bonnie Campbell plodded through the snow.

Once inside, Miles wrapped a warm fur around her slim shoulders and sat her down in front of the fire.

"Mr. Hillier will take you to the Hudson's Bay post," Miles mumbled. He felt ill at ease and decidedly confused by the morning's events. Dealing with a single girl in the wilderness was a challenge he had not bargained for.

Bonnie Campbell looked up at Miles with swollen, red, tear-filled eyes. "They've disowned me," she murmured in a small voice. "They won't have me with them."

"But you didn't want to go with Finlay, did you?"

Bonnie shook her head. "Oh, no, no."

"There's a ship coming in the spring," Miles told her, not knowing what else to say. "You might be able to go on to the Red River with those settlers; they won't know you and I've been told there're more women among them, more women your own age. Perhaps you can get work with one of the families, perhaps . . ." Miles didn't finish his sentence. Bonnie Campbell had lowered her head and was staring at the floor.

Miles turned away from her. Clearly her mother and father had cause to be suspicious, or they would not have reacted so. But could a girl like this willingly give herself to so miserable a creature as Finlay? It seemed unlikely. I am not the type to handle situations like this, Miles thought. I can start fires in the rain, build shelters against the worst weather, survive in the wilderness, construct boats, but I do not understand women. Nor, being a Catholic myself, do I understand this rabid Puritan attitude among the settlers. Heaven guide me!

Bonnie Campbell wiped her cheek with her hand. "What will become of me?" Her wide blue eyes looked up at Miles and he felt totally helpless.

"We'll think of something," he mumbled.

Josh MacLean sat in the Auberge Le Vieux St. Gabriel in Montreal. It was a pleasant, warm inn that served fine food and offered neat, clean rooms. He might have gone to stay with his cousins the Frasers or he could have been visiting the Deschamps in Trois-Rivières. But Josh was in no mood for family visits; the impersonal atmosphere of the inn better met his requirements.

The inn was now owned by Mrs. Dolley Hart, the widow of a wealthy merchant, Aaron Hart. The Harts were Hebrews and Mrs. Hart was motherly in the extreme as well as a bit of an eccentric. She had converted the entire top floor of the inn into her personal living quarters. There, like a queen, she held court. In the morning, as well as in the afternoon and evening, Mrs. Hart dressed in formal attire and always was bejeweled and elaborately coiffed.

One might have thought that such a woman would have happily relaxed, giving herself over entirely to a life of relative leisure among her friends. Not so. Dressed in her finest dresses and wearing her largest diamonds, Mrs. Hart not only baked bread with her own hands for her guests, but also prepared and personally served a dazzling array of rich, delightfully delicious meals.

"You're a big man," Mrs. Hart told Josh on his first night in the inn. "And you're eating like a bird. What would your mother say? She would say that you came to stay in an inn owned by Dolley Hart and you didn't eat. Eat! I don't cook for my own amusement."

Smiling weakly, Josh had given in and eaten. Mrs. Hart was as irresistible as her food, and she was a good listener too. "You'll tell me your problems," she told Josh. "A nice young man like you shouldn't have any problems, but I can see that you do."

And so Josh had unburdened himself to her. He had left Lochiel on the Niagara in December and gone to Colleen's father, Richard Adams.

Richard Adams had completed his preparations for winter and Josh had found him holed up in the farmhouse in front of the fire, happily enjoying his Irish whiskey in solitude.

Josh had not known what to expect in the way of a reception, but Adams was hospitable even though he refused to explain the mystery of Colleen's sudden breaking of the engagement and her equally sudden departure.

111

"I don't understand," Josh had protested. "Did she tell you?"

"I understand," Richard Adams answered.

"You don't seem angry, upset, or unwilling to speak with me," Josh told Adams.

"No reason why I should be," Adams answered with a grin. "You're a nice young man."

"Then explain it to me! Explain why she went to Boston! Explain why she broke our engagement."

"Can't do that. She made me promise."

"Then I want to see her," Josh persisted. "Tell me where she is in Boston."

"I'm not certain, but I think she would have contacted her mother's people. I'll give you their name, but it won't do any good. Why can't you let it go? It's better."

Josh shook his head and pressed Richard Adams till he wrote out the name.

Then Josh had made the long journey from Lewiston to Boston. He followed the waterways and traveled through the mountain pass, finally reaching a snow-covered Boston in January.

The people whose name he had been given had seen Colleen only briefly. "Rented a room on Brimmer Street," Colleen's second cousin told him. Josh went there immediately only to find that Colleen had gone. "Didn't say where," the landlady informed him.

Dejected, weary, and feeling totally defeated, Josh had left Boston and headed north, up to Montreal.

When he finished his story, Mrs. Hart patted his knee. "This girl sounds as if she's looking for something—it's not like a woman to be traipsing to one place after another without a reason. Maybe when she finds what she's looking for, she'll come back."

"I hope you're right," Josh said.

Mrs. Hart had stood up and smoothed out her taffeta gown. "You go downstairs by the fire. I'll send down some nice Burgundy and some cheese."

So it was that Josh found himself in the drinking room of the Auberge Le Vieux St. Gabriel, sipping a lovely dark red Burgundy and watching as large snowflakes fell outside the louvered windows while behind him a fire roared in the giant fireplace.

"Josh MacLean?"

Josh set down his glass and looked up into the curious face of Claude Deschamps. Josh quickly stood and grasped his friend's hand. "I thought you would be in Trois-Rivières," Josh said almost apologetically. "If I'd known you were in Montreal . . ."

Claude pulled up a chair and sat down opposite Josh at the little table. "I've just come back from New York," Claude confided as he removed his dark gloves. "And you know how it is in late February, travel is difficult, the weather is unpredictable. But what, my friend, brings you to Montreal in the dead of winter? Is it not cold enough on the Niagara?"

"I've just come back from Boston, myself," Josh confided. "It's a difficult journey."

Claude smiled. "Not as difficult as it was in 1748 for Mathew Macleod, eh? Transportation is improved, there are towns and settlements everywhere. It hardly takes three weeks now!"

Josh nodded. Somehow he had forgotten his grandfather's historic journey to Quebec from Boston. "And how are my adopted cousins?" he asked, leaning over to Claude, who was the son of Madelaine Macleod's brother, Pierre Deschamps. The Deschamps children had been adopted by the Macleods, and Tom Macleod had married Madelaine Deschamps.

"We're all in excellent health," Claude replied.

"But it has not been so many months since we last met."

Josh briefly thought back to his grandmother's funeral. It seemed like a million years, though in fact it had been only three months.

"What took you to Boston?" Claude asked curiously.

"A lost love," Josh replied, shrugging.

Claude pressed his lips together and nodded knowingly. "I see from your low spirits that you did not find your lost love."

"You see correctly."

The barmaid approached and leaned over. "More wine?"

"*Oui*, and some more cheese and black bread as well." She bowed slightly and disappeared. "Well, Josh MacLean, you have several choices—as all those suffering from unrequited love have. You can go West with the North West Company or the Hudson's Bay Company; you can join the army; or you can do as the French do, and find another woman. But since you are Scots, I suspect you would not take that suggestion. I suspect you will either go West or join the army."

In spite of his weariness and his grim mood, Claude had coaxed a smile from Josh. "I ought to remind you that my other grandmother was Acadian. I am, therefore, part French."

"But is it the right part?" Claude said, laughing.

Josh blushed. "It's true that I have already made inquiries about buying a commission in the army."

"Now we know what part is French," Claude quipped.

Josh shook his head, aware that his face was red and that he was stuttering to explain himself. "Living on the Niagara, I had might as well be in the army—I mean, I will have to fight in any case and—"

"I understand," Claude assured him. "And really, your romanticism is quite charming."

The serving girl brought more wine and an assortment of cheeses. The two men broke the bread and ate the cheese as they drank. "Are you really certain you want to join the army?" Claude questioned again as they finished their repast. This time his expression was more serious.

"I am," Josh replied without hesitation.

"I'll make you a bargain, then." Claude was smiling. "Let me take you out tonight—one night of drinking and womanizing. Then tomorrow I will take you to Red George Macdonell. He's here, down from Quebec City to set up training facilities in Trois-Rivières for the new Glengarry Regiment. He'll be pleased to know you want to volunteer."

Josh nodded his head in agreement. "I accept, but I may not be the best of company," he warned. Josh thrust his hand in his pocket to retrieve some coins for the bill, but Claude restrained him.

"In Montreal you are my guest," Claude said and smiled.

"I didn't know there were such places in Montreal," Josh commented later that evening. Claude poured yet another glass of wine and Josh found himself tapping his foot in time to the fiddler's tune.

"Few *anglais* do know the finer spots of Montreal, which is all to the good, eh?"

Josh found that the wine had gone quickly to his head and he could not even recall how much he had drunk. Claude had come for him around nine. Then they had gone to several drinking establishments and ended up here, in a smoke-filled, overheated tavern room that was a part of the larger Auberge Rouge.

"I think you are ready," Claude said, smiling. "Indeed if you drink any more, you will be absolutely incapable."

"Incapable of what?" Josh asked, slurring.

Claude took his elbow and helped him to stand. "Come along," he motioned. "Our evening has only begun."

Claude Deschamps led Josh out of the drinking room and away from the noise of the fiddles. They moved down a corridor lit rosy red, but which was not as well heated as the drinking room. The cooler air sobered Josh somewhat.

"In here," Claude motioned. He opened a door and Josh all but jumped at the unexpected sight.

The room was dimly lit but richly furnished. On a settee, a girl with long black hair lounged casually. She wore a flimsy red satin gown trimmed in a black lace that matched the material the settee was covered in. Her long, quite visible white thighs were a striking contrast to the black covering on the settee.

On a light blue settee across the room, another girl dressed in virginal white sat primly. She had flaxen hair and her white chemise did little to cover her voluptuous body. In another corner, perched on the edge of a table, was a tall, strong Amazon type, covered only by a furry animal skin that was artfully draped over her outsized endowments. And in yet another corner, there was a young woman dressed in a low-necked gown in the Louis XIV style and wearing a crown.

"An idea imported from Paris," Claude explained. "At least the blockade doesn't keep out ideas. See, they're all dressed as fantasies. I hear it's a sort of post-Revolutionary craze. Very popular in the continental brothels."

"I imagine," Josh said, not able to take it all in and rather wishing he had not consumed quite so much wine.

"Which one do you want?" Claude asked. "Person-

116

ally, you're out of luck if you want her, because I'm taking her." Claude indicated the woman on the settee dressed in red and black.

Josh exhaled. There was no getting out of this. "Her, if she's willing." Josh pointed off toward the flaxen-haired beauty dressed in white.

"For what she's being paid, I daresay she's willing. I might have known you'd pick her. A bit virginal for my taste, but a man should be true to his illusions." Claude moved to his lady in red. "May I take you to our room?" he asked.

The girl in white did not wait for Josh to come to her. She glided to him and took his arm, leading him out of the room and down the corridor again.

Moments later they entered a small bedroom. Like the woman he had chosen, it was decorated in white. As soon as the door was closed, the girl came to him and, standing on tiptoe, put her arms around his neck. Her big blue eyes seemed to devour him, and reluctantly Josh let the image of Colleen flee his mind as he gave into the flesh-and-blood woman who stood before him.

"I'm Kira," she said sweetly. Hers was an accent unknown to Josh. And he had to admit she was most unusual-looking. Her hair was almost white, her eyes were blue-green like some distant northern sea, and her body was full and well-shaped, all a man could ask for.

"Kira," Josh repeated as he allowed himself to be led to the bed.

"I'm from Norway," she said as Josh stretched out, feeling his weight sink into the feather mattress. Kira undressed him slowly, running soft white hands over him and touching him expertly till he felt himself responding and yearning for her. Then Kira stood up and shed her diaphanous white chemise. Her skin was not milky white, but almost transparent, and her nipples were a pale, delicate pink, like

117

the pink of a new rosebud. She lay down beside him, and even in the dim light Josh could see the light blue veins beneath her silky skin as her nipples hardened and her breasts grew fuller under his touch.

He kissed her breasts tenderly, then looked into her blue-green eyes. "Do you miss Norway?" he asked, brushing some strands of her fine flaxen hair away from her tiny face.

"I miss the sea," Kira answered. "And the ice castles. We used to built ice castles. . . ." Josh silenced her pale lips with a kiss and began to stroke her white body with his hand, feeling her respond to him.

"You warm me," she breathed, heaving her breasts up toward him and throwing her arms around his neck.

Josh sunk into her and moved slowly up and down, but weariness and wine combined to defeat him. He felt the woman beneath him shiver and tremble not once, but three times while he tried to satisfy himself, but it was to no avail. At last, he moved away from her apologetically. "I've had too much to drink."

She laughed gently and pressed herself to him. "I liked it," she said and breathed into his ear. "But you are not yet happy."

Josh nodded even as he felt her white hands enclose him and begin to massage him gently. He lay back and closed his eyes, dreaming incoherently of a castle made of ice, a glimmering, shimmering castle where the only sound was a tinkling of crystal when a gentle wind blew. And in his mind, he conjured up the woman who now lay next to him. In his dream, her white-blond hair fell to her slender waist, and she stood stark naked, her pink nipples urging him to make love to her. He moved to her side and touched her, tracing a blue-white vein from her

118

throat to the tip of her left breast. He kissed the nipple and ran his hands between her white thighs. "And me too," a voice in his dream interrupted. There, on the red plush seat of a sleigh made out of ice, Colleen sat, holding out her arms to him, her tiny, perfect breasts uncovered, her lovely buttocks sitting on a fur cloak. Her eyes were dark blue and her hair was not flaxen, but nearly jet black. Somehow, in his dream, Josh did not let go of Kira, even as he reached out for Colleen. As he felt her skin beneath his hand, he pulsated forth, suddenly aware of the throbbing satisfaction brought to him by Kira's experienced hand. Mercifully, she said nothing and Josh was only aware of the candle being extinguished and of a warm body nestling next to his.

Colleen cursed herself for having sent the carriage away. "How could I be so stupid!" she said aloud. She was standing on the porch of a house in Georgetown, a house that bore the address she had been given in Boston. Somehow Colleen had not expected a woman over seventy to be out, and therefore she had climbed out of the carriage with her satchel and her carpetbag and sent the carriage away. She had knocked and knocked on the front door, but no one had answered. "Now I'm marooned," she sighed. It was a residential area; in fact, it seemed almost deserted. Her common sense told her that there would be no rooming houses or hotels in this area, and on what street there might be an inn she did not know. It was late afternoon. Colleen pulled her shawl around her shoulders and set down her carpetbag. Then she sat down on the step. "I'll just have to wait," she said to herself. "There's absolutely nothing else to do."

Colleen had been sitting for about half an hour when the great front door of the house opened behind her. "What you doing on the step, missy?" a deep voice asked.

Colleen snapped around and jumped to her feet, peering into the dark face of Righteous, Mason James MacLean's butler.

"I knocked loudly and no one answered the door," Colleen said in a somewhat annoyed voice.

"It's washday," Righteous answered. "We's all out back hangin' the wash."

Colleen frowned and then decided to ignore both the explanation and her own annoyance at having sat on the front step for so long. "I've come to see Mrs. Sharp," Colleen explained. "Is she at home?"

"Mrs. Sharp?" Righteous repeated the name thoughtfully. "I don't know no Mrs. Sharp."

Colleen frowned and looked at the number on the door. "This is the address that was given to me; this is No. 52, is it not?"

Righteous peered at the numbers over the door. "If that's what it says," he answered. "Righteous can't read no numbers."

"Who employs you?" Colleen queried. "Who lives here?"

Righteous smiled broadly. "I don't have no employer, no. I'm a slave," Righteous explained. "I serve Mr. Mason James MacLean. He live here in this house!"

"MacLean?" Colleen stared at Righteous. She had been traveling for months, she had come from Lewiston to Boston and from Boston to Washington. She had been running away from the memory of Josh and desperately trying to find out more about their blood relationship. Now, by some coincidence she had ended up at the door of a man bearing the same last name as Josh. And just hearing the name filled her with sadness. Tears started to well in her eyes and she grasped the door to steady herself. "Mrs. Sharp doesn't live here?"

"No, ma'am, Mr. Mason James MacLean live here."

Colleen felt suddenly ill as well as overcome by misery. She bit on her lower lip, but it was no use, there was a kind of darkness taking her over, she felt light-headed and her feet hardly seemed to be touching the ground.

"Missy?" was the last thing Colleen heard. She fainted dead away.

CHAPTER VI

March 1812

Mason James leaned back in his black carriage. "I shall never forget this day," he muttered aloud to no one. "Never as long as I live."

He had accepted Mrs. Madison's invitation to a private lunch at the Executive Mansion, and while he certainly had expected something to happen, he could not even in his wildest dreams have predicted the events of the morning and early afternoon. He leaned back and recalled them now.

"More coffee," Mrs. Madison had drawled. She was looking at him with hungry eyes, much the same way she looked at the watercress sandwiches. She had been flirting with him for weeks, but thus far Mason James had not returned her boldness except for some smart repartee and a few *double entendres*. Of course, he contemplated, Dolley Madison might just be one of those women who openly flirted till she'd totally captivated a man, and then ran as fast as possible in the other direction when it appeared desire was about to come to fruition. He half hoped that would be the case.

So far Mason James could congratulate himself on playing extraordinarily hard to get. It was an easy game for him. It wasn't that he found Dolley unattractive; on the contrary, she was quite appealing and something of a curiosity as well. Her endowments fascinated him, even if he was not usually taken with women.

He leaned over conspiratorially. "Madame, you are teasing me."

Dolley had answered with a wide-eyed stare. "Why, whatever do you mean, Mr. MacLean, dear?"

He leaned over the small table that separated them. "I mean you torture me by your closeness. I am a prisoner of your captivating beauty, I am held fast to your side by your charms, your wit, and your intelligence. And, madame, if you continue to lean so far forward, I shall be unable to control myself."

"I'd like that," Dolley whispered. She paused and looked around to see if any of the servants were within earshot. "I must show you something—a painting. Come along, Mr. MacLean, dear. You are such an art expert! I know you will be so much help to me!" Dolley slipped her arm into his and Mason James found himself being propelled along a dark corridor.

"Shan't we be noticed?" he remembered stammering. "It's the middle of the day, right after lunch!" He had been totally taken aback by the sudden turn of events and even now, as he sat in his carriage, he remembered that all the way down the corridor he had kept looking over his shoulder apprehensively, lest they were being followed by the servants.

"I imagine we will be noticed," Dolley chattered. "But then, Mr. MacLean, dear, you have so much to learn about the art of dalliance! The more open one is, the less suspicious one's actions. And after all, there is nothing really wrong with the middle of the day, is there? Don't you like sunshine, Mr. MacLean, dear?"

Mason James noted that they turned a corner and came to stop in front of a door that Dolley quickly opened, all but pushing him inside.

Dolley closed the large oak door behind them and

Mason James heard the small bolt click into place. He blinked into the sunlit room. The die is cast, Mason James remembered thinking. I can't back out now.

"Stand still, Mr. MacLean, dear. Just wait till I uncover the painting."

Mason James stood stark still, trying to take in the strange room as well as the situation that had developed far too quickly for him. He had expected to arrange an adventure in his own home, or perhaps a rendezvous one night when the President was away. Even a visit to New Orleans. But here? . . . Here in what appeared to be a storeroom in the Executive Mansion—here while only a few rooms away James Madison was at work? Mason James MacLean was shocked.

The room was cluttered with furniture and paintings, many of which were still wrapped up or draped with white sheets. The furniture was dusty, but on one side of the room was a large four-poster bed with a high canopy. It looked to be made up with fresh linens.

"It's our storeroom," Dolley explained as she stepped over a hand-carved footstool to reach the closet. "I just can't keep up with it all. You know, finding the right place for everything—they're gifts for the Executive Mansion. Now, see, what would I do with that?" She pointed to a square object that seemed to be a birdbath. "It's made of marble, but aren't birdbaths supposed to be round? What on earth would possess someone to give us a square birdbath? You have no idea, Mr. MacLean, dear, no idea at all! Why, only last year, we were given two elephants! Imagine! What am I to do with two elephants? Why, my goodness, the gardeners have enough trouble cleaning up after the horses and the passersby. . . . Oh, here it is!"

Mason James peered at Dolley Madison as he began to relax. Perhaps he had misunderstood everything. But why had she locked the door?

"You do know something about art, don't you?"

"Quite," he had replied.

"Perhaps you could become my art adviser, Mr. MacLean, dear. You could help me decide where to hang certain paintings and what to do with some of this statuary. In fact, I suspect you have just darling taste."

Mason James remembered thinking: Was I invited here to help decorate the Executive Mansion?

"It's your clothes, I can tell by the way you dress, yes. Absolutely darling taste!" Dolley lifted a large painting out of the closet. It was draped with a white sheet. "Now close your eyes, Mr. MacLean, dear."

Mason did as he was bid.

"Now!" Dolley proclaimed with triumph as she whipped the sheet off the painting.

Mason James MacLean opened his eyes and his mouth at once. It was clearly a painting of Mrs. Madison, and she was nude from the waist up. It revealed her great mammary glands to be as voluptuous as anyone could imagine.

"Do you like it?" Dolley asked coyly. "Where in the Executive Mansion should I hang it?" Then, unable to control herself, she burst into laughter.

"It's quite breathtaking," Mason James observed, trying to show some reserve.

Dolley sighed. "I shan't be able to hang it, of course. It's even bad for Mr. Madison's heart. He gets so excited when he sees it! But I do show it to special people." She moved to his side and looked up into his face. "You're a special person, Mr. MacLean, dear. Quite special."

Mason James moved his eyes from the painting to the woman. "Does the artist do you justice?" he asked, a broad smirk on his handsome face.

"Judge for yourself, Mr. MacLean, dear." Dolley's

small hands flew to her bodice, and without further conversation she undid the ribbons that held it together, slowly parting her gown to reveal the reality represented in the painting.

Mason James raised one eyebrow appraisingly. "They really are quite stunning." He took a step toward her, knowing—or thinking that he knew—what she wanted and what was expected of him.

Dolley Madison, however, sidestepped him and went directly to the bed, where she sat down. Mason James followed her, thinking that he really found her quite exciting, although he wasn't at all sure why. It was quite true that he didn't usually yearn after women, but on the other hand, one of his earliest memories was watching slave women nurse their babies. He himself had been wet-nursed by such a woman, a woman with gigantic teats. And, he contemplated, if he enjoyed nothing else, he enjoyed suckling. There was something generally comforting about it.

He sat down next to Dolley, who now was lying on the bed. Her large dark eyes were closed, her mouth rounded expectantly. Mason James reached out and touched her twin prides. Large though his hands were, he could not grasp all of her. He leaned over and drew one nipple into his mouth. Dolley groaned.

Then, as many men would, he moved his other hand beneath her long skirts, seeking more intimacy. But Dolley stiffened and sat up, pushing him rudely away.

"Mr. MacLean, dear. What are you doing?" Her voice was filled with shock and her expression was one of amazement. Mason James' face went bright red for the first time in his whole life. He could feel his own excitement and desire and now he felt befuddled and confused. "I was about to—to make love to you," he stuttered.

126

Dolley blinked. "I do not allow such intimacies! What kind of woman do you think I am?"

"Desirable," was all he could manage to say.

Dolley smiled sweetly. "Why, thank you, Mr. Mac-Lean, dear. But you must understand the rules. Clearly you do not understand the rules."

"Rules?" Mason James MacLean repeated. Good God, all he wanted was to tumble her backward onto the bed and finish what he had started, or to be more accurate, what she had started.

"You can touch me only on top," she stated flatly. "I know what you want, and I'm certain if you try, you can manage it on top. Now, Mr. MacLean, you must let me introduce you to the finer art of love-making . . . to do it without actually doing it. It's really quite simple."

Mason's mouth felt dry and he watched her with wide eyes as she withdrew a small vial from the drawer of the bedside table. She uncorked it and poured it on her breast. It was a heavily perfumed oil that smelled of musk, or some oriental aroma. "Now do rub it on, using both hands."

Mason found himself as intrigued as he was stunned. He did as she bid him and Dolley moved beneath his massaging fingers, her flesh warmed by the oil. Again her eyes closed and Mason watched as her nipples hardened and, unbelievably, her huge breasts seemed to grow even larger with her excitement. Her breath came in small, short gasps and Mason James felt himself on the brink of total frustration. "Madame," he stuttered again, "I am quite, quite aroused."

Dolley lifted her hands and drew her great swollen breasts together. "Place your manhood here," she breathed heavily as she indicated her deep cleavage.

Mason could wait no longer and so again he did as

he was told. Surprisingly, she seemed to engulf him in warmth. The musk oil made it easy for him to move to and fro till he burst forth uncontrollably. Dolley, in turn, seemed to shake beneath him, quite as if the center of her pleasure were between her breasts rather than where it was in other women he had experienced.

"Good heavens, Mrs. Madison!" he exclaimed after some moments.

"You see?" Dolley looked up at him smiling, her face flushed.

"A most unusual experience," Mason said, uncertain of how in fact he actually did feel.

Dolley scrambled out from beneath him and stood up. She smoothed out her long skirt and tucked herself back into her dress, doing up her bodice. "You see . . . ingenious. We American women know how to lose ourselves and keep ourselves at the same time. And, of course, you can't make babies this way."

"Don't you ever . . . ever . . . ?" Mason asked, unable actually to say it.

"Once when I wanted a baby." She smiled and let out a little laugh. "Mr. Madison likes this much better. He says it's not so tiring."

Mason nodded.

"Now, Mr. MacLean, dear, you must agree to become my art adviser. Something simply must be done with all these gifts!"

"No, I'll never forget today," Mason James said again as the carriage came to a halt in front of his Georgetown house. As usual, he was helped from the carriage and, also as usual, Righteous opened the door, ushering him into the house.

"Lord!" Mason James said before the butler could utter a word, "get me a strong drink, a very strong drink!"

Righteous nodded and half bowed. "Master, some-one's here."

Mason James peered around the corner and into the parlor. "Where?" he said, frowning.

"Upstairs in the bedroom, master. She done come calling and fainted dead away on the front steps. I didn't know what to do, master. I couldn't leave no white lady on the steps fainted dead away."

Mason James lifted his hand to his temple. Not all in one day—why did things seem to happen like this? "Is she awake now?" Mason James ventured.

"Not yet, master," Righteous answered, "but she's sleepin' peaceful."

Mason James grumbled. "Well then, bring me my drink and send her down when she wakes up. We wouldn't want to disturb any young ladies who feel they should drop around here for a rest!"

Righteous backed off, padding toward the pantry and the liquor. The master did not seem to be in the best of all possible moods.

A full two hours passed. Mason James had not one, but three drinks. Then he went to his small dining room and was in the middle of his dinner when Righteous ushered the mysterious young woman into the room.

"Do sit down," Mason James invited. He was feeling mellow from the drinks and in general was in a much better mood than when he had arrived home. "It is not every day that someone passes out on my front steps."

Colleen sat down. "I'm terribly sorry," she murmured.

"Bring an extra plate, Righteous! Allow me to introduce myself. I'm Mason James MacLean." He bowed slightly toward her. "And with whom do I have the honor of having dinner?"

"I'm Colleen Adams," she answered. "You're very

129

kind, but I'm afraid I have made a mistake. I thought this was the home of Mrs. Sharp. I sent the carriage away—I was fatigued and dizzy, or something. I just fainted."

Mason James nodded with some interest. She was quite an attractive girl, though dressed in bad taste. And there was something else about her as well: She seemed distinctly distressed.

"Mrs. Sharp died sometime last year. I bought the house from her estate."

"Oh," Colleen answered almost in a whisper. "I feared as much."

"You're not eating," Mason James said, pointing to the pilaf. "It's really very good, a special Louisiana dish."

Colleen stared at him. "MacLean. I know someone with that name. Do you have relatives on the frontier? In Canada?

Mason James burst into laughter. "I'm from Louisiana! Dear, dear, relatives on the frontier? Nothing so common!"

"Oh," Colleen answered.

"You've said that several times. You don't have a large vocabulary, do you?"

Colleen blinked and suddenly burst into tears, sobbing uncontrollably.

Mason James dropped his fork and got up, stumbling to her side. It always distressed him to see women crying. "There, there now. I didn't mean it personally—look what you're doing. You're crying into your pilaf—it's really quite well salted already. I'm a very sarcastic man. I can't help myself."

Colleen continued to sob. "It's not that! I don't care about that! It's your name! And you don't look like him exactly, but you're both tall and you both have the same broad shoulders and there's . . . just something. I thought for one horrible moment you were related. It's—it's your name!"

130

Mason James scowled. "MacLean is a rather common name."

"I know, I'm foolish. You must forgive me. I've been looking for someone, and now I have no hope of finding her. I've left my home, I'm alone, and—and—" Her voice trailed off and she covered her face with her hands, adding, "And I'm sorry, you're a stranger and I have no right to burden you with my story."

"That is quite true," Mason James agreed. "But it's all right because I'm really quite magnanimous. I'm the art adviser to the President's wife and I'm on the delegation from the future state of Louisiana," Mason James bragged. He was just slightly drunk.

"The President of what?" Colleen asked between sobs.

"Of the United States of America!" Mason James said with some irritation. But his answer only brought another wail.

"I'm sorry again," Mason James said. "Miss—Miss Adams, is it?"

She nodded in the affirmative. "Colleen Adams."

"Miss Adams, it is much too late to take you to an inn. May I suggest you remain here, in the guest room? We will talk in the morning, when I hope we both will be in a better mood."

"It isn't proper for me to stay here," Colleen argued.

Mason James shook his head back and forth. He had little or no desire for women in the first place, and Mrs. Madison had sapped him of his last bit of energy in any case.

"You may stay or you may not stay," he said calmly. "But if you stay, I warn you, you will find my door locked!"

Colleen stared at him, and through her tears he saw a smile move across her lips. Then, quite unexpectedly, she burst into laughter.

Mason James turned away. His head was aching, but he too suppressed a smile. At least, he conceded, she had a sense of humor.

President James Madison was dwarfed by his mahogany desk. It was a desk that his predecessor, Thomas Jefferson, hadn't used very much. In fact, he hadn't used his office very much, or even the Executive Mansion, for that matter. Jefferson had conducted much of his business from his home, Monticello, in order to be near his creole mistress, whom he obviously could not bring to Washington. Then too, he was a man who had a bad habit of conducting most Cabinet meetings in the stable, "To be near the horses," he would announce. "If I sit at a desk at all, it is to write!"

President Madison had a great deal of respect for former President Jefferson, the principal author of the Declaration of Independence and the third President of the Republic. But Madison did not think work should be done from the home, he thought it should be done from the office in the Executive Mansion, and from behind his mammoth desk.

"There's whiskey in the cabinet and ice in the bucket," Madison announced. "Are you gentlemen comfortable?"

Henry Clay nodded, but Calhoun already was on his feet, headed toward the cabinet. "Are we to help ourselves, Mr. President?"

"Surely, surely. But while you're there, could you pour me some as well?"

"An honor," Calhoun replied as he nearly filled the tumbler with whiskey. "Always been a thirsty man," he announced. "Damn thirsty!"

Clay was leaning back in his chair, his feet propped up on another. "Well, what are we going to do, Mr. President? This can't go on, you know. The public's getting mighty angry!"

"We can hardly allow those lousy limies to continue to harass our men at sea! Lord! Enough is enough!"

"The navy is doing its best—you know, we have a damn good navy! There haven't been half as many impressments as reported in the newspapers," Madison claimed.

Clay burst into laughter. "Of course not! But how else are you going to get the people mad enough to go to war and knock the bejesus out of the British?"

"New York State, the New England states—they only want us to break the blockade on the high seas. They say if we actually go to war, actually invade British North America, they'll secede from the Union!"

"Nullification!" Clay spit.

"Idle threats," Calhoun mumbled darkly. "You don't see the South threatening things like that!"

"Well, we can't actually do much about the British at sea," Madison interjected. "Our navy is just too small."

Calhoun pushed himself up in the chair, seizing its upholstered arms and leaning forward. "Doing something on the high seas isn't the idea—using British actions to outrage the American public is what it's all about. By God, it gives us the golden opportunity to invade Canada! To bring all that territory under our control."

Clay turned a little sideways and looked at Calhoun almost benevolently as a slight religious glint sparkled in his dark eyes. "We're a chosen people, a people who will create a model society for the world. It's our destiny! It is manifest!"

"The clear and unmistakable task God has bestowed on us," Calhoun chimed in.

"But what has invading Canada to do with impressment of seamen?" Madison persisted.

"The impressment of our seamen is only the excuse we need—we have a duty to offer the Canadians freedom! We have a duty to unite this hemisphere from sea to sea and from the farthest point north to the farthest point south!"

"There are negotiations underway with the British minister, Augustus Foster. But they only concern impressment."

"And that is all they need to concern," Clay said, lifting his glass to his lips and taking a long, noisy gulp.

"The British have backed themselves into a corner. They are deep into a protracted war with Napoleon, they passed the Orders in Council in their Parliament to try to bluff the French and to control us. If they back down, they lose everything. No, they can't afford to change their policy."

"I suppose not," Madison allowed. "But do you think we have the wherewithal to invade Canada?"

"We don't need it," Clay said with determination. "You can't think the people of Upper and Lower Canada want to live under British rule. From everything I hear, we have only to offer them freedom and they will flock to join us!"

"Half of them are American anyway. Hell, what's the difference?" Calhoun asked.

"The vast majority are United Empire Loyalists who fled this country during the Revolution," Madison said, tapping his pen on the side of his desk. "The rest are French Canadian."

"Well, the United Empire Loyalists have had time to change their minds. And the Frenchies—well, hell, France is allied with us, or will be if we go to war with Britain."

Madison started to protest, but he didn't. In truth, he didn't know enough about the people of Upper and Lower Canada even to have an argument on the subject. Indeed, for Madison Canada was only a vast pink blob on a map, a place where it snowed a lot and where his beaver collars came from.

"I'll have to continue negotiations for a while," Madison told them.

"And perhaps there will be some incident, something that will anger people more, get them riled up."

"Some more impressments, at least," Calhoun added.

Madison didn't look up but continued to stare at the wood grain on his huge desktop. "They'll call it Madison's war," he said softly.

"Or maybe Madison's glory!" Calhoun announced brightly. "Come on, Jim, it won't be a long war and the chances are none of it will be fought on American territory. We'll seize the initiative and it'll soon be over. The French either will join us or not fight; the English-speaking Canadians will surrender by the thousands. And frankly, there are very few British regulars in Canada."

"I suppose you're right," Madison gave in. "In any case, I hope you're right."

The sky was a blanket of gray cloud, except for a long pinkish line across the eastern horizon that held out the hope that tomorrow might be sunny.

At least it's not raining, Josh thought. Still it was damp from the previous day's rain and, as was typical of mid-March, it still was freezing at night and cool during the days. He glanced upward, surveying the sky, then turned his canoe and headed for shore. It might take him another two hours to reach Kingston on his way to Niagara, and by then it would be dark. True enough, he then could go to his sister's house and have a hot bath and sleep in a real bed. But somehow Josh still did not feel like encountering relatives. He sought the solitude of the woods,

135

the quiet of camping even if the weather was adverse.

Josh guided the canoe to shore and climbed out, dragging up the craft behind him. Then he tipped it and bent down, lifting it up and over his head. He carried it for some distance to a spot in the woods where the trees sheltered the ground.

Josh went about making camp quickly. He tipped the canoe, setting each end on a tree stump, then he brought out his canvas and erected a crawl-in tent over and around the canoe.

That done, he stashed his pack and gathered some dry wood from under larger pieces. He opened his pack and withdrew a bundle of dry kindling he had gathered that morning. In a short time Josh had a fire blazing, though the dampness of the wood gave off too much smoke.

Then Josh built a small spit and began to roast the partridge he had downed earlier. He leaned back against a large rock and sighed. There was something wonderfully peaceful about the roaring fire and the sound of fat as it hit the flames. There was something about being alone in the deep woods, something about the smells and the sounds. . . . "I've had enough of cities," Josh said aloud.

He thought about his trip from Lewiston to Boston. It was a far different trip than the journey from Niagara to Montreal. Once you got to Albany, there were villages and people everywhere. There were large white frame houses and neat town squares with steepled churches. The roads were filled with carts going hither and yon, there was hardly any wilderness left in the East. But the Canadas, Upper and Lower, were different. You had only to leave Montreal to be in the wilderness, and most of Upper Canada outside of settlements like Kingston, York, and Newark was wilderness. Oh, there were farms, but they were far apart. And even the settlements were different.

The towns in New England seemed more modern; the houses were close together and had a look of permanency. Lochiel had that look, but it was an exception. While New England towns were laid out in actual streets and the roads were crowded with people and wagons and fine carriages, Canadian settlements were spread out and consisted mostly of log cabins widely separated. A man could wait a day to see another wagon on the road to York above the Niagara! It was true that Quebec was more densely populated, but even Quebec did not compare to what Josh had seen in Boston. Only Montreal did compare, but then it was well settled and was the largest city in the Canadas.

No, Josh thought, Upper Canada did not offer what Montreal and Boston offered. It seemed that Upper Canada was a hundred years behind in some ways. In Boston families had had time to accumulate immense wealth, and they flaunted that wealth. In Upper Canada there were few families who could boast wealth. His own, he knew, was an exception. But like all good Scots families, his family had invested their funds, putting them into property and businesses that would, in time, earn more. They did not use their money in obvious ways, they lived without luxuries, without servants, and without slaves.

"I don't want those things either," Josh said aloud as he poked the fire with a long green branch. "I'd rather have the peace of the woods, the quiet of the night." Civilization, as the Americans called it, was a nice place to visit, but Josh preferred the less harried life in Upper Canada.

Josh's thoughts returned to Colleen. I want her back, but it might never be. I'm in the army now and God knows what will happen or where I'll end up.

After this is over, I could be sent to India or to Australia. He recalled his recent interview with Red George Macdonell and some of the higher-ups among the British regulars.

"Oh, this time there will be war," Red George Macdonell had said. "No doubt about it, none at all."

Josh expressed his desire to buy a commission and it was agreed on immediately. "I want to send you back to Niagara for now," Red George told him, "because you know the country and can be of great help to the regulars at Fort George."

"I'll like being close to home," Josh told him. "Makes it easier to fight if one has something special to defend."

"I see your father was born in the Louisiana Territory," Lieutenant Revelstoke commented as he examined Josh's documents.

"That's right. My grandfather, Robert MacLean, traveled out of the Niagara and followed the route of the early explorers all the way to New Orleans. He married an Acadian refugee."

Captain Revelstoke met Josh's eyes with a steady gaze. He was a man who obviously did not allow historic guilt to overcome him. Either that, or he did not know the history of the Acadian deportations —which Josh found a bit hard to believe.

"Louisiana is about to become a state, part of the Union. Have you any living relatives there—cousins, aunts, uncles?"

"No, sir. Not that I know of, sir."

The lieutenant nodded, and a pleased expression crossed his face. "You're well spoken," he observed. "And you write well. Do you speak any languages besides English?"

"French, Mohawk, some Spanish . . ."

The lieutenant raised his eyebrow. "You'll return

to the Niagara now, as suggested. But I think I might have use for you in Intelligence work later. Are you averse to spying?"

Josh thought for a minute. It was not something that had ever occurred to him. Finally he replied, "No, sir. I don't think so."

The British officer made a humming sound. "Have you traveled in any of the former colonies?"

"New York, Massachusetts, Pennsylvania . . ."

"You might like Washington," the lieutenant said and smiled.

"I might," Josh replied.

"Well, it's nothing hard and fast now. Just a contingency plan. Go back to the Niagara, but if and when there is war, you can expect to hear from me."

Josh stared into the fire as he recalled that conversation. He stretched his arms upward as if reaching for the stars in the sky, then let his body go slack as he pulled his blanket up around him. The partridge was done and he carefully removed it from the spit, placing it on a tin plate. He tore off a leg and began eating the rich, gamey fowl.

Colleen was gone and probably would never come back. Britain and the new nation south of the border were on the brink of war. Ian had gone to Scotland and would be headed West when he returned. Josh felt alone.

At the moment all he had was the memory of his recent brief encounter in Montreal. The woman hadn't been his Colleen, but he had thought of Colleen and he still thought of her. She was no longer on the raw surface of his mind day after day; now her memory had receded, emerging only occasionally to suffuse him with a feeling of sadness and loss.

Josh finished picking at the partridge and buried the bones some distance from where he had built his tent. Wearily, he crawled inside and pulled his heavy blankets up around his neck just as he heard the first few drops of rain begin to fall.

Mason James MacLean reveled in what he had done. "I must," he conceded, "have a heart of pure gold buried beneath this rough exterior."

Following the arrival of Miss Colleen Adams, Mason James had felt somewhat guilty for being so sarcastic to her, although he vowed it would not keep him from being sarcastic in the future.

Nonetheless, after she had rested, he prevailed upon her to tell him her story of woe, and woe it was.

Though Miss Adams was not penniless, she was quite alone and, regrettably, with child.

The child was something Mason James preferred not to think about. He loathed children, feeling little but contempt for the small cookie crumblers who always seemed to be bleating about this and that. Children, it seemed to Mason James, went from totally soppy and dependent to sassy, irreverent, and much too independent without spending the slightest moment in between. "I never was a child," Mason James was fond of saying. "I could never have been anything so crass."

But, he rationalized, the child would not be born for many months and certainly it could be placed in care of a nurse. In any case, the child fit into his plan.

At first he felt pity for Colleen upon hearing her story, an unusual experience for him. He soon came to his senses, however, and realized that he could help her and solve one of his major problems to the satisfaction of everyone concerned.

Ever since his father's visit, Mason James had been troubled by the old man's veiled threat to sire a child in order to create an heir to the MacLean plantation. "I will have to share everything!" Mason

James declared while looking at himself in the mirror. "And I don't share! Ever."

After Colleen had finished telling him everything, he had invited her to stay for a few days and rest. "You'll find the inns in Washington quite dreadful and, my dear, you really couldn't tolerate the trip back to Boston so soon."

Colleen had thanked him and agreed to stay only after Mason James had told her that Mrs. Sharp, the former occupant of the house, had left trunks in the attic and that there might be something of interest in them.

"But they must belong to the estate," Colleen had protested.

"I am sure they do," Mason James had replied. "But I have notified them on several occasions that they are here and no one ever comes for them."

After that, Colleen had agreed and had remained for three days before she confessed that there was nothing of any value to her quest in the trunks and that he had already been too kind in putting up with her.

It was then that Mason James did the extraordinary. It had come to him in an absolute flash of genius. "My dear Miss Adams," he had begun, "you are not the only one with dreadful personal problems. May I confide in you?"

Colleen's great blue eyes had grown large and motherly. "Of course you can," she told him kindly. "You have gone out of your way to be hospitable to me."

Mason James poured himself a whiskey. "I am not the person I appear," he began. "I have strange tastes, some might call them weaknesses. . . ."

Colleen watched him carefully. She was quite unsure of what he was talking about. "Yes, do go on," she prodded.

"I think I am a Greek at heart," Mason James hedged.

"A Greek?" Colleen frowned. "You're not from Louisiana?"

Mason James waved his hand in the air. "Oh, I am. That's not what I mean. Oh, how can I put it? I don't find myself attracted to women—I mean, sometimes I sleep with them, but usually I don't desire them."

"Then why do you sleep with them?" Colleen asked.

"Because it is expected."

Colleen leaned back in the chair. "I do not expect it," she said, hoping that this is what he wanted her to say. Even so, it was quite true. She not only did not expect it, she wasn't even marginally interested. There was something about Mason James . . . she liked him and he was wonderfully suave, humorous, and even fun. But she did not find herself physically drawn to him. Of course, she did not find herself physically drawn to anyone but Josh.

"I know you do not expect it," Mason James went on, "but most women do. And my father does too. My father expects me to marry and furnish an heir for our plantation."

"And you don't want to marry?"

Mason James thought for a moment about how to phrase it. He rejected the idea of answering simply, "Well, not a woman."

"Madame, I find physical activity with women upsetting and unfulfilling. Sometimes I am attracted to men, as were the ancient Greeks. I do not mind having women around, and I don't mind having an occasional affair with a woman, but I find the idea of marriage unthinkable and the idea of siring a child abhorrent in the extreme!" To his relief, she didn't look shocked or upset.

142

"I have heard of such men," Colleen finally said. "But you are kind and I like you for what you are."

"I'm very sarcastic," he had admitted. "And some say arrogant."

"I find your arrogance a bit humorous," Colleen countered.

"I know you do, madame. That is why you may be able to help me solve my problem."

Colleen stood up and smoothed out her long dress. "I believe I'll have the drink you offered me now."

Mason James sighed. Somehow the worst was over; now he had only to make her see the logic of his suggestion. He went to the sideboard and fixed her a drink. "Not too strong," he said, handing it to her. "Too much liquor will make your waist thick."

Colleen smiled slightly. "Go on," she urged, sitting down again.

"Well," Mason James continued, "the way I see it, we have a problem that can be solved if we cooperate. You are pregnant and unmarried. That's normally a disgraceful state of affairs. I have to get married and produce a child for my father, except, of course, that I have no desire to do that. Now, if you remained here and we said we were married, you could have your child in peace without incurring the reputation of a fallen woman and I—I could make my father happy beyond his wildest dreams. Of course, I shall look after you and the child, but you in turn will sign a document promising not to make any claims on my estate in your name or the child's.

"Naturally, you will be quite free to have affairs with whomever you wish and I shall promise never to burden you with my physical presence."

"And are you going to have affairs?" Colleen asked.

"I shall not bring them home. Of course, I am having a dalliance with the President's wife now, but it could not exactly be described as an affair."

"You just told me you didn't like women."

"Well, this one is an exception of sorts. She's most unusual and arouses in me some primordial desire to suckle. It's the only way I can explain it."

Colleen burst into laughter. "You make her sound like a cow."

"She is," Mason James whispered. "But an influential one. Besides, I told you I have odd tastes."

"You're a very strange man," Colleen said, leaning back in her chair. Strong or not, the drink Mason James had fixed her made her dizzy and warm.

"And you are beautiful enough to make my father happy," Mason James replied. "But, of course, you'll have to learn how to dress."

"And you're going to help me learn?"

"I have excellent taste in clothes," Mason James replied.

Well, that had been some weeks ago, and Colleen had agreed to his plan. Mason James had written to his father immediately and told him the happy news. "I have found the woman of my dreams," he wrote, "a creature of exquisite charm and fine humor." Now he could not quite believe he had done it, though in truth he was quite satisfied with the bargain.

Ian MacLean walked briskly along Glasgow's main street. The densely populated city spread out onto both banks of the Clyde. It once had been a wealthy city, the center of tobacco production before the American Revolution. Now it was beginning to manufacture cotton, but that trade was small, curtailed by the protracted war between France and Britain.

So the city-of-might-have-been was the gathering

144

place of the dispossessed crofters from the Highlands
as well as home to a large unemployed native population. Glasgow was like a giant closet into which
the refuse of humanity had been stashed. Its streets
smelled of urine and feces; it's alleyways and houses
were filled to overflowing and, more often than not,
one found whole families huddling in doorways.
What charity there was, was taxed beyond belief.
The soup kitchens were full, people waited in long
lines for scraps of bread.

But Glasgow had its rich too, men who had benefited from trade and shipbuilding, men who knew
how to make money and keep it; men who were able
to weather the temporary inconvenience of war and
blockades.

"Have you a coin, lad?"

Ian stopped short and squinted into the darkness.
It was unusual to encounter beggars in this part of
town. But here was one. He was short and bent, hov-
ering in a doorway with a tattered blanket pulled up
about him.

"Everyone in Glasgow wants a coin," Ian replied,
trying hard to make out the man's face.

"Everyone in Glasgow is not of my advanced age,"
the man answered. "I'm a forty-sixer, you know. I'll
die soon, and I'd rather die with a full belly."

Ian looked harder into the darkness. "A forty-
sixer?" he repeated.

"Aye," the man retorted. "Aye, a forty-sixer."

"Come out of the doorway, old man," Ian re-
quested. "Come out and I'll buy you some hot grog
and as much as you can eat."

"Will you now." The old man shuffled out of the
doorway. His face looked like a bleached prune and
he had a mop of silver-gray hair that was dirty and
matted.

Ian extended his arm and helped the old man

along. They came to a pub and Ian escorted the old man inside, seeking out a table apart. He ordered hot grog and a plate of mutton stew.

"My grandmother was a forty-sixer," Ian said with some pride. "A Cameron who married a Macleod."

"A Cameron!" The old man giggled.

"What's so funny? She was the ward of Donald Cameron, leader of the clan, owner of Lochiel."

The old man giggled again. "Poor Donald and his brother! Always accused of stealing Cluny's gold, they were. But they didn't. If they had, they would not have died penniless." He paused. "Maybe your grandmother stole it." Then he burst again into senile giggles.

"Maybe she did," Ian said cheerfully, thinking of his grandmother's gold. It was a family legend. It was part of what now was invested in the Hudson's Bay Company.

"Well, it doesn't matter. It wouldn't have helped old Bonnie Prince Charlie anyway! Where's your grandmother now?"

"She died recently," Ian said. "She was in her eighties."

The old man slurped a spoonful of stew and gummed the mutton. "I'm seventy-five," he confessed. "I was a herdboy in '46 and I was there—" He leaned forward and winked at Ian.

"At Culloden?" Ian asked.

"Aye, at Culloden. I was there on the moor, I was. I saw it all."

"I'm going there in a few days," Ian admitted. "I wanted to go before I left Scotland."

"It's a long journey to Inverness."

Ian smiled. People in Scotland might think it a long journey, but distances in Scotland were nothing when compared to Canada. "It will be worth it," Ian replied.

146

The old man gulped down the rest of his grog, draining his mug.

"What's your name?" The man seemed quite alert except for his giggle, which was funny rather than annoying. He was, Ian thought, a bit of living history.

"Andrew Stuart," the old man answered.

"Ian MacLean." He extended his hand across the table and shook Andrew Stuart's wizened hand. "Mr. Stuart, are you, shall I say, unemployed?"

Again the old man nodded. "Aye," he finally said. "Down on my luck, lad."

"I shall pay you," Ian offered, "if you will come to Inverness with me."

"And you'll pay me way to Inverness by coach?"

"I shall," Ian promised.

CHAPTER VII

April 1812

Ian MacLean and old Andrew Stuart left Inverness
before the sun rose over the moor. Now they stood in
the early-morning mist, watching as the dawn broke
in the east, a slender line of silver against the dark,
gray-clouded sky. Before them on the grassy knoll,
the heather moved in the morning breeze. It was
April 16, 1812.

"It's the sixty-sixth anniversary," Ian said. "Almost to the hour."

Andrew Stuart pulled the coat that Ian had
bought more tightly around himself. "I was only a
lad, but I never could forget—not one part of it." The
old man laughed, but it was not his characteristic
giggle. It was a laugh of irony, perhaps a laugh of his
youth. "I was a herdboy," he told Ian. "We'd come to
watch the battle, we had. We hid in the high heather
right over there, see. Look where the ground rises up
a bit. Then your grandmother's guardian, Donald
Cameron, he came and shooed us all away. Told us
we'd be cannon fodder unless we ran away and
watched from farther off."

"Where were the Highlanders?" Ian asked.

"Lined up over there. All the clans in one great
long line. The Macdonalds, the Roy Stewarts, Clan
Chatten, Clan Fraser, Clan Appin, the mixed clans,
and the men of Atholl."

Ian looked where old Stuart pointed. In Ian's imagination he almost could see the lines the clans formed.

"And the English came from over there, from the direction of the Nairn." Stuart pointed off and away. Ian could all but hear the pipes in his ears. He had heard this story often, but suddenly he felt part of it, as if ghosts walked the moors and spoke to him, as if through the eyes of old Andrew Stuart he was seeing it now.

"They played their pipes as never before. Oh, Lord, how they wailed that day!"

Ian closed his eyes. Here, on this inhospitable moor, he thought, thousands of Scots were slaughtered and left to die of their wounds in the rain and the cold.

"See that stream." Stuart pointed to a rushing, winding stream. Its banks were green and fertile-looking. "Some four hundred crawled on their bellies to that stream, just to get a last drink of water before they died the slow death. Took some more than four days to die. They say that stream flowed red with blood for two days. And you know why the grass is so green, so rich? It's a mass grave and the land is fertilized with the bones of the Highlanders."

"This *is* Scotland," Ian said. "This is where thousands will come for hundreds of years. They'll come to remember, to reaffirm their heritage, to speak with their ancestors. This is an everlasting place and while there's a Scot alive, its story will not be forgotten."

"Aye," old Stuart said. "You can take a Scot away from Scotland, but you can't take the Scots out of him."

Ian felt tears in his eyes. He took a leather pouch from his pocket and bent down, lifting the soft earth with his fingers and putting it into the pouch. "For your grave, Grandmother. You couldn't come home,

149

so I'll bring a bit of Scotland to you." Ian stood up. The wind whistled and he felt a strange exhilaration from having established this connection with the past.

"You're a good lad," old Stuart said. He grinned, exposing his toothless gums. "You talk funny, but you're a real Scots."

"MacLean on one side, Macleod on the other," Ian said as he followed the old man.

"That's where they lined up the cannon. . . ."

Ian listened and Ian thought. The glory was not in the battle, but in the survival. "I'll not forget, Grandmother," Ian whispered under his breath. "Never."

"I really can't tell you how pleased I am," Dolley drawled. Her large eyes were fastened once again on Mason James' face.

"It's a proud day," Mason James returned, beaming. He felt twelve feet tall. Louisiana had just been made a state. "I like the date, April 30! It's so appropriate for future celebrations—April always is so nice in New Orleans."

"Well, I don't think we should wait for the future. A new state is cause for a celebration. Come along, Mr. MacLean, dear, you must help me make up a list of who should be invited. You know absolutely everyone."

Mason James followed the First Lady from the congressional gallery to her carriage. Then they rode together from Congress to the Executive Mansion.

"I have a new secretary," Dolley told Mason James. He's just a darling boy. A bit flitty at times, but otherwise just simply darling."

Dolley ushered Mason James into the smaller receiving room off the main gallery. "Henry!" she called out to one of the servants. "Do send in Jason." Dolley flopped down on the settee as close to Mason

James as she could position herself. "Jason, isn't that cute? It rhymes, Mason and Jason."

Inwardly, Mason James sighed. He fought off a number of unkind remarks that entered his head. It would be unwise to be too caustic with the President's wife. She was the one woman with whom he felt the need to be entirely pleasant at all times.

"It's a charming coincidence," he allowed.

"I've brought my pen and paper." Mason looked up to greet the young man who stood in the doorway. He was in his late twenties, tall and willowy, and he had pale blue eyes, a full mouth, and a bottom which was, to say the least, well rounded. Mason felt a sudden surge of pure wanton desire.

"This is my secretary, Mr. Jason Talbot. And dear Mr. Talbot, this is Mr. Mason James MacLean, my art adviser and one of the gentlemen in the Louisiana delegation—the new state, did you hear?"

"I did," Jason Talbot replied, extending his long, graceful hand to Mason James. "My most heartfelt congratulations, sir."

Mason took the proffered hand and felt the little extra squeeze that Jason gave it. He smiled his most seductive smile.

"There, I just knew you two would get along and I'm always right about things like that. Now, Mr. MacLean, dear, let us begin. There'll be Mr. Clay and Mr. Calhoun, of course. And all the representatives from the southern states, and—am I going too fast for you, Jason, dear?"

Jason looked to be writing quickly enough, but his eyes had not left Mason's who couldn't look away himself. An unexpected blessing in this dreary world, Mason thought. Ah, Mason and Jason. If only it didn't sound so cute.

President Madison made a steeple with his long fingers and stared at it. He tried to pretend that the dull, relentless throbbing in his temples didn't exist. It isn't a real malady, he told himself; rather his assorted pains were caused by endless meetings and constant pressure. It had come to him slowly, almost through a fog of self-importance, that members of Congress actually nagged. Yes, he thought, they nagged like fishermen's wives and they haggled as if they all had been brought up behind a pushcart selling wares. Jefferson had tried to warn him, but Madison had been too full of the self-importance of the presidency to listen and to understand. But now it came to him in the full flush of reality—issues often were invented to make the members of the government feel necessary, and grown men nagged. Madison idly massaged his temples. His headaches all magically fled when he went home to Montpelier, and in the rare moments he had alone with Dolley.

But there was no doubt the style of their life together had changed. Presidents ought to be celibate, they ought to be relieved of the pressures of everyday life. But, of course, the public seemed interested only in everyday life. They didn't care what bill was signed into law or what you said to Congress—they wanted to know the name of your horse and what color your bedroom was decorated in. Stupid busybody people won't let a man alone long enough to run a country, Madison concluded.

He had only recently removed himself from the bedchamber he and Dolley had shared, because he was unable to sleep at night and he feared his constant tossing and turning would keep Dolley up as well. They even had given up eating their main meal at midday because it caused him to grow weary and fall asleep at his desk, often at crucial moments. Ah, how wide awake he was in the darkness of the quiet night and how tired and worn he felt at two in the afternoon. I am sixty-one, Madison rationalized. But it was not a satisfying rationalization because, in truth, he felt closer to one hundred years old.

The month of May had been terrible. It had consisted of day after day of tedious meetings with Clay and Calhoun, both of whom always said the same thing and both of whom consumed incredible amounts of whiskey. Madison still considered war with Great Britain as a last resort. And the last resort was inching closer and closer.

In addition to Clay and Calhoun, there were endless meetings with the British minister, Augustus John Foster, a pompous young man of thirty-one who, it was rumored, called the Americans "the scum of every nation of earth" and "consummate rascals and adventurers."

But to Madison's face, Minister Foster was the model of decorum. He listened reverently to the American complaints and responded with his own list of complaints.

Madison had come to regard the man as a feathered parrot attired in a somber morning coat. Repetition was the order of each and every day. The British steadfastly refused to withdraw the Orders in Council that the British Parliament had passed. The Orders in Council allowed the British Navy to stop American vessels, to seize and search them on the high seas, and to take off their crews and confiscate their cargos in order to prevent them from reaching French ports.

Still, the vital questions of war and the realities of preparation for it haunted Madison, even as his headaches throbbed on.

The New England Federalists stubbornly refused to cooperate with the federal government. The navy was capable of considerable fighting brilliance, but the army was poorly led, poorly fed, ill trained, and inadequately supplied. It was made up of men who preferred drinking to fighting.

On the one hand, Madison was faced with Southerners and Westerners who seemed to regard war as some sort of sport. Indeed, they saw the impressment of seamen as an excuse to invade the Canadas and further their dream of governing a hemisphere. On the other hand, the New Englanders and the New Yorkers did not want war. In fact, their attitude toward participating in a militia was that it was all right if there was absolutely nothing else to do. They actually cried out and protested.

Madison recalled his meeting with Major General Dearborn and Major General Hull. Dearborn was a distinguished veteran of the Revolution, but he was old and more a diplomat than a soldier. Dearborn insisted that operations against the British could easily be begun on three or four fronts simultaneously.

"Montreal, Kingston, Niagara . . . they will all be ours in a matter of a day," Dearborn intoned with an air of frightening confidence that almost convinced Madison himself.

And Hull repeated exactly what Clay and Calhoun had said: "My God, there's nothing to it! Our army of liberation will be welcomed in Upper Canada; the inhabitants are sick to death of the British!"

Madison listened to the one-day plan to take Montreal, Kingston, and the Niagara. He squelched his desire to point out that the army that would be led by them might not be quite up to their expectations or able to carry out their grandiose plans.

And as for the matter of the Canadians surrendering the moment they sighted the Americans, Madison was not certain whether Dearborn and Hull had left that impression with Clay and Calhoun, or if in fact it was the other way around. Certainly they were all meeting with one another as well as with him. I wish I knew more about the Canadas, Madison thought to himself. An American President ought to know something about the place.

Madison leaned back and allowed his hands to go slack on his huge desk. Then, slightly agitated again, he leaned forward and lifted the half-filled glass of water on his desk. He took a sip and wished it were whiskey. He felt as if each of his limbs were tied to a different horse and that the horses all were running in different directions.

On his desk, quite hidden beneath a sheaf of papers of lesser importance, was a declaration of war against Britain. He had only to scrawl his name to it and send it to Congress where, without too many questions, it would be passed after some long, patriotic speeches and a wave of futile protest from New York. And across from him, in somber morning coat, the British minister, Mr. Augustus John Foster, droned on. It was the same conversation they had engaged in yesterday; it was so familiar that Madison did not even have to concentrate.

"My government cannot withdraw the Orders in Council when there still is strong evidence that the French continue to menace trade." It was the minister's final statement, it was always his final statement, *ad nauseam.*

And now for my final line, Madison thought. "Even those Americans who do not wish war are angered by impressment of our seamen." But today he felt like a change. He added, "We no longer can endure the continued violation of American neutral rights on the high seas, or the violation of territorial waters in order to harass commerce." It was nearly a direct quote from the declaration of war.

The British minister met President Madison's reply without so much as a sign of distress on his young, arrogant face. "My government is under great pressure," he answered.

Pressure. Madison silently repeated the word to

himself. Yes, he understood pressure. Heaven knew
he had his own pressure. Calhoun, Clay, and Congress yapping for war; Vermont and New York
mumbling about secession; the public furious over
British actions; two generals who thought they could
go to sleep one night and wake up with instant victory with an untested army . . . Pressure? Madison's
eyes caught the edge of the parchment on which the
declaration of war was written—just another scrap of
paper among the others on his desk. He lifted the
quill pen from the inkpot and, hardly daring to think
about it, shuffled the papers so that the line for his
signature on the declaration was accessible. Without
looking up, Madison scrawled his name on the document. The horses that had been mentally pulling
him came to an abrupt halt and time seemed to stand
still, as if suspended by his sudden, decisive action.
By this simple act, Madison thought, I have passed
on the responsibility to Congress. And he reasoned,
it *was* their responsibility. If the people were to go to
war, let their representatives take them there.

He lifted his eyes and met the British minister's
puzzled gaze with a half smile. "I think there is nothing more for us to say to one another." He spoke the
words evenly and flatly.

"And?" the British minister asked.

"Things will take their own course," Madison replied. "These matters are out of my hands and yours.
What will happen, will happen."

The British minister stood up, his face a little pale.
He smoothed out his morning coat, as he always did.
It was a delaying gesture, and it always annoyed
Madison. Today it irritated him more than usual.
"Shall we have further meetings?" the minister
asked.

"I think not," Madison answered. He stood up and
felt a sudden tingle in his legs; they had gone to
sleep, even if he had managed to stay more or less

awake. His eyes strayed to the window. The leaves on the trees were a new, deep green. The sky was blue and clear. It was spring—June 1, 1812. He suddenly longed for the peace of Montpelier and wondered, not for the first time, why he had wanted to be President.

"Good day," he said, eyes returning to the British minister. The man turned and left the room. Madison sat back down and stared across the empty chamber. Then he fumbled around and picked up the declaration of war. The ink had dried and his signature stood out, bold and strong. "John!" he called out for his secretary. The younger man soon appeared. "Send this over to Congress right away." He handed over the document. "It ought to be harder to declare war," he said aloud when John had left the room. It was a thought he would recall later.

Mason James MacLean sat on the very edge of his chair in the gallery during the roll-call vote. The declaration of war had passed the House of Representatives thirteen days ago by a vote of seventy-nine to forty-nine, but the Senate had proved more thoughtful. The Federalists and some of the older Republicans tried to amend the declaration of war in order to approve only a "limited" war at sea, a war by privateers. But this had failed and now the vote for war stood nearly tied. "Virginia!" the Speaker called out and the answer was returned. Mason clapped his hands in glee. "It's a most exciting moment, a most historic moment!" he said to Mrs. Madison, who sat next to him.

"Most exciting, Mr. MacLean," she whispered back breathlessly.

The speaker banged his gavel. "Thirteen against," he intoned solemnly, "nineteen in favor!" His voice rose and pandemonium broke out in the gallery as southern supporters rose to cheer, newspaper reporters bolted the room and headed for their horses, and lobbyists shoved their way forward.

"It'll have to go back to the House of Representatives for amendments," Dolley said and sighed without moving or acknowledging the movement around her.

"But surely it will just shoo right on through," Mason James said. "We do, after all, control the House."

Dolley nodded. "I do hope Mr. Madison will rest better now." She fidgeted with the drawstrings on her satchel. "I do think I must persuade him to take a little rest, come home to Montpelier for a week or maybe two."

Mason glanced at Dolley's heaving breasts and thought briefly that he too needed a rest. "When will you leave Washington?" he asked.

Dolley turned and touched his hand lightly. "In a short time," she murmured. "After all, there's a war to get on with, not that it will last too terribly long."

"I have every confidence we shall have a rapid victory."

Dolley stood up. "I'll be going to Mr. Madison now," she said and smiled. "And do come on Wednesday, dear Mr. MacLean. I have need to discuss more artwork with you."

Claude Deschamps sat behind his wooden desk in the first-floor office of the North West Company. The large warehouse was on the corner of St. Thérèse and Vaudreuil in Montreal and was shared equally with the South West Company, owned by John Jacob Astor.

It had been five months ago, back in February, that Claude had had his long, drawn-out political discussion with John Jacob Astor in New York. Thoughts of Astor brought back thoughts of his chance meeting with Josh MacLean as well. Poor

Josh, not even the most expensive brothel in Montreal had plucked him from his depression. Well, Claude thought, now he will have a distraction.

Claude leaned back in his chair and looked at his desk. It was a wonderful desk with a hundred slots and a lovely roll top. Claude lifted his feet and put them up on the broad expanse of oak. He lifted the message once again and reread it. It brought a smile to his lips.

"The proof of the pudding is in the eating thereof," he said aloud, quoting his favorite British saying. Well, the dispatch before him was the proof of the pudding—or, more accurately, the proof that John Jacob Astor had the best communications network in all of the Americas.

It was June 24 and Claude Deschamps, sitting in Montreal, had just received a message from a breathless courier that on June 18 the Congress of the United States of America had declared war on the British. One hundred forty-four hours from Washington to Montreal! It was an all-time record and possible only because the entire rapid-river relay system had been worked out carefully in advance.

Claude Deschamps chuckled. The message contained more than the simple confirmation of a declaration of war, it also informed him that the same message was on the way to Fort St. Joseph on Lake Huron. And that Claude Deschamps found most amusing of all. Fort St. Joseph was near the American Fort Michilimackinac. Both were absolutely vital links in the fur trade.

The Americans, as one might have suspected, had chosen to notify all their military units and commanders of the declaration of war by regular mail. That meant that the British, given Astor's information, might well know about the war several weeks before the Americans who had declared it.

"A small, amusing, and delightful advantage,"

159

Claude mumbled happily. "With a little luck, it might all be over on the Great Lakes before the Americans even find out they've declared war." And congratulated himself for doing his part. I have sent this message on to the British generals.

This Declaration of War would have certain effects in Quebec. It would momentarily end the struggle between the *Château Clique*—that small group of predominantly English-Scots merchants who controlled the executive councils and the economic life of the province—and the Legislative Assembly, who were mostly French and represented the traditional agrarian way of life.

Of course, the Legislative Assembly had little power, but they kindled the fires of French nationalism. Alas, nothing in Quebec ever was simple, Claude thought. The actions of the powerless Legislative Assembly were not so much a question of disloyalty to the British Crown as a desire to obtain power for the Assembly so that the majority of the population might protect its interests. Claude knew the situation in Upper Canada was similar, but lacking the dynamic of language differences. In Upper Canada, a small group called the Family Compact controlled the province.

Claude thought back to the discussion with Astor in February; Claude had tried to explain the contradiction of being a French Canadian, especially one of a rarefied group who had business dealings with the British and who were totally bilingual. The British would call on him and say, "Let us hear from a French Canadian!" But Claude knew their error. His own views were not representative of the majority of the French-speaking people of the province. He shared their disdain for Napoleon and he had a guarded interest in reform of the present system of government. On the other hand, he rejected their slavish practice of religion and rejected their conservatism. At the same time, he was far from British.

Claude Deschamps instead chose a seldom-walked path. He chose to be rich, to be educated, to be broad-minded, to be cultured. He chose to play the British for what they were worth and to seek the support of his fellow French. In some men, such a split sense of being would have led to destruction, but in a man as sharp and intelligent as Claude Deschamps it resulted only in arrogance and a rapier wit. He always would be superior to his French-speaking compatriots because he was wealthy, well-educated, bilingual, and cosmopolitan. He always would be superior to the English because the poor clods seemed unable to master two languages, lacked Gallic charm, and were, to Claude's way of thinking, nearly all constipated—if not physically, then morally.

Claude Deschamps considered it his fate—indeed, his destiny—to move forward with British North America while retaining his distinctive French heritage and to ignore all those who would, for whatever reason, allow Quebec to stagnate. He vowed to pull Quebec into the nineteenth century, shrieking and screaming if necessary. Like a river, he told himself, Quebec had to be placid along the shore and rushing forward in the center.

Claude stretched and brought his feet down from the desktop with a thud. How soon would the Nor-Westers at Fort St. Joseph receive Astor's message? Soon enough, Claude decided. Soon enough to make a joke out of the Americans.

A warm July breeze filled with the scent of spruce, hemlock, cedar, and fish cooking hit Toussaint Pothier as he paddled his canoe the remaining few hundred yards to the shore. He yelled a friendly, "Yo-ho!" to those Indians who had left their cooking fires to greet him. How convenient, Pothier thought. I have arrived in time for the noon meal. Fish, of course.

Toussaint Pothier was an agent for Astor's South West Company and had been traveling nonstop out of Amherstburg with news for Captain Roberts of Fort St. Joseph. Three days without sleep, three days of continuous exertion, three days with only dried foodstuffs—his arrival was a miracle! I am, he thought, a *voyageur* with wings on my canoe!

"Hey! Toussaint! What brings you up here? Did you come to fight the Americans?" bellowed Richard Dickson in his thick Scots brogue. He was a tall man, heavy-set, with bright red hair; a fur trader, an adventurer, and an explorer of some reputation. He was highly respected by the Indians, who often called him Flaming Skull, and intensely disliked by the Americans, who called him a bastard, a son-of-a-whore, and a fucking Indian-lover, among other endearments. "Well, I have my names for them too," Dickson said when told what he was called.

The Americans disliked Richard Dickson because the Indians respected him and he respected the Indians, while they regarded the Indians as savages, a nuisance to be eliminated. The Americans saw the Indians as roadblocks to expansion, as impediments to settlement. Richard Dickson hated the Americans and he was at Fort St. Joseph to fight for the British and for his Indian wife and half-breed children. "Ours is a way of life that will be destroyed if the Americans ever take over British North America," Dickson declared.

Toussaint Pothier beached his canoe with the help of Dickson and two Indians. They flipped it over, and Dickson fell in step with Pothier as the wily Frenchman headed up the beach toward the fort. "Well, have you come to fight the Americans?" Dickson repeated.

162

"Well, why not, eh? They're going to fight me. I have a message for Captain Charles Roberts. Seems the Americans have declared war on us."

"Jumping shit!" Dickson said, slapping his buckskins, then pounding Toussaint on the back. "Hey, there!" Dickson shouted to the Indians who had returned to their fires. "War!" He gave the universal sign for war and smiled again as a cry came up from the assembled Sioux, Winnebago, Menominee, and Chippewa.

"Good of them to declare war in summer," Toussaint declared. "This place is hell in winter."

"The Siberia of Upper Canada," Dickson said.

"Where's Siberia?" Toussaint asked. The joke was lost on him.

Dickson shrugged. "In Russia," he answered.

They passed through the gates of the fort and headed directly for Roberts' office. Fort St. Joseph was not a place of military decorum. Its log quarters were airy and lacked all but the barest of necessities, though they were built on stone foundations. The fort was manned by some forty soldiers of the newly formed 10th Royal Veteran Battalion, most of whom were in their late forties and early fifties. They were not in the best of condition. They drank excessively, suffered from assorted social diseases, and had a variety of infirmities acquired in various skirmishes, battles, wars, and tavern brawls. Last but not least, they suffered from physical inactivity, save assorted sexual acts with Indian women and stray animals.

The land around the fort presently was occupied by Dickson's Indians and more than one hundred *voyageurs* from Astor's South West Company.

Toussaint and Dickson climbed the steps to the captain's quarters. A sergeant snapped to attention. "Sirs?" he questioned.

"A message," Dickson said without further explanation.

The sergeant opened the door and peered in. Behind his table, Captain Roberts sat eating his noon meal. "Messenger, sir!" The sergeant tried to sound official.

Captain Roberts sighed. "Show him in," he said, his mouth still filled with fish.

Captain Roberts was a thin little man, as disheveled as his sergeant. Only Roberts' dark brown eyes held a glint of liveliness. "I hope it's good news," he said, his words still garbled from chewing. He stood halfway up and awkwardly tucked in his shirt, trying to look somewhat neater for his guests.

"Captain, this is Toussaint Pothier of the South West Company, come all the way from Amherstburg with an urgent message."

Roberts leaned forward. "Spit it out, son," he said to Toussaint, who was not all that young.

"The Americans have declared war, sir." Toussaint fumbled in his pack, seeking the pouch that contained the written message in more detailed form.

Roberts broke the pouch open and, squinting his eyes, held out the message and read it from a distance of two feet. "From old Astor himself," Roberts observed. "Concerned more about his furs and provisions than about what the Americans are up to. I'd make a bet on that, I would." Roberts paused and ran a nervous hand through his thin gray hair. "Now we're going to get some action! Jeez!" He shook his head again. "Gotta sober up the men, shake 'em out of the squaws' bedrolls, and send them over to Fort Michilimackinac to take it away from the Americans. Then we can be all by ourselves up here." Roberts paused, suddenly remembering that he was in the army and was no longer a free agent. "Jeez, I'll have to wait for orders from General Brock."

"Hope they don't take too long," Toussaint commented.

Roberts sank back into his chair and it groaned ominously, threatening to fall apart and send him sprawling. "Maybe it'll be like it was back in Ceylon and India, 'cept there aren't any pretty women who wear bells. That's what I remember about India: pretty, delicate little brown girls with bells."

"Perhaps we should formulate a plan of attack," Dickson suggested. Roberts mumbled under his breath and, opening the drawer of his desk, pulled out a rolled map. He spread it out, holding one corner down with his dirty lunch plate and the other corner down with a skin of whiskey.

Dickson, Toussaint, and Roberts all hovered over the map of the Great Lakes region. "Here we are," Roberts mumbled as he pointed to St. Joseph's Island at the top of Lake Huron. He ran his finger across the lake, some forty miles west, till it rested in the middle of the narrows between Lake Superior and Lake Huron. "Mackinac Island," Roberts indicated.

"The key to the western fur trade," Toussaint intoned almost reverently.

"I like the idea of a surprise attack. Say, you know as fast as Toussaint got here, I have an idea the brave defenders of Mackinac don't even know there's a war." Dickson chuckled at the thought.

"I know the terrain," Toussaint told them. "Here, hand me that piece of charcoal so I can draw a little." Toussaint took the charcoal and drew a shape like a rough arrowhead. "Here's the fort. It's totally surrounded with high, rugged cliffs." He pointed to the south end of the island. "And here's one possible landing place on the west side where the cliff is not too difficult to scale."

Roberts scratched his stubble again. "The Indians

have canoes. We have ten *bateaux* and I'll comman-
deer the North West Company's gunboat, the good
old *Caledonia*."

"I say we start preparations right now."

"Preparations only. We can't go till I get orders
from General Brock," Roberts stressed.

"Now that the Indians know Congress made it all
legal, I don't know how long I can keep them from
going out there and scalping all the Americans,"
Dickson warned. "So you better hope Brock's orders
come soon, or we're going to have our own little free-
for-all."

Mr. Hillier stood staring into the embers of the
burning fire. He thought, and doubtless would have
mumbled aloud had he been a mumbling man, that
there was no justice in this world for some people.
None at all.

Bonnie Campbell sat at the wooden table in the
center of his cabin staring into a cup of cold tea. Her
young, lovely face was tear-stained, and occasionally,
unable to control herself, she let out an audible sob.

After Bonnie had been moved to the fort at York
Factory, Miles Macdonell had seen to it that she was
housed in a small room and assigned certain chores
to keep her occupied. She cleaned Mr. Hillier's quarters and cooked and sewed for him as well. In addition, Miles had set her to work rolling bandages and
preparing emergency kits for the colonists who
would be heading South. As long as Bonnie Campbell was kept working, she appeared content.

But the morning when the colonists departed, led
by Miles Madonell, Bonnie had stood apart and
watched with tear-filled eyes. Miles, her friend and
defender, was gone; her parents were gone too and
with them went any hope of reconciliation. Moreover, there was no more work to keep Bonnie occu-

pied, save the small chore of cooking and cleaning for Mr. Hillier.

I was not meant to deal with weeping females, Hillier thought. I was hired to make this post profitable, to barter with the Indians, to fight if necessary, to provide law in a godless outpost of civilization. I was hired to teach newcomers to endure the winters and relish the short summers. I was not hired to deal with women who have problems and who are both rejected and dejected. Hillier sighed inwardly, not wanting to turn to look at Bonnie Campbell again. I am not guilty of not trying, he told himself. I have talked and talked to her, tried to comfort her, and it all was to no avail. If he spoke softly and logically, she wept; if he was authoritarian and angry, she wept harder.

"You can go with the next batch of settlers," Hillier had promised her.

"Alone? What shall I do in a wilderness alone?" Again she had cried.

"Well then, you can return to Scotland on the next ship." It was his most reasonable solution, for in his heart he agreed she ought not go down the Nelson without a husband.

"I'll starve in Scotland!" she had quickly retorted. "I cannot go back!"

"Then perhaps you shall marry one of the colonists; most of them are men in need of women."

"I cannot just marry anyone!" The wailing began again. It was not that Hillier was an unsympathetic man, it was that he had no answer to her dilemma and felt put upon because he had been left with this quite beautiful and quite charming problem child.

He heard her lift the teacup and he turned around. Her large eyes greeted him. They were not as red as they had been, but clearly there wasn't much improvement in her mood either.

"You could have married Finlay," Hillier said, regretting it almost as soon as the words escaped his mouth.

"He's a pig! He forced me! Why is it my fault? Why is every man on this earth so—so unreasonable and stupid?" Her eyes flashed, and Hillier felt almost encouraged. At least her temper showed that she was not an entirely beaten creature.

"Leaving that aside," he said evenly, "can you read?"

She blinked at him. The question was unexpected and seemed to have little to do with her plight. "Yes," she answered sullenly. "I can read the Bible."

"But you've read no other books?" Hillier should have known without asking. Girls were not often taught to read, and he supposed it fortunate enough that she could read the Bible. "I have some books, actually quite a few books. Why don't you begin reading them? How are you with numbers?"

Bonnie shook her head. "I can't do sums."

Hillier rubbed his chin. "I don't have much to do before the next batch of colonists arrive. I'll teach you," he suggested. After all, she was a pretty lass and he hoped she was intelligent as well. "A few hours a day," he added. "A little bookkeeping, useful things. Maybe you could teach."

"Teach?" Bonnie Campbell had a tone of awe in her voice.

"If you could learn to teach you might be able to support yourself. Then too, you might be able to do bookkeeping. It is a skill, Miss Campbell, a possible way out of your situation."

"Do you think I could learn?" Her voice brightened at the possibility.

"With the Scots, education is next to godliness. I think you can do anything you want, but you must want to do it, Miss Campbell. You have to stop your

168

incessant weeping and develop some pride." His voice had taken on an air of both optimism and authority. He felt again in control and he congratulated himself on being the most well rounded of all the factors who ran the Hudson's Bay Company posts. He suddenly felt that he could solve any and all human problems.

"We shall begin tomorrow," he announced, turning to his bookshelf. "You shall, in the meantime, content yourself with this history of England and this—it's from the United States, a Franklin reader." He handed her the two books, blowing the dust off of them.

"Go practice your alphabet," he suggested. "You must learn to write neatly and in a good hand. Tomorrow I'll begin teaching you numbers. We'll start with the account books at the post . . . good and practical, what?"

Bonnie Campbell actually smiled. "You're a kind person," she murmured.

Hillier felt gratified and a kind of warmth filled him. She is attractive, he thought. Small wonder Finlay pursued her so. And as Hillier watched Bonnie leave the room, his thoughts crossed the barriers he usually erected for himself. He wondered how easy a girl Bonnie really was. He contemplated her father's accusations and her denials. Hillier decided that the truth lay somewhere between, and it crossed his mind how terribly tiresome Indian women had become for him.

"It's a fine July night," Mason James observed. He and Colleen were dining on the terrace by candlelight. Mason James had ordered up roast capon in what he decided was a divine orange sauce, and he served a fine white wine with it, a deep red wine with dessert, and a heady liqueur after that. Colleen felt herself quite lightheaded by the time coffee was served. "A special brew," Mason James told her. "It's from Haiti and I have it sent directly to me from the importer in New Orleans."

Colleen sipped the brew and found that it cleared her head and woke her up almost immediately. "It's very strong," she commented. Her face still was a little flushed from the wine, and her eyes studied him.

"My father received my letter and I received his reply today," Mason James said. "He's overjoyed, simply overjoyed. Though I doubt he would be impressed with your fine figure at the moment."

Colleen smiled. Mason James was ever the flatterer. Only last night he had told her she looked like a cow, and the night before he cautioned her as she came down the stairs, telling her she might fall forward on her face because her stomach was so round and full of child.

"I'm certain I shall go back to my normal self after the baby," she smiled, ignoring his barbs as usual. He was good to her. Meals were an adventure. He insisted on her looking at new fashions even though she could not yet wear them, and he brushed her hair endlessly, playing with it and fixing it in new styles.

"I do hope you won't become fat," he said. "You're much more charming thin."

Colleen sighed. She felt she weighed three hundred pounds at the moment. "I hate confinement," she mumbled. "I should at least like to be able to go out once in a while."

"Soon," Mason James said. "Next month, is it?"

Colleen nodded. "Next month," she replied. And to herself, Colleen said a silent prayer that the baby would be healthy. Dear Lord, I know it's a sin for cousins to have children, but don't punish us, we didn't know.

"You look distressed again. I thought you were all over that."

170

"I was just hoping the baby will be healthy."

"Well, of course it will be! Whatever makes you say such a thing?"

"Because, as you know, Josh and I are cousins. Inbreeding isn't good."

Mason James let his laughter peal out. Colleen called this inbreeding! What would she have said had he told her his own background? But he did not. It was something he never discussed, not with anyone.

"Please, dear girl. I've grown quite fond of you. Now simply try to enjoy life and look forward to the best. Forget your long-lost love and concentrate on the future."

Colleen nodded silently. Forget Josh? She never could forget Josh! And she had decided she would spend her life doing penance for having made love with him.

CHAPTER VIII

July 8, 1812

Exhausted, panting, and still shaking, the buckskin-clad courier handed the message pouch to Captain Roberts.

"It's about time you got here!" Roberts was in no mood to feel sympathy for the man who had traveled nonstop from Fort York. Roberts opened the pouch and pulled out the message from General Brock that read: "War has been declared. Act accordingly."

Roberts looked up from the message only because of the thud. "Oh," he said under his breath. The messenger had collapsed, slipping rather awkwardly from the chair to the floor of the cabin.

"Sergeant!" Roberts bellowed. The sergeant appeared, wiping his mouth with his sleeve.

"Poor bugger," he mumbled, lifting the man slightly from under the arms and dragging him to the door.

"Yes, get him out of here," Roberts instructed. "See that he gets some rest, a double ration of rum, and an Indian woman for his other needs. Phew, and tell him to take a bath. He smells even for this place!"

The sergeant grunted his answer as he dragged the messenger from the cabin and Roberts called out the open doorway, "Fetch Dickson! Fetch Toussaint!"

By the time the sergeant returned, Dickson, Toussaint, Crawford, and Askin had arrived. Roberts was fairly dancing around his office, and with good reason. Lewis Crawford, who was with the South West Company, had organized 125 *voyageurs* for the battle, while John Askin, Jr., headed the Ottawa and Chippewa Indians who offered to join in.

"I'm seizing the *Caledonia*, impressing its crew into service." The *Caledonia* belonged to the North West Company and she was as neat a little vessel as sailed the lakes. Her usual cargo was furs, but Roberts had realized she could easily be converted into a man-of-war.

"What are your orders?" Dickson asked. "Are we to attack?"

Roberts could not suppress his smile. "My orders are: 'Act accordingly.' How's that for leeway?"

"I'd say it covered most contingencies," Dickson replied. This, he could not help thinking, would be some expedition. An elderly officer would command a division of near-geriatric veterans, men whom the Crown had failed to kill off in other wars. And the *voyageurs* were not to be forgotten. They were a rough, tough, dirty, drunken lot. Hardly one was under fifty, save for a few métis. Then too, no one, neither himself nor the regulars nor the assorted volunteers, was exactly in top-notch condition.

"It's going to take some time to sober up the regulars," Dickson commented.

"Four days," Roberts said. "More than that and nobody could fight 'cause they'd be too sober. Four days and off we go!"

The four days passed quickly in disorganized preparations. "Goddam arthritis," Sergeant Field cursed as he leaned one-legged against his musket. "You'd think it'd loosen up a bit in summer!"

It was July 12 and the atmosphere at Fort St. Joseph was one of confused excitement at the

173

thought of the coming battle and, not to be forgotten, the victory party after success. But for Sergeant Field, it could all be reduced to a pain in the leg, a pain he usually associated with the damp, cold rains of fall.

Captain Roberts was all but ready to embark on his great adventure when another messenger arrived. This one was not as tired as the first; he did not collapse, but rather stood against a tall fir tree and stared out toward the beach, trying to take in all the activity preparatory to the invasion of Fort Michilimackinac.

"Horseshit!" Roberts cursed. He stomped his foot and then literally screamed at the top of his lungs. The others had already gathered around.

"What now?" Dickson queried. He was chewing tobacco, and yellow spittle glistened on one side of his mouth.

"It's from that pansy Brock! Now he says, 'Do nothing'! Shit!"

"*Merde!*" Toussaint mumbled. "I don't know how we're going to keep the Indians down. They're raring to go!"

Dickson too cursed. "Do these people know what they're doing? Fuck, we have a real opportunity to catch the Americans asleep!"

Roberts scowled. "Gotta obey orders. This is the army. Oh, hell, give everybody a couple rations of rum. That'll shut 'em up at least. Give plenty to the Indians too, knock 'em out for a while."

The rum was passed out and the drinking began. For three days the drinking continued, but even so, Fort St. Joseph was a beehive of activity. There was excitement, frustration, and anger. Each night, the fires around which the *voyageurs* gathered with the Indians grew larger and brighter. And the war drums beat more loudly and more intensely than the night before. The Sioux and the Chippewa drank too much and began, drunkenly, to rekindle old animosities. Richard Dickson found himself kept quite busy keeping them apart.

On July 15 more news finally arrived from General Brock. This dispatch was delivered by Michel Deschamps, a young métis, son of René Deschamps. Michel neither collapsed nor leaned against a tree dumbly. Indeed, he was fully prepared to take part in the attack, should there be one.

Roberts opened the pouch and read and reread the message. "I am ordered to adopt the most prudent measures either of offense or defense which circumstances indicate."

"Eh?" Toussaint queried. "Can't the pansy speak the English?" Everyone laughed.

"It's army English," Roberts declared. "A little yes, a little no, and it all comes down to the fact that Brock doesn't know what the hell to do himself!"

"And what are you going to do?" Michel Deschamps asked. He winked a dark eye and smiled cheerfully.

"I say, let's go!" Dickson interjected.

"With the first light of dawn," Roberts agreed. "I say we attack Mackinac Island. It's the most prudent defense measure I can think of."

Cheers went up along the beach as Roberts' decision was passed along. And there was more rum as well. "Maybe we'll do better drunk," Roberts allowed. "Anyway, it's a hell of a time to stop drinking!"

With the morning light, to the wail of Dickson's bagpipes, the pounding of war drums, and the whooping of Indians, the force embarked. It was, Michel Deschamps thought, a sight to behold.

Captain Roberts and his regulars marched onto the *Caledonia* wearing their red kilts. One hundred eighty *voyageurs* poured onto their *bateaux* dressed in buckskins and wearing sashes around their waists, colorful silk scarves around their necks, and long cloaks falling from their shoulders.

Michel himself wore buckskins, a bright green sash around his waist, and a printed silk scarf around his neck. He was thirty-two years of age and boasted a strange family history. His father was René Deschamps, who had come West many years ago, leaving a wealthy family in Trois-Rivières. His cousin was, in fact, Claude Deschamps, one of the wealthy investors in the North West Company, for which Michel worked now and again.

Michel's Indian mother was from Pembina and had been extraordinarily beautiful in her youth. Michel had inherited the best of his parents' looks. His hair was black and his handsome face was bearded. He had his mother's golden-red skin, his father's merry eyes. Born in the Dakota Territory, Michel had traveled with his métis compatriots to the foothills of the Rocky Mountains and had participated in many a buffalo hunt but never in a battle. The scene before him was fascinating, and Michel took it all in.

In addition to the British regulars, none of whom appeared in good condition to Michel, there were fifty feathered Sioux in full war paint; Chippewa whose heads were shaved and whose faces had been blackened the color of coal with charcoal from the evening's fires; some forty Menominee; twenty-four Winnebago; and thirty Ottawa led by another métis, Amable Chevelier. It was one of those names, Michel thought. Those who spoke English pronounced it 'Am able' and thought it was the result of a compliment rather than a proper French name.

Michel chose to go with the *voyageurs* on the *bateaux.* The bright sun glinted off the small waves as the large flotilla of men and boats cut through the waters of Lake Huron. Their single objective was to reach Mackinac Island by dawn the following morning.

Night on the lake was a dazzling sight. The half moon cast a long reflection on the water, providing enough light to see the outlines of the canoes, the *bateaux*, and the gunboat *Caledonia*.

"Eh? What's that?" Richard Dickson whispered to his Indian companion, Joseph Two Feathers.

"Man in canoe," Two Feathers signaled back, making a motion with his hands to the other canoes. Almost instantly, some twenty canoes fell into formation and bore down on the single canoe.

"Hey! Don't shoot!" The single man in the small canoe straightened up quickly, almost as if he had been asleep.

Richard Dickson stared through the darkness, feeling he knew the voice. He raised his hand to give a signal to the Indians not to shoot.

"Michael? Michael Dousman? Is that you? You stupid son-of-a-bitch! What are you doing out here, anyway? Are you spying?"

"Dickson? You fat old Scot bastard! It's me, Michael Dousman of the South West Company. Don't let those savages shoot, huh?"

"Let's go aboard the *Caledonia*," Dickson suggested. He gave a signal and Dousman's canoe was taken in tow.

Aboard the *Caledonia*, Michael Dousman was warmly greeted by Toussaint, Crawford, and Askin, his fellow traders. "Eh, what you doing out here?" Toussaint asked.

"I came out to have a look-see along the border. I heard some rumors, something about a war being declared." Michael Dousman was an American, but one whose main concern was trade and money.

"The Americans have declared war on the British. How do you like that, eh?" Toussaint said and laughed.

"Huh?" the American trader replied, scratching

his head. "Well, nobody's told the Americans yet," he added, taking a belt of rum from the skin offered him by Dickson.

"We're going to attack them at dawn," Captain Roberts announced proudly. "A purely defensive measure, you understand. It's even reasonable."

"I suppose it is," Dousman answered dumbly. He had thought it was the British who had declared war. If the Americans had declared war, how come the Americans didn't know about it? But then, he had had a lot of rum, it was late, and perhaps he might understand it all in the morning.

"How many cannon do they have?" Roberts was asking. "Where are they placed?"

Michael Dousman sat down on the deck. "Got anything more to drink?" The rum skin was passed. "You know," he said slowly, thinking of all Astor's supplies at Fort Michilimackinac as well as of the vast liquor stash in the storeroom, "you might be able to do this without actually fighting. Wouldn't want a lot of innocent people to get killed by the Indians. God, you know how they are when they get excited."

"What have you in mind?" Roberts asked.

"Well here, I'll draw you all the fortifications and then I'll go on ashore and get the civilians out of the way and show you how to surround the fort. Then I'll just go in and tell Lieutenant Hanks.

"Is he reasonable?" Roberts asked.

"Oh, very," Dousman confirmed.

The flotilla of soldiers landed on the beach of Mackinac Island at three in the morning. Dousman himself went around to every house in the village, and the inhabitants were moved to safety in case the Indians got carried away. Dousman's ox team was brought and the British cannon was taken up the cliffs. Before dawn all was in place. The British guns were on a hill overlooking the fort and the British had marched their collection of men into place.

Dousman, good as his word, went into the fort and straight to Lieutenant Hanks. "The British are outside the fort," he said coolly. "With three hundred Indians, regular troops, and more than a hundred *voyageurs*."

"Huh?" Hanks said in typical American fashion. Then, recovering himself slightly, he asked, "When did the British declare war on us?"

"Washington declared war on them," Dousman said, repeating all that he had learned.

But Lieutenant Hanks' face already had gone pale. "Would be nice if the dear Congress notified the United States Army before it told the British!" he shrieked in a growing rage. Then, just to check, he walked to the fort's tower.

It was all as Dousman had said.

"Washington!" Hanks spit as he stared at the British emplacements. Then, without further comment, he ordered the white flag of surrender to be flown.

"Great!" shouted Dickson as he observed the white flag fluttering in the breeze.

"Now what do we do with the Indians?" Roberts asked.

"Give them some more rum. I hear there's plenty in the American stores."

"This calls for a victory celebration party," Roberts slurred.

A cheer went up from the rank and file as they marched and limped toward the fort and the casks of rum that lay in the cellar beneath it. Sergeant Field rubbed his leg as he moved along. They weren't the sharpest battalion in the British Army, but they sure knew how to have a good time. And by God, they had captured the most strategic trading fort without shedding a single drop of blood. Not bad for a bunch of twenty-year veterans, he told himself.

Michel Deschamps followed Dickson and the others into the fort. He thought he would stay for part of the celebration, since he was hardly averse to some rest and some rum at American expense. But he already had decided to leave in two days' time. He would be heading off to the Red River territory, heading home.

On August 26, the ship *Robert Taylor* anchored at York Factory. It carried seventy-one would-be colonists recruited by Owen Keveney in Ulster and by Ian in Scotland. Two more ships followed.

This second group was judged more useful than the first, despite the fact that they were as puritanical in their outlook and were primarily Protestant fundamentalists, rather than the more liberal Anglicans and Catholics.

Included was Andrew MacDermott, who wished to become a trader and a merchant; James Heron, a hardworking man of mixed talents and good humor; Michael Hayden Smith, who was a blacksmith by trade; and Robert MacVicar, a young carpenter.

The prospective colonists mumbled and murmured about the desolate post of York Factory. "There's cabins aplenty at the Nelson Encampment," Hillier told Owen Keveney and Ian MacLean. "Miles had the first lot who had to winter here do all the work. So they wouldn't get cabin fever, you know. Have to keep them busy."

"And boats?" Owen asked.

"And boats," Hillier confirmed. "I see no reason why you can't leave for the Red River within, say, two weeks. I think they need that long at least to recover from such a long voyage."

"Today's August 27. That means leaving on September 9," Owen said brightly. "Yes, that ought to get us to the Red River by October."

"Late October," Ian reminded him. "It's damn cold out on that prairie. These people aren't used to it and arriving so late won't give them time to make preparations for winter."

"The others are expecting us. Miles will make provisions."

Ian nodded abstractedly. Winter at York Factory was not a great improvement over winter on the Red River. The only question was one of housing. But of course, Miles might well see to the building of cabins on the Red too.

Hillier watched as Owen lined up the colonists and their meager possessions, which were loaded onto sledges. He would move out the colonists to the Nelson Encampment right away so they could get settled before nightfall.

"I have this problem," Hillier confessed to Ian. "Let Owen go on ahead. I'd like to discuss it with you."

Ian followed Hillier into the office of the Hudson's Bay Company post. It was a small, cluttered office. "Your offices are all alike," Ian commented. He recalled visiting Hillier once when he was working at a post on Lake Superior.

Hillier moved some things off a chair and motioned Ian to sit down. He himself sat at his desk. "I have this young girl," Hillier announced, leaning forward and looking deadly serious.

Ian laughed. "Is that a problem? I wish I had a young girl. Provided, of course, that she wasn't too young."

Hillier's face turned bright red with embarrassment. "No, no, no. I didn't mean *have* her in the biblical sense. I mean, she was left here and I don't know what to do with her. It's not personal, it's—it's—" Hillier actually was stuttering.

"Why, Hillier, I thought you were a man of the world. You don't know what to do with a girl?" Hillier was such a proper man, Ian could not resist teasing him. "Just how young is young?" Ian asked.

Hillier shrugged. "Seventeen, eighteen, I'm not sure."

"That," Ian corrected, "is a young woman, not a young girl."

Hillier caught the good-natured twinkle in Ian's eye and decided to ignore the teasing and get on with the story.

"Her father's a strict man, a very strict man."

"A good Scots Presbyterian?" Ian interjected.

"Yes," Hillier confirmed. "And so was his wife and most of the settlers Miles had with him. In any case, this man—a most unsavory man—he claimed to have, ah, well, had this girl, to have known her in the biblical sense. And when the man told everyone, the girl didn't deny it, but claimed she was attacked. But her father believed the man because apparently they had some reason to think the girl had entertained the man when they were away. In any case, they disowned her and she was turned out by the others as well."

Ian shook his head. "They all cast her out?"

"Well, the womenfolk. None of the men would have cast her out, but that would have caused a whole set of other problems. No one was willing to marry her. They all seemed to regard her as a whore. She wouldn't go with the man and his friends and anyway, I'm sending the lot of them back for punishment. The soldiers are rounding them up now. Miles doesn't need that sort of trash in the Red River settlement."

"Being attacked by a man doesn't make a woman a whore," Ian said indignantly. "It may make the man a coward and a bastard, but it doesn't make the woman a whore."

"Tell it to a Presbyterian, my friend. Whatever, they consider her used goods and therefore no good."

Ian shook his head. "Owen and I and the settlers we brought will be joining the others, you know. She can go South with us, but when we get to Pembina, they'll just shun her again and cast her out of the community. She'll be disowned all over again."

"I told her she could go South with your party. She's a lot stronger than she was. I've taught her some numbers and she can read well now. She could teach, you know."

Ian shook his head. "Are people going to send their children to a woman they think is a whore? Or should she get a horse and follow the métis from camp to camp teaching them? Honestly, Hillier, you know an unmarried woman can't go into that territory. She'll have to go back to Scotland."

"She says she'll starve. I can't tell her that, I've raised her hopes." Hillier looked totally dejected.

Ian stood up and stretched. It felt good to have solid ground under his feet after so many days at sea. And the air at York Factory was clear and crisp. Suddenly he felt quite tired. "I'll tell her," Ian said, feeling quite sorry for Hillier, who obviously was not used to dealing with women.

"And where is this wilderness waif?" Ian asked.

"At the fort," Hillier answered. No, he thought. I don't want to tell her she's going back to Scotland, I don't even want to be there when she's told."

"Can it wait till tomorrow?" Ian asked. "I ought to be with Owen, and I am tired. I didn't realize how tired."

Hillier stood up and jammed his hands into his pockets. "Sorry," he mumbled, his mind still on Bonnie Campbell. "Tomorrow will be fine."

"Mason James! Mason James! Oh, God! Come quick!" Colleen's cry ripped through the silence of

183

the night, and Mason James jolted upright in bed, his white nightcap askew and his white nightshirt twisted halfway around his body.

He leaped from the high canopied bed and let out a yelp as his bare feet touched the floor. "Righteous!" he screamed out. "Righteous, where are you?"

"Mason James!" Again Colleen's voice called out. It was a worried voice. As quickly as he could, Mason James lit a candle, then padded off down the hall. "I'm coming! Whatever it is, I'm coming!"

"Ouch! Damn!" Mason James turned into Colleen's room and stubbed his big toe on the doorsill. He jumped into the room on one leg, cursing loudly.

"Damn! Oh, the pain! It's my toe, I've broken my toe!"

"You've probably just stubbed it," Colleen said. "Anyway, there's no time for your toe!"

Mason James scurried to her side, awkwardly hopping on one foot. Even as he reached the side of her bed, he bellowed out once again, "Righteous! Get up here!"

Mason James lifted the candle to cast more light on the situation. "My heavens! What a horrible, sickening mess! What have you done?"

"My water's broken," Colleen wailed even as she doubled over. "And I've got the pains. I saw a woman have a baby once. My water's broken and the baby's coming. Mason James, I don't know what to do!"

Mason James stared at her. The white sheet was covered with a thick, slimy liquid. "Ugh!" he said with disgust.

"You called, master?" Righteous stood in the doorway. He carried a lamp and was dressed in a long, bright red nightshirt.

"Thank heaven," Mason James said and sighed. He turned to Colleen with an air of sudden calm. "Righteous will know what to do. The Negroes all know how to deliver babies. They always have such large families."

"I don't have a large family," Righteous chimed in. "I don't know nothin' about havin' babies."

"Nonsense!" Mason James snapped. "You must have watched when your brothers and sisters were born."

"I don't have no brothers or sisters," Righteous retorted. "And no wife either."

"A darkie who's an only child! Impossible!"

"Sorry," Righteous said, hanging his head sheepishly.

"Oh!" Colleen let out a scream and threw herself backward on the bed. "It's coming, I tell you, it's coming!"

Mason James looked at Colleen's pale face in the lamplight. "I don't know what to do," he said helplessly.

"Well, wash your hands and sterilize some water and get some towels. And hurry!"

"Goodness," Mason James said. Then he turned to Righteous. "Well, you heard her, fetch those things."

Righteous scampered from the room. And Mason James approached the bed as if Colleen had the plague, or worse. He gingerly reached over her head and fluffed the pillows. "Lie back," he commanded. "And if you'll excuse my asking, spread your legs."

"I think I'm supposed to lift my knees," Colleen suggested.

"If you must," Mason James retorted, moving downward and peering into the darkness beneath her nightdress. "I haven't enough light," he concluded. Hurriedly, Mason James pulled over a table to the foot of the bed and then, one by one, he lit all the lamps in the room till it was ablaze with light. Then he returned and peered under her dress again.

185

"Looked better in the dark," he said, staring at Colleen's huge, swollen, angry purple vagina. "The trouble with women is that all their parts are on the inside."

"Oh, oh!" Colleen screamed once again and her hands gripped the headboard as her whole body tensed and she panted like a small puppy.

"I have everything, master, even the water!" Righteous ran into the room, panting himself. "Lordy!" he exclaimed under his breath.

"Put them on the table," Mason James said with irritation. The whole sight was sickening and he only wanted it over. "I think you're supposed to push when you have the pains," he guessed as he washed his hands in the basin Righteous had brought.

Colleen let forth with yet another scream and Mason James positioned himself. "Now push!" he directed, probing slightly. "Oh, I feel it! I feel it!"

Colleen screamed again, this time a long, agonized scream. "Push, push, push!" The small head appeared and Mason James grasped it, easing out the bloodied infant, which instantly shrieked. "Oh, I knew it was going to cry!" Mason James said with some distaste. He laid down the infant on the bed, seeing that its cord still was attached to something that had not yet come out.

Colleen screamed again. "I think there's another! I feel something!"

Mason James was on the verge of mentioning the afterbirth when he saw yet another tiny head appear. "My God! You're having twins!" He reached in and eased the baby out. It came as easily as the first. And happily, it was followed by the afterbirth.

"We gotta cut that," Righteous, who up until now had offered no advice at all, announced. "You cut it with somethin' sharp sterilized in the fire and then you gotta tie it in a knot."

"I thought you didn't know anything about this,"

Mason James said amid the din of the two crying infants.

"Well, I know that," Righteous grumbled. "Everybody know that."

Mason James sighed deeply and sent for his razor. He sterilized it in the flame and cut the cord, tying each one, and then wrapping the two infants separately and handing them over to Colleen.

"I think you're supposed to feed them. Righteous, empty out those drawers and fix them up as little beds for now. Twins! How could you? They'll cry all the time, you know I loathe children. God, I should have known better than to have taken in a wide-hipped Irish girl. Built for having babies! I suppose I'm fortunate they're not triplets!"

Colleen giggled. She was tired and overwrought, but even so, Mason James was not hard to see through. "You're silly and don't loathe children. Come here and look at them now. See how lovely they are, my two little boys."

Mason James approached them. One was already hungrily suckling on Colleen's breast, the other was nuzzled close to her. Mason James reached down to pull up the cover, and the infant's flailing little hand wrapped tightly around his thumb. "Oh, my," Mason James whispered, "I think he likes me." Then, pausing and smiling just a little, he added, "I suppose they're all right if you like babies."

As was so often the case in the wilderness, tomorrow became six days. Ian had been unable to return to the Hudson's Bay Company post because he and Owen Keveney had their hands full settling the colonists into the log cabins vacated by Miles Macdonell's group, who had departed on the long trek down the river system. Furthermore, Ian had been delayed by rain.

Finally, on the morning of September 2, the rain

gave way to light gray skies, and Owen joked, "It's threatening to clear up."

"And what should we do with Mr. Hillier's problem?" Ian asked. He had explained everything to Owen just to make certain they were in agreement. Owen shrugged, more concerned with the coming trek to the Red River than with Mr. Hillier's young lady. "I'll go along with whatever your decision is," Owen said. "If you think she ought to come with us, we'll take her. If you think she should be returned to Scotland, then she will be returned."

"You're a great help, Owen my friend," Ian said, waving as he headed off for the Hudson's Bay Company post. Not that he really needed Owen's thoughts on the matter. He already had told Hillier the girl should go back, and he had not really changed his mind.

It was a silver day, Ian thought as he traveled along. As on so many days in early autumn, there was a mist over the water, a mist that hovered in low-lying areas and hung eerily in the forest of tall pine and cedar. It was a two-and-a-half-mile walk to the Hudson's Bay Company post from the Nelson Encampment and Ian paced himself, taking long strides and breathing deeply. He enjoyed walks such as this because there was no need to carry much of a pack and there was no need to blaze a trail because the path was well trodden. Moreover, Ian thought, it was certain that there would be a mug of fine rum waiting at the end of this early-morning exercise.

Ian loved and enjoyed the woods. But when he walked with someone, or led a group, there always was the sound of human voices in conversation or simply grunting as men exerted themselves. But alone at dawn in the woods, a man could listen. He could hear the wind in the trees, the sound of nearby water as it bashed against a rocky shore, the scampering of small animals, the occasional chirping of the birds. This was a walk of pure pleasure, and as Ian saw the fort looming in the distance across the clearing, he felt almost sad it had come to an end. But he consoled himself that there would be many mornings like this. He had agreed to travel ahead of Owen and the main body of settlers. His job on the trek would be to act as scout, to lay the trail, to mark camping points.

The huts that surrounded the post were small, and the morning cooking fires belched smoke from their chimneys. The smell of fish prevailed, though it mixed with the odor of skins being tanned. The Hudson's Bay Company post maintained minimal security, since the Indians were friendly and industrious, and an attack could come only from the sea.

As Ian passed by the huts, an old Indian woman wrapped in her Hudson's Bay Company blanket waved at him, smiled a toothless grin, and called out a greeting. She has a wonderful face, Ian thought. It was lined like a walnut, but it was not round. She had magnificent high cheekbones and bright, happy eyes that seemed to wink at him. As he looked at her, Ian felt once again, not for the first time, a kinship with the Indians as he looked at her. They worked endlessly, they were one with the land, and, he thought, in reality it's their land.

When he was a boy, his father had taken him and his brother Josh into the woods on a long three-month trek. During that time, they had spent many weeks with an Indian tribe. The chief, a good friend of the MacLeans and the Macleods, had taken Ian and Josh on long walks, showing them signs on the forest floor, teaching them to listen as few white men listened. "Walk softly on the land," the chief had told them. "Build your shelter only when you have listened to the wind and you know from which direction it blows." The Indians, Ian thought, had taught him and Josh much. "One day," the old chief had

189

told them, "the furs will be gone. There will be no more pelts. When that day comes, the white man will go away, he will give us back our land."

Maybe that's why they help us, Ian thought. They believe in their hearts that we will go. They do not yet understand. But the eastern Indians who had been pushed off their land by the Americans knew. There were no more pelts in the Mohawk Valley, but there were no Mohawk either. They all had fled to Upper Canada and there, under the protection of the Crown, they survived, though not the way they once had.

And where do I belong? Ian had been forced to ask himself. There was terrible waste in the fur trade. He could comfort himself that his present assignment from the Hudson's Bay Company did not involve furs, but rather settlers. Farmers would, in time, give back productivity to the land, a productivity stolen by the pelt hunters. But settlers were also a double-edged sword. They would push the Indians farther west, they would take more Indian land.

Ian MacLean, who loved both the Indians and the land, was deeply moved by these conflicting concerns. He was of this land, born here and reared here. He had lived among the Indians and he understood both their fears and their dreams. "Walk softly on the land," he repeated aloud in a half whisper. "I shall," he promised the wind that blew out of the southwest. No, there was no way of stopping the tide of immigration to the Canadas or into the vast area of Rupert's Land. But we must keep some of it unspoiled, Ian thought. And the Indians must have their share.

The gates of the Hudson's Bay Company post and fort were unguarded, and Ian strode through them and toward the quarters of Mr. Hillier. He knocked on the door, and within a moment Hillier himself opened it.

"Good you're up!" Ian said, winking.

Hillier frowned. "I always get up with the sun and go to bed at ten. Except, of course, in winter, when the sun shines for only an hour or so."

"I wasn't serious," Ian explained. Hillier nodded and motioned him inside. The fire already was burning and Hillier was having morning tea.

"Tea?" he invited. "Or something stronger?"

"Rum," Ian answered, and sat down at the table, straddling the bench with his long legs. "I've had a good, brisk morning walk."

"I presume you've come to talk with the girl," Hillier observed. He poured some rum into a cup.

"I have," Ian replied. "Discussed it with Owen and he's prepared to stand by whatever I decide."

"Thought you'd already decided."

"I have, essentially. But I ought to meet her, speak with her. It's the least I can do."

"I'll call her," Hillier suggested, walking to the door at the far end of the room and passing through it into a long corridor. Ian could hear him whispering to someone.

"I've sent for her," Hillier explained as he returned. "Her name is Bonnie Campbell."

"Campbell?" Ian grimaced. Never since he could remember had anyone in his family spoken to a Campbell in friendship. And for Ian, so recently returned from his visit to Culloden Moor, the dastardly deeds of the Campbells against their fellow Highlanders were all too fresh in his mind.

Unkindly he thought, Yes, we'll send her home to Scotland. Who cares if she starves? But he did not express these feelings aloud. He just shook his head and said, "Macdonell must have loved shepherding Campbells down to the Red River!"

Hillier's face took on the expression of a little old schoolteacher bristling with morality. "Don't pass the sins of the fathers to the children," he cautioned

191

Ian. "She's quite nice, works hard, and had nothing to do with the Battle of Culloden."

Ian lifted the rum to his lips and took a long, satisfying sip. "The Campbells betrayed Scotland," he intoned.

"And now all the Highland chiefs betray her people! We're cast off our land for sheep!"

Ian whirled around to meet the deep blue eyes of the undeniably beautiful creature who stood in the doorway to the corridor. Her waist-length, chestnut-colored hair was held loosely by a red ribbon, and her eyes were a cornflower blue, clear and at this moment filled with disdain for him.

Ian smiled. Her feet were positioned a little apart, her hands were on her well-rounded hips, her lower lip was thrust a little outward. She looked for all the world like a young woman ready to do battle. "I take it you're Bonnie Campbell," Ian guessed, his eyes frankly admiring her.

"And you, I assume, are Mr. MacLean."

"Ian," he corrected her. Again she looked at him with a stony gaze.

"I'll call you Mr. MacLean," she said icily. "We wouldn't want the world to know that a MacLean and a Campbell were friendly."

Ian met her glare with amusement.

"Don't laugh at me!" Bonnie Campbell said sternly. "I'll not have it! Because if truth be known, Mr. MacLean, I've had enough from you and your kind."

She paused a moment and wiped a stray strand of wavy brown hair off her high forehead. "Except for Mr. Hillier, who's been most kind, I can't say my opinion of men is very high."

"Not all men are alike," Ian offered.

"You are quite right, I imagine. Nor, Mr. MacLean, are all Campbells alike!"

Ian felt his face grow red. He was about to counter when she continued, "But I expect you are like the men I don't like, Mr. MacLean. You have a most distinct look of lust in your eyes!"

"Lust?" Ian swallowed hard. She was right, of course. She was damn beautiful and he would have had to be dead not to lust after her. Or as old and prim as Hillier. Still, Ian had no intention of admitting his lust to this obviously hot-tempered little wench. "Lust?" he repeated. "After a Campbell? Not really."

An awkward silence fell over the room. Hillier had been sitting with his hands clenched. He eased himself up, teacup in hand. "I think I'll leave you two to talk," he said in a small voice as he all but fled the room.

"I'm told you are the person from whom I must obtain permission to join the expedition down to the Red River. I want to go, Mr. MacLean."

Her sudden shift of subject left Ian in the corner he now felt he had backed himself into. "It's out of the question," he snapped. "When we get to the Red River we'll be moving on to Pembina, where both groups of settlers will join up for the winter. You will have the same problem there that you had here. It's far better you go back to Scotland, being a single woman and all."

Bonnie Campbell stared at him. She did not burst into tears as she felt like doing. Instead, she stood stiffly and met Ian's comments with defiance. "I'll not go back to Scotland!" she shouted stubbornly. "Time has passed, more time will pass before we arrive. My parents may not have me back, but the others will accept me. From what I've heard of the Red River, Mr. MacLean, the settlers ought to have other things to worry about. Food and shelter, to name two."

Ian hardly could deny that. It was more the thought of a single woman on the long trek that bothered him.

"Who will carry your canoe on portages and paddle upstream? Who will build your fire at night and look after you? Can you carry your pack on the long portages? And when we get to the Red River, who will build a cabin for you, Miss Campbell? You are a woman and cannot do these things. You cannot hunt to provide your food! You can't survive without a male companion."

"I'll take care of myself, Mr. MacLean. And if I am as attractive as you seem to think, it should not take me long to find a suitable husband."

Ian scowled at her. But he couldn't maintain his scowl for very long. He remembered Glasgow and its starving inhabitants and was overcome by a wave of guilt. Without moving his lips, he swore.

"I'm going to be the scout," he said evenly. "I suppose I could take you with me, but you will have to promise to let me look after you."

"I can look after myself! I couldn't before, but I can now." Bonnie Campbell nearly spit out her words.

Ian stood up and walked over to her. She looked up at him defiantly. "You can come only if you agree to come with me and agree to allow me to look after you."

"I'll agree to that if you agree never to touch me."

"I wouldn't touch a Campbell woman with a ten-foot canoe paddle," Ian replied. "And you'd do well to be less arrogant!"

"Arrogant? You thickheaded Scots Highland Catholic bastard! You should not talk about arrogance!"

Hillier banged on the doorway. "Enough!" he shouted in a strained voice.

Bonnie took a step backward toward the door. "When shall we be leaving?" she queried.

"The eighth, early in the morning," Ian replied. "And Hillier, see that she brings a proper pack!"

Bonnie bit her lip and whirled around, disappearing down the corridor without pausing for an instant.

CHAPTER IX

September 1812

Fort George stood on the bluffs above the Niagara River. The walls of its stockade were constructed of thick, massive timbers and its huge gate, which opened outward, was reinforced with iron spikes. At the top of the stockade there were musket slits, and outside the stockade a waterless moat surrounded the fort and could be swept with cannon fire from the corner bastions.

Inside the fort's walls was a guardhouse; six bastions, one on each corner and two facing the river and the American settlements on the far shore; a building which served as the officers' quarters; another that served as the officers' kitchen; the artifactor's building, where the blacksmith and carpenter resided; the powder magazine; two ravelins for the storage of artillery; the sawpit; three blockhouses, where the troops were billeted; and a house where the officers slept. At full complement, the fort could house several thousand men.

The three large blockhouses were built for battle, not for comfort. The upper story of each overhung the lower floor, enabling men on the top floor to fire down on any enemy soldiers who might try to take shelter against the wall of the building. Like the outer wall of the fort, both the bottom floor and the top floor had musket slits along the entire perimeter.

In the winter the wind off the river howled in through the musket slits, and the soldiers covered themselves with heavy blankets or tried to stuff the slits with cloth.

Inside the blockhouses every available bit of floor space was taken up with row on row of double-decked beds measuring exactly five feet, ten inches long and three feet wide. Since the same beds were used by the officers, Josh MacLean could pity the taller enlisted men who served under him. At six feet, two inches, he had tried the various alternatives, one of which consisted of rolling himself into a ball, and another of which was allowing his feet to dangle over the side. But it was no use; the beds were not built to accommodate those above average height. At least, Josh thought, his bed in the officers' house had a proper mattress; the mattresses on the beds in the blockhouse were filled with straw. Moreover, the men had to store all their possessions in a small pack that could be suspended from a peg on the wall. Apart from the inconveniences of overcrowding, living conditions at Fort George were not bad. Laundry was done once a month, and the food rations were more than adequate. It was, to Josh's mind, an ideal fort. Though all the British forts and Hudson's Bay Company forts looked roughly the same from the outside, few were as comfortable, as well managed, and as self-contained as Fort George.

Built on the high ground, Fort George stood guard over the river channel and the growing town of Newark, which many of its inhabitants called Niagara-on-the-Lake. A winding dirt road followed the bluffs. It was intersected by a number of smaller lanes that led off to the rich farms beyond. A few miles from Niagara-on-the-Lake, but at the foot of the high bluffs that rose from the Niagara River gorge, was the village of Queenston, where the British maintained a small naval base. From Queenston, a road and several pathways wound their way upward toward the towering heights and intersected with the road that ran along the top of the bluffs.

No area could be more familiar to Josh MacLean. His parents, Will and Jenna MacLean, lived in the village of Queenston, and Lochiel was off the road that ran along the top of the bluffs. As a child, Josh had both walked and ridden the trails. He knew the woods around the Queenston heights so well he might have had personal names for the trees. Being at Fort George was like being at home for Josh MacLean.

As an officer, Josh MacLean was afforded a number of privileges he would not have had as a volunteer enlisted man. He was able to bunk at home when he was off duty, and he could visit Lochiel often.

"I think you ought to move up to Lochiel," he told his mother earnestly on his first visit home. They were in the pleasant, warm kitchen, and Jenna was preparing the evening meal. His father still was at the trading post down on the riverfront.

"Your father can't leave," Jenna answered, covering the pan in which the fish were frying. "And I'm not going anywhere without him."

Josh tapped on the table. "When Father is called by the militia, he'll have to go. Then you'll be alone here, and I don't like that. Neither does Father. There are a limited number of places the Americans can cross the river, and this is one of them."

"So they'll cross the river." Jenna plopped down a bowl of carrots on the table and sat down and began peeling them.

"If the Americans don't shoot at me, I'll invite them in for some nice, warm butter tarts and tea; and if they do shoot at me, I'll take down the musket and shoot back." She paused and looked up, sensing he was annoyed by her attitude. "Josh, when you live in a place you love, you do not pick up and run away and hide. Laura says they won't bother civilians anyway. Laura says we could be of great use if we all just watched and listened."

Laura Ingersoll Secord lived a few houses away. She was a transplanted Bostonian and a dedicated United Empire Loyalist. "I should simply die if I had to live under *their* disgusting Republic!" she would say. "There's no one left who is worth anything, you know. All the best people left. Only tobacco-chewing, lowbred ruffians remained. There is no culture left in America, no breeding, no charm."

"Laura doesn't know everything," Josh reminded his mother. "You actually are living in the path of a possible invasion. Father wants you to go to Lochiel, I want you to go to Lochiel."

Jenna shook her head. "I have a root cellar full of provisions and I have other provisions which are hidden. There's a secret passage out of the house and into the woods. Josh, I feel perfectly safe here and I intend to stay, that's all there is to it. Besides, I really don't think the Americans will attack."

"They are hopping mad that the British found out their Congress declared war before they did. They're furious over the loss of Fort Michilimackinac up on Lake Huron. The war is on, Mother. They will attack."

"I'm still not moving. Anyway, I think it's funny. Fancy not telling your own army you've declared war." Jenna laughed.

Josh made a motion of surrender to his mother. He ought to know by this time that she was willful and stubborn and that it would take more than his grim predictions to move her from her house.

"How are you feeling?" Jenna asked pointedly. It was one of her probes, Josh thought. She didn't want to ask, "Have you heard anything of Colleen?" or, "Have you gotten over Colleen?"

"I'm not distraught enough to put my body in front of an American bullet," Josh answered truthfully.

Jenna looked up wide-eyed. "I should hope not! What a thing to say!"

"But after this is over—the war, I mean—I intend to locate Colleen and find out everything there is to know."

Jenna merely nodded. Josh's stubbornness was much like her own. No, Jenna thought, Josh can't put Colleen out of his mind till he understands, and even then he might not be able to forget her.

"Dinner's almost ready," Jenna announced, changing the subject. "Josh, could you go down to the trading post and get your father?" She wiped her hands on her apron and then touched his sleeve. "Things will work out if they are meant to," she said softly. "Believe me, Josh. I know."

The colonists began their trek at dawn on September 9, just as Owen, Ian, and Mr. Hillier had planned it. It was a hazy morning, but the warmth of August still was in the air. The boats had all been loaded the night before and Ian assigned the passengers their places, set the schedules for rowing, and outlined the day's journey. As Miles Macdonell had done before them, Owen Keveney had provisions transported as far upriver as "The Rock," a spot where Hill River fell into the Hayes River. The first sixty miles, Ian well knew, was a good, steady pull upstream. Ian smiled to himself. His grandfather had traveled south down the Mississippi, going with the current because the major rivers on the other side of the border ran south. But the rivers here ran north into Hudson Bay, so the trip south to the Red River was upstream all the way. It would be easier to go south, Ian thought, if the rivers here ran south as they did in the United States.

The party would follow a long and difficult route

from one river to another and across a number of lakes. At times, all the cargo would have to be unloaded and carried, as would the large York boats. The birchbark canoes were nothing on such a portage, but the York boats were heavy and cumbersome. Moreover, although the men outnumbered the women, there were on the trek a number of "noneffectives," as Owen called them, women and children who could carry neither cargo nor boats.

Ian and Bonnie Campbell had left on the morning of the eighth so that Ian, who was to scout ahead of the colonists, would have the benefit of a one-day head start.

Bonnie Campbell, as instructed, appeared at the Nelson Encampment early in the morning. Clearly, the women colonists who had come to bid Ian goodbye found her appearance shocking.

Bonnie had braided her long chestnut hair, Indianstyle, and she clothed herself in men's buckskins. No woman among the colonists was dressed in such a fashion, but Ian had to admit to himself that her attire was infinitely more practical than a long skirt, slippers, and a bonnet would have been.

"I could take her," Owen suggested before they left, when he and Ian were alone for a moment. "It's quite clear that there's animosity between you two."

"She's a Campbell to the core," Ian answered. "Stubborn, arrogant, ill-tempered, and trying to be just what she is not, a self-sufficient person instead of a helpless young woman. But it's quite all right. I will take her south and after her first five portages I guarantee I'll have the woman prepared to take the first opportunity to return either to Upper Canada or to Scotland. She'll not want to be alone on the frontier after a few days in the bush."

"Oh, there's method in your madness." Owen raised an eyebrow. "Well, be sure you can handle

201

her. She seems a right stubborn young lass and, if I may say so, a bit unconventional."

"Once we're in the bush, she'll be quite dependent," Ian said with confidence, "and I think I can handle a slip of a girl."

Bonnie Campbell looked suspiciously at the long birchbark canoe as it bobbed in the water. Ian lifted his paddle and demonstrated how she should get in by laying the paddle across the gunnels.

"Here's a cushion for your knees," he said, throwing her a buckskin folded in half.

Bonnie climbed into the canoe awkwardly and took a kneeling position in the bow. She faced Ian, who was steadying the canoe at the stern. Her paddle was across the gunnels as Ian had instructed.

Ian cocked an eyebrow. "Miss Campbell, you are in the bow and I am in the stern and the way you are sitting we will be paddling against one another and going nowhere as rapidly as possible. As the captain of this ship, I would ask you to turn about, please."

Bonnie scowled at him. "I know that," she mumbled, then added in a louder voice, "and it wouldn't be the first time a Campbell and a MacLean were going against each other!"

"And going nowhere," Ian retorted. He restrained a laugh at the sight of Bonnie's ample backside weaving back and forth with the wobbling canoe as she turned toward the bow with the paddle stuck between her legs and caught on the ribs of the canoe. All he could hear was a series of muffled curses, "Mother of God . . . Who created these things? Woo . . . ouch!"

"It won't be the last time, Miss Campbell. You will be saying 'ouch' till you master the art of embarking and disembarking properly." Ian smiled at her back. "Are you comfortable, Miss Campbell?"

"Curses no, Mr. MacLean! But I could do without your mouth!"

"You'll get used to it," Ian said calmly as he pushed off. "Please hold your paddle as I showed you. Stroke, keep low, watch your right hand."

"Ouch!"

Ian did not laugh. "You scraped your hand on the gunnel, didn't you? I tried to warn you. Are you all right?" The canoe rocked ominously. "Be careful or you'll dump us!" Ian called out. "Stop squirming around up there!"

Ian could hear those on the shore laughing, and no doubt Bonnie could too. Gritting her teeth in pain, anger, and frustration, Bonnie turned around, blue eyes glaring and tears running down her cheeks. "I will not dump this canoe, but if this paddle were long enough, I would gladly swat you over your head! Not that it would do damage to your brain. That's nonexistent!"

"I am glad you know how to swat. That is what I would like you to do to the water—swat it." Ian watched and felt a little pride as she mastered the stroke. Her stubbornness would stand her in good stead, he thought. It was all a matter of directing it.

In no time Bonnie and Ian settled into a steady, unified stroke. Within the hour they were in the quiet wilderness, far away from the Nelson Encampment.

Several times, Ian felt his novice shift around in the bow. "Are you all right?" he called out.

"As all right as you!" she answered crisply in her thick Scots brogue.

"I have no desire to make a cripple out of you," Ian said. "Tomorrow we have long portages and you have a heavy pack to carry. If your legs are stiff, we can rest."

"Are your legs stiff? Are you tired?" she asked in a sarcastic tone which matched his.

"I was raised in a canoe," Ian answered. "I'm used to it."

"And you think a woman can't do it!" Bonnie twisted about and peered at him angrily.

"I know damn well a woman can do it," Ian answered. "My mother is one of the best canoeists around. She and my father canoed all the way from Illinois to the Niagara."

Bonnie Campbell fell silent for a while, and Ian, fully prepared to break her stubborn streak early in the trip, did not stop till late afternoon, when they had arrived at the spot he intended to make camp. Nevertheless, he stopped sooner than he would have had he not been with Bonnie Campbell. The next part of the journey took them past some incredibly beautiful vistas and he felt Bonnie Campbell ought to see it by daylight.

Ian guided the canoe to shore, and as it bobbed in shallow water, he said, "Miss Campbell, you may get out first."

Bonnie slowly raised herself, using her arms on either side of the canoe. She could not feel her legs from the knees down. She waited for a long minute and then felt the return of circulation. It came unpleasantly, like a thousand pins and needles all stabbing at once. Then came the feeling of weakness, of no control. Bonnie's face contorted with pain as she lifted herself onto the narrow cross support bar of the canoe that was directly behind her. She moved her ankles and again her face contorted in pain. Slowly, Bonnie put one leg over the side of the canoe and as she took her hand off the gunnel to lift out her other foot, the bow sprang upward with the weight of Ian in the stern and knocked her flat on her backside into shallow water and wet sand.

Ian shook his head as he scrambled out of the canoe. Without further thought, he bent down and picked her up, carrying her to a nearby flat rock still warm from the heat of the sun. Bonnie Campbell was quiet for once. She didn't struggle in his arms; in fact, she didn't respond in the slightest. Her pretty face was pale and she was visibly shaken.

Silently, Ian built a fire and placed the canoe on two rocks, building a small shelter. He arranged the bedrolls and began preparing strong tea.

"Come sit by the fire," he invited. "I have tea for you." He waited and watched as Bonnie painfully stood up and then limped over, collapsing in front of the fire, her legs extended to one side of her body. "I shouldn't have come so far today," Ian said with a tone of regret in his voice. "But you should have told me your legs hurt."

Bonnie stared at the sand. "I am fine, thank you, Mr. MacLean. I'm just a wee bit sore, but I don't want your sympathy."

Ian felt a twinge of admiration for her pride. He had not in fact intended her to suffer as she was doing now, nor the way she would suffer later, when she really began to stiffen up.

"You did well today, Miss Campbell." Ian poured her tea and crawled around to where she was sitting to give it to her. "Do not mistake honest consideration for sympathy, Miss Campbell."

Bonnie took the tea with a shaking hand.

"Let me rub your legs," Ian suggested. "Sometimes it will keep you from waking up stiff in the morning."

Bonnie lifted her eyes and Ian was surprised by her expression. She looked suspicious, but for the first time since they had met, not at all defiant.

He didn't wait for her answer, but instead rolled up her buckskins and began gently to massage her long, lovely, well-shaped calves and feet. He moved the muscles and rubbed slowly, feeling her relax and then, to his surprise, seeing her lean back and close her eyes. Then suddenly Bonnie raised her head and looked at him steadily. "Don't get any ideas, Mr. MacLean, or you will have a mouth full of my foot." Then she leaned back again and Ian, smiling to himself, finished his massage.

"It feels good," Bonnie finally admitted, wondering how many ladies allowed strange men to rub their legs.

Ian finished and sat up. He reached for his own pack and withdrew a skin of rum. He poured some into a mug and held it out. "It's even better than tea," he suggested. Then he poured himself some. Bonnie lifted it to her lips and took a drink, then made a face and coughed. Ian laughed lightly. "Not so much in one gulp," he advised.

"Are you going to get drunk?" Bonnie asked. Ian shook his head and smiled. "No," he assured her.

Ian waited for a few minutes, then extended his hand to her. "Can a Campbell and a MacLean make a truce for the rest of this trip?"

Bonnie blinked at him and then reached out, accepting his hand. "We could try," she allowed.

"You have very pretty legs," Ian praised. In the firelight he could see her face turn pink.

"You promised not to molest me. I shouldn't have let you touch me."

"I'm not going to molest you," Ian assured her. "How can you expect a man not to compliment you? Not all men who find you attractive are going to force themselves on you. And, I might add, you're headed for the Red River country. Women—white women—are practically nonexistent. You are going to find men forward and rude and sometimes dangerous."

Bonnie looked away from his eyes. "I know it's no place for a single woman. People keep saying I should marry. But I don't want to get married till I fall in love. I don't want to marry just so someone will take care of me and protect me."

Ian looked at her earnestly. "It is rough country. I appreciate your feelings, but you have to be realistic too."

"So do you," Bonnie replied quickly. "If I went back to Scotland I'd soon be selling my body on the street to get bread. No, Mr. MacLean, no matter. I could not be worse off in your Red River country. I don't think I could be worse off, no matter what."

"Perhaps not," Ian allowed.

Bonnie finished her rum and crawled over to the bedroll. She snuggled inside and turned over, curling herself into a ball. "Thank you for the compliment," she said to Ian just before closing her eyes.

In the morning, Bonnie Campbell was awakened by the mouth-watering smell of frying fish. She opened her eyes and stretched as much as she could under the roll of blankets.

"How are the legs?" Ian called out to her, seeing that she was awake.

"A little stiff, but not too bad." Bonnie stood up and looked down, smiling. "At least I can stand up straight on them."

"Breakfast's ready," Ian informed her. "Sleep well?"

"The sleep of the dead." Bonnie sat down and took the tin plate Ian extended. The fish smelled wonderful, and the hot brew Ian offered her tasted better than any she remembered. "Mmm, best fish I ever tasted. You know, that's the first night I ever slept on the ground."

"Food tastes better out-of-doors," Ian confirmed. "And you'll find you sleep better too, unless it's really cold."

Bonnie smiled shyly and Ian thought it was the first time he had seen her really smile. "We'll be changing rivers this morning. For a while we'll be passing between what's known as the clay banks. Some of them rise a hundred feet above the river and they're chalk-white—they're eerie and quite a beautiful sight. I thought you might like to pass that way during the daylight hours."

"Thank you," Bonnie answered.

Ian laughed boyishly and tossed his head back. "Think of it as a treat to compensate for yesterday and tomorrow."

"Tomorrow?" Bonnie queried. "Will it be a hard day?"

"Uphill," Ian said. "A lot of rapids and long, difficult portages."

Ian was true to his promise. The clay cliffs they passed between later that morning were quite astounding and not, Bonnie thought, unlike descriptions she had heard of the White Cliffs of Dover.

"They're magnificent," Bonnie said. "I've never seen anything so magnificent."

"Does it make you think of anything?" Ian asked.

"Oh, the setting for a hundred eerie folk stories . . . Scots tales."

Ian laughed heartily. "I've heard those tales, but of course the Campbells always are the villains."

"Not the way I tell them," Bonnie retorted without malice. "We have different endings."

Fort Niagara was identical to the British Fort George across the river. But obviously it was not as well run, James MacLean thought. If it had been, the running joke among the American troops would not have been that in order to get a decent meal one had to join the British army. The British and Canadians, on the other hand, were known to jest that in order to get a drink one had to join the American army. A few continentalists were known to hold their views only out of a desire to have both good food and strong drink available to them.

Nonetheless, James MacLean had settled down at Fort Niagara. "The only other decent officer in this man's army appears to be Winfield Scott!" James MacLean proclaimed to a selected few. But he did not proclaim it too loudly, since he did not want to make enemies of the officers from the northern states. He realized that the vast majority of them were either too old, too ill trained, or too inexperienced to lead men into battle. Still, he wanted political gain from the commission he had purchased, and it would not do to make out-and-out enemies of men who still curried favor in the Executive Mansion and with Congress. Not that James MacLean felt much but sheer disdain for the occupant of the Executive Mansion. Had Madison any guts at all, he would have had John Jacob Astor shot for treason. The shame of the British finding out the Americans had declared war before the Americans themselves were told was an outrage!

But naturally John Jacob Astor was not tried for treason. And the reason was all too obvious. Mr. Astor was capable of controlling more of Congress than the President. Thus Astor went absolutely free, claiming that the sorry incident was an accident. He simply shrugged the whole thing off and mumbled in his German accent, "The declaration of war was public. How was I to know Congress would take so long to tell the United States Army? Was I to know my messengers traveled faster than the mail?" The whole affair made James MacLean sick. "Six days from Washington to Montreal! Even if men could fly, that probably would be an all-time record for mail between the Canadas and the United States!"

Of course, James MacLean reasoned, it wouldn't have mattered much if the American Army had been told they were at war. Even today, over three months since the declaration of war, the American Army was undisciplined, badly equipped, disgracefully uniformed, and disorganized in the extreme.

Nevertheless, it did appear that something was about to happen. It was nearly the end of September, and James MacLean and Winfield Scott had been sent on a long trip to scout the river. Information was being gathered to help the American generals decide when and where to cross the Niagara.

"What do you think?" James MacLean queried.

Lieutenant Colonel Winfield Scott spoke with a typical Virginia accent, slow and refined, drawing out each word. But Winfield Scott was not the refined Virginian he appeared to be. He was not cut from the same ineffectual elite mold as George Washington, nor the intellectual mold of President Madison. If the truth be known, Scott was a mountain boy at heart, a lad raised with a musket over one shoulder and a cup for moonshine strapped to his belt. His air of refinement was carefully cultivated and used around Easterners and influential Southerners. At twenty-seven, Winfield Scott understood the U.S. Army. General Wadsworth would go home when this war was over, Mr. James MacLean would go back to his plantation, but he, Winfield Scott, would make the army his career. Because he intended to make it his career, he needed to make friends in high places, friends who could help him get the right promotions and the right assignments at the right time; friends who would see to it that America entered enough wars to keep her soldiers well paid and in practice.

War was important to the new nation, Scott believed. War brought glory to politicians, and war brought more territory. Like his friends, Clay and Calhoun, Winfield Scott believed in the destiny of the United States, and that destiny was to bring morality to lesser people. Countries to both the north and south would be annexed and thus benefit from the American way of life even if they were unready actually to become part of the new nation. He believed with all his heart that British North America should be the first territory annexed and that this war was merely a mopping-up operation left from the previous War of Independence. "Just stopped the last one too soon," Scott was fond of saying. Then he would add, "First the Canadas, then Mexico."

Winfield Scott scratched his head and looked up at James MacLean, who was twenty-two years his senior. MacLean was his inferior in terms of rank, but outside the army he was a man Scott might need sometime. Doubtless MacLean had purchased a commission in order to further his political aims. Nonetheless, Scott and MacLean got along well together, and in spite of the age difference, MacLean seemed to respect him.

"I would land my troops yonder in that little village, what's it called?" Winfield Scott ran his finger along the map. He had opened it up and laid it out on a large flat rock. "Ah, yes, Queenston. I would guess that from that village there must be a well-worn path up to the heights, and of course once we are on the heights we would have the advantage of the high ground."

James MacLean nodded. "Wonder who lives there?" He didn't expect an answer and he didn't get one. When he asked the question he was more than half wondering about two particular people. Ever since the army had assigned him to Fort Niagara he had fought to suppress his excitement, but his growing anticipation made it more difficult by the day.

This was the Niagara! This was the Thundergate of Jenna Macleod's stories. This is where Jenna had fled with his own twin brother, Will MacLean. It had been thirty-one years since the two of them had run

211

off, leaving him humiliated and tied up in the trading post down by the Mississippi River. James felt a burning hatred for Will. James felt it even though Will never had come back to claim his half of the family fortune. James hated him because Will had taken Jenna, and James MacLean never had forgotten Jenna Macleod. She was not a woman a man forgot.

James always had believed that Jenna really loved him and that if Will had not come home when he did, Jenna would have adjusted, would have married him, would have become the mistress of Skye, his sprawling, rich plantation outside Vidalia.

As it turned out, there was no mistress of Skye. James MacLean had bedded many women, but the only one who had borne him a child was his own sister, Maria.

After Will had stolen Jenna away, Maria seemed to return to near normalcy. She devoted herself to James, keeping house for him, cooking for him, and helping him accumulate the money to buy the needed slaves.

Then Maria had come to him and he had given in, though he hadn't intended to. She crawled silently into his bed early one morning before the cock crowed, urgently seeking his affection like some lost creature.

James MacLean was only too aware of his weaknesses. The warmth of her flesh, her quick caresses, the way she fell on him while he was between sleep and consciousness had combined to weaken his resolve and cause him to partake in their grievous sin.

Weeks and months passed and James, ashamed, sought to ignore his sister and avoid her whenever possible. Then her stomach swelled with child and James MacLean knew that their sin was to give issue.

During the nine months of pregnancy, Maria was like an animal. Her wild insanity returned and she frightened James so, he kept her locked up, a prisoner in their home. Maria ranted and raved, then held herself and rocked back and forth, moaning and speaking only to herself.

During the birth of Mason James, Maria had screamed continually, and after the birth, she turned her back to the wall, not even looking when the wet nurse took away the child.

James felt a sense of relief when the child seemed healthy and normal. He liked the child and was happy that the child looked like him rather than like Maria.

But there was no respite. The day after Mason James' birth, Maria rolled from her bed and ran head on into the wall, shrieking and pulling at her hair. "She's coming! This time she's coming!" Her eyes blazed with her madness and fear, her face grew so hideous that James shrank from the sight of her. The slaves called her a witch and a devil, so full of evil that it finally was killing her. At last, on the fourth nightmare day after Mason James' birth, Maria's womb opened up and she bled to death amid shrieks and curses.

It had been a dreadful experience, but in spite of Maria's madness, Mason James MacLean had grown into a healthy young man. He was too sensitive for his father's tastes, and too eccentric. But James MacLean could be glad of one thing: His fears about his son's sexual tastes appeared groundless. The latest letter from Mason James informed him that his wife, Colleen, had given birth to twins. And twins, as James MacLean well knew, ran in the family.

Still, he wondered how it would have been had he not lost Jenna. His mind drifted off again—lovely, redheaded Jenna with her flowing locks and her

213

milk-white skin. He thought now of the way her hard pink nipples and her white flesh looked in the moonlight, he remembered how she would cry out for him to satisfy her with an expression of pure passion on her face. Thoughts of Jenna sometimes came to him during the day, but more often they dominated his night fantasies. More nights than he could count, he had lain in bed massaging himself while thoughts of Jenna raced through his mind.

"Are you all right, MacLean?" Winfield Scott's voice cut through James MacLean's daydream.

"Yes," James quickly replied, pulling himself back to the here and now.

"Here, take the glass. You can see across the river. You actually can see people coming and going. You know, from what I hear, the inhabitants will welcome us. I hear they're anxious to be liberated."

James took the glass and looked through it. He focused on the dock down at the water's edge across the river. He moved the glass a bit to the left. A small lad was fishing in the river. He moved the glass to the right and lifted it slightly, focusing just above the dock. He focused on a woman. She was looking out across the river, almost as if she were looking directly at him.

Her long red-gold hair was gathered up and framed her beautiful face. But there was no mistaking that face! It was Jenna! James MacLean whispered her name under his breath.

"What?" Scott asked, turning toward him.

"Nothing," James said, hardly even aware that Scott was next to him. "They look so close, are you certain they can't see us?"

"Not unless they are observing us through a ship's glass too," Scott replied.

James MacLean couldn't move. He felt rooted to the spot. Jenna moved slightly and he saw her put her arm around the child. Could a child so young be hers? She was the same age as he, forty-nine. But, he acknowledged, she looked ten years younger. Her figure still was outstanding, her face still beautiful. He yearned to fly across the river and confront her. He yearned to rip the clothes from her body and once again have her subservient beneath him.

"Well, what do you think?" Scott said in an irritated voice.

James dropped the glass slightly and shook his head. He handed back the glass to Scott and forced himself to stand up straight. "Queenston seems an ideal place to land," he confirmed, trying not to reveal any of his anxiety. "Absolutely ideal."

"It's really lovely here," Bonnie said as she leaned back and away from the fire. Across the river a jagged, rocky bluff rose up nearly a hundred feet. They had made camp on a grassy rise facing the river and the opposite bluff. Behind them, dense brush obscured the rise and fall of gentle hills.

"We'll be on the prairie soon," Ian told her. He had torn off a long piece of grass and was sucking on it, like a boy. "It's flat there, so flat you can see for a hundred miles on a clear day."

"I'll be glad to be somewhere," Bonnie joked. "I'd like a hot bath."

Ian stood up and stretched. It was dark and only the shadow of the bluff was evident by the moonlight. The fire crackled as the duck he had shot earlier in the day roasted.

"Nature calls," he said. "I'll be back in a few minutes."

Bonnie smiled as he ambled off into the brush. She moved to the other side of the fire and sat down, crossing her legs Indian fashion and holding her hands to warm them over the fire. Softly she began to sing to herself in Gaelic.

She stopped short for an instant and listened. It

was Ian. That devil, she thought. We may have a truce, but he's still trying to frighten me. Well, I won't be frightened. He's just trying to sneak up on me and go "Boo!" Bonnie ignored the soft sound of the footsteps behind her and continued to sing, this time more loudly. The footsteps came closer. I will not acknowledge him, she thought proudly. No matter what silly thing he does, I will not turn around and I will not jump. Just let his little joke fall flat!

Then he nudged her none too gently in the back. Bonnie still did not turn, but instead stared straight ahead into the fire. "You think you're so smart," Bonnie said aloud. "Well, Mr. MacLean, it will take more than having you sneak up behind me in the dark to frighten me. I'm a Campbell and we Campbells don't frighten easily. But I do hope you're going to apologize. It may be good boyish sport, but it really isn't very nice to go around deliberately trying to scare women." She paused and smiled to herself. "Well?" she said more sharply as she felt him nudge her again.

"Don't move! Don't move a muscle!"

Bonnie jerked her head up and opened her mouth. Ian was standing on the other side of the fire, on the edge of the bush. If he was there, what was in back of her?

"Don't move!" Ian repeated his instructions more calmly.

"Wha-a-at?" Bonnie began to shake, then unable to stand it an instant longer, she whipped around to come face to face with a small-eyed, pointy-nosed black bear. "Oh! My God!" She let out a piercing scream and the bear jumped backward and turned, loping off into the brush.

Bonnie in turn ran toward Ian and fell into his arms. Then, almost as if she remembered some promise she had made herself, she straightened up and excused herself. "I'm sorry. It frightened me."

216

"Frightened you. I heard you talking to it. Now, didn't I tell you it wasn't safe to talk to strangers?"

"You're making fun of me again!" Bonnie looked into his face. "It's not funny. It might have killed me."

But Ian was convulsed by laughter. "You thought it was me! My God, you Campbells are a suspicious lot!"

Bonnie stomped her foot on the ground and returned to the fire, sitting a little sideways so she could see behind her. Then she smiled slightly. "I suppose it is funny," she allowed. "But I should have known it wasn't you. He was quite gentle."

CHAPTER X

October 13, 1812

For a few days Major General Isaac Brock had asked the same question over and over: "When and where?" It was a question Josh MacLean would have liked to be able to answer with some assurance, but in all honesty he could do no better than venture an educated guess.

Brock had divided his major firepower and a large number of men into three groups. One group of men and arms was located at Fort Erie, another at Chippewa above the falls, where a crossing would be the easiest, and the third, of course, at Fort George.

Two flank companies of the 49th Foot and an equal number of the Lincoln Militia were positioned in and around Queenston. One reasonably large cannon was skillfully hidden on the north slope leading from the village of Queenston to the heights above. It had been placed below a crest so that it could not be seen by the American guns at Lewiston across the river. Another, larger gun, manned by Solomon Vrooman, was placed farther downriver on a point. That gun too was hidden.

Josh thought back to the night of October 9, the night that gave away the intentions of the American commanders.

Lieutenant Jesse D. Elliott of the United States Navy had managed to knock two British vessels out of combat. One, the *Caledonia*, which had been used to secure Fort Michilimackinac a few months earlier, had been towed to captivity by the Americans and the other, a larger vessel called the *Detroit*, had run aground trying to escape. But the crew of the *Detroit* had acted with haste and when the good ship was grounded, they burned her rather than allow her to be captured by the Americans.

Everyone on both sides had to admit that the small American Navy had done its job well. But Josh and his British compatriots under Brock's command still could rejoice. The U.S. Army, commanded by Major General Van Rensselaer, had blundered badly and managed to undo most if not all of the U.S. Navy's accomplishments.

On the night of October 10, Van Rensselaer had tried to seize the advantage given him by the naval victory to cross the river, departing from Lewiston. But his men were inexperienced and had not drilled in the boats. Moreover, only after they had loaded themselves into the bobbing vessels had they discovered that they had no oars. Before they could scramble ashore, inclement weather in the form of a heavy, cold rain drenched one and all, and the entire would-be attack force retreated back to camp, mumbling and cursing.

This ill-organized attack gave further credence to Josh's belief that the next attack would be at Queenston. But General Brock was not entirely convinced. On the one hand, Brock was perfectly aware of the importance of Queenston and the heights above. He knew that from the vantage point of the heights it was possible to control the traffic on the Niagara River; losing Queenston and the heights might well mean losing all of Upper Canada eventually. On the other hand, he believed that the Americans might launch their major attack at Fort George, using their batteries at Fort Niagara, across the river, for support. Thus Brock and his staff remained at Fort George and waited like poised runners on their marks, ready to respond wherever the attack occurred.

Several peaceful days after the abortive American attempt to attack from Lewiston, Josh MacLean began to unwind and to think that perhaps the Americans would not attack at all, at least not until next summer, when their forces might be stronger.

On the night of October 13, he slept nestled in his mattress and covered with a large quilt he had brought from home. Since his aunts had made it, it was long enough to accommodate his height. As usual, one leg was extended and hung over the side of his bunk. He slept with his hand on his genitals, much the way young boys sleep.

Colleen's long, sinuous legs were wrapped around him and he was still removing the clothing from her body, slowly, piece by piece. Then miraculously, as can happen only in a dream, she stood in front of him nude and holding out her arms. Her long, jet-black hair cascaded over her white shoulders and caressed the rosy tips of her perfect breasts. Her blue eyes invited him to grasp her, to pull her to him. She smiled seductively and he pulled her on top of him, then pushed up into her as she spread her legs, straddling him. Josh exploded at the same time that the room rocked and his bunk shook suddenly. Josh snapped open his eyes, aware of the dampness from his all-too-vivid dream and then of cannon fire from across the river.

He swung his long legs over the side of the bunk and grappled for his clothes. "I hear cannon!" he shouted. "We're being fired on!" Josh pulled on his socks and his pants, followed by his heavy shirt, jacket, and boots. In the dark his fellow officers cursed and mumbled as they scrambled from the their beds.

Josh stumbled through the officers' quarters in the dark, reaching the center room with difficulty. There he grabbed the huge tin gong and began beating it furiously. It sounded the alarm that woke the enlisted men in the blockhouse, should there be some who were not already awake.

Somewhere in the darkness that still enveloped the fort's drill yard and buildings he heard the night watch officer shouting at the top of his lungs: "The Americans are coming! The Americans are coming! Put out the signal lanterns! They're attacking at Queenston!"

Jenna had been curled up in a tight little ball, her head resting on her arm, her body curved into Will's body. The first cannon fire from across the river shook the entire house and lit up the bedroom as if it were broad daylight.

Will literally jumped from the bed, shaking Jenna. "Wake up! Wake up!"

Jenna opened her eyes and looked about just as another burst of cannon fire shook the house. "Lord," she whispered, "they do make a lot of noise!"

"Get up and get dressed in something warm. Hurry!" Jenna scrambled from the bed and put on her shoes and a heavy wool dress. The cannon fire continued. Jenna peered out the window. She could see a fire down by the shore and hear the sound of villagers screaming and running. Will joined her at the window.

"Good thing this house is set against the hill," he observed. "Looks as if a couple of houses have been hit."

"The ones right down by the shore," Jenna said. "I'll have to set up something downstairs, invite people in."

They hurried down the stairs together. As they reached the kitchen, another burst of cannon shook the house. One of Jenna's lovely china plates fell from the cupboard and broke, sending chips in all directions. Jenna stamped her foot. "Oh, damn! Now see what those stupid Americans have done!"

Will was loading his musket. "I have to round up the local militia," he said. "I doubt that civilians are in any danger, mind you, but you know where the pistol is."

"But we must get those people whose houses have been hit in here," Jenna replied.

"I really wish you'd go up to Lochiel," Will pressed. "I could take you up to the top of the bluffs now and you could ride on from there."

"Well, I don't want to go to Lochiel," Jenna answered with determination. "I wouldn't miss this for the world. We have a cellar if need be, and besides, I'm mad enough about that plate to strangle the gunner bare-handed!"

Will suppressed a smile. Jenna was as headstrong now as when she was younger and, he thought, every bit as pretty.

It was a little after three in the morning, still as black as pitch outside and cold and drizzly to boot, Josh noted. He could see the soft orange glow of the cannon fire off in the distance. He felt tense, wondering if his mother and father were all right.

"MacLean! Get your mount and accompany the general and his aides." The order came out of the darkness, and Josh just turned and headed for the stables. He found that General Brock and his aides already were mounted. The general's horse, Alfred, seemed skittish.

"Ready, Macdonell? Ready, MacLean?"

Josh nodded. Macdonell was John Macdonell, a relative of Red George and of Miles as well. The entire area was populated with Macdonells. The entire clan had immigrated to Upper Canada.

John Macdonell was struggling with his sword and coat while at the same time trying to mount. "MacLean! Come along! Macdonell will catch up with us!"

Brock was an anxious man. "I have to find out if this is the main attack or merely a diversion!" Josh felt like answering the question, but he knew Brock would not take his word for it.

The two of them galloped off into the mist. It was a seven-mile ride to Queenston.

"You lead the way, MacLean!" Brock bellowed, allowing Josh to take the lead.

It is my backyard, Josh thought. I've lived here all my life, I helped clear the land for this road. "Lanterns ahead!" Josh called back to Brock. "When we're closer I'll ask for identification," he added.

Josh waited a few seconds as the lanterns grew closer.

"Who goes?" he called out into the darkness.

"Militia!" His father's voice rang back.

"Only the rest of my family," Josh joked as he turned back to Brock. In seconds Brock and Josh MacLean were among the lantern-bearing militia. Will MacLean rode next to the militia's commander, John Robinson.

"Is our house all right?" Josh asked. "Has Mother gone to Lochiel?"

"When I left, the house was fine. It's pretty far back, out of the line of cannon fire, it seems. As for your mother, no, she will not go to Lochiel. She's waiting with a musket to kill the man who fired the cannon because he broke her best china plate!" There was a roar of laughter from the men in the militia, many of whom were uncles and cousins of Josh and all of whom knew the fiery Jenna MacLean.

"God pity the man!" someone mumbled.

"At least the last thing he'll see will be a pretty face," another quipped.

223

"Carry on!" Brock advised the York Militia with a wave of his plumed hat. Josh, Brock and the militia rode together into the early-morning light. They began to encounter a long line of wounded American prisoners marching toward Fort George.

"Pinned down by the redan gun as they landed, sir," the young officer in charge of them reported. "They got out of their boats and couldn't go anywhere so they surrendered."

"Good show!" Brock enthused. "Take them back to Fort George!" He paused. "And carry back this message like a good chap. Tell General Sheaffe to bring as much of the garrison as possible. Tell him this is the main attack. I have no doubt about it now."

Down on the shore, not far from the village of Queenston, the American landing party was flat out, having sought shelter wherever possible. The houses of the village were in sight, but the village itself was not the objective; rather, the heights were. The hill that rose to the heights was steep and wooded, and somewhere, hidden on the hill, was the redan gun that was doing so much damage to the American landing parties as they clambered out of their boats to establish a beachhead.

General Van Rensselaer's brother, Colonel Solomon Van Rensselaer, was writhing in agony, having been hit some five times during the landing. Apart from the severely wounded Van Rensselaer, not one American commander had made it to the Canadian side of the river. Captain Wool of the U.S. 13th Infantry was the ranking officer. Being better acquainted with the territory than any of the other American regulars, he knew the winding path that led to the redan gun.

Captain Wool leaned over Solomon Van Rensselaer. "I grew up in this area, sir. I think I know how to get at that gun."

Van Rensselaer nodded. A trickle of blood ran out of the corner of his mouth. "Go to it," he ordered, breathing heavily.

On the heights, far above the desperate Americans, Josh rode next to Brock. Four hours had passed since the first cannon fire directed at the village of Queenston. It now was 7:00 A.M. and though it still was cloudy, the eastern sky was beginning to lighten up.

"You're silent," Brock said, looking at Josh.

"Thinking," Josh said abstractedly. His eyes scanned the dense brush. It was difficult geographically both for defense and offense. It was steep, heavily wooded, rugged. A great deal depended on knowledge of the terrain, more than most people would care to admit. "I suggest we take the far path, ride down to Queenston, and check on the 49th Foot, see how they're doing."

They turned their horses, heading for the far path that led down the steep hill and into Queenston. When at last they reached level ground, they rode into the village at a full gallop and were greeted by the boisterous cheers of the 49th Foot. Those Americans who had landed were in the woods on the other side of the village and most were unable to move owing to the redan gun and the sharpshooters scattered on the higher ground. Nonetheless, they had the woods to hide their movements. "Knowledge of the terrain," Josh whispered. The thought haunted him. The far path was well fortified and guarded by the 49th Foot. The other path, the one that led to the redan gun, was not well known . . . but it would be known to anyone who had ever lived in the village.

Brock was giving orders to John Macdonell to

225

bring the rest of the 49th down from the heights to support the Grenadiers. Then the general turned away for a moment and looked up at the heights. "There aren't that many who got ashore and into the woods," he said, rubbing his chin. "They couldn't get up that incline. C'mon, MacLean, let's take the path up and have a look at the redan gun."

Josh followed as Brock boldly led. The two guided their horses up the steep incline along a narrow, rock-strewn path. Josh glanced upward, toward the heights. The bushes were leafless, but in the early-morning light they were shrouded in low-lying fog. The rocks along the edge of the heights jutted outward. Josh felt a moment of anxiety as they approached the redan gun from one side. "Sir, I . . ."

Josh did not finish his sentence. Major General Brock had turned and was looking out on the panoramic scene offered from the vantage of the ledge on which the redan gun was positioned. It was a long strip of slanting land, a level space roughly halfway between the river below and the highest promontory above. When climbing as a boy, how often had Josh MacLean stopped on this strip of land to rest. It offered a fine view. He and Brock both could see the smoke from the eighteen-pound cannon firing from the point across the river at Fort Niagara. In the water, they could see American boats bobbing up and down and, on the opposite shore, they could make out the lines of troops waiting to cross the river and relieve their comrades on the Canadian side.

"Sir," Josh insisted, "some of those boats could easily have landed. Americans may be scaling these heights now."

Brock laughed. "Oh, I hardly think so. The path is hidden and rugged, the light is simply dreadful."

Brock squeezed Alfred with his legs, urging the animal toward the redan gun. The redan on which the gun was placed was reasonably wide, and the side of the hill above overhung the weapon slightly.

The smell of cedar was strong in the early-morning air. Many of the tall birch trees had lost their leaves, but most of the smaller trees and all of the shrubs on the bluffs still had their foliage. A bush to Josh's left had all its bright red leaves. The color of blood, Josh thought. Then he erased the image, thinking quickly of something else. "Never think of dying or of death before battle," his father had told him once.

Brock had left Josh and gone on up to the artillerymen manning the redan gun. "Good work!" he said in a loud voice. "You've kept the enemy at bay!"

Josh had been looking upward when a special feeling came over him. It was a feeling he had experienced often in his life, the feeling of being watched. It was, he reckoned, a kind of Indian sixth sense, something he had developed from often being alone in the woods, some kind of strange instinct that was well developed in those who had trained him as a woodsman. As surely as he stood where he did, Josh MacLean felt eyes on him—unfriendly eyes.

Then Josh caught a hint of movement from the corner of his eye. He let out a warning cry and dropped behind the brush almost at the same second as the first shots crackled through the air. "The Americans did scale the heights! They're coming down on us!" he cried.

Brock snapped his head around. His face momentarily bore the same stunned expression as that of the frightened gunners.

"Spike that gun!" Josh ordered. "Get the spike into the touchhole, render her useless!" A horrible vision of the redan gun being turned on the helpless village of Queenston below ripped across his mind. He took a deep breath when the gun fell silent. He prayed it had been properly spiked.

227

Josh turned in time to see the Americans swarming down the hill, yelling as they came toward the redan gun.

Josh shouldered his musket and fired. He saw the Americans who were within range scramble for cover. They had not expected a sharpshooter to be guarding the redan gun. He heard Brock ordering his men down the hill and into the tiny village of Queenston.

Josh dismounted and slapped his horse. The sound of firing so close had spooked the animal in any case. He slapped her again. "Go home, girl," he ordered, knowing that if and when he got back down the hill, his horse would be waiting.

From that moment on, Josh tried to move and provide cover fire for Brock and the gunners at the same time. He was relieved when he saw them disappear into the woods. But now the Americans were close, too close.

"It's cool," Bonnie Campbell observed. They were on a large lake, and Ian was keeping the canoe close to the shoreline. In the past week the scenery had changed radically. They had passed from the northern rugged desolation of Rupert's Land to the low, rolling plains that characterized the prairie. Ian was right, Bonnie thought. You could see for a hundred miles. There was no forest here, no fir trees, and no cedar. There were only a few poplars along the edges of the lakes and rivers, but otherwise nothing save low bushes and grassland. In some places the grass was almost as tall as Bonnie Campbell herself, and in October it was brown and brittle, preparing to lie down under the snow of winter and sleep. But to Bonnie Campbell, the most striking feature of the prairie was the wind. It howled and wailed a funeral dirge for the summer past and acted as a harbinger for the coming winter.

"There's nothing to stop the wind," Ian told her. "It sweeps across the prairie till it beats itself into a frenzy against the base of the great mountains."

Out on the prairie, Bonnie Campbell could not even imagine mountains. From horizon to horizon the land was like a table, punctuated only by small rises and tiny dips where a river or a lake wound its way through the land.

"Ayi! Ayi! Ayi!" Bonnie Campbell stiffened in sudden fright at the unexpected sound. She gripped her canoe paddle more as a weapon than as means of locomotion. Her eyes traveled the shore, following the ungodly sound.

Then, to her surprise, Ian returned the cry in kind. "Stop paddling," he told her. "They're métis. We'll beach the canoe."

Ian guided the canoe to shore, jumped out, and pulled the canoe aground. Then he helped Bonnie out, offering her his hand. Over the rise, a large group of men on horseback appeared, men such as Bonnie Campbell never had seen.

There were nine of them in all. They had shoulder-length hair, wild, bearded faces, and were unkempt and uncombed. Their skin was copper-colored and their eyes were bright like shiny shoe buttons, set into angular faces with high cheekbones. They dressed in buckskins like Bonnie and Ian, but they wore colorful head scarves, wild hats with tall feathers, bright red and orange sashes. They looked a little like Indians to Bonnie, but also a little like white men. They sat proudly on their horses, as if they had been born on them. They all displayed weapons, long muskets and glittering knives that were partially exposed and unsheathed.

They eyed Bonnie Campbell with long looks that ranged from curiosity to undisguised lechery. So bold were their looks that a chill of apprehension ran down her spine. These men seemed somehow uncivilized to her and they were nine while she and Ian were only two.

"Ian MacLean, scout for Owen Keveney?" one of the men asked in French.

"*Oui,*" Ian answered. "Headed for the settlement at the Forks."

"Miles Macdonell took the entire party to winter at Pembina. You go to Pembina too, we'll send back messages to Keveney."

Ian nodded and waved his hand. Then one of the men moved his horse closer to Bonnie Campbell and, leaning over, poked her in the ribs as if she were a sheep and he were trying to determine her readiness for slaughter. She jumped slightly and scowled at him.

"Nice squaw," the man said and laughed, then let out an ungodly whoop and a loud holler. The others followed his lead. To Bonnie it seemed somehow like a round of applause.

"My squaw," Ian answered cheerfully.

"I am not your squaw!" Bonnie snapped. Ian turned to her still smiling, and he patted her hair with a long, loving stroke. "Shut up, my dear," he said without breaking the expression on his face. "After all, my sweet, if you are not my squaw, they might decide to make you their squaw. Fortunately, love, they do not speak English well enough to follow this conversation. Smile at me, edge a little closer."

Bonnie's expression went from outrage to fear to resigned cooperation. "Yes, my darling," she said through her own clenched teeth.

Ian circled her waist with his arm, giving her a little squeeze. "We'll be heading for Pembina," Ian said to the riders. Without another word, the métis horsemen, who rode with only a blanket for a saddle, turned their animals and galloped off. With another whoop and holler, their guns hoisted in the air, they

230

turned and waved a farewell. To Bonnie it seemed they were hardly holding onto their horses at all.

"Métis," Ian explained. "French métis. There are Scots métis too."

Bonnie frowned. "What are métis?"

"Years and years ago," Ian explained, "French *voyageurs* and Scots *voyageurs* traveled west to this country to explore, and in search of furs. There were no women, so they married Indian women. Their children are the métis—the Burnt Wood People. Some call them the People of the Buffalo. They are the finest horsemen in the world and they live off the buffalo."

"They're like wild men!" Bonnie said.

Ian laughed. "No," he corrected. "They speak French, sometimes a little English, always the Indian tongue of their mothers. They're not wild. They have their own code, it's different from ours, but it exists and it's enforced. Many of the métis are Catholics, devout Catholics. They do consider the Indians their blood brothers. The métis are a new race."

"Well, they seem wild," Bonnie argued, "and a little frightening."

"Until Miles arrived in August, there was only one white woman west of Upper Canada. You're an unusual sight, and frankly I ought to be angry with you. Pride or no pride, you must try to follow my lead. You don't understand this country, its people, or its customs. Please, don't be so ready to judge."

"Next you'll be threatening to spank me," Bonnie said mockingly.

Ian shook his head. "Spanking might be all right for small children, but you are a woman. In fact, you're a beautiful woman and I suspect an intelligent woman beneath your bad temper and stubbornness. I have no need to tame you, Bonnie Campbell. This land will tame you."

231

"Ian MacLean, you are insufferable! You have a Highland ego as big as this prairie!"

"We have a truce," he reminded her. "We also have a long trip."

Bonnie climbed back into the canoe with all the expertise she had gained over the past weeks. She took up her position in the bow of the canoe and dipped her paddle into the water as Ian pushed them off into the lake. I can feel his eyes on my back, she thought, as if they were boring straight through me. The thought caused her face to glow a little, and a feeling of warmth filled her. So Mr. Ian MacLean thought she was beautiful and intelligent. Bonnie Campbell would not admit it, but the knowledge pleased her.

Up on the heights, Captain Wool's men charged down the hill hooting and yelling. Captian Wool was immensely pleased with his sneak attack on the redan gun from above.

"Great balls of fire!" he exclaimed joyfully, "we did it!"

"They've spiked the gun!" one of the Americans wailed. "Shit! She's spiked good, useless!" Wool shook his head and looked up at the heights behind him. Nothing could stop the Canadians from doing what he had just done. They could climb the far path, walk along the top for some distance, and swoop down on the redan. "I'll need reinforcements on the top of the heights as well as down here if we hope to hold this position," he said aloud.

Josh had remained behind long enough to recognize Captain Wool as a person who once had lived in the village of Queenston, a man whose family had moved away some years ago. That's how they scaled the heights, Josh thought. Wool knew the terrain.

After making that discovery, Josh had eased off

232

and away, prowling down the hillside as rapidly and as quietly as possible. When he reached the bottom of the far path, he burst into a full run.

At the far end of the village of Queenston, Josh found Brock organizing the 49th Regiment together with the tired and somewhat dazed remnants of the Lincoln Militia.

Josh shook his head and moved in among the 49th and the Lincoln, looking for his father. When at last he found him, they embraced silently, then simply stood looking into each other's faces for a second before they spoke.

"Mother?" Josh inquired.

"Your mother has set up a temporary hospital in the living room," Will replied. "Laura Secord is with her, though she's quite upset because her husband is badly wounded."

"We're going to spend the day running up and down that damn hill," Josh observed. "We have to take back the redan gun before the Americans can consolidate their position."

"I'm glad to see you've taken off your uniform jacket," Will said and smiled. "Damn dumb thing to send men out to fight in."

"I tore it coming down the hill, but I would have taken it off anyway," Josh said and laughed.

"Well, you've got more brains than your commander," Will said under his breath. He didn't really care for General Brock and never made any bones about it. "Just look at that," he added, shaking his head in mild disgust.

Major General Brock was perched dramatically on Alfred. His run down the hill had neither mussed his clothing nor shattered his confidence. He wore a stylish cocked hat, a bright red coat, gold epaulettes, and a colorful scarf given to him by the great Indian Chief Tecumseh after the capture of Detroit.

233

To one side an army artist sketched General Brock's picture, while on the other side a young lad brushed Alfred's hindquarter.

"I shall return!" Brock said theatrically. "The redan gun must be retaken! The heights must be retaken!"

"You're right," Josh said to his father. "He's a perfect target in that getup."

"Couldn't be better if he had a circle painted on his back," Will added.

Josh reached out and clasped his father's hand. "I'll have to rejoin Brock now," he said softly. "Take care."

"You take care," Will said, smiling. "Keep your head down."

It was an old family joke, and Josh laughed and waved as he walked toward General Brock. Josh and Ian both had been gangling teens, forever banging their heads on the low doorways of the house. "You'll be fine when you learn to keep your head down," Will would tell them.

Josh made his way to Brock's side. They were two hundred in strength as they moved off toward the heights. The Americans were not at full strength, but now they did have the high ground.

"Classic," Josh mumbled under his breath. The militia, experienced men all, crawled up the hill almost silently, taking cover in the brush, moving like the Indians. The British regulars were hopeless. They walked upright, making a great deal of noise, so much noise that Josh half expected them to break into song at any moment.

"Keep your heads down!" Josh cautioned them just as his father had jokingly cautioned him.

Overhead, bullets whistled though the trees, often just missing their fleshy targets.

"Damned Yankee sharpshooters," Josh whispered. He had just said it when Brock let out a cry.

"You've been hit!" Josh was at his side in one long step.

But General Brock only shook his head vigorously. He had taken off the scarf that Tecumseh had given him at Detroit and tightly wrapped it around his wrist. "It's nothing, nothing!"

Fear engulfed many of the 49th and they began to fall back, taking shelter where they could. Brock called out, "Fight on! We must take the redan!" Josh was behind Brock, who still was mounted on Alfred. He saw Brock's chest heave, then he saw him go entirely limp and slump, falling from the saddle. Josh ran and knelt at Brock's side.

"He's been hit!" Josh signaled for some men. Again the Americans were behind them. Josh wiped Brock's brow. "Take him back down the hill," Josh instructed the several men who had come to help. He's dead, Josh thought, there's no doubt about it. The men carried the limp form of General Brock away and Josh looked up to see a welcome sight. It was Lieutenant Colonel John Macdonell, Brock's aide-de-camp, with two flank companies of the York Militia. Somewhere near the back of the advancing column a bagpipe wailed and Josh MacLean, waiting no longer, ran to join Macdonell and his men, who were primarily Scots. Behind him, Josh could hear the others following, his father surely among them.

Josh reached Macdonell. "Sir, General Brock is dead."

John Macdonell had been Brock's aide-de-camp for some time and he understood the man. He blinked disbelievingly for a moment, then straightening up, he announced, "Well, we must avenge him then."

"Indian-style?" Josh asked, hoping they would abandon this absurd formality that was causing unnecessary loss of life.

Macdonell nodded. "Indian-style," he confirmed.

* * *

235

Unpleasant hours passed, hours filled with the smell of smoke, the hiss of bullets, the cries of wounded men, and the jolting sound of cannon in the distance. Lieutenant Colonel Winfield Scott and Lieutenant James MacLean looked at the badly wounded Captain Wool. The Canadians and the British had retaken the redan gun, and Winfield Scott had led the Americans in taking it back again. Now the Canadians and the British had retreated to the gun down on the point, which was manned by Vrooman and his men. There the Canadians and the British seemed to be waiting for reinforcements from Fort George.

At one point General Van Rensselaer had come by to visit the position held. Then he had withdrawn and left Brigadier General William Wadsworth in charge.

General Wadsworth was not a choice that pleased either Winfield Scott or James MacLean, both of whom hoped for a decisive victory. And James MacLean would have added to that the opportunity to search the houses of Queenston and to find Jenna.

As misfortune would have it, neither James MacLean nor any American had gotten near the little village.

"I do not understand, General Wadsworth, I do not understand at all," Winfield Scott was saying. For once he had abandoned his slow speech, and he spoke crisply and somewhat angrily. He had retaken the heights and rumor had it that John Macdonell was severely if not fatally wounded and that General Brock was dead. Now the same spies brought information that the York Militia was on its way from Fort George. But General Wadsworth was not planning the defense for the heights, nor was he encouraging more American troops to cross the river in order to take advantage of the victory already achieved. No, Wadsworth was doing none of these things and Winfield Scott did not understand.

"Our troops should be consolidating our position!" Scott said firmly.

"Indeed!" shouted James MacLean.

Wadsworth looked unmoved. "You gentlemen are from the South. You, Scott, are regular army, a career man. Those men aren't!" He pointed off across the river where more Americans waited. "They've been conscripted and, frankly, they want to go home."

"Go home! In the face of victory! They're in the middle of a decisive battle, they're winning! What the hell do you mean, they want to go home?" Scott's voice thundered through the trees. He was torn between anger and total disbelief. "No Virginian would do such a thing! It wouldn't even cross his mind!"

"They have a legal right," Wadsworth intoned.

"Legal right?" James MacLean shot back. "They should be shot for treason!" He was shaking slightly. If the reinforcements didn't come across the river, they would all be taken prisoner when the British and Canadian reinforcements arrived.

"Just what kind of legal rights do these New York pig farmers think they have?" James MacLean asked, spitting out the words.

"According to the terms of their conscription, they are legally bound only to defend the United States. They say that no one has invaded the United States, that by crossing the river they are fighting on foreign soil and that is not defense, but offense. They say they are defensive troops only."

"Sons-of-bitches!" James Maclean exclaimed.

"Shit," Winfield Scott added. Not only had the Canadians not surrendered on sight as he expected, but also the stupid Americans from New York wanted to go home to milk their cows. "That leaves us with some four hundred regulars holding the heights, and thanks to those who have returned to their farms and their stores, our men are running out of ammunition." Scott bit his lip and turned, "Come on, MacLean! We're going to defend the heights as long as we can in spite of these absurd desertions. Damn fools! They should have planned this attack with men who would fight where they were told. You can't defend the United States unless you're prepared to invade and fight every country in the world! Foreign soil, shit! For an American the only foreign soil is heaven!"

James MacLean turned and shouted back at General Wadsworth, "You can be sure the President will hear of this!"

Josh watched as his father was placed in the wagon. "He'll be fine," the orderly assured him. "Just a nasty shoulder wound. The doctor will fix him up just fine."

Those wounded near the shore had been taken down to Queenston for immediate care. Those wounded on the heights were put in wagons and taken directly to Fort George.

Josh patted his father's arm gently. "Didn't keep your head down, did you?" he said, trying to smile.

Will laughed, then grimaced slightly. "Should have kept my whole body down." He paused, then looked at Josh pleadingly. "Be sure to tell your mother it's nothing serious. You know how she is." Josh nodded and squeezed his father's hand.

"Come along, MacLean. We've got more prisoners than we can deal with." The officer led Josh away. There were lines and lines of American prisoners, mostly militia who had just surrendered and who now were grumbling about having been forced to cross the river to fight on foreign soil.

Meanwhile, on the heights, the American regulars still were giving stiff resistance to the York volunteers.

"Josh—Josh MacLean!" Josh turned toward the long line of prisoners. They all looked disgruntled and tired. There among them, waving at him, was none other than Richard Adams, Colleen's father.

"A friend?" the officer inquired.

Josh nodded. "I doubt there are many of us who don't have friends on the other side of the border. May I speak to him?"

The officer nodded. "I imagine we'll have to send them all home anyway. Go ahead."

Josh moved to Adams' side and thought that the man looked friendly enough, more friendly and more cooperative than when he had tried to find out about Colleen.

"What are they going to do with us?" Adams asked anxiously. "Jeez, I didn't want to come over here at all, shootin' things up. First thing I knew, I was conscripted; second thing I knew, I was bein' pushed into some boat."

"Where's Colleen?" Josh asked, ignoring Adam's explanations. "I went to Boston, but she wasn't there."

Adams shrugged. "She's moved to Washington. Living in Georgetown. I have the address at home."

Josh bit his lower lip; the man was utterly maddening. He felt as if he could strangle him on the spot, a feeling that had nothing to do with the battle. He leaned over. "You want to go home?"

Adams blinked. "Sure, the cow needs milkin', the farm needs tendin'. Hell, it's the only thing I've ever owned and even though I do have some money now, I still care about the farm more than anythin'. I don't want to fight, especially with you or your family."

Josh leaned over Adams. "Tell me why she ran away. Tell me straight. I could arrange for you to sit

239

out this war in a British stockade—damn it, Adams, tell me!"

"She made me promise not to, leastways till she was gone." He frowned and looked at the ground. "She was afraid you'd follow her, try to stop her, the whole thing is painful enough."

"Tell me," Josh persisted. "Tell me now."

Adams nodded dumbly. "I got a trunk from my grandmother . . . picked it up the last day you visited, back in early December."

"I remember you weren't home," Josh said. Remember? He and Colleen had made love, they had cherished those hours alone. "What has the trunk got to do with Colleen and me?" he pressed.

"It had my grandmother's diary. Her name was Megan O'Flynn. Seems your grandfather, Mathew Macleod, had an affair with her; seems he's my father."

Josh's face formed an expression of utter disbelief. "My mother is your half sister?" he stuttered. "I don't believe that! My grandparents were— were—always loyal to one another. My God, their love was a family legend!"

"Legend or no, the diary tells how she loved Mathew Macleod and how she left Fort Niagara before Janet Macleod came back from Quebec. It's all there, it's all written down. Colleen's your first cousin, and first cousins can't marry. It's not healthy."

"I don't believe this," Josh repeated, though in fact he didn't credit Adams with the imagination to make up such a story either.

"It doesn't matter, Colleen believed it and she's gone," Adams said. "She didn't want to cause your family any grief with this story. She didn't want to see you, because she knew you couldn't marry her."

She did love him! It was close to the only thought

240

in Josh's mind. She had left only because of the scandal, because she believed they were cousins.

"Will I be able to go home?" Adams asked.

"I imagine," Josh answered. His thoughts were wildly scattered and moved from one thing to another in rapid succession. He turned to Adams and patted his arm. "Don't worry," Josh said abstractedly.

"They've opened up a new flank with reinforcements from Chippewa, they're behind us!" The young American soldier who brought the news to the regulars on the heights was breathless. "We don't know how many there are, sir. They have a lot of Indians fighting with them! Sir, we're badly outnumbered."

Winfield Scott searched the gray sky. It was late afternoon, perhaps three o'clock. This farce had begun twelve hours ago; he was hungry, his men were hungry and exhausted.

"Woeeee!" Suddenly all hell broke loose as whoops and shrieks filled the air and mixed with musket fire. The Indians were coming down on them together with the British and the Canadians. Scott hit the dirt along with James MacLean. Then a soldier fell right across Scott, dead weight. Scott rolled out from under. The man's wide-open eyes held a blank, lifeless stare, his mouth was agape. Scott fired his musket in the direction of the attackers and with the others began to crawl backward down the slope.

"Fall back!" Scott ordered. There was no question about it, his position was being overrun with British-Canadian troops and whooping savages.

Many of Scott's men had staggered to their feet and were running down the hill screaming in full retreat to the river's edge. "Stupid New Yorkers!" he cried after them, knowing full well they could have come to his aid.

241

James MacLean shivered. The river was too swift and too cold to swim. "We ought to surrender," he suggested. It was all right to enjoy war, he reasoned, but there was no need to be suicidal. Apparently Scott agreed. He waved his handkerchief in the air. They deserved to surrender, James MacLean thought. The whole invasion was ill-planned. The troops didn't want to fight, they were all ill-trained and poorly supplied. Morale was abysmal.

"Hands on top of your head!" Josh called out.

James MacLean stared at the young man in the British uniform. His mouth fell slightly open. He looked exactly like Will! No, he looked as Will had looked thirty years ago!

"Josh, John Brant would like to see you. He wants you to meet with some of the Six Nations Indians he brought. And you're wanted back at Fort George as soon as you can get there."

Josh nodded at the young officer who had brought him the message. Josh turned and disappeared into the woods, leaving James MacLean, hands on top of his head, with his mouth open.

"Forward! March!" The officers of the York volunteers marched the line of weary prisoners off and down into the village of Queenston.

In Queenston, Jenna MacLean and the other women of the village stared at the long lines of American prisoners as they were marched by.

"I hear they've got more American prisoners than troops at Fort George," someone whispered.

"What is going to be done with them?" Jenna asked one of the British regulars.

"Oh, they'll be asked to sign papers promising not to fight, then we'll have to send 'em home. Hell, we got more prisoners than men!" A roar of laughter went up.

Jenna's eyes moved along the line of prisoners and

suddenly she froze. The eyes that boldly met hers were unmistakable, and the leering smile on his lips took her back to the most horrible period of her life. It was James MacLean! She nearly reached out to grasp the arm of the young soldier standing nearby. James MacLean! Josh's real father! She felt terribly dizzy, but she broke the look between them and whirled around, running toward her house, wanting to stay forever behind its locked doors!

CHAPTER XI

October 14, 1812

Major General Roger Sheaffe looked at the papers he held in his hands and then at Josh. "I have your orders from British Intelligence," he announced, handing Josh a sealed envelope. "Those are your new identity papers. You are to be sent back across the Niagara River with the prisoners. It's a rather ideal way to slip you into the United States."

"When?" Josh asked. He wanted desperately to speak with his mother, to tell her Adams' story.

"We've been sending them in small lots after questioning. Tomorrow morning is the best time, I'd think. That gives you a whole day to find shelter, to get farther away from the border."

Josh nodded absently. "Can I go home tonight?"

"Why not? But you must be careful. Your orders are written out, you have to memorize the names of your contacts and burn the list before you leave."

Josh glanced at the envelope in his hand, then remembered Richard Adams. "One of the prisoners knows me. His name is Richard Adams. Make certain he's sent back today. It wouldn't do if we were together."

Major General Roger Sheaffe nodded. "Quite," he agreed.

"May I go now?" Josh asked.

Sheaffe nodded and waved him away.

It took Josh less than an hour to ride to Queenston. He had seen his mother only briefly before returning to Fort George yesterday. But he knew his father had been sent home, so he expected she was quite calm.

"Mama!" Josh called out as he opened the front door.

"I'm here!" Jenna called back. She came into the parlor from the kitchen and flew into his arms, embracing him. "Oh, I've been so worried about you!"

"Worried? But you knew I was all right." Josh held her back and laughed.

Jenna stared at him. Ever since she'd seen James MacLean she'd been a wreck, a bundle of nerves. Will was asleep upstairs. He hadn't been awake long enough over the preceding twenty-four hours to notice her agitation. But she couldn't hide it from Josh and she knew that as soon as Will was feeling better, she wouldn't be able to hide it from him either. In truth, it was Josh she feared for, yet she knew that fear was irrational. James MacLean didn't know he was Josh's father! She had to keep telling and telling herself that. He didn't know.

"I need your help," Josh said. "Come, sit down with me."

Jenna followed him dumbly to the settee. And Josh, almost unaware of her agitation, began his story.

In spite of herself and in spite of being distracted in the beginning, Jenna quickly grew interested in Josh's story. When he'd finished, she leaned back and said, "That's astonishing! But I don't believe it!"

"Mama," Josh pressed, "it is true that Grandmother was in Quebec City and that she returned to Fort Niagara after the Battle of the Plains of Abraham. Isn't that right?"

Jenna nodded. "That's right. Of course, I wasn't born then. . . . I was born later."

245

"But how could Richard Adams have known that?" Josh's eyes bored into Jenna's. "Why, that's right!" she exclaimed in her amazement.

"There must be some truth somewhere," Josh said. "Mama, I have to find it."

Jenna nodded. "You'll have to talk to Helena and Madelaine. They're older than I am. They might remember."

Josh agreed and, kissing his mother good-bye, he hurried to Lochiel.

He arrived breathless about an hour after breakfast. "Where's Auntie Helena?" he asked John Fraser, whose main concern was yesterday's battle.

"Upstairs making beds."

Josh bounded up the stairs. "Aunt Helena, you have to help me," he announced, interrupting her in the middle of her work. "I'm afraid I don't have much time."

"Young people never do," she retorted quickly.

Josh ignored her bad humor and poured out his story.

"I know you find this hard to believe, young man, but I was once six years old." Helena pounded the pillows with vigor.

"But do you remember anything about 1759?"

Helena shook out the quilt and laid it over the top of the bed and stepped back, her hands on her ample hips. "I remember there was a war. Mama was in Quebec City with your grandfather, Robert MacLean. Papa was working at Fort Niagara. We were here, only here wasn't here. Here was a log cabin."

Josh inhaled, afraid his exasperation was about to show. "Does the name Megan O'Flynn mean anything to you?"

Helena turned and scowled. "Megan," she repeated the name. "Megan, Megan . . . was that her name?"

246

"Whose name?" Josh pressed.

Helena shook her head. "Lord, it was over fifty years ago and I was six years old! I honestly can't remember. Why are you plaguing me so, anyway?"

Josh shook his head. "Nothing."

"Nothing doesn't bring you from the fort and nothing doesn't make you follow me around in the morning when I have chores to do asking me questions about fifty some-odd years ago. Go ask your Aunt Madelaine. Remember, she was near twelve then. She might remember."

Josh waved and left the room. "Thanks!" he called out as he ran down the staircase. Madelaine was in the kitchen, clearing the breakfast dishes.

"Back for seconds?" Madelaine turned around. Her small, dark eyes twinkled; one could tell what a pretty woman she had been.

"Do you remember what happened in 1759?"

Madelaine smiled. "Are you testing to see if I'm senile yet?"

"Of course not. Please, Auntie Madelaine, it's serious, very serious to me. It concerns Colleen. Do you remember 1759?"

"Yes, I think so. We were all here, your grandmother was away."

"Do you remember a Megan, a Megan O'Flynn?"

Madelaine sat down. "Megan, yes. O'Flynn, no. That wasn't Megan's last name. Her name was Coulon."

"Was she Irish?"

"Yes, I believe she was. But she was married to the man at the fort."

Josh sat down opposite Madelaine. "Did Grandfather Mathew have an affair with Megan?"

"What?" Madelaine raised an eyebrow. "How can you ask such a silly question? Your grandfather loved Janet Macleod, and 'loved' is the very right word. There just wasn't anyone else. Ever."

"There was Anne Macdonald, Tom's mother," Josh reminded her.

"That was when Mathew thought Janet was dead. But no, not after they were married, no one."

"How did you know that?" Josh prodded.

"She took care of us. . . . I remember, she moved in for a while, brought us here . . . when the fort was destroyed. No, before it was destroyed," she corrected herself.

Josh felt his heart sinking. What would a twelve-year-old know . . . if they lived in the same house to-together. "Auntie Madelaine, how do you know they didn't—didn't make love?"

"I just know," she answered. "But why take my word for it? Your grandfather left an account of it all. I seem to remember something about her being a spy. Anyway, he spent a long time writing it all down. Besides, your grandmother knew all about it. They used to laugh about it sometimes."

Josh had moved to the edge of the chair and was leaning forward. He felt like lurching across the table and hugging Madelaine. "Where is the account?"

Madelaine thought for a few minutes. "In the attic, I think. Yes, I remember, that's where we put all those things."

Josh already was standing. "You've been a great help, Auntie Madelaine."

"That's good. When you get old, you like to think you can help sometimes."

Josh was off and running. He would have to get the lantern because the attic would be dark, but somewhere amid the old gowns and the family mementos there was a key to Megan O'Flynn—and with it perhaps the solution to his own mystery.

Pembina was a dusty settlement. It had a fort of sorts, a trading post, a collection of log cabins, shacks, huts, and tipis. Since arriving in Pembina, Miles Macdonell had been engaged in building housing for the settlers, a place where they could survive the winter together before heading out to their farms to clear, till, and plant in the spring.

"Of course, the two groups will have to winter together," Miles told Ian. "There's just no other choice. You say Owen is behind you? How many days?"

"Two at the most," Ian replied.

"There's plenty of buffalo meat for the winter," Macdonell told Ian and Bonnie. "And we expect to be finished with this"—he waved his arm to indicate the building behind him—"by the end of November."

Macdonell looked at Bonnie and then at Ian. "They still won't accept her," Miles said. "And the women in the first group will gossip to the women in the second group. I could force them, of course, but she'd have a hard time of it—too hard."

"I don't think I want her subjected to that kind of mindless prejudice," Ian replied. "Besides, by the end of winter they'll be even meaner from being inside so long."

"I would be pleased if you would not discuss me as if I weren't here!" Bonnie stamped her foot as if to gain their attention.

"I have métis friends," Ian said. "We can stay with them till spring."

"People like those savages we encountered?" She looked at him in amazement.

"At least they're civilized enough to welcome you among them."

Bonnie looked down. He was right, of course. "And then what?" she asked. "I still want to teach."

"And teach you might, on the Niagara. In the spring I can take you to Upper Canada."

Bonnie continued to stare at the floor of Miles Macdonell's unfinished headquarters. She could not claim that she was impressed with the prairie; it was not what she had expected. Nor could she say that she really wanted to stay among the colonists, who glared at her and gave her dirty looks and whispered. Now, she thought, they would whisper that she was living with a man she wasn't married to. Perhaps Ian was right.

On the other hand, she could not imagine a winter with the métis, the wild men they had encountered by the lake. There were more wandering around Pembina, these mysterious so-called Buffalo People.

"Can you ride?" Ian asked.

Bonnie Campbell shook her head in the affirmative.

"Good," Ian said and smiled. "We may have to ride." Then he turned to Miles. "Can she stay here for a bit? I have to make some inquiries."

Miles waved him off and Ian stepped out onto the dusty path that was Pembina's main street. He had blood brothers among the métis, relatives he had not seen.

Ian returned within a hour, and the smile on his face showed considerable relief. "I have solved our problem," he announced.

Bonnie Campbell seemed almost to be pouting, though Ian knew that she was not the pouting type. Doubtless she felt sorry for herself, and certainly she must be tired. The journey had been long and she had just suffered considerable rejection.

"I've found a place for us to stay. Come along, night's coming."

"Us?" Bonnie questioned.

"Us," Ian confirmed. "Listen, you must understand by this time. You can't be left alone."

"Where are we going?" the ever-suspicious Bonnie asked.

"There's a French family—not métis, French Ca-

250

nadian. The woman's name is Madame Lagimonière, and she is well known, you might even say famous. She journeyed here from Trois-Rivières in Lower Canada in 1808. Until the arrival of the colonists in August, she was the only white woman in the West. She and her husband and children have only just returned from farther west. They returned because they heard of the Selkirk settlement."

"And they will take me in?" Bonnie asked.

Ian shook his head. "They have a small cabin, and near it, less than half a mile away, is a second cabin. Both cabins belonged to some cousins of mine who are farther west and will not return this winter. We are welcome to the other cabin, but it needs some fixing up and we'll have to get a Red River wagon and take some supplies out there."

"How can I live with you? What will people say?" Bonnie's eyes were wide.

Ian almost laughed, but he suppressed it. "You've already been disowned. What difference does it make? The métis won't care. The Lagimonières won't care. The Indians won't care. And heaven knows, I know what a Puritan you are! Besides, the only person you are likely to see much of is Madame Lagimonière."

"And you won't bother me?" Bonnie looked at him steadily.

"Have I ever?" Ian replied.

Bonnie shook her head and thought about being alone with no one to talk to save a French Canadian woman. "My French is wretched."

"It will improve," Ian promised. "And I hope your cooking will improve as well." A devilish glint came into his eyes. "A man who gets no love at least requires a good dinner."

Bonnie glared at him. I would like to love you, she thought bitterly, but you never would love me. You

251

could make love to me, but you couldn't love a Campbell. No, my pride would not allow you just to make
love to me without really loving me.

Jenna was down on her hands and knees scrub-
bing the floor with a vengeance. Indeed, it seemed as
if she might scrub the very boards away. It had been
exactly fourteen days since the Battle of Queenston
Heights. Upstairs, Will lay in the bedroom, still recovering from his shoulder wound.

Josh had come to her all excited because of the diaries he had found. But he had to leave almost as soon
as he came. "Where are you going?" she had asked
him repeatedly. But he had refused to tell her.

"Military secret," he answered. "I won't be back
for some time."

All of that was two weeks behind her now, and
Jenna still had not dared to tell Will about seeing his
brother James MacLean. She had wanted to scream
out, "He's across the river! Your brother is fighting
with the Americans! He knows I'm here!" But she
couldn't. Jenna held her tongue and her secret. She
prayed never to see or hear of James MacLean again,
but in her heart she knew he would come back somehow, she knew he meant to have her.

In her frustration, Jenna had cleaned very inch of
the house. She had used her nervous energy to scrub
floors, to wash windows, even to clean and load all
the muskets.

"Jenna!" Will's voice called from upstairs.
"Jenna!"

"In a minute," she called back. Then, wearily
climbing the stairs, she went to her husband. "Honestly, if you ever get shot again, I don't know what
I'll do. Do you know how many times I've climbed
those stairs?" She had her hands on her ample hips
and her long red-gold hair was hanging loose, instead of the way she usually wore it, up in a huge

bun. Her voice was filled with mock anger, and Will burst out laughing.

"I see you've been playing Irish washerwoman again." He was sitting up, his hands folded outside the covers.

"Well, there's work to do," Jenna complained.

"Not as much as you're making, my dear." Will winked at her. "Come here, sit down, kiss your old invalid husband."

"The doctor says you can get up next week." Jenna sat down on the edge of the bed and primly folded her hands.

"Does he now? And when does he say I can make love to my wife again?"

Jenna blushed. "He didn't," she answered in a small voice.

"Something's been troubling you," Will observed. "Woman, I've been living with you for thirty years. You never clean like this unless something is wrong. Now, what is it?"

"Nothing. Oh, maybe I'm a little worried about Josh . . . about the war."

"Josh isn't the one who was wounded. And you weren't so worried before."

"I know," Jenna replied. She was looking away, out the window and toward the bluffs and the woods. "It's starting to snow," she observed.

Will reached out and pulled her down to him, kissing her mouth and then her neck. "You're still bedridden," Jenna protested. Will laughed aloud and dipped his hand into her loose-fitting dress. "This is not your most seductive dress," he commented.

"It's my scrub dress. How should I dress to clean the house?"

"But I don't want you to clean the house, not now." His face was impish once again, and Jenna felt a surge of desire, suddenly realizing that it had been over two weeks since they made love.

253

"I have a lovely idea," Will said, rubbing his chin thoughtfully.

"Yes?" Jenna arched an eyebrow in expectation, knowing her husband was in a playful mood.

"Why don't you put on the gown that we bought in Montreal, the one sent from Paris so many years ago."

Jenna's face flushed a deep red. "It looks like it was meant for a lady in a brothel, it's a shocking dress."

"But you still keep it in the trunk. Anyway, it certainly was meant for a high-class brothel." Will was holding her hands and rubbing them gently. "Go put it on," he urged. "Let's have a little diversion from this dreary existence."

"Are you really well enough?" Jenna asked, her eyes sparkling wickedly at the thought of their little game.

"If you don't mind an old man with a shoulder still swathed in bandages, I think I can manage to arouse you sufficiently."

Jenna got up and went to the trunk at the foot of the bed. Carefully, she found her way to the ravishing black gown that rested on the very bottom of the trunk. "I shall have to put it on in the other room," she said, looking coquettish.

Will fluffed up the pillows and pulled himself up in bed. "Don't be too long," he joked.

Jenna disappeared into the other room, quickly discarding the plain gray woolen dress she had been wearing. In its place she put on the black dress trimmed in red ribbons, ribbons that laced up the front, barely drawing together the thin, fragile material of the bodice. "It's a miracle it still fits," Jenna said aloud to herself. And she thought, it's our secret gown. Much too shocking for any other use, it had only been worn for Will. He adored making love to her when she wore it. Jenna herself had to admit to

254

being excited by it and thought to herself, perhaps I have a secret desire to be a whore instead of a staid wife and mother. Quickly she loosened her hair, allowing it to fall on her shoulders. Then she returned to Will.

She stood at the foot of the bed and allowed him to look at her, his eyes slowly traveling the curvature of her body. "You still could pass for thirty," he said admiringly, "and as a whore in any fine Parisian brothel, I'm certain."

Jenna came to his side and Will pulled her down to him, gently kissing her neck, her ears, her mouth. His hands moved across the almost transparent material, material thin enough that Jenna could feel his every movement. He in turn watched as her full breasts swelled beneath the netted bodice in anticipation. Her hands rubbed his back as he leaned over her, caressing her thighs, returning again and again to press her mound gently while she writhed with growing desire and whispered how much she loved him. "Oh, now," Jenna breathed into Will's ear.

But Will moved his hand away teasingly. "No, not now," he breathed back into her ear, "not for a while yet."

Jenna groaned. He knew so well how to control her mounting pleasure, how to make certain that when at last he allowed her full pleasure she would cry out and shiver in his arms, a full victim of desire. But that would not happen until Will entered her, and often Jenna wondered at his self-control. He was a masterful lover; he understood her well.

"You are driving me mad," she said, pressing against him. But Will's only answer was a satisfied hum. He was loosening the red ribbons now, uncovering her white breasts, breasts grown soft and mature, breasts still tipped with rosebuds, breasts that to Will were sweet to the taste and soft and arousing to the touch. He caressed her with his tongue, bit her

255

gently and massaged her, moving ever downward seeking the warmth and moisture of that softest of all spots, marveling at her movements, growing himself as she moved against him wanton and desirous.

Will moved into her with incredible ease, amazed as he always was at the sensation that rushed through him as she surrounded him and they became one. Jenna groaned as his movements increased her need, but she was aware of him, aware of his unusually rapid heartbeat, aware that his breath came in shorter gasps. Then she was lost, shaking in his arms, vibrating against his flesh, and they moved together in a thunderous climax that was like tumbling down a steep hill in one another's arms.

"Mmm," was all Jenna could say for a long moment as they collapsed together against the pillows.

"Not bad for a wounded man, what?" Will asked.

"Not bad at all," Jenna conceded. "But it's really the dress."

Will kissed her on the lips and squeezed her. "Don't pack it so far down in the trunk," he joked. "And when you go to Lochiel, take it. I wouldn't want it to fall into American hands."

Jenna didn't answer, but only looked into Will's eyes. Lochiel . . . he was going to make her go this time. He was going to insist because he felt being on the riverfront was far too dangerous. Jenna bit her lip and lay down on his shoulder. She felt wonderfully secure in Will's arms and she noted that this was the first time she had felt truly secure since she had seen James MacLean. Again, Jenna wondered if she should tell Will. But again, she didn't.

The cabin was twelve feet square, and one entire wall was taken up by a fieldstone fireplace. "It's a fine cabin," Ian said as he opened the door. "It's far better than the accommodations the colonists will have for the winter."

Bonnie's legs ached from the long horseback ride. It had been a while since she had ridden, and even then she had not been an accomplished rider. "It's isolated," she complained. "Quite a way out of the settlement." She had a hard time thinking of Pembina as a settlement. True enough, there were some buildings already standing and more being built to house the colonists, but Pembina mostly was a collection of huts occupied by the roving métis and a gathering of tipis occupied by the Indians who came to trade.

"It's close to Madame Lagimonière." Ian did not say the obvious. Since Bonnie had been cast out and disowned, she would have been isolated in any case.

"I suppose it's not too bad," she allowed, "though it needs a good cleaning."

"Considering how short a time we have before it really gets cold, I'd say the cleaning can wait." Ian watched as Bonnie moved around the empty cabin. Her pride was very much on the surface today, probably because he had bought the supplies, which were outside piled high on a Red River wagon, one of those distinctive two-wheeled carts used by the métis and so ideally suited to the barren, rutted prairie.

While Ian purchased the supplies at the trading post, Bonnie had been distant and sullen. She left Ian to buy the table, the benches, the furs, and additional cooking utensils as well as the foodstuffs. It was because I paid, Ian thought. She feels kept. And further, it crossed his mind that the crofter's hut she had lived in in Scotland probably had not been as fine as this cabin. But that was all something Bonnie Campbell wouldn't admit.

"I could have made the table and benches," Ian said absently as he carried things into the cabin. "But there's so much to do, it didn't seem worth the time."

"Besides, you're made of money," Bonnie said

coldly. She was standing in front of the fireplace. She turned to him, her blue eyes large, her jaw set stubbornly in the way Ian had come to know. "I'll pay you back for everything," she said. "As soon as I have some money. But I don't want you to think that because—because . . . you'll sleep over there." She pointed off to one corner. "And I'll sleep over there." She pointed off to the opposite corner.

"I shouldn't want you to do otherwise," he answered, mocking her own cold tone. "And pay me back when you want. Of course," Ian rubbed his chin thoughtfully, "I'll expect you to work."

"Work?" Bonnie questioned.

"Missy, if we are going to live under one twelve-foot roof and I am going to be working in town, I expect meals to be cooked for me, I expect my clothing to be kept clean and in good repair, and I expect some occasional—mind you, occasional—civil conversation. Do you think a Campbell might manage that?"

Bonnie scowled. "As long as that's all you expect, I think I can manage."

"Good," Ian replied. "Now, we have a wagon full of goods outside. Perhaps Her Majesty, the Queen of Scotland, would stoop to help me unload them."

Bonnie did not answer, but she followed Ian outside into the fading twilight. They brought in the furs, the food, the utensils, and the bucket.

"When we go to the Lagimonières', you must put on your dress," Ian instructed her. "Madame Lagimonière is a proper lady."

"And what would a proper lady be doing here?" Bonnie was arranging her own belongings, laying her bedroll along one side of the cabin.

"She traveled from Trois-Rivières with her husband, over two thousand miles by canoe and portage. Her first baby was born in a wigwam four years ago. Marie-Anne Lagimonière is a most unusual woman—you'll hear the métis speak of her almost reverently. She rides like a man, shots straight as any sharpshooter in the buffalo hunt, is a fine woodsman. She carries her infant in a moss bag as the Indian women do, and most of the Indians here and as far west as the Rockies consider her a good omen. But you'll see, she is a lady—a lady who can teach you a great deal about this territory, about the Indians, the métis, and what you have to know to get along."

"And how do you know this Marie-Anne Lagimonière so well?"

Ian smiled. "Before she was married, she was Marie-Anne Gaboury. She is the sister of the woman married to Claude Deschamps of the North West Company. And Claude is my cousin—well, he is sort of my cousin. His Uncle René owns this cabin."

Bonnie looked puzzled. "I thought you were Scots."

Ian nodded. "My grandparents adopted the Deschamps children when they were orphaned—my grandmother had been their tutor. And when they grew up, Pierre, the eldest, moved back to Trois-Rivières and René moved West and married an Indian woman. But we have always kept in touch and remained close in spite of the miles between us." Ian shook out a large fur. "Here, you better take this. You'll need it for your bedroll."

Bonnie took it and spread it out over the other blankets. Then she returned to trying to arrange the utensils.

"Put the utensils on the mantel," Ian suggested. "Maybe later I'll make a shelf for them."

Bonnie continued to put things away, stacking some of the food stores in one corner temporarily. Ian brought in a large sack of grain, shouldering it carefully and then putting it down so as not to burst it.

"I don't suppose they have any books in Pembina, do they?" Bonnie had stopped and was looking at

Ian. "I was reading a lot in York Factory. Mr. Hillier had books."

Ian frowned. The métis were a gypsylike people, always on the move. Few were literate. They were the main customers at the Hudson's Bay Company post and at the North West Company post, and both carried only vital supplies, things needed for survival. Finding even a single book could present a real challenge. "I'll see what I can do," Ian promised. Surprisingly, Bonnie smiled.

Josh MacLean had been ferried across the river with a small group of prisoners scheduled to be released on the morning of October 15. His identification papers gave him the name of Joshua Henry and described him as an unemployed teacher. His orders instructed him to travel overland to Washington, D.C. Once there, he was to meet his contact, a young man by the name of Jason Talbot, who was none other than the secretary to the President's wife, Mrs. Dolley Madison. Mr. Talbot would pass vital information to Josh, who in turn would code it and carry it to another contact for transmission to the Royal Navy, whose ships were often off the coast of the United States and easily reached by small craft.

Josh had memorized the details of his future rendezvous. Then, as instructed, he had destroyed his orders. If the truth be known, Josh all but danced for joy when he read his orders: Of all the places in the United States he might have been sent, Washington was the only place he really wanted to go.

Moreover, his orders suggested that he travel to Washington by a circuitous route so that no one would suspect the released prisoner who suddenly arrived in upper New York State and then immediately sought transportation to the nation's capital.

On the way across the choppy Niagara River, Josh

decided to make a slight detour. He decided to go to Colleen's father's farm in Lewiston.

Josh had arrived, tired and worn out, on the evening of the fifteenth.

"What on earth are you doing here?" Richard Adams questioned when Josh arrived. "You're in the British Army, I'm a conscripted militiaman—I could be tried for treason. You're a spy, and if you're not a spy, you're a fool for coming here!"

Josh looked at Richard Adams steadily. "We both love your daughter," he said quietly. "Whatever I'm doing on this side of the border, I've come here in peace. Colleen does love me, doesn't she?"

Richard Adams nodded. "Suppose she does," he allowed.

"I'm not her cousin," Josh announced. "Tell me, in the diaries left by your grandmother, Megan O'Flynn, what is the date given for your birth?"

"December 1760, in Boston," he replied.

Josh grinned. "Your grandmother left the Niagara in October of 1759. You could not be Mathew Macleod's son."

Richard Adams sat down and stared into the fire. "I don't know if I'm glad or not," he finally commented. "But for you and Colleen, I guess I'm glad. Though I liked thinking I knew who both my parents were . . ." His words trailed off, and Josh had risen from his chair and patted Adams on the shoulder. "Your family and mine go back a long way," Josh said. "It's an astonishing tale, one our grandparents didn't even know about. Only when the diaries of Janet Macleod, Mathew Macleod, and Megan O'Flynn are put together does it all become clear."

Adams looked at Josh. "Tell me the tale," he urged.

Josh began the long story. He told Adams how Janet Cameron had escaped Scotland and gone to France with little Robert MacLean and Richard

O'Flynn who, according to Megan's diaries, was a master spy. Janet and O'Flynn had had a tempestuous affair, possible only because Janet believed Mathew to be dead. Then Janet had come to Quebec. Later, during the Seven Years' War, Megan had joined her father as a spy. She traveled to Fort Niagara as Megan Coulon and was responsible for the sneak attack that allowed the fort to be taken. She had cared for the Macleod children when Janet had gone to Quebec and, true enough, she had fallen in love with Mathew and tried to seduce him. But then, when she failed, she left Fort Niagara before Janet returned. Janet returned in October.

"Ah, a family of spies," Adams said. "Of course, she admits it in her diaries. And tell me, Janet Macleod and Mathew Macleod never knew that Megan was the daughter of Richard O'Flynn?"

"Never," Josh confirmed. "That's what was so eerie abut reading their diaries. To think that over sixty years later, we would know something they did not."

Adams shook his head. "Strange," he muttered.

"Will you tell me where in Washington Colleen is?"

"Why not?" Adams asked. He stretched and stood up. "I guess it's all right if you stay." He peered out the window and saw that it was snowing hard. "Ain't goin' nowhere tonight anyway."

James MacLean had been watching as the boats unloaded their cargo of returning prisoners. He instantly recognized Josh MacLean as the young man he had seen in British uniform and known as his brother Will's son. James had beckoned two enlisted men and, together, they had followed Josh to the farm of Richard Adams outside Lewiston.

"I want them taken alive," James MacLean told the two enlisted men. "I have good reason to suspect there's spying going on here."

262

The abrupt knock on the door startled Richard Adams. "Got more company tonight than I've had in two years," he muttered. "Any chance you were followed?"

"No, I don't think that's likely. Open the door and act normal."

Adams did as he was told—and that was the beginning of Josh's nightmare.

The three soldiers burst into the room with their pistols drawn.

"Ah, young MacLean, I take it?" the oldest and highest-ranking among them said in a cool southern accent.

Astonished, Josh had stared at the tall, dark, nasty-looking man. His face was totally unfamiliar to him. How could this stranger from so far away know who he was?

"Don't bother to deny it," the man said. "I know perfectly well who you are."

"That puts you at an advantage," Josh replied, trying to sound calmer than he actually was. Had he jeopardized his life, Colleen's father's life, and his whole mission by coming here? Silently he cursed himself.

"I know you're Will MacLean's son. And I presume you're a spy."

"I'm not a spy," Josh lied. "I have personal business with Mr. Adams. I'm engaged to his daughter."

"And where is this alleged daughter?"

"Visiting friends in the East," Adams interjected.

"Tie them up!" James MacLean waved his pistol.

"Are we going back to the fort, sir?" one of the enlisted men asked.

"Not right away," James MacLean answered. "Besides, it looks more comfortable here. Tie them up and separate them."

"And then what are you going to do with us?" Josh asked, not certain he wanted to hear the answer and

263

praying that he would not be searched and his false identification found. The penalty for spying was hanging. And whoever this strange man was, he knew that Josh was not Joshua Henry. He knew he was Josh Maclean and that he was Canadian.

"I'm going to send for your mama," James Mac-Lean said. "Now, you'll like that, won't you?"

"My mother?" Josh was outraged and he started up from his chair, but he saw the pistol held by one of the enlisted men pointed directly at him, and he felt the restraining hand of the other on his shoulder. "What has my mother got to do with anything?"

"I just want to see her again," James MacLean said, as he removed his black leather gloves. "Just to say hello."

Josh struggled on the bed, but struggling only made the knots tighter. James MacLean had taken him prisoner two weeks earlier. In all of those two weeks, he had not seen Richard Adams. And he had been tied most of the time, except for a short exercise period twice a day and during meals when only his hands were undone. All Josh had managed to learn was that the man who had taken him captive bore the same last name as he, and Josh made the assumption that James Maclean was some distant relative of his father, a relative who had a grudge, a relative who knew his mother.

"She won't come," Josh said during the evening meal. "It's been two weeks."

"Can't get here because of the weather," James MacLean replied. "But you're wrong, she's coming. I had a letter pouch this morning. Mrs. Jenna Mac-Lean is coming."

CHAPTER XII

November 1812

Marie-Anne Lagimonière was a delicate-looking woman; indeed, her fine-boned build belied the legend of her strength. Bonnie Campbell could hardly visualize this tiny raven-haired beauty riding bareback across the plains, gun in hand, pursuing buffalo.

On this evening, Marie-Anne wore a black wool skirt with a bright red sash and a kind of dark tunic atop a long-sleeved, bright green garment. Her thick, curly hair was tied behind her head, and her black eyes were intense. Around her long, slim neck, Marie-Anne wore a thick gold cross, and Bonnie could not help thinking that it was the gold cross that linked Marie-Anne's two quite different worlds.

"It is a pleasure to meet you," Marie-Anne said and smiled. "I'm told there are other white women in Pembina now. I shall go soon to meet them. It is why we came back, you know. We came back because there will be a settlement here."

Bonnie glanced around the cabin. It was larger than the one she and Ian shared. It had at least three rooms and certainly it had more furniture.

"Do you bring all this when you travel?" Bonnie asked in halting, broken French. Her accent was different from Marie-Anne's.

"No. We leave it with the Indians. When we travel we take only necessities."

"And you like this life?" Bonnie asked incredulously. The trip from York Factory had been long and tiring. The ground was hard and the nights were cold. If she looked back on it, it was hard to remember anything save the pain of the long hours in the canoe. Except, she thought wistfully, for the trip through the great white clay cliffs. And the waterfalls. She liked waterfalls.

"Let us say that I would want no other life," Marie-Anne replied.

"But it's so isolated," Bonnie observed. "There are few other women."

Marie-Anne smiled. "There are Indian women."

"But they're different. . . ."

"Not so different," Marie-Anne corrected. "They love, they give birth, they know pain. Remember, I speak their language, I know them." She took a long breath. "But they are different. I will tell you how. Indian women are strong and their men depend on them. They can be anything they want to be within the tribe; nothing is forbidden if they can master it. They can be hunters and hunt with the men. Inheritances are passed on through the mothers, not through the fathers. Indian women do not feel useless, as white women often feel. They are not china dolls for their men. They are useful and needed. They are flesh and blood."

Bonnie listened and thought about what Marie-Anne said. She was fascinated by Marie-Anne's point of view.

"Isolation," Marie-Anne concluded, "is of one's own making."

Bonnie lowered her head and looked at the floor of the cabin. Each of the boards was set together perfectly so that there were no cracks. It should be that way between people, she thought. They should fit together, they shouldn't fight or allow things to come between them. "The settlers," Bonnie said suddenly. "They will tell you stories about me that are not true. They are very religious, very strict and proper. My father cast me out of my family. My parents say I am dead."

Marie-Anne laughed. "They will learn not to say much of anything about others after a time. Here on the prairie, life is a matter of depending on others. They will have to live among the métis and the Indians; they will see a morality that is strange to them. But you—you are young and you must be more adventurous. You must be self-sufficient."

"It's all new to me," Bonnie said softly. She could thank Ian for taking Marie-Anne's husband outside to look at some horses. It was good to talk to another woman alone, good to meet a woman who was strong and at peace with herself, a woman who seemed to have a sense of her own worth and of her place in the world. She was a woman who could love children and do what other women did, but she also could do things many men did. She was not afraid to break the mold.

"Even the land is strange," Bonnie confessed. "I'm used to rolling hills, to mountains, to the moors. . . ."

"I do not know moors," Marie-Anne said and smiled. "But I have traveled to where the plains rise and finally to where there are mountains so high that their tops still are in the clouds. I have seen herds of buffalo so dense that they were a thundering, dark movement in the distance and it looked as if the land itself actually were moving.

"And birds—I have seen bluebirds and great black ravens. This is a wondrous land, and I can only thank God that I have seen it as no other white woman has. I have seen its majesty and its beauty."

"And you are not lonely?" Bonnie pressed.

267

Marie-Anne shook her head. "I have a fine, healthy daughter, I have a good son. And I have a man who matches this land: changeable, strong, good. I have learned the medicine of the Indians, and when I had my children the Indian women were there helping me, showing me."

Bonnie nodded silently. Marie-Anne was different from any woman she had ever known before. Marie-Anne had left a comfortable home in Trois-Rivières because the man she loved had a dream to go West. She had not asked him to give up that dream, she had become a part of its fulfillment.

"You are not to be pitied," Marie-Anne said, taking Bonnie's hand in hers. "You have a fine young man. He is strong and brave and you love each other."

Bonnie blinked at Marie-Anne. "Oh, no! You misunderstand. Ian and I—he's a MacLean, I'm a Campbell. He doesn't even like me very much. And he —he's arrogant."

Marie-Anne's expression was one of benign amusement. "A Campbell and a MacLean. A family feud?"

Bonnie nodded her head in the affirmative.

Again Marie-Anne's warm laughter filled the room. "But he looks after you. What kind of feud is this?"

"I suppose he thinks looking after me is his duty."

"Well, I have lived to see the French embrace the Mohawk, and the Cree accept the Sioux. Even the French and the English come together now and again. I do not think this family feud will last. Besides, I pride myself on being a good observer. I see what I see in your eyes. . . ."

Bonnie was about to answer when the door of the cabin burst open.

"We're ready for a drink, eh? And some buffalo meat!" Jean Lagimonière announced in a loud, merry voice. Marie-Anne met her husband's entrance with a warm, loving smile. She stood up and smoothed out her long woolen skirt.

"I think it is ready."

"It smells ready," Ian inhaled deeply as he commented. On the stove a great iron pot steamed, giving off the aroma of meat cooking.

"You have eaten the meat of the buffalo before?" Marie-Anne asked Bonnie.

"Not yet, but it smells delicious."

"I have made a kind of stew. I hope you will like it, but it is different. It takes some getting used to."

"You will come to like this beast!" Jean Lagimonière roared. "It will clothe you and feed you. Its fat will make tallow for the candles and soap. It is the sustenance of the métis and the Indian."

They sat down at the table and Marie-Anne placed large bowls in front of them. When all had been served, Marie-Anne sat down and recited a short prayer. Then she looked up warmly and said, "Enjoy your meal."

Bonnie waited, then dipped her spoon into the stew. She took a mouthful and chewed on the meat. Then she took another. It was stronger than beef and somewhat stringier, but it was good.

"It's tasty," Bonnie said. "Please tell me how to cook buffalo meat."

"Oh, please do," Ian begged, "or I might starve over the winter."

Marie-Anne laughed. "I'll make her into a frontier woman."

Bonnie blushed and looked into her bowl of stew, vaguely aware that she felt warm and comfortable and at ease. She felt better than she had in a long while.

Jenna MacLean had taken the leather pouch from the messenger and opened it with a strange feeling

269

of apprehension. When she read it, it was like a bad dream come true.

My dear Jenna,
    I am holding your son Josh MacLean on charges of spying. These, I am sure you realize, are most grave charges. Naturally, I want to give you the opportunity of seeing him before I return him to Fort Niagara for hanging. Enclosed is a safe-conduct pass. Please come alone.
    I am looking forward to our reunion.
                            Love always,
                            James MacLean

A chill ran through Jenna and she shook violently. She moved around the room as if she were in a trance—James had Josh! "I must go to him," she said aloud. "Oh, my God! I must do something!"

But the next two weeks were a living horror. The weather closed in and a blizzard engulfed the Niagara peninsula, making the trip to Lewiston impossible.

Jenna was only grateful that the person who knew her best, her husband, was staying with the militia at Fort George. "I must deal with this myself," she said over and over. "Will must not find out."

She sent a message to James MacLean declaring her intention to come. She prayed it would reach him, though she didn't hold out much hope. Still she rationalized. He will know it's the weather that delays me. Oh, please let him know that, she prayed silently.

Finally the weather cleared and Jenna was able to get a boatman to take her across the river. Once there, she rented a horse-drawn sled to take her to the Adams farm. What was Josh doing there? How had James found him? Her mind was filled with a never-ending series of questions for which she had no answers.

"We ought to take them back to the fort now that the weather's cleared," one of the enlisted men suggested.

"I have sent messages to the fort," James MacLean replied arrogantly. "I'm in charge here. You will not question me or my actions. I have an important investigation to carry out." James MacLean stared at Josh, who was tied to the chair opposite, a gag in his mouth. "Where's the other one?" he asked.

"In the barn," the enlisted man informed him. "Nice and warm with the pigs."

"Remove his gag and leave us," James ordered. Jenna would be coming soon, James thought. It was time now to have a talk with Josh.

Josh ran his tongue over his lips. "Can I have some water?" he asked.

James filled a cup and went over to Josh. He held the cup to the young man's lips and let him drink. It was nice to see the image of Will all tied up the way James himself had been years ago when Will took Jenna and ran away.

Josh shook his head, indicating he was finished drinking.

"Where were you headed?" James asked almost casually.

"I'm not a spy," Josh said evenly. Unbelievably, they still had not searched him. There was something irregular about all of this. And why did this man want to see his mother?

James rocked back on the rear legs of his chair, balancing himself by holding onto the table with one hand. He sucked air through his teeth. "We're related," he revealed. "I guess you figured that out since we have the same last name."

"Who are you?" Josh questioned. "How did you know who I was?"

"You're the spitting image of Will," James replied. Then he smirked. "I'm you're uncle, son. Your father's twin brother."

Josh's mouth fell slightly open. "My father's brother." He repeated the words, then shook his head. "I don't understand." No one ever had mentioned his father having a brother!

"I sent for your mother because we're old friends, very old friends. You know, your father took her away from me. Trussed me all up the way you're trussed up now. Ran off with her, he did. Shit, she was the best lay I ever had!"

"You're a lying, foulmouthed son-of-a-whore!" Josh shouted angrily. "Don't you talk about my mother that way!"

James laughed loudly and picked up the glass of whiskey he had been drinking. "I know every curve of your mother's body—she was mine first!"

Josh's face had gone nearly purple with rage. "That's a lie!"

"I met her in a brothel in New Orleans," James told Josh, laughing with bravado.

"You didn't!" Josh spat out the words, though he knew his mother had been in New Orleans and that his father had been born in the Louisiana Territory.

James poured himself another drink. "Loved your mother," he slurred, "in my own way. I'm a selfish man. It's not easy for me to love anyone."

"You're a liar!" Josh still was shaking. He could kill this man bare-handed.

"Oh, I'm not lying. When she comes I'll put you in the bedroom, let you listen. I want to be with your mother one more time for old times' sake."

"I'll kill you!" Josh raged.

James MacLean laughed. "We'll see who'll do the killing. You know, if she'd married me, I'd have

272

made her mistress of Skye, finest plantation on the river. She'd have had slaves to dress her, to comb her hair, to keep her beautiful. She'd be a rich woman, pampered and well dressed. I might even have taken her right into the Executive Mansion of this country. Jenna Macleod could have been something very special. . . ." James' eyes took on a strange glow that sent a terrible chill through Josh. This man didn't really think he was a spy. This all has to do with my mother, he decided.

It was November 2 and the sun shone brightly in a cloudless sky. The rolling hills around Lewiston were covered with a deep, white snow and it was cold and crisp.

The young enlisted man ushered Jenna into the parlor of the Adams farmhouse where James MacLean sat at the table, his feet up, relaxed and looking rested.

"Where's Josh?" Jenna asked before she took a step across the threshold. Her eyes traveled quickly around the room, taking in the leftover food on the table and the general mess. James MacLean and the soldiers who were with him had been here for some time, she gathered. How many were there? she wondered. She had seen one out by the barn, and one had shown her into the house. Counting James, were they three altogether? Of course, there might have been others inside the barn. I have to find out, Jenna thought. I have to know how many there are and where they are.

"Where's Josh?" Jenna repeated.

James didn't answer immediately. His dark, wicked eyes traveled up and down her slowly as he savored his moment of power.

"You look nice," James complimented her, "but you'd look better if you weren't dressed so plainly. Still, you look like you prettied up to come here."

"I did no such thing," Jenna replied, icily.

James straightened up and his heavy-booted legs dropped to the floor with a thud. "Go on! Leave us!" he shouted to the young enlisted man who hovered in the doorway. "I'll question the spy's mother. I know her."

"He is not a spy," Jenna protested. Actually, she thought he might be. He had been so mysterious when he left.

But her proclamation fell on deaf ears. The young enlisted man had left and closed the door behind him. James clearly did not care if Josh were a spy or not.

"Where is he?" Jenna demanded again. "I want to see my son. You haven't hurt him, have you?"

"He's out in the barn," James informed her. "I haven't harmed a hair on his head. Of course, I expect the noose to break his neck. Looks a lot like Will, doesn't he?"

"Yes," Jenna answered softly, "a lot like Will."

She tried to ignore his terrible comments about hanging. He's trying to terrify me, she thought. I mustn't let him get the best of me.

"You've had a long journey, my dear. Take off your cloak and sit down."

"This is not a social call," Jenna replied.

"Of course not. You've come to beg for your son's life. It's touching, really touching."

"Will never did a thing to hurt you, James MacLean. He never pressed the authorities for his share of Robert's land and money, never had you punished. He went away and left you with all of it. What's the matter, James, wasn't all of it enough? Why do you have to come back now to hurt him? To hurt me? And Josh—Josh is perfectly innocent of everything that happened thirty years ago."

"Will took you," James said, leaning forward.

Jenna stared at him. He had been drinking heavily, she could smell it on his breath. Perhaps he

274

would get reckless. "I love Will," Jenna answered. "I never could have loved you the way I love him. Not after I found out how cruel you were, how dishonest . . ."

James laughed sardonically. "I remember your lying in my arms and begging me to touch you. Ah, Jenna, my love, you were such a hot little tart. I trust you still are."

Jenna's face flushed. A vague image of Will and her making love flashed across her mind. "I'm not seventeen now," she replied, trying to sound as cold and remote as possible. "I had a certain physical attraction toward you, but that's all it was. I was young, James. Will taught me what love is. People change, I've changed."

James' eyes were greedy. "You're a fully ripe woman now." He leered at her and she felt he could see through her dress.

"Don't talk to me this way. I'm your brother's wife!"

Jenna came a step closer to James. She tossed her cloak over a bench and sat down. Through the doorway Jenna could see the kitchen of the farmhouse. On the table were dirty dishes from the morning meal. There were three places . . . they probably fed Josh and Richard Adams in the barn. There were only three of them!

"You ought to have been my wife!" James stormed, reaching out toward her.

Jenna moved artfully backward, avoiding his grasp. "James, I remember the day your father drowned. I remember you tried to save him, I remember how you suffered. James, you are not evil. . . ."

"Not like Maria," James offered. "But I'm not good either, certainly not compared to Will! Will is a saint!"

Jenna covered her eyes with her hand, "Oh, James . . ." Her voice now was more sad than angry.

275

"You would have been happier with me, you'd have had a wonderful life! You'd have had slaves! We'd have gone to Europe! Look at your hands, Jenna! It's disgraceful that a woman as beautiful as you should ever have had to work a day in her life!"

"I am not a doll," Jenna answered. "I don't want to be one. I never did. Don't you understand?"

"I understand that I have your son. I understand that I can have him hung or even shot immediately. Of course, I also could let him go."

Jenna sat on the edge of her chair. She had been waiting for him to make her an offer. She knew that James would try to bargain with her. She knew too that it would be an evil bargain.

"You will let him go?" Jenna questioned.

"If I can have you," James suggested. His mouth turned up slightly at the side, his fingertips seemed to dig into the table in anticipation. "I want to feel your skin again, know the smell of your flesh, kiss your nipples, feel you shaking beneath me. . . . I want to . . . I want to. . . ."

"Stop!" Jenna shouted. Her green eyes were fastened firmly on the floor. "Are you seriously suggesting that you will trade my son's life if I agree to allow you to make love to me?"

"Just a few times," James smiled. "Once now, once or twice after he's gone. Then you can go home to darling Will, and I will have had my sweet revenge."

"And you would kill my son for that?" Jenna's green eyes were wide with disbelief.

"He's Will's son too," James added. "I might even enjoy seeing him hang."

"The truth shall make you free. . . ." The quote ran through Jenna's mind. She jumped up to her feet, and the stool she had been sitting on fell over. "He's not Will's son!" Jenna burst out, tears forming in the corners of her eyes. "It's a trick of nature that he looks like Will—they say children often look like their uncles and aunts rather than like their parents. . . . Josh is your son, James. Yours and mine!"

James leaped to his feet and seized her shoulders. "What do you mean? What are you saying!"

Tears flowed down Jenna's cheeks as she trembled. "It's true, its true. You want to hang your own son! He's ours, James, he's ours!"

James released her shoulders, and Jenna's arms dropped loosely to her sides. She couldn't—no, wouldn't look at his face. A silence fell between them and Jenna retreated weakly to where she had been sitting. She looked up only when James spoke.

"All these years . . . all these years and my rightful son was kept from me! My God! You don't know, you just don't know!" He rose again and came over to her. He grabbed her roughly and jerked her to her feet. He drew back his arm and Jenna tried to move, but found she was frozen to the spot. His slap sent her to her knees in front of him. "All these years!" he shouted as he fell on her, forcing her to the floor.

"You kept my son from me!" He attacked her in both anger and passion, ripping her dress wildly with his hands. "You kept me from my son! You're my son, Josh MacLean! Did you hear your mother's confession? You're mine! I'm going to possess your mother now! Listen to her scream! Know how you were conceived! You can listen!"

"Listen!" Jenna screamed. "What are you saying?" She struggled beneath him, terrified not by his actions so much as by his words.

"And you!" James shouted. "God, how I longed for you!" His hands grasped her breasts, which now were bare. His massive knee was on her midsection. Jenna stared up at him. He looked like some crazed creature of the wild as he kneaded her breasts roughly and moaned aloud, his conversation having disintegrated into grunts and groans.

"What do you mean?" Jenna shrieked. "Tell me what you mean!" Jenna turned her head sideways. There was the door to the bedroom. Josh . . . was Josh beyond the door?

James' hand was under her skirt now and he was pulling at her undergarments.

"Josh!" she screamed out her son's name, and her agony, both emotional and physical, filled the room. "Oh, Josh, forgive me!" Jenna cried out.

"He's in the other room!" James panted. "He can hear every word, Jenna. He's heard it from your own lips. He's my son!"

Jenna let out a long, tormented wail of terror and pain. James' probings meant nothing. She could hardly feel them she was so filled with emotion over the thought of Josh knowing the dreaded secret. She had begged Will to tell him, now he had found out this way! And from her own lips!

James pulled away her undergarments and forced her legs apart. Jenna couldn't even struggle she was so staggered by the thought of Josh in the next room.

Jenna screamed again.

"Yes, scream, Jenna. Let our son hear you scream!" James sounded hateful.

Jenna bit her lip and thought, I shall not scream again, I shall not give him the satisfaction. She closed her eyes as he forced his way into her. He loomed above her, panting like an animal. Jenna felt totally numb.

She opened her eyes and looked at his face. He was surely about to reach his ghastly moment of satisfaction. He was hurting her terribly, but strangely she felt impervious to it. She turned her head to avoid the foul smell of his whiskey breath and saw her purse on the floor. The knife! She had carried it since one of her neighbors had been seriously injured when the horse on her buggy ran away. "If she'd have had a knife, she would have been able to cut the horse free," Will had said. It was then that Jenna had begun carrying her mother's old hunting knife.

Jenna groped around and opened her purse, withdrawing the knife and unsheathing it.

James started to gasp, started to shiver above her. Then Jenna grasped the handle and lifted her arm, plunging the knife into James' back.

Still shaking with his climax, James MacLean jolted upright like a mad dog; spittle ran down his mouth, and his eyes bulged with pain. Jenna pushed with all her might and squirmed from beneath him. She jumped away, even as his large arms flailed in the air.

"You've stabbed me!" He wailed out his pain like a wounded bush dog.

Jenna darted to the table and grasped the pistol. "Shut up or I'll kill you!" she threatened.

"You've stabbed me," James repeated with disbelief. He was trying to clutch at his back. His pants were around his ankles; his limp member dangled absurdly.

Jenna kept the pistol trained on him. She stepped gingerly to the window and looked out. She saw no one and there still was a light in the barn. She stepped back, and with one hand pulled the remnants of her dress up and around her, covering herself. Jenna backed into the bedroom. On the bed, bound and gagged, Josh struggled to free himself. His face was deathly pale, and Jenna could tell he was tense with anger.

James staggered after her. "Stay away!" Jenna screamed. "Stay away from me! Don't come another step toward me. I know how to shoot, James. I'll kill you!"

James stopped short, grasping the doorjamb for balance. His face was bright red, his eyes rolled in pain, his breath came in short gasps. Jenna held the pistol in one hand, as she struggled with the knots that held Josh.

James waited and then, sensing that she was distracted with one of the knots, lunged forward. Jenna jolted backward and, quickly turning away from the knots, fired the pistol, hitting James in the upper left thigh and sending him sprawling backward with yet another cry of pain.

Jenna panted and waited, poised like a cat. But when James did not move, she set down the pistol and quickly removed Josh's gag. "Oh, God. Someone must have heard that shot!"

Josh coughed and pulled himself upright as Jenna succeeded in undoing his hands. He bent forward and freed his own legs.

Josh fairly tumbled off the bed, running to James' side. He prodded him with the toe of his boot. "He's still alive," Josh said, turning to her.

James groaned and blinked up into Josh's face. James' dark, large eyes were filled with pain. "I can't take the knife out," Josh said softly. "If I do, he'll bleed too much."

"Shh! Someone's coming!" Jenna had moved to the door. She bolted it from the inside.

"Lieutenant MacLean, sir? Are you all right? I thought I heard a gunshot."

Jenna bit her lip. Then in as syrupy voice as she could muster, she answered, "We'd like to be alone. Tell him we'd like to be alone, honey. . . ."

"Get out of here!" Josh said in a voice that sounded incredibly like James MacLean's.

Jenna leaned by the door and listened in relief to the receding footsteps of the enlisted man.

In the meantime, Josh had laid down the pistol

and, staggering, half lifted, half dragged James Mac-Lean to the bedroom. Josh pulled him to the bed and lay him on his stomach.

"He needs a doctor," Josh whispered to Jenna, who now stood motionless in the doorway. "His breath isn't good."

The color had drained from Jenna's face and she leaned against the sideboard. "I've killed him," she murmured. "He's going to die."

"Don't faint," Josh ordered as he looked at her. "Don't you faint!"

Jenna closed her eyes for a moment. She wanted to give way to the dizzying sensation, she wanted nothing more than to close her eyes, wake up, and find out it all had been a terrible dream.

"Mama!"

Jenna's eyes snapped open in response to Josh's command.

"Get some cloth, we'll have to bandage his leg."

"What about the knife?" Jenna trembled.

"How long is it?" Josh looked at the handle, but he couldn't visualize the blade.

Jenna made a measure with her hands, indicating four inches.

"Maybe I can get it out," Josh said. "Boil some water and get something we can use for bandages, and bring some cool water for his head."

Jenna moved around the farmhouse as if she were drugged. She put another log on the fire and filled the pot. Then she busied herself with looking for clean rags. In time, Jenna found the sterile, absorbent cloths that Colleen must have kept ready for her monthly blood.

Jenna brought the cool water, and Josh laid a compress on James' forehead, turning his head sideways. James groaned and blinked open his dark eyes.

"Don't cry out," Josh warned. He looked at James coldly. "Stuff this in your mouth. I'm going to remove the knife."

James nodded and opened his mouth so Josh could put in the cloth.

"Don't want you to bite your tongue or cry out in pain," Josh explained. He then grasped the knife handle and jerked the knife out of James. For a second blood spurted like a fountain.

Josh clamped a bandage down over the deep puncture wound and held it tight, applying as much pressure as he could. James MacLean groaned.

Jenna leaned against the doorway and watched as her son administered to his biological father. What was Josh thinking? Fear filled her: Josh spoke to her coldly, he seemed angry—or was it anger? So much was happening at once that Jenna could not sort out her own emotions. How could she hope to guess what Josh's were?

Josh removed the cloth from James' mouth. "Lie still!" Josh commanded. He gingerly released some of the pressure he was applying and lifted the corner of the cloth. The wound had stopped gushing. James let go of the pressure pad altogether. He dressed the wound tightly.

That done, Josh turned his attention to James' thigh. "Need a doctor to get the bullet out," he observed. "Best I can do is bandage you up."

James nodded in silent comprehension.

"I ought to kill you," Josh said evenly, "for what you did to my mother. I'd hoped you would die when she shot you, but she didn't aim to kill. Now I can't kill you because that would be cold-blooded murder, but if you could stand up to hold a pistol and walk the ten paces we could have a duel and then I could kill you."

Jenna wordlessly grasped the skirts of her dress

during the exchange between father and son, praying for some clue as to how Josh felt about her. Could he ever forgive her? Quiet tears ran down her cheeks.

James' fingers clung to Josh's jacket. His mouth was partly open. "I'm your father," he gasped. "You're my son!"

Josh closed his eyes, unable to look into James' face. "I am the son of Will MacLean. He is the only father I have. I am his son, no matter what. I am his son."

Jenna let out her breath slowly as she heard Josh's declaration. "I wanted to tell you," Jenna said in a small voice. "I wanted to tell you so many times. . . ."

Josh turned to look at his mother. She was shaking, but he could not accuse her of being a coward. She had come to offer herself to this man in exchange for his life.

"You would have slept with him to save me?" Josh asked, seeking her eyes.

Jenna couldn't answer, but she nodded her head in the affirmative, looking away.

Josh closed his eyes for an instant, ignoring James MacLean, who lay still, his eyes looking from Jenna to Josh. His mother had been through a terrible ordeal. The animal on the bed had raped her, she was exhausted, and he thought she must be on the verge of hysteria as a result of her emotional turmoil. Whatever his parents had kept from him, whatever his mother's past, he loved her more now than ever. He opened his eyes and looked at his mother. "I love you," he said. "No matter what."

Jenna blinked back tears and ran to him, falling on her knees and burying her head in his lap. "Oh, Josh," she sobbed, "I wanted to tell you."

He patted her hair. "It's all right. Come on, Mama, we have to get out of here, we have to get you back across the border."

Jenna lifted her head and with enormous effort pulled herself to her feet.

"How many did you see when you came in? How many men were with him?"

"Two," Jenna answered. "There were three places set at the table in the kitchen. But where is Mr. Adams?"

"In the barn," Josh replied. "Come on, I think there's a musket in the kitchen closet. And we've got the pistol. We have to get Richard Adams, we can't leave without him."

Josh tied James MacLean loosely so his wounds would not trouble him too much. "We'll send someone for you," Josh said as he left the bedroom.

"It's pitch dark," Josh said to his mother. "James MacLean and I are built alike. I'm going to put on his uniform and I'm going to escort you to your sleigh. You're going to get in and take the sleigh down the road a bit, out of sight. Go to where it's wooded and get the carriage off the road, then hide it and unharness the horses. Wait for me and don't make a single sound till you hear the Indian whistle. You remember it?"

Jenna nodded. "Josh, you must be careful. There are two of them."

"I have the element of surprise."

Josh watched as his mother turned the sleigh and headed off down the road. He then turned and walked toward the barn, seeing one of the two enlisted men walking toward him across the field.

"Hey there, Lieutenant MacLean! Find out what you needed to know?"

Josh couldn't see it, but he was certain the man had a smirk on his face. Stupid son-of-a-whore, he thought. But he did not answer the man's call, he only waved his arm in greeting. Josh stopped and waited till the man got closer, then he turned and stood with his back to the approaching man, looking up into the night sky, hoping that from the rear his silhouette would look enough like James MacLean's to be convincing.

Josh was hardly breathing as he listened to the man's footsteps crunching across the open space, coming closer and closer. When Josh felt the man directly behind him, he whirled around, hitting him in the gut with all his strength. The man gasped and doubled over. Josh delivered a second vicious blow to the back of the head and without more than a muffled groan, the guard fell forward, unconscious.

Josh waited an instant, then looked around, but evidently the other soldier had heard nothing. Josh hoisted the unconscious man over his shoulder and carried him toward the farmhouse. Once there, he gagged and bound him, locking him in the kitchen closet and leaving him.

Josh then discarded James' uniform and donned his own clothes. He retrieved his hunting knife and sheathed it; he brought the pistol and the musket. He made his way silently to the barn, approaching it from the rear. Through a small hay window in the back, he peered inside.

The second soldier crouched before a small fire he had made. In one corner, Richard Adams sat bound and gagged.

Josh drew the pistol and waited till the guard was in the right position. Taking careful aim, Josh pulled the trigger and hit the guard in the shoulder.

Josh ran quickly to the front door of the barn and inside. "Don't move a muscle," he warned. The guard grasped his bleeding shoulder and nodded dumbly.

Josh moved closer and looked at the wound. It

seemed more painful than serious. He poked the young soldier with his pistol. "Untie him at once!"

The soldier stumbled to Richard Adams and untied him with one hand. Then he pulled out the gag.

"Shit!" Adams spit and jumped to his feet. He stretched and swore again.

"Tie him up," Josh said. "Come on, hurry up. The night is not young."

Adams did as he was told. "I'm American," he protested.

"I'm sorry," Josh apologized. "But no one will believe you, they'll hang you. Besides, you don't like being conscripted to fight. Come on, man, there's plenty of good land in Canada." Josh paused and smiled. "Besides, you'll be nearer to your grandchildren."

"Colleen's in Washington."

"And I'm going to find her and bring her home."

Adams shrugged. "Canadian, American—what difference does it make?

"At the moment six feet of rope," Josh answered. "Here, you take the pistol." He extended the weapon to Adams.

"Long live the King," Adams muttered under his breath. Then he added, "There are some things I have to get in the house."

"You'll have to hurry, we haven't much time. My mother's waiting and you two have to be gotten across the river before it's light."

Adams nodded and hurried off toward the house. There were jewels there, things he had found in Megan's trunk, things that had to be brought.

He flung open the door of the house and rummaged through the left drawer of the dresser. There, in a square case, were the jewels. He withdrew the case and put it inside his shirt.

"Don't move!"

Richard Adams whirled to face James MacLean,

whose expression showed his pain. He stood on one leg, braced against the door. But he did have a pistol. Adams made some quick deductions: MacLean had been tied up in the bedroom, so the pistol must have come from the drawer in the bedside table. It belonged to Adams and he knew it wasn't loaded. He made a sudden move and drew out the pistol Josh had given him. Adams fired even as James MacLean's pistol with its empty chamber clicked dully.

James MacLean's face bore an expression of total surprise. His eyes bulged, then he crumpled like a doll on the floor.

Within two minutes of the shot, Josh came running into the house, musket ready. He looked at his biological father lying in a pool of blood and he saw Richard Adams leaning over him.

"He's dead," Adams reported.

Josh shook his head. "It's better," he whispered in a hardly audible voice.

Josh and Richard Adams hurried down the road and soon found Jenna waiting in the woods. They mounted the horses and headed for the river.

"Can you handle the crossing?" Josh asked Adams.

"I've crossed this river more times than I can count."

"You're not coming?" Jenna looked up into her son's face. "Oh, Josh, you must come home."

Josh shook his head. "I have work to do." He turned to Adams. "Take care of her, see that she gets home."

Adams shook his head and motioned Jenna toward the boat. "We have to hurry," he said. "Otherwise we'll be caught by the Americans or blown out of the water by the British!"

Josh leaned down and kissed his mother on the forehead. "Don't worry," he whispered, "about anything."

CHAPTER XIII

December 1812

Dolley Madison was not wearing one of her famous turbans on the morning of December 1. Instead, her hair was loose and uncovered, forming endless tight little ringlets around her face. Dolley's cheeks were pink with anger, as were her little pink ears, the end of her nose, and the area just above her breasts.

"Mr. Madison's war! That's what they call it! Mason James MacLean, they call it Mr. Madison's war!" She thrust out her lower lip and pouted. "I could personally strangle every Federalist newspaper editor! It's not bad enough that they rant on with their filthy lies about me and Mr. Jefferson! God knows if Mr. Jefferson would even look at me, he's so smitten with the darkie woman who's his mistress. . . . I hate them, Mr. MacLean, dear. I hate them—every one! Why can't they call it Mr. Clay's war? Or Mr. Calhoun's war?"

Mason James tried to concentrate, but it was difficult because Jason Talbot was bending over the tea tray just a few feet away. Then too, Mason James was not as sympathetic as he might have been. Mrs. Madison would not have been upset at all to have it called Mr. Madison's war, were it not for the fact that it was such a fiasco. But to have a circus named after one's husband was upsetting.

First there was the defeat at Fort Michilimackinac, then the defeat at Detroit, then the three attempts to cross the Niagara River into Upper Canada. The attempt in early October had resulted in a resounding defeat, and the other two, attempted late in November by Smythe, had fizzled out before the river even was crossed. It was all quite pathetic, though even Mason James would have to admit that it was not as pathetic as the recent battle near Montreal.

On the night of November 19, a detachment of American regulars crossed the border and fought a skirmish on the Lacolle River in Lower Canada. They actually captured a blockhouse, but the Canadian troops who were bunked in it escaped into the darkness. What ensued probably would not go down in the military history of the new nation. The Americans became more confused than usual in the dark and systematically began killing one another. It was one of their great successes. By morning there was one American survivor, giving the Canadians yet another victory.

"The militia is badly trained," Mason James observed as Jason Talbot slipped out of the room. "And naturally, as the war is going—well, not as well as we expected it to—the press is blaming your husband."

Dolley shook her curls. "No. It's not just the militia! The regulars are not one bit better." She flounced herself down on the settee. They were in the main reception room of the Executive Mansion. It was a large, partially empty room and their voices seemed to echo off the walls.

"Outside of dear Mr. Madison, this country has precious few leaders," Dolley lamented. "General Dearborn did nothing, and General Hull, intelligent man that he is, gets so confused when there's a crisis, he doesn't know his ears from his toes! And General Smythe! Well, General Smythe is the master of sheer folly!"

"And so our plans to invade Canada have come to a halt," Jason Talbot interjected as he set down the tea tray and then took a chair himself.

"For the time being," Dolley agreed in an exasperated tone. "I'm just so frustrated, Mr. MacLean, dear. I just cannot decide what to do." Dolley cupped her chin in her hand while her eyes roamed the walls and settled on the Gilbert Stuart painting of General George Washington. "I wonder what he would have done?" Dolley asked with a sigh.

Mason James glanced at the portrait of Washington. He did not answer, because he had no answer. If the truth be known, he was as perplexed over the progress of the war as she was.

"I should be planning a Christmas party," Dolley finally said. "Something charitable—people should do something charitable at Christmas. Oh, speaking of charity, how is that little girl you took in, Mr. MacLean?"

Mason blushed. "Quite well," he replied vaguely. What could one say about a woman as robust as Colleen and two babies? "But of course, she means nothing to me," he added. That at least was the truth, though in fact, he liked the babies in spite of himself.

Dolley sighed again. "I'm so exhausted today. This war is so distracting!"

Mason James inhaled and stole a look at Jason. He was glad Dolley was exhausted. Heaven knew, he was tired of her and her strange desires.

Mason James sipped his tea. "To return to the subject," he said carefully, "I do think the red drapes would be right for this room." Mason James put down his teacup and moved around the reception room. "Red would pick up the colors in the flag

290

here—I do believe we should try to be as thematic as possible."

Dolley made a face. "I don't like the flag! It's got the same old colors as the British flag. Red, white, and blue—posh! I always thought Mr. Washington did the wrong thing having that flag made red, white, and blue like the old British flag. It ought to be more distinctive. I love turquoise and orange! I just don't know why it couldn't have been turquoise and orange."

Mason James smiled benignly. The flag was the farthest thing from his mind. At this moment, he was thinking only of Jason's adorable little round bottom.

"Is Mr. MacLean here?" The servant stood stiffly in the entranceway.

"He is," Dolley called out.

"A message has been delivered here for you," the servant announced. He walked across the room and handed Mason James the official-looking letter pouch. "It's from the Secretary of the Army," the servant explained.

Mason James took the proffered pouch and looked at it a moment before opening it. Then he broke the sealing wax and withdrew a parchment. His face paled.

"What is it, Mr. MacLean, dear?" Dolley looked concerned, and Jason Talbot was leaning forward.

"My daddy's been killed," Mason James said in a whisper. And it suddenly ran through his mind that he no longer had to worry about his father producing another heir, or about pretending to be married.

"That's shocking. Oh, Mr. MacLean, dear, you had better sit down."

Jason Talbot took his arm, and Mason smiled gratefully into his face as he allowed himself to be helped to a chair. "He died a hero," Mason James

291

said under his breath, "trying to interrogate some spies."

"Spies?" Jason questioned.

"They escaped," Mason James breathed, "after they shot my daddy."

"Horrifying!" Dolley said. "Oh, Mr. MacLean, dear, I can't tell you how terrible I feel. And I can't even stay. I have to be with Mr. Madison this afternoon. Can you ever forgive me?"

Mason James nodded. "It will be all right," he uttered. "It's just such a shock."

"Of course it is, but you should not be alone." Dolley paused, then burst into a wide smile. "I know, you take the afternoon off and stay with Mr. MacLean, Jason. You two get along so well!"

The cabin that Bonnie and Ian lived in was built for the long, cold prairie winters. It had two slits in place of windows and it was dominated by the fireplace, which was the sole source of heat.

Bonnie Campbell watched through one of the slits as Ian headed off toward Pembina for another day's work. He and Miles Macdonell and Owen Keveney were supervising the building of a new trading post and the strengthening of the fort. "One day," Ian had told her, "there will be houses, schools, churches, and a blacksmith. This will be a real community," he stressed. "It's on the Red River and there will be trade with the Dakotas as well as with Upper and Lower Canada and Britain."

She smiled as Ian's bundled-up form disappeared into the distance. He rode his horse almost casually, and his gun was slung over his shoulder. As he totally vanished from her sight, Bonnie felt a sudden surge of loneliness.

It was snowing hard and the wind was crying as it blew around the corner of the cabin. Ian had warned her to remain inside and not even to venture as far as Marie-Anne's. "This could turn into a prairie howler," he joked. "And they can be treacherous."

"And what about you?" Bonnie had questioned. "Are MacLeans invincible?"

"I'm certain I'll be home for dinner," Ian had said, smiling. He ignored her jibes and she always regretted being sarcastic as soon as the words escaped her mouth. If only Ian MacLean did not treat her as a child, if only he didn't have the capacity to make her so angry . . .

Bonnie turned back to the cabin, walking casually over to the hearth and staring into it. Was Marie-Anne right? Was there something between her and Ian? No, Bonnie decided. Marie-Anne was wrong. She was only a romantic who thought she saw something that was not there. Ian doesn't even like me, Bonnie thought. He has deep-rooted prejudice against all Campbells.

For a time following Ian's departure, Bonnie sewed. Then, tiring of that, she took to cooking. I'll make a surprise for Ian's dinner, she decided. Bonnie toiled for hours pounding the buffalo meat and combining the other ingredients to prepare the stew Marie-Anne had shown her how to make. When she was finished and the stew was set over the fire for slow cooking, she made two loaves of bread and placed them on the mantel to rise.

All that done, Bonnie heated some water and washed her hair, drying it before the fire. Then she adorned herself in her only dress.

Tonight, Bonnie promised herself, she would not be so sharp-tongued. Tonight she and Ian would have an extra-special nice dinner and they would talk.

"Ian MacLean!" Ian turned around at the sound of the friendly greeting. He smiled into the high-cheek-boned, copper-colored face of Michel Deschamps.

Michel was in his midthirties, the son of old René Deschamps and an Indian woman. He himself was married to Wind Willow, a lovely Cree woman. Like his father, Michel was a *voyageur,* and he and Ian had met once up near the Sault, where Lake Superior and Lake Huron meet. Now the two men embraced, and Michel asked enthusiastically, "What are you doing here?"

Ian explained and then, somewhat red-faced, added, "I have moved into the cabin belonging to your father. I thought you all were farther west."

Michel slapped him on the back. "We're staying with the Indians. I would not have stayed there anyway. Come on, let's have a drink together."

Ian nodded and surveyed the sky. "The storm still is bad," he observed. "Just as well to wait awhile before going back."

The two of them headed for Miles Macdonell's quite comfortable headquarters. "Where exactly have you come from?" Ian asked.

"From Fort St. Joseph and Fort Michilimackinac."

"Fort Michilimackinac is American," Ian said and smiled. "What took you there?"

"It's not American anymore. It's Canadian now. We liberated it."

Ian laughed. He had known that the Americans had declared war. "So now we control the trading routes."

"By some miracle," Michel answered. "You wouldn't believe it. The Americans didn't notify their army that they had declared war, but we got our information from Astor's couriers. So the whole lot of *voyageurs* who were there, together with the soldiers and the *Indians,* took Fort Michilimackinac without a shot being fired. Imagine? You must know that everyone at Fort St. Joseph was a geriatric and an alcoholic to boot. It all turned into one long party."

"This war doesn't sound too serious," Ian said.

"It's serious but not here."

Ian nodded and wondered about Lochiel and his family. "Have you heard anything about the Niagara?"

Michel shrugged. "Only that it's still Canadian. The Americans attacked a few times last month. I heard that from one of the traders. But they were repulsed."

"Good," Ian said under his breath. They reached Miles' headquarters, and Ian knocked on the door. Miles invited them in and there were introductions all around. "Came to drink some of your liquor stores," Ian told him. "And wait out the storm."

They sat for the better part of four hours drinking and talking. "You're as drunk as a prairie dog that's been slurping whiskey!" Miles proclaimed, slapping Ian on the leg.

Ian looked at the two empty bottles on the table. The whole room seemed to be weaving back and forth.

"It's good to get drunk," Ian slurred. "Once in a while."

"You should have been at Michilimackinac," Michel chimed in. He was slouched over, gripping his glass, and smiling happily. "You'd've fit right in, 'cept you and me are about twenty years younger than the army up there. Hell, even the Indians were old!"

Miles laughed loudly. It was a good evening. Michel Deschamps was full of stories, and the sideboard was full of whiskey.

"How's your mistress?" Miles asked, burping just before he finished his sentence.

"Not my mistress. We have an—an honor—an honorbound—an honorable relationship. That's it, honorable." Ian waved his glass around. "Is there more?"

"If you have an honorable relationship you need more! There's always more! What's winter in Pembina without a lot to drink?"

"Dull," Michel answered.

Magically, Miles wove his way to the sideboard, found another skin of whiskey, and returned to the table without falling. He bit off the top and took a swig directly from the skin before passing it on to Ian.

"She sleeps on one side of the cabin and I sleep on the other," he said, staring at the floor.

"That's not natural," Michel mumbled. "You better do something about that."

"She's pretty," Ian said, filling his glass. "Damn scornful wench, but pretty."

"If she's already slept with one man, how come she won't keep your bed warm?" Miles burbled.

" 'Cause I haven't asked her. Anyway, you know I think that Finlay did attack her. Hell, she's pure and proper!"

Miles shrugged. He couldn't think straight, the room was moving too fast. "I'm a Catholic," he finally said. "I don't understand Presbyterians." He paused, then looked around and smiled. "I think I have to pass out," he told the others. Then, without further ado, Miles Macdonell staggered to his bedroll in the corner, lay down, curled himself into a ball, and fell instantly asleep.

Michel Deschamps virtually slipped out of his chair and onto the floor. He too fell asleep.

Ian stood up. He was tired and groggy. "Why am I here?" he said aloud to no one. "Oh, yes, because it was snowing too hard to go home earlier." He shook his head and peered out the window. The snow had stopped, the wind was still, and the night was cold and bright. Ian put on his heavy clothes, pulled down his fur hat around his ears, and wrapped his scarf tightly around his neck and face. He went to the barn to get his horse, his footprints zigzagging drunkenly across the deep snow.

He mounted the horse and headed off into the night, the cold air sobering him only slightly.

The sound of the door jolted a fully dressed Bonnie Campbell from a light, distressed sleep. Her cornflower-blue eyes were wide, first from being startled, second from the sight of Ian, who staggered into the cabin.

"Where have you been?" she demanded, standing up. "I've been frantic! Where have you been?"

Ian stood absolutely still and stared at her. She was beautiful! He saw her long hair hanging loose for the first time—and behold! She no longer was dressed in buckskins but in a proper dress. Her eyes shone. Oh, her eyes are pretty, he thought. But Ian was, in spite of the night air, a man still filled with whiskey. "It was snowing . . ." He didn't finish his sentence, but instead literally crumpled before her.

"You're drunk!" Bonnie screamed to unhearing ears. "I thought you were frozen in the snow! I thought you'd been killed! But you're not dead! You're drunk!" Her hands were doubled into angry fists. She bent over Ian's unconscious form and pounded on his shoulder. "I fixed a special dinner! I dressed up for you! I even washed my hair! I waited and waited! I worried about you! And you're drunk, you miserable bastard! You're drunk!"

Ian MacLean woke to a throbbing head, a churning stomach, and the sound of Bonnie Campbell sobbing. He was still wearing his furs, and he found himself in a puddle of water where the snow from them and his boots had melted in the warm cabin.

He stretched and was not surprised to find himself stiff. As he attempted to sit up, he felt the vomit rising in his throat. Grasping the side of the table leg, he half crawled, half pulled himself to the door, pushing it open and throwing up again and again onto the snow on the doorstep.

"You're letting cold air into the house," Bonnie said.

Ian turned. He was pale and dizzy, but he felt a little better for having been sick, though he suspected this was not the end of it.

Bonnie's long, loose hair was tangled, her lovely blue eyes were red from crying. Ian exhaled, then inhaled, trying to steady himself. Then, deciding he was finished being sick for the time being, he pulled himself back inside and closed the door.

"You deserve to be sick," Bonnie said. Then she repeated her accusations of the night before, her anger and frustration pouring out. "And you came home dead drunk! After I worked so hard!"

Ian heard her out, leaning against the wall by the door. Never had he had such a headache, or such an upset stomach. Never had he felt such a surge of mixed emotions. Bonnie Campbell's blue eyes seemed to penetrate his whole being. God, he thought, she really is beautiful.

"Well, what have you to say for yourself?" Her hands were on her hips, her cheeks were rosy, her lips inviting . . . or at least they would have been inviting if Ian had not felt so ill.

"I couldn't leave because of the snow. I got to drinking with a long-lost relative and with Miles. I came home when the snow stopped."

"Hours after it stopped! I was frantic!"

"Were you now?" Ian asked.

Bonnie suddenly blushed and looked away. Through a wave of absolute nausea, Ian suddenly knew the truth. She cared about him. They had been together for months and she really cared!

"Living with a woman you want to make love to, a woman you love, and not being able to touch her or get near her is enough to drive any man to drink," Ian stumbled.

Bonnie lifted her head and their eyes met. "What?" she said, amazed.

"I love you—I'd make love to you this minute, but damnit, I'm going to be sick again!" With that, Ian again flung open the door and stepped outside. Lord, I'm turning inside out, he thought.

"You could love a Campbell?" he heard her say. She was standing behind him, unconcerned that he was retching. Ian continued being ill, then turned to her. His face was pale. "Yes, I could love a Campbell! I do love a Campbell! But not right now, damnit!"

Ian staggered back inside and Bonnie took his elbow. "Lie down for a while," she advised. Ian smiled weakly at her and allowed himself to be led to his bedroll. She helped him off with his furs and covered him when he sank onto the bedroll. Ian closed his eyes, feeling Bonnie's hand on his.

He opened his eyes and found the cabin dark except for a few dying embers in the fireplace. Quickly, Ian pulled himself out from under the pile of furs and went to the fire. He placed more logs on it and stoked it, lest it die. The room was chilly and it occurred to Ian that he and Bonnie had slept all day. He had been exhausted from drinking and being ill, she had been weary from waiting up all night for him to return.

Ian washed his face in the little basin and lit the lantern. He rinsed out his mouth and took a long drink of water. He felt normal again—and hungry and thirsty.

Bonnie moaned slightly in her sleep and rolled over on her back, only half awake. He walked over to her and looked down. She blinked her eyes open and smiled at him. "Are you better now?" she asked.

Ian bent over and touched her cheek softly with the back of his hand. Then he kissed her cheek tenderly. "Much," he replied, stretching his long body out next to hers on the pile of furs. "Were you really so worried?"

Bonnie shook her head in the affirmative. "And then I was angry."

Ian kissed her nose, her neck, and then her lovely full lips. He felt her return the kiss, putting her arms around his neck and hugging him. "I wanted to kiss you long ago," Ian whispered in her ear. "But you kept a wall between us."

"I thought you hated Campbells."

Ian returned to her lips and gave her a long, slow kiss, moving his mouth sensuously against hers. She in turn clung to him.

"I guess there is one Campbell I will have to learn to love." He again kissed her neck, then gently rolled her over on her stomach and proceeded to undo the long line of buttons that held her dress together.

"Learn?" Bonnie questioned without moving.

"I have to love the woman I'm going to marry," Ian said. "And, of course, she'll reproduce and we'll have a lot of little half Campbells. I'll have to learn to like and love them too." He smiled mischievously and pushed the material of her dress away, kissing her bare back from the base of her spine upward beneath her flowing chestnut tresses.

"Should I marry you?" Bonnie asked.

"Since you are going to be the mother of my children, it seems only right," Ian replied, pulling off her dress, leaving her only in her white undergarments.

"And how many children are we to have?" Bonnie asked playfully.

"There's a lot of land in the West," Ian smiled. "A dozen or so at least."

He rolled her over on her back and kissed her throat. His fingers toyed with the ribbons on her undergarments. Then, still kissing her, he undid them, slipping them away. He wiggled out of his own clothes and soon they lay body to body, warming each other with caresses. Ian kissed her firm breasts, her stomach, and her navel, then caressed the soft patch of downy hair that curled over her mound. He parted the hair and his caresses aroused her to a glowing passion. When Bonnie was warm and rosy all over and he felt her breath coming in short gasps of anticipation, Ian rolled her over once again and lifted her rounded buttocks to enter her. She moved with him, moaning now and again, lost in a world of pleasure. When she let out a long final sigh of fulfillment, Ian allowed himself release. They lay together for a long while, curled in each other's arms.

"That was nice," Bonnie said after a time. "It is nice when you feel something special. . . ."

"And you've waited so long," Ian added, kissing her again. "You know, I used to lie across the room at night and listen to you breathe. I used to think of you breathing in my ear, I used to imagine holding you like this, caressing you, touching you. . . ."

Bonnie's hands moved across his hairy chest and then downward, setting him afire again. "I wondered about you too," she confessed. "I wanted you to hold me, to love me. . . . I was frightened after that man—I didn't think it could be like this, though I wanted it to be."

Ian touched the tip of her breast and felt it harden. He bent his head down and took her nipple into his mouth, aware of her growing excitement as he did so.

301

Then he returned his hand to her mound, massaging her into a frenzy of desire. To his delight, she returned the intimate caresses, holding him till he was again hard and ready. Then Ian pulled her on top of him and Bonnie straddled him, closing her eyes and groaning as he pushed up into her. Her lovely breasts hung over his face, and Ian took one in each hand, teasing her nipples until she moaned and arched her back. Ian watched, loving the expression of satisfaction on her face, then he too exploded. They tumbled together onto the furs, laughing.

"I do love you," Bonnie confessed. "I love you!"

"And I you," Ian replied. "And we'll be married in the spring when the priest comes . . . in the spring, Bonnie, though we're just as good as married now, under métis custom."

Josh sat in the tavern opposite Jason Talbot. "You haven't touched your drink," Josh observed.

"I really don't like liquor," the young man retorted. "I much prefer a nice cool fruit punch."

Josh nodded and acknowledged the heat. It was late May, but already the sun shone brightly and the air was filled with humidity.

It had been a long trip from Lewiston to Washington, a trip with many delays. He had arrived only an hour earlier and in spite of his desire to go directly to the house where he knew Colleen was living, he had vowed to make his contact with Jason Talbot immediately.

"So you will be giving me what information you have to pass on," Josh finished explaining.

"I shall have a pouch prepared by the end of the week," Jason informed him. "You seem anxious about something."

Josh smiled. Jason Talbot seemed efficient, but there was something about him. He was not exactly handsome, but rather, pretty in a kind of feminine way. Still, he smiled kindly and he seemed interested.

"I am anxious," Josh admitted. "I have to find my fiancée. She's here, she's in Washington—well, Georgetown, actually. I really don't know my way around."

"What's the address?" Jason asked, taking a sip of his drink and then making a face.

Josh fished into his pocket and brought out a crumpled piece of paper, which he handed to Jason. Reading it, Jason's eyes opened up wide. "That's Mason's address!"

Josh frowned. "Mason who?" he asked. "I thought a Mrs. Sharp lived there."

Jason shook his head like a disgruntled old woman. "No, no, no . . . Mason James MacLean lives there. Is your fiancée named Colleen?"

"Mason James MacLean?" Josh repeated the name and quickly reminded himself that Jason Talbot did not know his real last name, because, following his orders, he had given the name on his identity papers. "And who is Mason James MacLean?"

Jason heard the jealousy in Josh's voice. "Oh, it's all right," he quickly said. "They live together, but they don't live together, if you understand. I mean they don't know each other in the biblical sense."

Josh still was frowning. He could scarcely imagine a man living with Colleen and not making love to her.

Jason's eyes suddenly widened. "You must be Josh MacLean!"

Josh leaned back. "That is my real name," he said in a near whisper. "You seem to know a lot about me."

Jason smiled almost benevolently. "Well, Mason James is my . . . my . . . friend; yes, dear friend. And

303

Colleen . . . I go there often for dinner, and Colleen always is speaking of you. Good Lord! You must be the father of the twins!"

Josh blinked. Twins? He was losing his mind. The room was starting to spin. Jason reached across the table and patted his hand. "There, there now . . . they're lovely twins. Mason and I are ever so fond of them!"

Mason and I . . . ah, Josh thought, trying to pull himself together, that was it! He felt a mixed sense of relief and amazement. "And who is Mason James MacLean?" he asked again.

"Oh, the son of James' MacLean of Louisiana. A very rich man, very rich. He took poor Colleen in to fool his father—I mean, he didn't want to get married, but his father insisted on an heir. Oh, dear, it's such a long story. Anyway, now his father is dead."

Josh closed his eyes and drank every drop left in his glass. Mason James MacLean was his half brother! He let out his breath and signaled the waiter to fill up his glass.

"Are you all right?" Jason Talbot questioned.

"I'm in shock," Josh said honestly. "How is it that Mason James MacLean lives in Mrs. Sharp's house? I don't understand any of this. Colleen came here to find Mrs. Sharp—that's what her father told me."

"Oh, Mrs. Sharp died some time ago and Mason James bought the house."

Josh only nodded at that piece of incidental information. "Will you take me there?" he asked.

"Oh, I'd be delighted," Jason Talbot cooed. "Absolutely delighted."

It was a May morning, with eerie little fog patches hanging here and there. The ground was soggy from the April rains, and new grass was beginning to appear, fresh and green.

But with the sprouting of the seedlings and the return of the birds from the South, with this coming of spring, there also was war.

In the beginning it had been a halfhearted seesaw war of attempts and failures; both sides had been unprepared. Now, in spite of the original failures, the U.S. Navy had become a power to reckon with on the Great Lakes. Under the leadership of the brilliant Commodore Chauncey, the tiny American fleet managed to wreak havoc along the shore.

Will MacLean was third in command of the Canadian militia units serving in the Niagara. He was gone more than he was home, and now he didn't argue, he made Jenna move to Lochiel.

"Lochiel won't be safe either," Jenna had protested.

"A least you will be with the family. I won't have to worry." Will had stared into her emerald-green eyes. "Do as I say," he ordered.

"All right," Jenna gave in. Seldom did Will order her, and she went to Lochiel out of love for her husband more than for safety or comfort.

The dreaded shelling from Commodore Chauncey's fleet began on the morning of May 25. It was directed at Fort George.

Within a few hours, the log buildings within the fort were ablaze. The defenders of the fort were a mixed force and included some one thousand men of all ranks from the 8th and 49th Foot, the Royal Newfoundland and Glengarry Light Infantry Fencibles.

Brigadier General John Vincent, now in charge of Fort George, divided the garrison into three groups. He hoped to launch a counterattack wherever a landing might be made by the Americans. He preferred that strategy to being caught in an indefensible fort that now had most of its buildings burned or burning.

But the plan, whatever its merits, was not good enough. The Americans landed on the morning of

May 27 and the British troops and the Indians were forced to fall back. The first ashore was Winfield Scott and his attack force.

"This fort cannot be defended," Vincent told his men. "Our Intelligence sources indicate the assault force is made up of some five thousand men."

There was a ripple of comment among the assembled men. "We'll have to blow the ammunition and spike the guns," Vincent told them. "Then we'll drop back; they'll have difficulty if they have to pursue us on our own territory, their supply lines will be too long." Vincent paused. "I'll be taking the British regulars, but I'm dismissing the militia and sending them to their homes and farms."

Will MacLean let out a sigh of relief. Andrew Macleod was an old man and so was Tom. Middle-aged men and those in the prime of life were serving with the army in other parts of Upper Canada. The men serving here in the militia were older. Will himself was one of the youngest, at fifty. It's good that I can go back to Lochiel, he thought. At Lochiel there were many young children and women of all ages. They would need help with the crops.

Will bid his friends among the regulars farewell. He rode with a regular soldier as far as the road that led to Lochiel, then he gave the man his horse and took off on foot the last quarter mile down the road.

Will felt odd. It was spring and he felt almost lighthearted. He was on his way to Jenna, and even with the cannons thundering in the background and Fort George burning, he felt good. Lochiel loomed up in the distance and Will quickened his pace, walking faster till he broke into a half run.

Jenna threw open the front door and ran out to meet him. Her hair was loose and shining in the morning sun. It had been five months since Jenna's terrible encounter with James MacLean. Will had been stunned when she told him about it; he had felt strangely relieved to learn his brother was dead. But James' death and Josh finding out about his true parentage had brought a new kind of peace between him and Jenna. The one flaw in their relationship had vanished. Josh still was his son, Jenna still was his wife, and now there were no more secrets.

"You're home!" She threw her arms around his neck and together they walked toward the house. "I could see the smoke from the upstairs windows! And hear the cannons! The children are all frightened." Jenna squeezed his hand.

"The Americans have landed," Will told her. "Come along into the house."

He led her up the front steps. "Everyone's here," Jenna explained with a wave of her hand. "We've stored and hidden provisions; we have guns, ammunition."

Will shook his head. "No. We can't fight off five thousand Americans. The British have pulled back. This is not a time for fighting. They won't bother us."

Jenna pressed his hand. "You're in the militia," she said, biting her lip. "Will, I'm not certain they won't bother us."

CHAPTER XIV

June 1813

"Heaven save us!" Mason James' voice was filled with amazement. He sat in his huge green tapestried chair with his feet up and gulped down his Bourbon and branch water. Josh had just finished his tale, but he would soon have to repeat it because Colleen was not at home. It gave him the opportunity to talk to Mason James first.

For his part, Mason James had listened wide-eyed to his newly discovered half brother. And if he was troubled by anything, it was at the vague thought he might have to share his vast inheritance.

"I didn't kill your father," Josh concluded. "He was shot by another man." Josh didn't say the other man was Colleen's father. Enough was enough.

Josh studied Mason James' face and thought he saw what really was troubling him. "I don't want any of your money," he said firmly. "If that's what you're thinking."

Mason James suddenly beamed and felt the flush of temporary generosity. "That's wonderful of you," he blurted out, "but of course you and Colleen and the twins will need a place to live. I trust you will go on accepting my hospitality."

Josh raised an eyebrow. "That could cause you some difficulty, for I have just confessed to you that I am not who my identity papers say I am."

"Are you a spy?" Mason James questioned. His face had gone a little pale. "But I cannot harbor a spy! I'm a loyal, patriotic American!"

"Of course you can, you silly man," Jason interrupted. "There are many things you can do with a spy—and do do." He winked.

"What?" Mason James' eyes had grown quite large. "I don't understand."

"I will help you to understand," Jason said and smiled. "Just let us not think of unpleasant things like our love letters falling into the wrong hands. Things like that can—well, ruin a political career!"

"My God!" Mason James intoned. "I'm in the lair of spies! I'm surrounded!"

"You love it!" Jason smiled his most devastating smile as Josh shifted uncomfortably in his chair.

"Oh, I hear Colleen's carriage." Mason stood up and parted the curtain that hung over the front window. "I suppose you want to be alone with her."

"If possible," Josh replied.

"I think we should be alone," Jason said pointedly, taking Mason's arm. "Come along. We have things to discuss, you and I."

The two of them disappeared into the back courtyard, leaving Josh standing alone as the door opened and Colleen came in. She set down her packages on a table in the entranceway and turned, her mouth falling open as she stared into the parlor and saw Josh.

"It's me," he said. "Don't pass out." Josh took two long steps across the room and caught her in his arms, pulling her to him. "I am not your cousin," he said and smiled. "And I have a great deal to tell you."

Josh didn't wait, but pulled her to the settee and kissed her. Then he told her his story. "And you see," he concluded, "your father was born some fourteen months after Megan left the Niagara. Mathew Macleod could not have been his father."

309

Colleen leaned against Josh's shoulder. "Mason told you about the twins?"

"They run in the family," Josh told her. "My father was one of twins. Mason James is my half brother."

"Wh-what?" Colleen looked at him in astonishment. "But he said he had no relatives in Canada, he said . . ."

Josh was shaking his head. "He didn't know," he finally said.

Colleen sat up straight and looked at him skeptically. "Mason James MacLean is a dear man in spite of himself. I'm very fond of him, but he is—ah, well, different."

Josh slapped his knee and leaned back laughing. All his tension and weariness disappeared. "And you're worried about his half brother?" His eyes were wildly flirtatious. He turned and kissed her.

"No," she said after a minute, "you aren't at all alike." She looked down and away for a moment. "Can you forgive me for running away?"

"I love you, I want you," Josh answered.

Colleen smiled her wonderful smile and touched his arm. "You know, Mason really has been very good to me."

"His side of the family owes mine," Josh joked.

Together they climbed the stairs and went to the nursery Righteous had fixed up.

"They're still asleep," Colleen said, looking down at her sons. "That one is Colin and that's Trace."

"Trace?" Josh questioned. He squeezed her waist. "I like the sound of it, but what the hell does it mean?"

Colleen giggled. "I wanted to name one of them after Mason James, but he wouldn't let me. So we named the baby after the place he comes from, the Natchez Trace."

"Trace MacLean," Josh said. "Has a good sound

about it." He turned and kissed her. "I love our babies," he said proudly. Then winking, he added, "Let's make some more!"

Two days passed and Fort George ceased to be British. The Americans set up camp and began to visit homes and farms in search of the younger men who had been released from the militia. The rumors traveled faster than the soldiers. The Americans, it seemed, were asking for money to ensure the lives and well-being of the former militiamen. They called it "parole" and took it instead of arresting the Canadians and locking them in the stockade.

On the morning of June 13 Jenna MacLean took the older children into the fields to begin readying the ground for planting. She wore a long gingham dress and a large bonnet to protect her fair skin from the sun. Like the others, she was hoeing, chopping the soil into small pieces after the recent rains.

"Soldiers coming!" one of the children called out. "Look, they have an American flag!"

Jenna straightened up and stared at the approaching soldiers. There were ten in all. She gripped her hoe tightly.

The soldiers reined in their horses. "Winfield Scott at your service, ma'am." Their leader introduced himself and bent from the waist.

Jenna looked up into his face. "I do not require anything," she said coldly. "Why have you come here?"

"Hear tell there's a militiaman about. You can pay parole for him, or we'll be coming back tomorrow and taking him on up to the stockade."

"I'll go back to the house with you now," Jenna told him.

Winfield Scott nodded and extended his hand to her, helping her up behind him. "Wouldn't have a lady walk," he said gallantly.

311

At the house, all the family resident at Lochiel assembled in the living room. Winfield Scott inspected the men and concluded that only Will could have served in the militia.

Good, Jenna thought. He's dismissed Andrew and Tom as too old. But what he doesn't know won't put money into his pockets. "And how much is this, this parole?" she asked.

Winfield Scott snapped his fingers and a young orderly withdrew a sheaf of papers. "We have documents to fill out," Scott answered. He looked at Will. "Name?" he questioned.

"Will MacLean."

Winfield Scott tapped his foot. "MacLean . . ." he repeated. The spy who had escaped and who was responsible for his friend James MacLean's death had been named MacLean too. "Do you have sons?" Scott asked.

Will looked at him curiously and then decided it would do no harm to answer. "Josh, who is elsewhere with the British Army, and Ian, who is out West."

"Josh MacLean." That was the name James had sent along to the fort to explain his long absence, that was the name of the spy he had been interrogating.

"Your son Josh murdered James MacLean. He's a spy and he got away! Where did he go?" Winfield Scott's face had grown red and angry. "Where did he go?" he demanded.

"He got away." Will smiled and quite suddenly all of the assembled family clapped.

"Josh'll keep the Yankees out of Canada!" Ronald Fraser called out.

"Long live the King!" shouted Ronald Macleod. It was all he could think of to shout, but it seemed appropriate.

"There will be no parole from this house!" Winfield Scott said and sneered. His red face surveyed

312

the amused faces of the family. "How the hell can people who look so American be so goddamned subversive?" he shouted. "Get everyone out of here!" He stomped his foot. "Burn this house to the ground! By God, I'll set an example here! Raze it!"

The Macleods and the MacLeans were herded outside and made to watch. "I'll smack the first person who sheds a tear," Helena said harshly. Then she turned to Winfield Scott. "Why don't you shoot an old lady as an example, you filthy southern swine?"

Winfield Scott stared at her. "You're a foul-mouthed old harpy!" Scott said and sneered.

But Helena did not blink an eyelash, she simply spit at him and marched off. "Don't give them the satisfaction of seeing you cry!" she muttered.

Madelaine leaned against Tom's arm.

"The shell will still be there," he said, trying to comfort her. "It's stone."

"We'll rebuild," Helena said defiantly. "I promised Mama we would."

Jenna pressed herself to Will and fought back tears. "At least they didn't arrest you," she murmured. "God, they're so destructive!"

Young Ronald Macleod tugged on Jenna's skirt. "Josh will get even for us," he said confidently. "He'll get even with the Yankee scum!"

Because the winter months passed so slowly on the great prairie, spring was especially welcome. "I can't believe how beautiful it is!" Bonnie Campbell said as she pressed Ian's hand. They walked arm in arm across a carpet of wildflowers.

Ian looked down on his love and stroked her long hair. "I could take you to the base of the great mountains and beyond," he said. "Bonnie, I want to go farther west. All the way to the Pacific—there's trade with the Haida. We'd be a real pioneer family! Will you come? Would you travel like that?"

313

Bonnie's eyes sparkled and she squeezed Ian's arm. "I'll come," she promised. "I'd follow you to the ends of the earth."

That had been in April. In June the priest came and Bonnie Campbell and Ian MacLean were married in a Catholic ceremony, speaking their vows in French under a canopy in the middle of a field. They were surrounded by gaily decked-out métis horsemen, mounted and rowdy even before the priest spoke the last sentence of the short ceremony.

Then with whoops and hollers, the métis rode in circles, laughing and joking in French as they demonstrated their prowess in the saddle by dipping to pick flowers for the bride.

"You see," Marie-Anne explained, "we know how to marry someone. If you had been married in Pembina, among the colonists, there would have been whispers. Here, among the métis and the Indians, there is only happiness, only festivities."

"I shall miss you, Marie-Anne Lagimonière, I shall miss you a great deal when Ian and I have gone, traveling in the wilderness."

"We shall meet again," Marie-Anne smiled. "It's a large land, but we are few."

"And you are famous," Bonnie said.

Marie-Anne laughed her enchanting laugh again. "I am told by the Indian shaman that our grandsons will mold this land; that one will be French and Indian and that he will be famous."

Bonnie nodded; she did not always know how to react to Marie-Anne's beliefs.

"We too are going for a time," Marie-Anne confided. "We are going back to Isle la Crosse, north in the land of the Plains Cree."

"And you will not be lonely?"

"No, no. There is a big fur trading post there; we will bring furs and we will visit the Riels. They are almost like us. Madame is a métis, but she is half

314

French, half Montagnais. The Montagnais are Quebec Indians and she is as far from her home as I am from my own."

"I shall be far from mine too," Bonnie said softly, "though it won't matter anymore. Ian says I will stand on the Pacific shore, that we shall have our first child there."

"When I came here," Marie-Anne confided, "I was the only one. Now, you see, there are more, and still more to come. It will be the same with you. In a few years there will be many settlers. You will be surprised!"

Ian moved up behind his bride. "You two are having much too serious a conversation. A wedding should have dancing!"

Almost as if by command, one of the métis produced a fiddle, and a curious blend of folk dances began. It consisted of dances from Quebec, dances from Scotland, and something original. And as Ian and Bonnie danced, Indian children made garlands of grass for Bonnie and clapped their hands and sang.

"Do you feel cast among strangers?" Ian asked.

Bonnie shook her head. "I shall learn to love it!"

Josh and Colleen and the twins continued to live in Mason James' house in Georgetown under the watchful care of Righteous. Mason James came and went, spending many of his nights in Washington with Jason Talbot. Josh was gone now and again as he took Jason's information and passed it on to the British naval spies. Farms on the Niagara were burned and Josh, after many months, learned that Lochiel was among them.

In retaliation, the British Navy struck repeatedly at the coast of the United States. Again it was a seesaw war. York was burned and there was continued fighting in Upper Canada.

A year passed, a year of senseless destruction, of

killing, and of pillaging. It was August 18, 1814, when Josh received an urgent message.

"It would happen now," Colleen said. "On the children's birthday!"

Josh let the message drop from the pouch. He looked at the bright-eyed twins, who were two years old on this day. "You had better pack up," he told Colleen. "We're going to have to leave Washington. I think my usefulness is about finished here. We're to rendezvous with one of the British ships."

"To go home?" Colleen's eyes glistened.

"For now," Josh smiled. "To what's left of it."

Colleen looked at the twins. "Oh, Josh, we can't leave Righteous! The babies are so fond of him; besides, he could be free in Canada."

"Righteous in Canada?" Josh shrugged. "All right," he gave in. "Have him pack too. But hurry, we have to leave by carriage within the hour. We have precious little time to waste if we're to make the rendezvous."

"What about Mason James?"

"Jason has the same information I do. He'll take care of Mason James. That's one thing you don't have to worry about."

"Home," Colleen repeated. She bent down and hugged the twins. "What a nice birthday gift."

Dolley Madison turned uneasily in her giant canopied bed. Mr. Madison had gone out to observe the battleground and not returned. The thundering guns had kept her awake all night and finally she gave in and got up, stretching and putting on her lovely red silk robe, a gift from the French ambassador.

Why? was all Dolley Madison could ask herself. Why hadn't someone taken the time to see to the protection of the nation's capital! Brigadier General William H. Winder was supposed to have taken care of the defenses, but it was all too obvious that he had

316

done exactly nothing! Not even after the British had landed! "This is most inconvenient," Dolley said aloud.

"And everyone is going to say this is Mr. Madison's fault," she went on, talking to herself. "His and Mr. Monroe's. But surely it isn't." In her wildest dreams, Dolley could not imagine why this was all happening.

Five days earlier, on August 19, British Major General Ross had landed his troops and begun marching right up the Patuxent River, supported by Rear Admiral Cockburn with a naval division of light vessels. Then on August 27, Commodore Barney had been forced to destroy his own gunboats to keep them from falling into the hands of the advancing British. Now only heaven knew what was happening! The army had just come and gathered up every little old person capable of shouldering a gun! Even Jason Talbot and dear Mr. MacLean had been taken! Dolley pouted, feeling quite alone.

She made her way downstairs and lit a candle. She was about to go into the main reception area when she heard a loud banging that brought the one guard left scurrying to the door.

"Mason James MacLean and Jason Talbot to see the First Lady! For heaven's sake let us in, you dolt," Jason was protesting. "We have been sent by the President, man. The British are coming! My God, they're going to kill us all, burn down Washington!"

"Let him in, let him in!" Dolley swept into the foyer. "Oh, Mr. MacLean, dear. Oh, Jason! Where is Mr. Madison! Oh, tell me that he is safe, tell me!"

"Quite safe, madame," Mason James reassured her. "It is for you he worries. We were sent here to fetch you and to take you to the place where he and the Cabinet have taken refuge."

"We must go at once!" Jason Talbot said. "Absolutely at once!"

317

For a moment Dolley Madison stood like a statue. "I'm not dressed," she said. "What does one wear for an evacuation?"

Mason James stared at her. Her red satin robe glistened.

"Madame, we are in peril!" Mason James had welcomed the opportunity to leave the scene of the battle and of course he was more than glad to be with Jason, but Dolley sometimes was too exasperating to bear.

Dolley turned and headed up the great spiral staircase. "My blue gown, I think . . . yes, I'll try that one on first."

"We don't have time!" Mason James called after her.

"It's all right, Mr. MacLean, dear. Now, while I'm getting dressed, you and Jason fetch me all the wagons you can muster. I can't leave my artworks! I can't desert the history of the nation! Lordy! They belong to the people!"

"Artworks?" Mason James stood stunned before the retreating image of Dolley Madison. She paused at the top of the staircase and looked down.

"Tonight we will make history!" she proclaimed. "We must save what we can for posterity!"

"Don't argue," Jason advised. "You go for the wagons, I'll start gathering up things."

"You're not going to meet the British?"

"Oh, heavens, no, I'm going to stay with you! Now run off and get the wagons!"

Wagons? They were both mad, Mason decided. All of Washington was fleeing, people were setting fire to their own homes! The rabble were running amuck in the streets, shrieking and looting. They were behaving like—like rabble! Nothing worse than roused rabble. What the British didn't destroy, the discontented, poverty-stricken wretches who hovered in the doorways of the American capital would.

318

"Sir?" Wilson, the Executive Mansion's butler, stood ready to do his mistress' bidding. "Miss Dolley sent me to help you with the wagons."

Mason James summoned all the strength at his disposal. Jason was coming with him, Dolley needed him. "To the stables!" he proclaimed. He and Wilson ran to the stables behind the Executive Mansion. They roused two sleepy stable hands and assembled three wagons. As luck would have it, Mason James saw three more military wagons in the street as they drew up to the front portals of the Executive Mansion. He drew them to a halt and flashed his handwritten note from the President. "These are needed for the immediate evacuation of the Executive Mansion," he mumbled. Wisely, he did not mention the artworks that would be piled into them.

When Mason James returned with his ill-gotten caravan, he found Mrs. Madison resplendent in her blue gown standing on the front steps, while servants carried out paintings and vases, silverware and dishes, antique furniture and clothing under brave Jason's direction.

"Oh, my heavens!" Dolley exclaimed. "Oh, come, Mason James, I forgot the most important thing of all!"

Bewildered, Mason James followed Dolley back into the Executive Mansion. "I forgot Mr. Stuart's painting of George Washington!"

"We haven't much time!" Mason had no sooner said it than he heard one of many rockets bursting in the air.

"Oh, there's no room for the frame!"

"Madame, I must ask you to make haste. I think the building is on fire."

"Bother," Dolley replied with irritation. She opened her little satchel and withdrew a penknife. "Here, Mason James, you lift me up."

Mason James mentally began counting. But he

319

lifted her as high as he could and she adroitly cut the painting from its frame. "I certainly wouldn't want future generations of Americans not to know what the father of their country looked like."

Mason lowered her as she rolled up the painting. "I'm certain you'll be remembered for saving it," he said dully.

Dolley smiled brightly. "And for my ice-cream socials too . . . or, at least, I hope so."

Mason grasped her hand and pulled her back outside. He lifted her onto the wagon where Jason waited among the treasures of the Executive Mansion. "Go!" he shouted to the driver. "Hurry!"

"I do believe we have almost everything of value," Dolley said with satisfaction. The flames were dancing on the horizon and the Executive Mansion was ablaze.

"Everything," Mason said, patting Jason's hand.

"Oh, damn the British!" Dolley said.

Mason looked back on the burning city. He thought that it needed rebuilding in any case and that almost anything would be an improvement. As if echoing his thoughts, Dolley looked out at the city and shook her head.

"We'll have to rebuild almost everything. My heavens, the Executive Mansion too! What color do you think it ought to be, Mason James? Red brick? Fieldstone?"

"White," Mason James answered without a moment's hesitation. "White, like a great plantation house. Yes, Washington ought to be one giant plantation!"

The Macleods and MacLeans who had been living at Lochiel took refuge in the inn owned by Steven MacAndrew, whose wife, Susanna, was Jenna's youngest daughter.

"At least we have a roof over our heads!" Helena

said over and over, though it was quite obvious she was less than enthralled with the accommodations. Nonetheless, no one could complain that the inn wasn't convenient to Lochiel. It was less than half an hour's ride away, and that enabled the family to work in the fields over the summer.

"Americans or no Americans," Helena mumbled, "we'll have a harvest, a harvest festival, and food to eat over the winter!"

And so the first of November 1814 came. In the kitchen of the inn Auntie Madelaine, Jenna, Agnes, and Susanna worked under the watchful eye of Helena. There would be cooked apples, pies, pastries, brown bread, and even roast corn. And out back, in the open field behind the inn, the younger boys would play Highland games.

"I'll win this year," fourteen-year-old John Fraser Murray announced. "I'll win all the races!"

Ronald Macleod, who now was eight, looked at his cousin and laughed. "There's no competition this year! Josh is gone and so is Ian! You're the oldest one still at home, unless you count the really old ones."

"Are you saying I won't win fair?" John Fraser Murray looked indignant.

"No, I didn't say that," Ronald gave in. He shuffled his feet a bit and stared at his shoes. "If you win this year, who will you give your candy to?"

John Fraser Murray smiled. "Grandmother Helena," he answered confidentially, "for spitting in old Winfield Scott's face!" The two boys giggled and resumed their chore of carrying the logs to the pit where the great fire would be built for the corn roast.

"Glad to see you two hard at work," Helena said as she strode out the back door of the inn to inspect the preparations. "You had better bring more kindling though, because, as you know, it's hard to start a good fire with just big logs."

321

Ronald Macleod nodded and John Fraser Murray immediately headed off to gather kindling.

"When will we rebuild Lochiel?" Ronald asked as he carried another two logs over to the pit. "I miss it."

Helena wiped her hands on her apron and spontaneously took the eight-year-old in her arms, giving him a big hug. "I miss it too," she confessed. "And I promise you, the minute the Yankees and the British are through marching back and forth across the same piece of property—our property—we'll rebuild." Helena pressed her lips together and doubled her fist, shaking it at the sky. "And, by God, Lochiel will be bigger, grander, and richer than ever before! That's my promise, Ronald Macleod, I'll see that every member of this family works their fingers to the bone building a house that Mama—your great-grandmother—would have been proud of. And we'll show them, we'll show them we're not beaten so easily!"

Ronald smiled and hugged his Great-aunt Helena back.

"Helena!" Madelaine's voice called out the back door. "Guess what? You'll never guess!"

Helena turned and looked at Madelaine.

"A messenger just came! The British have burned Washington! They burned it in August! Imagine!"

Helena smiled what Ronald Macleod thought was the biggest smile he had ever seen on his great-aunt's face. "See, I told you Josh would get even!"

"For York and for our Lochiel," said Helena. Then, turning back toward Madelaine, "I hope they burned it all the way down to the ground! Damn Yankees!"

Madelaine closed the door and returned to the kitchen.

Agnes was peeling apples furiously. "I do wish she

wouldn't swear in front of the children," she mumbled.

Jenna laughed and Madelaine suppressed a smile. "Age has its privileges. Helena says what she wants when she wants. Anyway, they are damn Yankees!" Jenna wiped her hands and looked at Agnes, almost daring her to reply. But she just peeled the apples all the more furiously.

"It'll be over soon," Madelaine said, touching Jenna's arm. "And Josh will come home."

"I hope he's safe." Jenna looked at Madelaine for a long moment, then returned to the pie crusts.

Later that night, after the food had been consumed and the games had been played, the family stood around the bonfire. Helena's eyes followed the smoke as it curled upward into the night sky.

"They say truce negotiations are under way," Tom commented. He had heard it in town.

"Then we shall have a toast," Helena said. "Pour some wine and let's drink to next year at Lochiel." Helena lifted her glass. "From the ashes, victory!" she toasted.

"And from the wildfires, peace," Tom Macleod added.

"To Great-grandmother and next year," eight-year-old Ronald Macleod piped.

"There—there it is down through the trees." Ian pointed to an expanse of shimmering blue beyond the forest where the trees parted and the land dropped away, forming a steep cliff. Ian took Bonnie's hand and led her through the trees to the edge of the cliff.

It was late November and behind them lay snow-capped mountains, deep, lush valleys, fertile plains, fields carpeted with wildflowers. They had crossed a thousand rushing streams and more than one great river. They had passed through the rugged mountains and they had weathered a winter in the wilderness.

"That's the Pacific Ocean," Ian said, giving her a squeeze. Below the cliff were jagged rocks, and the waves crashed against them, white foam rising and then falling back into the sea.

"It's beautiful," Bonnie said. "I have never seen anywhere as beautiful as this spot."

Ian sat down on the grass in the warm sunshine. "I don't think I'll move for the next month."

Bonnie stretched out beside him on her back and looked up at the puffy white clouds against the deep blue sky. "You had better get up," she chided. Bonnie turned her head toward him, a mischievous smile on her face.

Ian propped up his head with one arm and looked down at her. "Oh?" he questioned. "And why do you want me to get up and work?"

Bonnie smiled and patted her stomach. "Because we'll need a place soon." Her smile broadened. "I'm pregnant," she sang out. "You said we'd have our child here!"

Ian blushed with pride and joy. He leaned over her and kissed her deeply. "I love you," he said. "And nothing ever will part us." Then Ian reached around his neck and slipped off the silver chain that held the Roman coin in its setting. "There are two of these," he told her. "Mathew Macleod gave one to Janet Cameron, and she gave hers to Robert, my grandfather. Mathew found Robert because of this coin, and Robert found Jenna because of her coin. I have one, Josh has the other. Now, Bonnie Campbell MacLean, I give you mine and you are to pass it on to our lastborn child."

Bonnie felt the cold silver as Ian hung the chain around her neck. "I always wondered why you never took this off," she said, reaching up and kissing his brow.

"It has a hundred wonderful stories."

Bonnie nestled in Ian's arms and knew that they were going to make love, here on the edge of the ocean. "I like long stories," she breathed.

"And I shall tell you all of them," Ian promised.